I close my eyes and think of home

written by

Clair Hamilton

with

Simon Bonsai

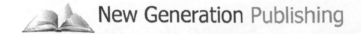

New Generation Publishing

Acknowledgements - I would like to thank my good friend Helen Stanger for all her help and assistance in proof reading this novel for me and finding the numerous mistakes I had made and overlooked in my many readings. Also, thanks to my brother, Stephen, and son, David, for their help and encouragement. And, last but not least, thanks to my girlfriend, Polly, for, well, being Polly.

About the Author

Lady Clair Hamilton lives in Hamilton Hall in Worcestershire with her children. She is a well known humanitarian and charity worker.

Simon Bonsai, though born in Worcestershire, now lives in Nottingham, where he grows and sells beautiful Bonsai trees.

They first met when Simon booked a table at a charity event organised by Lady Clair in August 2015 and they have remained firm friends since.

Prologue

I closed my eyes and felt despair overcome me. I thought of my home in England, and I thought of my children, and remembered us having a picnic on the back lawn on a warm summer's day.

I should be back home in Worcestershire, I thought, not sitting in the back seat of an old car, with my hands tied, guarded by 3 soldiers and on my way to be the love slave of a mega rich member of parliament. A fiction writer couldn't make it up.

Part 1 - Abacadia

Chapter 1 - Kidnapped

It was late on a Tuesday evening in June and I was feeling rather pleased with myself. The evening had gone extremely well, even if I say it myself, and I reckon we had raised over £4,000 for my own charity, the Lady Clair Hamilton Trust. To be honest, all my charity evenings went well. I worked hard and had a flair for organising.

So I had been told.

I had organised a raffle and a number of market stalls including a bloke with a beard called Simon who grew and sold beautiful Bonsai trees and a French lady who was married to an Italian and they cooked and sold Spanish paella and there was a couple of local singers but the highlight was a comedian, who had been unknown when I booked him but had since been on the BBC and had become an overnight success and had kept his promise to appear and was wonderful.

We had professionally filmed the comedian and had his permission to sell the resulting film to Channel 4 and keep 50% of any profit we made from that.

The evening had taken place at a rather glamorous hotel on the banks of the River Severn in Worcestershire, and the hotel, all 4*s, had allowed us to use the room for free, which was partly due to their kindness and partly due to my wily negotiating skills. Mind you, their name was included on all the posters, and would be included on the Channel 4 programme credits. More free publicity for them.

There were no games of whist.

So all in all, a good evening was had by all and as I drove home that balmy summer night, I had the radio on and was singing along to hits from the sixties and seventies.

"Wouldn't it be nice if we were lovers, wouldn't it be nice if we were friends, "I sang.

I was just a few miles from my home, Hamilton Hall, travelling along country lanes that I knew so well. Narrow and twisty, with alternating high hedges or, during daylight hours, wonderful views over the surrounding hills and woodland with occasional glimpses of the river.

Gods' own country.

I loved it.

I loved my car almost as much. A silver blue 45-year-old E Type Jaguar. Soft-top, and the roof was down now. The wind blew through my long blond hair, trailing it out behind me. I drove fairly quickly, I always had. I was a good driver, I reckoned. A clean licence, of course.

I passed someone standing at the side of the road. A man appeared to have some road signs with him, and was just about to put out what looked like a diversion sign, or he may just have taken them down. He had a phone or walkie-talkie by his ear. This was a fleeting thought, which quickly disappeared from my mind.

A few seconds later, I turned a corner and saw, to my astonishment, a small green car that appeared to have come off the road and was half stuck into a hedge. I can remember thinking to myself that it was a strange place to have an accident as it was by a very slow corner, but then I forgot those thoughts as the driver's door opened and a young woman crawled from the car. She appeared to have blood on her forehead, so I slowed down, stopped, and jumped out.

I ran over to her, and she looked up at me, with a look of horror on her face and whimpered rather pathetically. I knelt down beside her to see if I could help, then felt both my arms grabbed from behind. I looked around, glimpsed a man's face hidden by a scarf pulled up to his nose, then felt a prick in my arm. I tried to struggle, but I was being held too tightly, and I could feel myself losing conscious. I tried to shout but no noise came from my mouth.

The last thing I remember seeing was the face of the young woman, which was now completely blank.

Chapter 2 - Disappeared into thin air.

This story has two parts to it. There is my story, which I will tell myself, but there is also an alternative story, which runs alongside my story, and my eldest daughter, Alice, will tell this.

I, Alice, started getting a bit worried that Tuesday evening at about midnight when mother hadn't returned. I was sitting in the living room with my sister, Pauline, and my brother, Theo, watching a film on the television. The film finished, and I looked at my watch.

"Mother should be home by now," I said, slightly concerned. "I wonder where she is."

"She could have broken down," suggested Pauline, "Or maybe she's decided to stop with a friend."

Pauline, at 22, was 3 years younger than me. Out of the three of us, she was the tomcat. She played hockey for Stourport, one of the top hockey clubs in the country, had run marathons and climbed tall mountains and such.

Neither Pauline nor I had gone to university, much to our parent's disgust, but instead had set up our own business, based at Hamilton Hall, making and selling soaps through the internet. We called the company 'Lady Soap', in honour of our mother. The business kept us out of mischief, though we were never going to become millionaires through running it.

Theo, our baby brother, was 20. He was at Worcester University studying computing of some sort. It was his summer break and he had managed to get a part time job with a local printers in Kidderminster with the highly unoriginal name of 'Print-U-like'.

"She would have phoned us to let us know," I said.

I picked up my mobile.

"I'll try phoning her," but it went straight to her

answering machine.

"Mum," I said to it, "It's Alice. Please phone me as soon as you can. We're starting to get worried."

"I'll phone Marjory."

Marjory Hackett was mother's best friend and had been at the charity evening with her.

"She left as normal," Marjory told me when she answered her phone. "She was quite late leaving, but I saw her drive out of the car park in front of me. She should be home by now."

I put the phone down and stood up.

"Come on, "I said, "Let's drive to the hotel. There can only be one route she would have taken."

We all piled into my 1964 Morris Minor, and I drove to the hotel, but we saw nothing. Around every bend we expected to see mother's crashed E-type, but nothing. We arrived home an hour later, and I immediately phoned the police. They said they had nothing to report but would keep us informed. We eventually went to bed at about 2 o'clock and I found sleep hard to find. I just couldn't imagine what had happened to her.

In the morning the local police inspector, Inspector Hetherington Hector, phoned us, but only to say they had no news.

"Do you think she could have been kidnapped?" he asked.

We didn't think so for one minute and told him so. But we couldn't think of any other answer.

Pauline, Theo, and I decided to go over the route that our mother must surely have taken on returning from the charity event once again.

We drove to the hotel and enquired there, just in case she had decided to stay the night and had forgotten to tell us. Maybe she had met a bloke but the hotel couldn't tell us anything.

Her E-type was not in the car park.

We left the hotel and drove slowly back towards home. Cars hooted and flashed their lights at us for driving so slowly, but we ignored them. I was driving so I studied the road ahead. Theo looked to the right and Pauline to the left.

We were only a couple of miles from home when Theo shouted, "What's that?"

I stopped just past a gentle bend and we all climbed out of the car. We saw some tyre marks in the grass at the side of the road, and a few branches in the hedge were snapped.

"It looks like a car has parked into the hedge," said Theo. "If it had crashed, then there would have marks on the road and surely more branches would have snapped. There would be more damage."

"So you think someone parked here?" asked Pauline, "Why?"

"Maybe they made it look like a car crash to get mother to stop and then kidnapped her," Theo suggested but he looked a bit sceptical.

"We must get the police forensics here," I said, and phoned Inspector Hector, who said he would send somebody around as soon as he could.

Whilst we waited for them to arrive, we examined the area ourselves the best we could, without disturbing anything, we hoped, but found nothing. We weren't sure what we were looking for, but it was better than doing nothing.

The forensics eventually arrived, and we left them to their work and drove to Marjory's house. She was very concerned about mother's disappearance but couldn't tell us anything of help.

"She was in a really good mood when she left. The evening had gone really well," she told us as we sat in her lounge, drinking tea and nibbling on cakes. "I can't possibly imagine what has happened to her. Have you contacted the police?"

"Yes, we have told the police. They're working on it. Did she go off with anyone?" I asked but Marjory shook her head.

"No. At least I'm pretty sure she didn't."

"Was she extra friendly with anyone at all that evening?"

Marjory shook her head again.

"Not that I noticed. She was friendly with everyone just as she always is. I can't recall her paying any extra special attention to anyone."

"Did you notice anyone staring at her or anyone who looked a bit suspicious?" I asked, but she said she hadn't.

"It was just like a normal charity evening."
She shrugged.

"Sorry. What do you think has happened to her?" but we couldn't answer and left her promising to let her know if we heard anything and returned home.

The police told us they would check all the local hospitals but we did the same thing anyway. There was no sign of mother or the car. We studied maps and drove down every single lane in the area that she could possibly have driven along, but nothing.

We contacted all her friends and acquaintances, even those she only vaguely knew. We even phoned up everyone who had been or may have been at the charity evening, including the comedian, a French lady who was married to an Italian and Simon the Bonsai tree man, but nothing.

We, and I mean the police and the family by that, searched every single avenue and line of enquiry that we could, but nobody had seen or heard anything. She had just disappeared into thin air, and so had her beloved E-type.

Chapter 3 - Lady Clair

Sometime later after the kidnapping, I vaguely remember waking up and thinking I may be on a plane, but then I lost consciousness again.

When I eventually woke up properly, I was lying on a bed. My arms were tied above my head, and I couldn't move them. I twisted my neck and saw my wrists were tied to the bed headboard using what looked like a silk scarf. It was very unlikely I could undo the knot.

I closed my eyes and tried not to panic. I told myself to keep calm. I was Lady Clair Hamilton. I'd be all right. Whatever was going to happen to me, I would come through. I swore to myself, took a few deep breaths, and looked around me.

I appeared to be in a bedroom, but where I was, I had no idea. Possibly a hotel, but hotel rooms the world over looked very similar. At least I was fully dressed, in the clothes I had been wearing in the E-Type.

The room was very posh. The bed was large, possibly king size, and looked quite good quality, though it was hard to tell. It felt very comfortable. There was a large ceiling fan in the middle of the room, which was rotating slowly.

"They don't often have ceiling fans in Britain," I thought. "Surely I can't be abroad, can I?"

Paintings on the walls showed scenes of trees and hills and water. I liked them. There were two comfortable chairs, a wall-to-wall built in cupboard and a dressing table with a mirror.

On one wall were floor to ceiling curtains, with a pull cord at one end to open and close them. They were almost closed, giving the room a gloomy feel, which summed up my feelings as well.

Gloomy.

I wondered what the view was like through the window. All I could see was sky, which was a bright, bright blue, with no clouds visible. The curtains, like the rest of the room, were gentle pastel shades. Like many hotel rooms around the world.

There were two doors in the room. I assumed one led to an en-suite bathroom and the other probably to another room or maybe through to a corridor. I struggled with the scarves that bound my arms, but they wouldn't move.

My mouth felt very dry, and I tried to cry out. "Hello," came out as a soft croak, but immediately a door opened and a young-ish man walked into the room. He was tall and slim and rather good looking, with a neatly trimmed moustache. He wore a smart suit and tie, but it was his hat which told me where I was. It was a cross between a flat cap and a bowler and it was called a karatam and there was only one country in the world where a karatam was worn. Abacadia, in central Asia.

The man walked over and sat down on the edge of the bed.

"Lady Clair," he said, "I do apologise that you are tied to the bed. If you promise to keep calm, I will, of course, untie you immediately."

He raised his eyebrows, and I thought I had seen those eyes and eyebrows before. Was he the man who had been at the fake car crash in Worcestershire and had grabbed me from behind? I wasn't sure. I had only had the briefest of glimpses of him.

I nodded and he leant over me and undid the knots. I rubbed my wrists, and the man pushed two pillows behind my back. I made myself comfortable whilst he poured me a glass of water from a bottle. I gratefully took a long drink whilst the man just watched me. When I had finished, he took the glass from me and carefully put it back on the bedside table.

"Firstly, I really must apologise for what has happened to you. It was necessary, and I will explain why later. You are in a hotel room in Abacadia. You are, for the time being at least, a prisoner, but you will be well looked after. My name is Moldie Bedlam."

I was totally confused. What was going on? It was like a bad dream. I shook my head. I tried to keep calm and took some more deep breaths.

"Please explain to me what is happening," I asked him.

"You have been kidnapped," he said, looking directly into my eyes, "Because we think you can be a great help to our cause."

His English was excellent, though he had a slight Abacadian accent.

"I am a leading member of the Organisation for the Development of Effghania, the ODOE. Our entire aim is to improve the quality of living for our fellow Effghanians. We believe you can help us immensely."

I knew all about Effghania. Everyone did. It was a region of southern Abacadia and it was very, very poor. It was one of the areas of earth that was regularly on the news.

'And now a report from Paul Reporter, our Asian correspondent, who is live in Effghania and is interviewing some small, cute orphans holding puppies.'

"Am I to be ransomed?" I asked, "Because although I do have a small amount of money, I am not a rich woman. When my husband died four years ago, a lot of my money was taken in death duties. I'm sorry to say, you won't get much money from a ransom."

"I will explain tomorrow what we want from you, but we do know all about your husband, Lord Hamilton, and I do sympathise with you over his early death."

Alfie was just forty-eight when he was killed in a car crash, the same age as I was on that day I was kidnapped.

"We know all about the death duties. Ransom is not the reason we have kidnapped you. As I said earlier, I will explain to you tomorrow why you are here."

That made me wonder.

"What day is it?" I asked.

"It's Friday. Mid morning. You've been asleep for over 3 days."

Three days? I must have been drugged to sleep that long.

"How did I get here?"

Moldie Bedlam smiled and actually looked pleased with himself.

"That was all my doing," he said, proudly. "It took a bit of planning but I'll tell you all about it later."

"Why?" I asked.

"Tomorrow," said Moldie. "I'll tell you everything tomorrow. Now, you must be hungry. I'll go and get some food and wine. The bathroom is through that door. Maybe you would like to freshen up?"

I nodded and he walked over to the curtains and pulled the draw cord and the curtains opened and through the window I could see trees. Tall trees. It looked like I was on a first floor somewhere.

The man smiled at me and left the bedroom. He left the door ajar but then I heard a key being turned in another door. I walked over to the door he'd just walked through. My legs felt a bit wobbly and I was still rubbing my wrists. The carpet was thick and luxurious.

Through the door was a very elegant and spacious room, with an expensive 3-piece suite, a cabinet that obviously contained drinks, and a large flat-screen television and DVD player. There was also a small table with two chairs, which was set for dinner and in one corner a running machine.

In one of the cupboards I discovered a small fridge freezer, with some milk in the door and ice cubes in the freezer section. Next to it were some cups, saucers, some tea, coffee, sugar, biscuits, and a kettle.

One wall of the room was almost all window and through it was a panoramic view overlooking a small grassy area with woodland beyond and mountains in the background. A good view, one which, I randomly thought, I would never tire of.

There were no people or buildings or any sign of human habitation in sight.

I walked back to the bedroom and through the other door into a luxury bathroom. The soft pale carpet of the bedroom ran through to the bathroom.

There was a large two-person bath, with the taps in the middle, a separate large shower unit and a loo and even a bidet. Fluffy towels and expensive soaps were everywhere. On the ledge by the sink were shampoos, conditioners, bubble bath, toothpaste, and various other smellies. I recognised them all and was surprised to discover they were all the same ones I used at home. Someone had been doing some serious research on me, and then I remembered that I had included all this sort of thing on my Facebook page.

There were two light switches. One put on a bright light, the other much dimmer. I used only the dim light. Soft music was playing in the background. Moldie Bedlam was trying very hard to relax me, I reckoned.

I ran the bath, pouring in a liberal amount of bubbly. I undressed in the bedroom, and walked naked into the bathroom. I checked the temperature of the water to make sure it was perfect then climbed into the bath. I lay back, closed my eyes, and tried to make sense of what was happening.

I was Lady Clair Hamilton, 48 years old, in the prime of my life, healthy, athletic, slim but with a good figure, extremely pretty, so I had been told, with high cheekbones and large brown eyes. A full mouth with good white teeth and long straight blonde hair. I looked 20 years younger than I was and had often been mistaken for an older sister of my daughters.

I had been born in Kidderminster hospital in Worcestershire and christened Mary Clair Francis Eileen Pitt, but had always been called Clair, to wealthy and highborn influential parents. My Dad, Herbert Pitt, was distantly related to both the Queen and William Pitt, the first prime minister of Britain, and my Mum, Francis, was a direct descendent of Owen Glendower, the 14th century self-proclaimed Prince of Wales.

The family house was called Pittdown Manor and was more of a large country house than a manor house, set in 4 acres of land, and situated a few miles north of the beautiful Malvern Hills.

I had been a bright child, privately educated at home until I was 13. I had no brothers or sisters, mother having to undergo a hysterectomy after my birth, but entertained myself by exploring the woods and streams around the house and learning to swim in the River Severn.

At 13, I went to the Alice Ottley School in Worcester. I did well there, both academically and sportingly, achieving 10 GCSE's and 4 A levels, and captaining the school at lacrosse, tennis and swimming.

I was also Head Girl.

I went to Nottingham University where I obtained a 2nd Class honours degree in Business Studies. It would and should have been a 1st but I was too busy having a good time, representing the university at many sports and fighting off, half heartedly, the advances of many, many young men.

One of the young men I met was Alfred Hamilton, known to all as Alfie or Hammy. He was the son of Lord and Lady Hamilton, of Hamilton Hall near Bewdley. He was studying business but, naturally, at Cambridge University.

We met when Nottingham played Cambridge at mixed hockey, and we were in opposing teams. I was captivated by his good looks and extreme politeness, and when, at the end of the day, he asked me if we could meet again, I was delighted and instantly agreed.

He was in his final year whilst I was in my first, and when he qualified, with a first class honours degree, of course, he got a job working for his father in Worcester. However, we met up regularly until I finished at Nottingham.

The day after I heard that I had passed my degree, he took me for a walk on the Malvern Hills. He proposed to me on the top of the Worcestershire Beacon one evening, with the sun setting in a beautiful sunset.

The wedding was held at Hamilton Hall and we honeymooned in Kenya in East Africa. We stayed in a beach hut near Mombasa and a small cottage in the midst of the Tsavo National Park, where we saw all the major wild animals, which was nice.

I loved Kenya but my eyes were opened to the huge differences there between the rich and the poor. The rich had everything they could possibly want and lived a life of pure luxury. The poor had nothing. Literally, nothing and most of them lived lives of almost total misery and starvation.

There and then, I decided I would dedicate my life to helping the less fortunate people of the world.

Back home I founded, with Alfie's blessing and help, the Clair Hamilton Trust, later, after Alfie's parents were killed in a car crash and he inherited the title and the hall, to become the Lady Clair Hamilton Trust. I soon discovered, using my business studies skills and family connections, and with Alfie's help, that I was very, very good at organising charity events and raising money, and the trust won a number of charity awards. I became quite well known for my charity work.

Meanwhile, Alfie and I started a family, with three children, 2 girls and a boy. Life was going well until poor Alfie's death in yet another car crash 4 years ago.

Death duties took a huge amount of our money and the children and I were now struggling to make ends meet, which seems very unfair to me. We managed to keep Hamilton Hall, but only just, and only because both the girls worked. It was a struggle.

I had continued since then working hard at my charity, but I had been wondering if I needed to get some paid employment but hadn't thought of anything I could really do so hadn't done anything.

I figured my kidnapping must be something to do with my charity work. They must want me to see local conditions and use my contacts to raise some money for them.

But why kidnap me? I would have helped anyway. There must be something extra they wanted. At least Moldie seemed very nice and caring, but that could just be an act. I didn't seem to be in any immediate danger, which was one thing.

Oh well, I thought to myself. Things will no doubt soon be explained.

No need to panic.

Yet.

I thought of my family and friends back home. What were they thinking? They must be concerned. I would ask Moldie about it when I got the chance.

Moldie Bedlam. What a strange name. It was if somebody had

made it up. Maybe in Abacadia it was normal. A good name, though, I thought.

I had a good soak and washed my hair. I climbed out of the bath and dried myself on one of the tremendously fluffy towels. There was an even fluffier dressing gown hanging on the door. I put it on, wrapped a towel around my hair and walked into the bedroom. In one of the cupboards was a hairdryer and I sat by the dressing table and dried and brushed my hair.

I considered putting on some make-up but decided against it. I looked good without it, I reckoned, as I studied my face in the mirror.

When I had finished admiring myself, I walked through to the living room. Immediately there was a knock on the door, which opened without me even saying anything. Moldie Bedlam walked in.

"Ah," he said. "You're out of your bath. I hope you enjoyed it. Your hair looks nice."

I found out later that he damn well knew I had enjoyed my bath. He had been watching and filming me via some hidden cameras.

"Now," he said, "Would you like something to eat? I'm sure you must be hungry."

I suddenly realised that I was indeed rather ravenous. I hadn't eaten for over 3 days.

I nodded and Moldie rang a small hand bell and the door opened again. A young woman walked in carrying a tray with two plates of food. The food looked and smelled delicious. Moldie put his arm around me and I let him gently lead me to the dining table. He pulled out a chair for me, and sat down opposite. The young woman left, quietly closing the door behind her.

On the table was a bottle of rosé wine. It was a merlot rosé, brewed here in Abacadia by Cadia Vineyards, just about my favourite wine. What a coincidence having my favourite rosé wine!

Moldie poured out two glasses, and raised one to me.

"A toast to our successful venture, "he suggested.

"You are joking," I said. "You want me to toast my kidnapping? I don't think so!"

He looked a bit shocked and very disappointed.

"I'm so very sorry to disappoint you," I said, with a touch of sarcasm. "Do you mind if I propose my own toast instead?"

"Eh, no, of course not," he replied.

I held up my glass.

"Here's to my early escape and return to England," I said, and laughed when he looked even more shocked and more disappointed.

I turned to the food on my plate. It was a pâté starter. I loved pâté, and this pâté was as good as any I had ever had. It was served with apricot chutney and thick white toast and butter. We ate in silence.

When we had finished he rang the bell again. The young woman came in, took away the empty plates, and returned with two more plates. The meal was salmon in a cheesy sauce, with peas and broccoli. I love salmon in a cheesy sauce with peas and broccoli.

"These are all my favourite foods and my favourite wine," I accused Moldie. "And the bathroom is full of my favourite shampoos and perfumes. Pray explain."

Moldie didn't even look slightly embarrassed.

"We have been doing a lot of research about you. We probably know more about you than you know yourself."

"Why?" I asked again. "Why are you doing all this? What do you want me for?"

"I'll tell you...."

".......Tomorrow."

I finished the sentence for him.

He smiled.

"Now, stop worrying and enjoy your food."

So I did.

We chatted easily. I found him to be intelligent and amusing and I soon found myself beginning to like him, even though he had just kidnapped me and I hardly knew him. After talking about general things, mostly about me and my life in England, I asked him about his childhood and growing up in Effghania.

Chapter 4 -Moldie Bedlam

Moldie Bedlam's family were farmers and had been for generations. They had owned a medium sized farm of about 20 acres, with a small stream running through the land and a large area of woodland. They farmed a mixture of tea and coffee and some sugar with a few animals including some cows and goats and a few chickens.

Moldie was the fourth child of seven.

"The middle one," he explained, as if that was something special. "I had 3 older sisters and 3 younger brothers.

"My childhood was quite idyllic," he told me. "We all had to help out on the farm, but mum and dad made it all seem so much fun."

It was usual, it seems, for the men to run the farm and the women to look after the farmhouse, but Moldie's parents encouraged all their children to try their hand at everything and they taught them all to speak English.

"My brothers and I learnt to cook and the sisters learnt how to ride horses and milk the cows," explained Moldie proudly.

"My father died when I was only 14. He had a heart attack. It was a very sad time. He was a lovely man. Everyone liked him. Mother was heartbroken, we all were.

I was the oldest boy. I had to run the farm, I was only 14, but the rest of the family helped and we coped. Some of the neighbours rallied around and we managed for the next 3 years."

It was about then that a new government took over the running of the country. They didn't like Effghanians and one day Moldie and his farm were visited by government troops. They arrived at lunchtime. The whole family were in the dining room except for Moldie himself.

"I was in the field at the time, tending to a sick cow, and the soldiers didn't see me. However, I saw them. I got to the farm as quickly as I could but realised I had to keep out sight. "

He gave a sort of snort cum chuckle.

"My three sisters, who were all pretty and really should have been married by then, had all been dragged into the house and from the screams, I realised they were being raped by the soldiers. I think my mother was also raped. Later, all of them, including my three younger brothers, were bundled into the back of a wagon at gunpoint, and driven away. There was nothing I could do about it. Nothing."

He sighed, and looked at me.

"Nothing."

"That's dreadful," I said, and meant it. "Are they still alive, have you heard anything about them?"

"This was about fourteen years ago," said Moldie. "I tried to find out what had happened to them, but found out nothing. I have heard rumours that my mother is a cook in a government department in Snuka, the capital city. She used to make a lovely spicy goat stew."

He looked wistful.

"I haven't heard about any of the others but assume that the girls are either married off to soldiers or are prostitutes. I also assume that the boys are in the army. I hope so, because if they aren't then they will probably be dead."

I was horrified by the story. I had heard of such happenings, of course, but this was the first time I had ever talked to someone who was personally involved. I leant over and touched his arm.

"What did you do then, after the soldiers left with your family?"

"I waited in hiding until I was sure they had all gone, and then went into the farm. I packed up stuff I thought I might need and any valuables, and all the food I could carry and went and hid in the woods, in case they returned. I made my mind up there and then to dedicate my life to helping the Effghanian people."

"Why didn't they burn the farmhouse down?" I asked.

"It was a good farm," explained Moldie. "Well run by me and the family. They gave it to a government official and his family who moved in the following week. They still live there now, and, to be honest, it's still a good well run farm. I went back a few years ago to have a look. It hadn't changed much, but now the children running around playing are his family, not mine."

"I'm sorry," I said, meaning it.

He shrugged.

"These things happen. Anyway, back to the story. I wandered through the woods until eventually I met up with a small group of neighbours who had also been attacked. Some of their stories were even worse, with many old men and old women and very young children murdered on the spot. We decided to combine our meagre forces and try to form some sort of group to help our people.

That was when ODOE, the Organisation for the Development of Effghania, was dreamt up and formed. I was one of the original members. We decided right from the start that we would be non-violent. We didn't really have any weapons anyway, and almost certainly no guns.

To start with we just helped by repairing buildings, supplying food and medicines, doing what we could. Over the years the organisation grew in numbers and strength. Now we are the leading voice in Effghania.

We still do what we can to help but have built up a network of contacts and friends all over Abacadia and even abroad.

I'm one of the senior officials."

He shrugged and I decided we needed a change of subject.

"Could you tell me about my kidnapping, please," I asked. "Am I right in assuming that you were the mastermind behind it?"

Moldie looked pleased with that remark.

"I was indeed. It took a bit of organising, I must tell you. We have been following you on Facebook and Twitter for quite a while. You listed all the charity events you were organising or attending, and decided to kidnap you on the way back from one of them. Actually, this was the second attempt. We originally tried two weeks previously. You had been attending a meeting in Worcester but you drove home by a different route. I think you were giving somebody a lift home."

I nodded. I remembered well.

"The second time things went perfectly. We all had walkie-talkies and when we heard you had left the charity meeting, an Effghanian student in England set up the diversion signs so no one would drive down the lane where we had set up the fake car crash. When you were almost upon him, he took down the signs but immediately put them back when you had driven by.

There was another student with diversion signs and a walkie-talkie at the other end of the lane. The woman in the car was also an Effghanian student and it was me who injected you and I apologise about that. Two of the students drove your E-type away and it is now stored in a private garage, safe and sound.

The other one helped me load you into the fake crashed car and we then drove you to a small airport where you were loaded into a small private plane and flown to Abacadia.

Although I say it myself, I think I organised it all very well."

I neither agreed nor disagreed with his thought.

"Which airport was that?" I asked.

He smiled and shook his head.

"I'm sorry, Lady Clair, but that's a secret."

"How did you get me here then?"

"I'm sorry, but ......"

"........ That's also a secret," I finished, and he chuckled.

"That's true. It has taken ODOE years to set up our route."

"Right."

"We are worried though," he continued, "About how your friends and family are reacting back home in Worcestershire. We don't want anyone to be upset and worry too much about you and we've been wondering what we can do about it. We think we have come up with a plan. We really don't want you to talk directly to anyone, so we thought you could record a message, which we will send on to anyone, you like. We thought you could send a message, say, weekly."

"Weekly?" I asked. "How long do you intend keeping me here?"

"We're not sure. A few weeks possibly. We'll see how things go. Now, do you want to send a message to your family?"

"Of course I do," I answered with a sigh. "I'll think about it, and let you know in the morning."

I was pleased that he was willing to let me send home weekly messages. It gave me the impression that I wouldn't come to any harm.

He left me later, after coffee and a brandy, with the news that the door was locked and there were two guards outside. He told me to sleep well and said he would return in the morning.

On my bed I found a cream coloured knee-length cotton nightie, very similar to the one I wore at home. How did he know what I wore in bed? The maid must have put it there when we were eating dinner, I reckoned. I put it on. It fitted, perfectly, and was rather comfy.

I climbed into bed, and lay there, wondering what message I could send which may give my family some clue of where I was without Moldie realising what I was doing.

Eventually I came up with a message, which started with "I am very well, but have been kidnapped. I am not allowed to say where I am, but I am being treated very well and please don't worry about me. I am not sure how long I will be held captive but I'm fairly certain that no harm will come to me."

I then gave my love to everyone, and wished they were all well. I asked them to keep on with the charity work, and included the line "In this, my initial message to you, could I ask you a couple of favours. Ask Betty and Celia and deliver the invitations to Alan for the next charity whist drive."

The initial letters of the phrase spelt out Abacadia, almost, and as we had never had a whist drive, I hoped they would realise something was strange. I found a note pad in the bedroom and wrote the message down before I forgot it.

Chapter 5 - Reality or Nightmare

I actually slept quite well. I think I must have been mentally exhausted. Moldie joined me in the morning for breakfast. Poached eggs on lightly buttered toast, again one of my favourites, with coffee and some grapefruit. I showed him the message I wanted to send, and he found nothing wrong with it. He pulled out an iPod and I recorded it and he said he would include the previous evening's premiership football scores, just to prove that the message was sent that day.

After breakfast, Moldie left, telling me to get dressed for a trip into the country and he would return in an hour. In the cupboard in the bedroom I found many clothes, including a number of luxurious evening gowns hanging up in the cupboard and in a drawer I found some sexy underwear, and nighties. Why did I need all those? What were their plans for me? I was beginning to get suspicious.

Moldie returned after exactly 60 minutes. He was still smartly dressed.

"You look nice," he said, admiring me in the safari suit I had chosen. He looked me up and down, concentrating on my bare legs.

"Why are there numerous long dresses and sexy nighties in my bedroom?" I asked him.

"I'll explain later."

"Where are the clothes I was wearing when you kidnapped me?"

"The maid, Pebble, has taken them to be washed. You'll get them back tomorrow. Come on, let's go."

The two security guards escorted us into a lift and we went down two floors and exited through a small door, which I assumed was at the back of the hotel. Moldie led me to an old battered Landrover, and helped me to climb in to the passenger's seat then got into the driving seat. The guards climbed into the back. They were large hairy brutish looking

22

creatures who looked like they could handle themselves in a pub fight but might struggle to do the Times crossword.

"I want to show you many things today," he said, "Which I hope will help you to understand why you are here and why we want you to do what we want you to do."

He drove off along a dirt road and we passed through a dense woodland full of huge trees I didn't really recognise. They seemed to reach miles into the sky. As I looked up, I couldn't see the tops. I saw a number of colourful birds in the trees and thought I heard some animals barking which may have been some kind of monkey.

After about ten minutes, we entered a large clearing, which was full of tents, laid out in neat lines, into which people were coming and going. Most of the tents were quite small, they looked like pre-war army tents, but there were a couple of larger tents in the middle of the field.

"The large tent is the hospital tent," explained Moldie. "It is the only hospital of any kind in Effghania. It serves over 300,000 people. All the smaller tents are like wards, and are all full of sick and dying people. We have enough medicine to treat maybe 10% of them. Most of them have to manage with TLC. Many of them don't survive.

If we had even the most basic of drugs then I believe the survival rate would be much, much greater. But we just don't have them."

I looked around me in horror. I saw many obviously sick people staggering around, some were even crawling. They looked thin and in need of a good meal. It was like a refugee camp that you saw on the BBC 'News at Ten'.

"These are some of the lucky ones," continued Moldie. "They have covers over their heads and food to eat 'and medical attention. Ninety nine percent of our people have nothing. And I mean nothing. I'll show you."

We climbed back into the Landrover and Moldie drove away. I looked around as he drove, truly horrified by what I saw.

"How has this happened?"

"There are two tribes of people in Abacadia," he explained. "The Effghanians and the Jakalamnians. The two tribes have been at war for many, many years. Well, less a war, more a mutual hatred. And now the government are Jakalamnian.

We hate Jakalamnia and they hate Effghania. It's a tribal thing, which stretches back centuries, but recently, the latest Abacadian government have started using their power to make things as difficult for us as possible. They give us no aid, nothing, no food, medicine, education, nothing.

Then two years ago we had a drought, then dreadful floods and last year an earthquake shook the area. Most of the local buildings collapsed and many thousands of people were killed or injured. Maybe you heard about it. "

I did recall vaguely hearing something about it on the news but the report didn't mention anything about people dying.

"But worst of all, the government still don't care. They just don't care. They are all members of the Jakalamnian tribe, and they hate us. We get no help from them at all. None. Nothing."

I really was horrified.

"Why doesn't the rest of the world know about this?"

"The government keep it all a secret. Alternatively, if they do say anything, they just lie. Lies, lies and more lies. They say they give us some money but don't. They say they give us aid, but they never do. Anything that we want done, we have to do ourselves."

Moldie was getting quite worked up. He was obviously sincere in his motives.

We drove on in silence for a while, passing though more woodland, crossing a couple of bridges, through an abandoned village until we eventually arrived in another clearing.

This was a large clearing and was full of yet more small tents, again all laid out in neat rows. There must have been hundreds and hundreds of these tents, maybe thousands. Grown ups sat outside the tents on the ground and small children were running around. There were one or two stray dogs.

"Each tent contains a family," explained Moldie. "If there are more than 6 in a family then they are allowed 2 tents. Some have folding beds to sleep on, but most people sleep wrapped up in blankets on the bare ground.

They are fed once a day. There are a number of fires kept burning night and day, over which the food is cooked in large pots. When they're not cooking food, they are heating water. People can come for water whenever they like for tea.

Handcarts carrying a large pot full of broth and some bread are pushed around the area. Every person has a small dish and they get it filled up and a slice of bread. That is their food for the day.

There is a small river at the other side of the clearing where people can wash and bathe. I'll show you."

We drove off again, heading towards the river, and I was conscious of many, many eyes following us as we drove by. Many people were in the river, either washing clothes or pots or bathing. A few children were swimming or playing.

"This is the river Agii," said Moldie. "Nobody is allowed to drink the water from below this spot and no one is allowed to do anything except drink the water above here. This way, we hope, no one will drink contaminated water. We have managed to keep cholera and dysentery to a minimum, though there are always a few cases every week."

Moldie drove us down river a couple of hundred yards. Here, a wooden platform overhung the river. There were a number of holes cut into the platform. People were squatting over the holes, obviously having a shit. I could see hundreds of turds floating down the river.

I sensed Moldie looking at me.

"I know it's pretty disgusting, but what else could we do? There are no towns or villages on the river between here and the sea, about 15 miles away. Well, there used to be a couple but we have closed them down because of the health risks and moved the people who lived there up to here.

Anybody who is too ill to make it here, well, they shit into a bucket and someone carries the bucket here. It was the only solution we could come up with."

I was on one hand quite horrified by what I had seen, but on the other hand, impressed by the organisation. They had virtually nothing but were doing the best they could with virtually nothing. Everything was neat and tidy and I saw no litter.

"Is this all organised by ODOE?" I asked.

He nodded as he looked around.

"If it wasn't for ODOE," he said, "Many of these people would be dead."

Later, back at the hotel, Moldie and I were sitting down having some supper. Soup and sandwiches. Very nice. Again, my favourite leek and potato soup, and blue cheese and onion sandwiches on white bread. I was finding it hard to concentrate on the food though. I was thinking of the poor people I had seen.

"So what exactly do you want of me?" I asked eventually. "I will do anything I possibly can to help."

"I'm glad you said that," said Moldie. "I want to show you something."

He opened a briefcase and took out some Abacadian newspapers and magazines. He opened them up one by one and I was amazed to see that on every page there were photographs and articles about me. There were dozens of them, dating back, it seemed, many years. Most of the articles were in Abacadian, I assumed, but some were in English.

"What..." I stuttered.

"You are extremely popular in Abacadia," explained Moldie. "Everybody loves you here. We love you because of all the good work you do for everybody, because you are such a beautiful woman, and because you are an English rose. You are our number one pin up girl. Everyone loves you."

I was amazed. I had no idea. Why did I have no idea? It all seemed very strange.

"It started 4 years ago. An Abacadian journalist called Klock Wise went to England to interview you and produced a half hour programme all about you, which was shown on primetime television. He showed you in a wonderful light and ever since then you have been our number one pinup."

Vaguely I remembered a short interview I had given with a journalist from Abacadia. I couldn't remember his name but I did remember he was a bit odd. He must have been this Klock Wise that Moldie mentioned. It was, I recalled, not long after Alfie had been killed and I had other things on my mind, but I think I was polite with him. At least I hope I was. It seems now that I must have been.

"So tell me now," I told Moldie, "Why have you shown me all this? What do you want me to do?"

He took a big breath.

"If you go back to England, I know you will do everything you possibly can to let the world know about our problems, but any money you raise will go through the government and none or very little of the money will come to us. We need you to do something which will bring money straight here, to us."

I looked on suspiciously.

"What exactly do you mean?"

"Although there is a lot of poverty in Effghania, there are also many, many very rich men in Abacadia. Most of them would pay a huge amount of money to spend a night with you. When I say a huge amount, I mean $100,000 or even more. We have made inquiries and have over 20 men willing to pay that money to spend a night with you. That money would be paid straight to us in cash. With three men a week, in a month we can have over $1,000,000 to help all those people we saw today. So that's what we want of you."

All this lot came out in one mad rush, as if he was rather embarrassed to say it.

My mouth was well open. I know it was. I was in shock. Had I heard correctly? He wanted me to be a prostitute. He wanted me to sleep with three rich men a week, so that the money I earned could be used to help his people.

"You want me to be a prostitute?"

He nodded.

"Yes. Please. If you don't mind."

He sounded almost apologetic.

Yes please. If you don't mind. That's what he said. If you don't mind. Yes please.

"I do mind," I said, trying to sound outraged. "There's no way I'm going to do that. Even to help your people. I'll do anything else, but not that. No way."

"Lady Clair, we have racked our brains to think of another way to raise large amounts of money quickly to help our people, but we couldn't think of anything. We don't believe in violence. Please, for the sake of our people who you saw today, we would really like you to do this."

"No," I answered but Moldie held up his hand.

"Please let me explain a bit more what we have in mind. The 'shall we say gentleman' will arrive here at this hotel in the afternoon and come up to this room. You will be wearing one of the dresses in your cupboard. You will act as an English Lady all evening. The two of you will talk and posh food and wine brought up to you both. Later, the two of you will go to bed, and do what you do. In the morning, breakfast will be supplied and after that, the gentleman will leave. Everything will be done in the best possible taste. Please Lady Clair; we really want you to do this for us."

"What happens if I just refuse? You can't make me do it."

"We can't, I agree, but, as much as I admire you, my people are more important. We need money from you. We could try ransoming you, but before that, I'm afraid, we will whore you, except this time you will do as we say. We would only be able to get a few thousand dollars a time, maybe only a few hundred, so you will have to be fucked 5 or 6 times a day, 7 days a week, to earn any decent amount of money. The choice is yours, Lady Clair. Please make the correct choice, I beg you."

The way he said 'fucked 5 or 6 times a day, 7 days a week' left me feeling cold. It was that that made me realise that maybe he wasn't such a sweetie-pie after all.

I sighed. I needed time to think.

"I will let you know in the morning," I said, "I think you had better leave now," and he left, quietly closing the door behind him. No one came to take away the dirty dishes.

"Oh my God," I thought to myself as I lay in bed that night. But, of course, I had no choice. I couldn't escape, or could I? I thought about that. I was a very resourceful lady. Although I was 48 years old, I was still very fit and healthy. Could I get out of the hotel? I got up and checked all the windows. They were all double-glazed and securely locked and it looked like they were alarmed but I wasn't sure. The door that led out of the living room was locked, and there were the two guards waiting outside.

And supposing I did manage to escape from the hotel. What then? I was in a strange country, a white woman on her own, where, as far as I knew, virtually no one spoke English, with no money and no friends. It would be very difficult for me to get anywhere.

And no doubt, Moldie would send men after me. Almost certainly, I would be captured.

I thought about the Landrover we had used that morning. Could I steal that and drive it to somewhere? I knew that there was a way to start cars without the ignition key but I had no idea how to do that. With an older vehicle like that, it should be relatively easy for someone with the knowledge, but I had no idea at all what to do. You needed to rub two wires together but which two I hadn't the faintest.

And if I did manage to get it going and drive it away, what then? It probably only had a small petrol tank, so wouldn't go far, and I had no money to refuel. Then I would be on foot and totally lost.

I could hand myself in to the local police station, if there was one, but what would they do? Hand me back? Probably. They would all be Effghanian's, wouldn't they? Probably members of ODOE. Did they know about me, the police? I obviously didn't know. Oh God!

Attempting to escape seemed a hopeless option, at least for now. Maybe something would turn up later. I needed to bide my time.

And I obviously didn't want to become a common whore.

'Fucked 5 or 6 times a day, 7 days a week.'

The thought made me shiver with horror. I decided I just had to go along with his sordid plan. Upon reflection, I decided that it wouldn't be that bad. I was a healthy young woman, youngish, and having sex with rich men three times a week wasn't that horrendous. Was it?

I hadn't had that many lovers in my life. A few at university before I met my husband, Alfie. I had been completely faithful to him, totally, but I had had three or four casual relationships since his death. I enjoyed sex as much as the next woman and I knew I was good at it. I had been told so many times.

"Bugger," I thought to myself. Bugger was one of my favourite swear words.

"What would my children think? Surely they would understand. Wouldn't they? Of course they would. Oh bugger, bugger, bugger. How has this happened? Kidnapped and now this and all because I was so popular. It didn't seem fair. It didn't seem right.

But somehow it didn't seem so wrong either. I shivered. In fear? In anticipation? Probably a bit of both. And Moldie would look after me. He told me he would. Did I believe him? He seemed nice enough. Did I trust him? I think I had to trust him. Oh, more buggers. Bugger, bugger, bugger."

Eventually I talked myself into believing that it might actually be fun. I might actually enjoy myself. In the morning, I'd tell Moldie that I would go along with his sick plan. Maybe something would turn up. Just go with the flow Clair and keep yourself safe.

Eventually I fell asleep and I dreamt of my Alfie.

Chapter 6 - A hidden message

Three days later, the phone rang again at Hamilton Hall. It had rung many, many times, and each time when one of us picked it up, we were hoping it was mother, or news about her, but it never was. I was hoping this time as well.

I picked up the receiver and said, "Mother," but a man's voice which I didn't know ignored my question and said,

"We have a message from your mother. Please listen carefully. The message will not be repeated."

I grabbed the pen and paper that was always by the phone and wrote down the message as best I could. It was mother's voice but it was obviously a recording.

Then a man's voice read out some football scores, which I also wrote down, then he just hung up and the phone line went dead.

I called the others.

"I've just had a phone call from somebody, and then a recorded message from mother. I'm pretty sure it was recorded. She sounded calm enough. I've written the message down, the best I can," and we read it together.

"I am very well, but have been kidnapped. I am not allowed to say where I am, but I am being treated very well and please don't worry about me. I am not sure how long I will be held captive but I am certain no harm will come to me."

We looked at each other in astonishment. She'd been kidnapped. Our worse fears.

"At least she appears to be safe and sound," I said. "I wonder where she is. I wonder who's holding her. I wonder what they want. Ransom?"

There were so many questions.

"Let's have a look at the rest of the message," suggested Theo. "Maybe there's a hidden message in the message. She is very clever."

Theo was the nerdy one. I say nerdy in the nicest possible way.

We studied it.

"Why has she insisted we carry on with her charity work?" asked Pauline. "And why so much detail? And what's this bit about a whist drive? She's never organised a whist drive, has she?"

"In this, my initial message to you, could I ask you a couple of favours? Ask Betty and Celia and deliver all initial invitations to Alan for the next charity whist drive," I read. "Do you think there might be a clue in there?"

Theo picked up the pen and paper and wrote.

"ABACADAIITAFTNCWD. Those are the initials," he said. "She mentioned initials in the message, but that doesn't really make any sense."

"Yes it does," I said. "Swap the 'I' and the 'A' and it spells Abacadia. She probably had to make the message up in a hurry and that was the best she could come up with. I think she's in Abacadia."

"At the end of the message she say's that the kidnappers will allow her to send one message every week. At least that will assure us she's okay." Pauline was thinking. "But why would a kidnapper allow that? It all seems very strange. I've never heard of anything like this before."

"We know nothing about kidnappers, do we?" said Theo. "Maybe it happens all the time. We just don't know. I'm just going to check the premiership football scores."

"I'll phone Inspector Hector and let him know about the message," I said whilst Theo confirmed the scores.

The inspector arrived at the house less than an hour later. He asked me how I had come about the message and I told him.

"We'll try and trace the call," he said, "But I very much doubt it will tender any clues. We should have set it up so that every phone call to you is automatically recorded and traced. I will arrange that immediately. If that's acceptable with you?"

We assured him that that was perfectly acceptable.

He studied the message.

"Are you sure this is the message?" he asked me.

"The best I could do," I said. "It did come as a bit of a shock and I had to grab for a pen and a piece of paper. I think this was just about it."

"And you think she is in Abacadia. You could be right. It's all we've got to go on, I suppose. Let me take a copy to our encryption department and see if they can find anything else. At least it is a start. Have you any idea why they might be holding her? Ransom maybe?"

"We've been thinking about that," I replied, "And we think that is very unlikely. Since Dad died, and the death duties were paid, we have been relatively poor. But whether they know that, we don't know."

"Keep your thinking caps on and get back to me if you come up with any ideas, or if there are anymore phone calls," said Inspector Hector.

"Is there any news from forensics about the car in the hedge?" I asked, but the good inspector shook his head.

"Nothing," and off he went.

We looked gloomily at each other, and, with nothing better to do, made a pot of tea.

Chapter 7 - Becoming Friends

In the morning over breakfast, Moldie told me that my message had been sent.

"Did you get a reply?" I asked, but he just shook his head.

"We just sent the message and hung up," he said.

Then I told Moldie of my decision to go along with his plans. He seemed very pleased. Very, very pleased. In fact, delighted.

"I'm delighted, "he said. "I'm glad you saw sense. I'll try to arrange your first client in a couple of days. That'll give us time to get you ready."

"What do you mean, get me ready?" I asked indignantly.

"We want you to earn as much money for our people as you possibly can," he answered patiently, "And to do this you must entertain the men who come to see you the best you can. And to do this, you must do what they expect you to do. You must be Lady Clair Hamilton. They have a perception of what you are from the newspapers and magazines, and you must live up to that expectation. I need to advise you on how to do that."

"Are you talking about in the bed?" I growled at him angrily, "Because I think I know how to satisfy a man in bed."

"The sex is only part of it," he explained calmly. "The very rich men are paying for the whole experience of meeting you and spending time with you, and if they are pleased, they will come back again and also pass the news on to some of their equally rich friends. They may even tip you. The better you are, the more money we can get to help my people."

"Oh God," I sighed, "What have I done to deserve this?"

I put my head in my hands, and immediately he came around to my side of the table and put his arms around me. I lay my head against his chest. He stroked my hair.

"I'm sorry about this," he said tenderly, "But my people mean so much to me."

I gently pushed him away and sighed.

"I know," I said, "I know and I can't really blame you. Alright, let's get on with the training."

"When the client arrives," he explained, "You must look like Lady Clair. Your hair must be perfect, your make up must be perfect, and your clothes must be perfect. We have a woman who will come in to help you. Her name is Pebble. You have already met her. She's the woman who served our food last night. She's a good girl. Loyal and hardworking. You'll like her.

Anyway, you must act at all times like Lady Clair would act. You don't need any training for that bit. In bed, you must know what pleases Abacadian men. I think they have different yearnings from English men. It would be good if you learnt what they want."

"And who is going to teach me in bed?" I asked, sarcastically. "You?"

He looked shocked, probably at the anger in my voice.

"It was just a thought," he said quietly.

"Forget it. I know what to do in bed to please any man. I don't need any lessons from you or from anybody."

I was really angry now.

"Forget it."

He looked truly shocked now, but held up his hands in resignation.

"Okay," he said, "It was just a suggestion that's all."

He managed to control himself, and continued, after taking a big breath.

"And you need to learn the story you are to tell them as to why you are here."

"Story?" I asked. "Why not just tell them the truth?"

"Because most of the men who will come to see you are either members of the Jakalamnian government or rich Jakalamnian businessmen. They hate the Effghanian people, and if they knew their money was going to help us, they probably wouldn't be at all happy, and may ask for their money back. And they definitely wouldn't return.

And even worse, I'm sure they could find out where we are and send the police or even the army to arrest us all. And that would be the end of everything. No money to help my people. That's why."

"Oh. So what story do you want me to tell them?"

"You will tell them that you lost all your money in death duties when your husband died, which is sort of true. You need money quickly otherwise you will loose Hamilton Hall and when you learnt that you were a sex symbol here in Abacadia, you decided to come here and sell yourself. You booked this room in this posh hotel, and got an agent, me, to get rich men to spend a night with you. You think this is the best way to earn some quick money. I'm sure they'll believe you. Just make sure that you never mention that we are in Effghania."

I groaned. This was getting worse and worse. I just couldn't see it working. It was going to all go horribly wrong and I knew it would end in tears and they might be my tears. And I couldn't think of anything I could do except go along with it.

I shook my head.

"Moldie, do you really think this is going to work? Seriously. Do you think this is going to work?"

Moldie started to look worried and suddenly I felt sorry for him. He had this wonderful plan to earn a lot of money to help his people and here was me throwing doubt on it.

"We've already spent a lot of money getting you here," he said. "It has to work."

I couldn't believe what I said next. I still can't believe it.

I said, "Let's give it a go shall we, it might be okay. Come on, let's start on my lessons. I'll go and put on one of the dresses, and we'll have a pretend conversation. You wait here."

There was me encouraging him that his ridiculous plan might work. Just because I felt slightly sorry for him. He'd kidnapped me for goodness sake. Gee.

I walked into the bedroom and opened the wardrobe that was full of a dozen or more posh dresses. I counted them. I looked at them more carefully, and fingered some of the material. I pulled out two or three and held them up in front of me and looked in the full length mirror and sighed to myself.

A colourful dress caught my eye. It was basically navy blue but was covered with squares and triangles of many colours. It was made of some sort of silky polyester, I guessed, with a long zip down the back. I undressed then pulled the colourful dress on over my head. It slipped down my body easily, with a wonderful feel. I pulled up the zip and looked in the mirror again, and it fitted perfectly. It clung to me like a second skin, leaving little to the imagination.

I did look good in it. Just like a posh English Lady should look like. I sighed and walked back to Moldie.

"How do I look?" I asked him, tossing my hair, and blowing him a kiss.

He thought I looked wonderful. I could see it on his face. Oh God, I thought, don't say he's falling in love with me.

"Right," I said, "Let's start a conversation," and I saw him make a big effort to concentrate on talking.

So we spent the next hour chatting about what I should say. It was a two-way discussion. He told me I had to talk about being a lady in England, and I talked about my family and charity work and Hamilton Hall and the rich and influential celebrities I knew and some I didn't know.

"That's really good," he said. "They will love to hear things like that. Maybe you could make up a few stories or exaggerate rumours, make things a bit more spicy."

I sighed.

"You also need to learn a little bit about the clients," Moldie continued, "So that you can talk to them about their lives and they can talk about their lives as well. Men like to talk about themselves. I will supply you with some reading matter, and you need to do some homework."

I sighed again.

"It's been a long time since I did any homework. Okay, I'll do some homework."

"Do you mind if we talk about the bedroom time now?" he eventually asked and it was his tone of voice that made me suddenly realise he WAS actually in love with me. He had said that all Abacadian men loved me, and he was one of them. He was definitely in love with me and he wanted to sleep with me before I slept with the others. Maybe the whole idea of whoring me had come from his daydreams of sleeping with me.

So what was I going to do? Encourage him, or refuse him? Of course, he could have taken me any time he wanted to, but I sensed that that was not his way. He seemed like a decent man, and rape was not on his agenda. If I refused him, then he would be disappointed but would probably leave me alone.

However, I reckoned that would cause resentment and jealousy on his part. I needed him on my side. He was the only friend I had in Abacadia, if you could call him a friend. If I was to survive this nightmare, I needed all the help I could get. I would have to let him sleep with me, and it had to be soon. That evening. And I had to make it good for him.

The more I could make him fall in love with me, the better he would look after me and care for me and keep me from harm. I had to have him on my side.

All this went through my mind in an instant, but even so, I suddenly heard him saying, "Lady Clair, are you okay?"

"I'm sorry," I said, "I was miles away. Moldie, I've been thinking. I am a bit nervous about the whole situation. I want to do my best for you and your people, but I am worried I won't be good enough."

Immediately he showed concern. He put his hand on top of mine and gave a gently squeeze.

"You'll be fine," he said. "Just be yourself."

"I think I need some more practise. This evening, let's go through the whole thing again, and follow it through to the bedroom."

He inhaled sharply and groaned.

"Okay, if you think so."

He appeared to be trembling slightly.

"Give me some homework to do and this evening we'll go through it all again," I said firmly and he nodded. I could see he was pleased and excited. He left the room, remembering to lock the door behind him and I glimpsed one of the guards sitting outside.

I went to change out of my posh dress and put on some working clothes, jeans and a blouse, which had been provided. He returned shortly with a folder full of information about Abacadia and suggested I read it. He left again and I sat down with a glass of white wine and started reading.

The data came partly from ODOE but also the Abacadian Jakalamnian government. The two bits of information were so different that they could have been talking about separate countries. The official government said that everything was going fine whilst ODOE pointed out how things were going wrong.

I knew which of the two contradictory reports I believed.

A bit later, I went and had a shower and put the posh dress back on. There was a shy knock on the bedroom door, and, after I had answered, Pebble, the maid, entered. She didn't speak any English, but, by using sign language and a few giggles, indicated that she was there to put on some make up for me and brush my hair.

She seemed very friendly and I wondered if she realised what was going on. Why I was there. Probably not, I decided. Our inability to communicate was a problem. I needed to learn a few words or more of Abacadian. I would ask Moldie for an English Abacadian dictionary at the earliest opportunity.

Pebble was humming to herself as she brushed my hair. I wondered if somehow I could talk her into delivering a message for me somehow. It was a thought. A message to whom I did not know, but it was a thought.

She eventually left with a smile and a wave and I walked through to the living room. Moldie was waiting for me. He pretended he didn't know me, as we had decided, and introduced himself.

"My name is Moldie Bedlam," he said. "How do you do?"

I walked over to him and offered my hand. He took it and kissed it.

"I'm Lady Clair Hamilton," I said, using a very posh voice, "It's nice to meet you Moldie. Please sit down. May I get you a cup of tea or would you prefer something stronger?"

The evening carried on like this. We both role-played to our hearts delight. The main problem was trying to stop laughing. I think the evening might have been a small help to me, but probably not.

As bedtime approached, Moldie got quieter and quieter. Probably his sexual dream was soon to come true. I wondered should I tease him a bit, but decided not. We were getting on quite well, why upset him?

So eventually, I stood up, took his hand and said, "Come on Moldie, time for bed."

I led him into the bathroom. I stood in front of him and turned round and said, in a low, husky voice, "Please Moldie, will you unzip my dress for me," which he managed to do, though it took him a few seconds. I think his hands were shaking. I know his hands were shaking.

Then I stepped out of my dress and hung it over the side of the bath. Still with my back to him, I undid my bra, and then slowly pulled down my panties. I heard him gasp, and then I turned around to face him. His eyes were all over me but he kept his hands by his side.

I looked straight into his eyes but my fingers started undoing the buttons on his shirt, starting at the top until they were all undone. I slipped my hands inside the shirt, and ran my fingertips up his body.

He was standing perfectly still but I felt him shiver. I moved my hands around to his chest and up his neck to his cheeks, which I stroked gently.

"Lift your foot," I told him, and pulled off his shoes and socks, then, once again looking him in the eye, undid his flies, and pulled down his trousers and pants. If he had been nervous earlier, he certainly wasn't now.

I put my arms around his neck and pulled his face to mine and we kissed. Gently at first, but then with more passion. He wrapped his arms around me and held me close. After a few seconds, I pushed him gently away and turned and switched on the shower and, taking his hand, pulled him in with me.

I put some shower gel onto a big, soft sponge and started washing him all over and he stood there with his eyes closed, obviously thoroughly enjoying himself. Then I gave him the sponge and he washed me. I sighed with genuine pleasure as he sponged my back. My back has always been sensitive, and caressing my back has always made me feel gooey inside.

We didn't speak, just muttered endearments and encouragement.

"Mmmm, that's nice, oooh, that's lovely."

After just a few minutes, I switched off the shower and wrapped a big, very big and fluffy towel around him, and he wrapped one around me. We dried each other, and then I led him to the bedroom and pushed him down onto the bed.

"Lie still," I told him. "I'm in charge," and proceeded to spend the next 20 minutes showing him exactly how an English Lady pleases an English Lord in bed.

He seemed to quite enjoy it.

"Well," I asked when we had finished, "Was I good enough?"

"You are fantastic," he said, and I smiled to myself. "Are all English Ladies so sexy?"

"I don't know," I said, "I haven't slept with all of them. The one's I have slept with were all very wonderful but I should imagine the others are all pretty good as well. Lords and Earls and Knights of the Realm don't marry us just for our looks, you know!"

I kissed him on his cheek, leant over to switch off the side light, and cuddled up. I soon fell asleep, feeling a lot more content and relaxed than I had since I had been kidnapped. Maybe things could work out okay after all.

I slept very well in Moldie's arms, and in the morning, I bought him a cup of tea.

"Whilst you are up, will you open the curtains please?" suggested Moldie "Let a bit of daylight into the room so I can see you better."

I thought it was more romantic to keep them closed but I did as I was told. I didn't realise at the time, but I found out later that the reason he wanted them open was because he had positioned a number of hidden cameras around the room and everything was being filmed. The footage was then edited into a 3-minute film, which he used to promote me and get clients. He may have been in love with me, or not, but his people still came first.

"I need to have you in as many positions as possible," Moldie explained to me, "Just to check that you know them all and are competent."

What he really meant was the more positions the better would be the film he could send off to randy men.

I didn't know about the cameras then. I just enjoyed the sex. It was wonderful. I climbed on top, he climbed on top, we lay side by side, we lay head to toe, I knelt down and he knelt behind me and I had a number of lovely orgasms and eventually so did he. We both finished sweaty and panting and so went and shared another shower.

"Thank you very much for giving me that lesson," I told him, tongue in cheek. "I learnt so much and I hope I passed the test."

He told me I had.

"I'll arrange the first client as soon as possible," he said over breakfast, "So that we can earn some money and start improving the lives of my people. I'll try to sort something out for the day after tomorrow. We have a number of men keen to meet you."

I nodded.

"Whatever."

I remembered my idea the day before about talking to Pebble.

"Moldie," I asked, "I think it would be a good idea if I were to learn a few words of Abacadian. Do you think I could borrow an Abacadian-English dictionary?"

Moldie looked surprised but seemed pleased.

"They all speak English," he said. "At least I think they do but if you would like to learn our language, well, I think that's good. Everyone likes it if you make the effort to speak a few words. I've got one downstairs. I'll bring it up for you."

Moldie returned with a dictionary. He had obviously been thinking.

"I could help you, if you like. I understand that Abacadian is quite a difficult language for Western Europeans to learn. The structure is very different from the Latin based languages."

I thanked him, said that would be nice, and he spent the next two hours giving me a lesson. He was right, it was difficult, but he was a good teacher, and patient and I made a little bit of progress. After he had left, I attempted to learn a few phrases of Abacadian from the dictionary that I felt would help me, such as "What is the name of the local town?" and "Where is the nearest airport?"

Pebble visited again after lunch. Not only was she my make up artist and hair stylist, and the woman who served my meals, but she was also the cleaner. And, I hoped, my friend.

I attempted to talk to her in Abacadian but the conversation dissolved into bouts of giggles.

"Do you live near by?" I eventually managed to ask her, hoping she lived in the local town and would tell me the name.

"I live in Redik," she said.

I'd never heard of the place.

"How do you get to work?" I asked her. "Do you walk or catch a taxi?"

"I walk," she says, "It's only 20 minutes."

At least I think that's how the conversation went. However, I was fairly sure that I was being held near the town of Redik.

The next time I saw Moldie, I asked him, "Moldie, I've been thinking about home. I'm sure they must be worried about me. Could I send another message, please, just to reassure them that I'm fine?"

"Okay," he replied. "You're being very helpful so I think I should help you. What do you want to say?"

"I'll have a think and let you know later," I said, and went to the bedroom to compose another secret message. I wondered if my children had managed to work out my first message. I just had to assume that they had.

Eventually I came up with the following.

"This is the second message. I am still okay and being well looked after, both physically and mentally. I am not totally sure why I have been kidnapped and why I am being held here."

I really didn't want to tell them the real reason. I couldn't. I just couldn't and anyway, I didn't think Moldie would send such a message.

I carried the message on with, "In this, my second message after my initial message, please can I ask you once again to pass on some messages to some of the volunteers."

There were a number of messages giving actual advice and suggestions to real people with real problems. Then one of the messages said, "Concerning the whist drive, try letting Adrian Williams skype the others volunteers to convince them to work harder. Suggest a prize of the hot elephant water bottle. I'm sure they'll think it's a top rate present."

I finished the message with "I really am being very well looked after and my kidnappers have promised I can send another message in one week's time. I love you all and think about you every day."

I hoped the clues weren't too obscure for my family or too obvious for Moldie to spot them. Anyway, that evening, I recorded it, and Moldie didn't seem to notice and the next morning he told me he had sent the message to my daughter Alice.

"Did she say anything?" I asked him.

"No, we just sent the message and hung up," he said.

I would just have to be patient, I reckoned.

Chapter 8 - Wondering

Early the next morning, police Inspector Hector phoned.

"We have contacted every single airport in the country, public and private, and there were no unscheduled flights from any of them last week.

We have also contacted the Abacadian government, and they have no records of any unauthorised landings. If they did fly your mother out of the country and she really is in Abacadia, then it must have been done in total secret. With modern technology, I think this is highly unlikely.

To be honest, I think she is still in Britain somewhere. That message was just a coincidence or is deliberately misleading. That's my opinion."

We didn't think so, but how could we argue with him? We tried but he had made up his mind and wouldn't change.

Pauline, Theo, and I visited the local library and got out every book we could find about Abacadia. There weren't that many. We also read everything we could on Google and Theo used his friends at University to find out even more about the place.

It did us no good. All we found out was that Abacadia was a large country with a large population. If mother was being held captive there, then she could be anywhere and would be almost impossible to locate.

We tried to find out if there were any terrorist groups in Abacadia, or any gangs of any kind who may have captured her, but as far as we could discover and according to the Abacadian government, there were no such organisations. Everything seemed highly peaceful in the country.

Two days later and another message arrived from mother. This time, thanks to the inspector's recorder, we could all listen to the recording, and we did so a number of times.

"At least she sounds cheerful enough and in no danger," said Pauline. "It sounds like she is being well looked after. Is there another secret message for us?"

Theo had been studying the message carefully and had written it down on a piece of paper.

"She says that this is the second message after the initial message. In last week's message, she used the initial letters of a series of words to almost spell Abacadia. This time I think she wants us to use the second letters of words to spell out a message. And I think the sentence will be the one about the whist drive again.

'Concerning the whist drive, try letting Adrian Williams skype the other volunteers to convince them to volunteer. Suggest a prize of the hot elephant water bottle. I'm sure they'll think it's a top rate present.'

If we take the second letters of the sentence 'try letting Adrian Williams skype the others volunteers' it spells REDIKHTO. Is there a town or a place called Redikhto in Abacadia?"

We got out a world atlas, opened it at the index at the back, and looked up Redikhto.

"There isn't a Redikhto, but there is a Redik in Abacadia," I said. "That must be the town she means."

"And look at this," said Theo, "'Suggest a prize of the hot elephant water bottle. I'm sure they'll think it's a top rate present.' Hot elephant? Could that be hotel? And top rate present could mean she's being kept on the top floor!"

"Hum, possibly," I muttered, "But I don't think Inspector Hector will think much of that."

"I've googled Redik," said Theo, studying his computer screen. "There's a small entry in Wikipedia all about the place. It's in Effghania. It's quite a big town, over 150,000 population, but very, very poor. Surrounded by squatter camps. There's a lot of poverty. Just the sort of place that would attract mother. Do you think they've kidnapped her to get her to help them? It's what she's well known for and what she's really good at."

"Hmm. Possibly. " I wasn't convinced. "Does it list the names of any hotels in the town?" I asked.

"No," said Theo. "It doesn't say anything about hotels. I wonder if the name of the hotel is included in her message."

We all studied it, but couldn't come up with anything. We reluctantly agreed that that was the extent of the secret message.

"Maybe in the next message next week," suggested Pauline. "If they allow her to send one."

We passed the information on to Inspector Hector. Once again, he wasn't impressed but promised to contact the Abacadian government again.

"I'm not impressed with Inspector Hector," I said. "What can we do ourselves, I wonder?"

"We could fly out there," suggested Pauline.

"And do what?" asked Theo. "We are completely out of our depths here. We need help."

"Let's contact the British Embassy in Abacadia. Maybe they can help."

That was my suggestion.

"Surely Inspector hopeless Hector will have done that?" wondered Pauline, but Theo found the number on the internet and I phoned them anyway.

"Hello," answered a posh educated British voice. "British embassy. How may I help?"

I explained who I was and what our problem was.

"We think our mother has been kidnapped and smuggled into Abacadia," I explained. "We think she is being held in a hotel in Redik."

"And why do you think this?" asked the voice.

"We've had a message from her in code," I explained.

"You have, have you?" said the voice. "Have you contacted the police?"

"Yes."

"And what do they say?"

"They don't really believe us but we are pretty sure it's true," I answered, suddenly realising I was sounding rather pathetic.

There was a huge over-reacted sigh from the phone.

"Give me your details," said the sighing man, "And I'll see what I can do, though, to be honest, not a lot."

He asked me some questions, names and dates and phone contact, and then said, "I must warn you, Effghania is a dangerous place, and Redik is full of beggars and bandits. If you are thinking of visiting the place yourselves, be very careful. If I obtain any news, I will contact you," and at that, he hung up.

I looked at the others, who had been listening on, and shrugged.

"I don't think he believed me."

The others shook their heads.

"Plan B," I said, but we didn't have a Plan B.

We didn't even have a Plan A.

Chapter 9 - Lake Lucinda

The same evening I had recorded the message, and after Moldie and I had had yet another lovely dinner, I asked him if I could go for a visit somewhere in the countryside for the day.

"Tomorrow is a day off. I've done everything you've asked of me, plus one or two things extra." I winked at him. "How about the two of us going for a picnic? I would be very grateful!"

"Well," said Moldie, obviously surprised at the suggestion. "I suppose we could."

"I promise I won't try and escape," I promised. "If you're worried, you could bring along your two tame gorillas to keep an eye on me. However, that would put a bit of a dampener on the day! If you know what I mean?"

I could see that Moldie was very keen on the idea.

"I'll get back to you," he said.

I think he probably phoned somebody for permission, but permission he got because later that afternoon he gave me an answer over afternoon tea.

"We can leave after breakfast tomorrow if you like," he said, grinning. "There's a lovely lake about 40 minutes drive from here. It's surrounded by rolling hills and woods and is extremely pretty. We could even go swimming, if you like. I happen to know that you are a good swimmer!"

"That sounds lovely," I said, "Would the gorillas be with us?"

He nodded but shrugged. "I'm afraid so, but we can lose them for a while when we are there. I'll organise a picnic. Sandwiches and wine?"

Moldie left me alone for the rest of the day. There were plenty of books and magazines for me to read, plus more information about Abacadia, and there was a television and a DVD player, a radio, and some paper and a couple of pens. I spent an hour or so writing down my experiences. I decided I would try to keep a diary. You never know, if or when I got home, my story might just become a best seller.

Or probably not.

I also spent plenty of time on the running machine. I had always been athletic and was proud of my figure. I didn't want to become fat and podgy so I ran and thought and ran some more then had a shower.

I switched on the television. There were only two channels, both in Abacadian. I tried watching, thinking it might help me improve my knowledge of that language, but it didn't, so I gave up. The programmes seemed to be entirely game shows or soap operas. There wasn't even any news. I gave up.

At least Moldie had supplied me with some good films. In fact, all my favourites. These included Shirley Valentine, Notting Hill, Dave and The Life of Brian. Once again, I wondered where he got that information. Somebody, possibly Moldie, must have spent a lot of time researching me. The afternoon passed quickly, Pebble brought supper to me and I ate on my own and went to bed early.

I actually slept quite well, and was gently awoken in the morning by Moldie tapping on the bedroom door. He bought me a cup of tea, Earl Grey, my favourite, naturally. I could see him eyeing me up in my nightie, but I made it apparent that he wasn't going to get anything. I wanted to keep that for later.

After breakfast together, I shooed him out, had a shower, and got dressed. He rejoined me and we left the room, went downstairs in the lift, and out of the back door of the hotel once again. The two gorillas followed close behind. We got into the same battered old Landrover, the gorillas got into the back seat, I got in the passenger seat and Moldie drove off.

We passed through yet more beautiful countryside, but this time heading away from the town of Redik and all the squatter camps. Moldie gave me a running commentary of the area we were passing through.

"The hills are called the Hills of the Phantoms Caves. They are called that because of many sightings of ghosts and phantoms in many of the caves. Obviously, there are no ghosts in the caves. Caves exist, but ghosts don't.

They are not the highest hills in Abacadia by a long way, but many people think they are the prettiest. They have many beauty spots in them, with waterfalls, forests, viewpoints, and a number of small lakes and rivers. And caves. Maybe we could visit some of them at another date."

Later we passed a huge rock, which rose almost vertically, it seemed, towards the sky. The sides were smooth and grey, with occasional clumps of bushes or trees clinging precariously to anywhere they could get their roots into. Even by craning my neck, I couldn't see the top.

"It's called Elephant Rock," explained Moldie, watching me in amusement. "The top is almost flat, and is a home to a village of 35 people called Elephant village. There is a.path on the other side, which leads almost halfway up, but then they climb the rest of the way using rope ladders. Goods are hauled up and down using rope baskets. It is, I think, a unique way of life."

"How far is it to the top," I asked him.

"About 1300 feet," he said. "I've heard that the view from the top is quite spectacular. I've never been up, I'm not allowed. Traditionally, only villagers born on the summit are allowed up."

I looked back as Moldie drove away from Elephant Rock, and as we got further away, I reckoned I could see some huts on the summit, but maybe I was imagining.

Elephant village was the last village we saw until, eventually, after about 90 minutes driving, we arrived at the lake that Moldie was heading for. The lake wasn't very large, just a couple of hundred yards across, I guessed. The water was very blue, and the surface was covered with small ripples. It was surrounded by tall trees and rugged hills in the near distance, and was one of the most beautiful places I had ever been to in my life.

Despite all this beauty, the overriding impression was of birds. Water birds. Everywhere. The surface seemed to be covered with them. Many, many different species, and different colours and shapes and sizes.

They were a spectacular sight.

"This is called Lake Lucinda," said Moldie. "It was named

after an English Lady, like yourself, who unfortunately drowned here in the 1840's. It used to be one of Abacadia's most popular tourist resorts, and was a special favourite of bird watchers. However, since the enmity between Jakalamnia and Effghania and the earthquake and the famine, hardly anyone comes here now. Such a shame, but good for us."

He parked on a piece of grass beside the lake, and we all got out. I looked around me. There was no sign of human habitation anywhere. Moldie reached into the back of the Landrover and took out a large rucksack.

"This is ours," he said, talking to me.

"Your picnic is here."

He was now talking to the gorillas alone, and pointing to the Landrover.

"Lady Clair and I are going for a short walk around that headland," pointing to a headland. "We'll be a couple of hours. You two stop here, eat your lunch and relax. Just mind the Landrover."

The gorillas grinned and leered, Moldie chuckled, and I stuck my tongue out at them. That made them chuckle even more. I later found out that the reason for that chuckle was that in the back of the Landrover was a cine camera with a telephoto lens and the main reason they were there was to film Moldie and me but mainly me as I swam in the lake and anything else I got up to.

Moldie and I walked along the lakeside.

He said, "This is possibly my favourite place in the whole world. I love coming here whenever I get any spare time. Nobody lives here anymore. It's too far away from any towns, and there is no work for anyone. We won't be disturbed and just around the headland is a beautiful little cove. Come on."

We walked up and over the small headland and as soon as we were out of sight of the gorillas, Moldie took my hand, and smiled at me.

"This is a good idea of yours," he said.

He was very attractive when he smiled.

"Thank you for suggesting it."

We rounded the headland and I saw the cove he had mentioned in front of us. It really was lovely, with a tiny beach and lovely views over the lake and the surrounding hills and trees. There was a small river flowing out of the lake just the other side of the beach. I could just hear the sound of it gurgling away above the sound of birds singing.

Moldie took a blanket out of the rucksack and spread it onto the beach. We sat down, and I looked around.

"It really is a wonderful lake," I said. "The water is so calm and the sky is so blue."

Lake Lucinda wasn't large, and almost a perfect circle, but with the small headland spoiling or enhancing the symmetry to our right. On the far side of the lake the trees came right down to the water's edge, but where we were there was a small grassy area above the small beach.

All around the lake hills rose gently away and they were almost entirely covered with a mixture of different trees. The leaves were mainly green, of course, but I could see the occasional tree with red or orange leaves, and often some brightly coloured flowers.

There were one or two fluffy clouds in the sky, and these were reflected in the almost totally calm lake. However, much of the lake's surface was covered with swimming water birds. They swam and squawked but there was not a single bird flying anywhere. Every bird I could see was swimming.

I leant back on my arms and shook my head, and chuckled. A place like this almost made the last few days worthwhile.

"Would you like to go swimming?" Moldie interrupted my thoughts.

"It looks great," I said, "But I haven't got a swimming costume."

Moldie put his hand into the rucksack and pulled out what looked to me to be the smallest tiniest bright red bikini I had ever seen in my whole life.

He handed it to me, grinning.

"This isn't going to cover much," I muttered, "I might as well swim in the nude!"

Moldie laughed and I realised that was what he had in mind.

"Come on then," I said, and stripped off all my clothes and ran to the lake edge. I put a foot in. The temperature was lovely, so ran through the shallows until the water reached my waist and looked around. Moldie was right behind me, also nude. I squealed, and dived in.

As Moldie had earlier suggested, I was a good swimmer. Very good actually. I had swum for my county, Worcestershire, when I was at school, and now I reached out powerfully, but Moldie was after me. I looked over my shoulder and there he was, just a couple of body lengths behind. I changed direction and swam quicker, and he chased after me, never quite catching up. He was a good swimmer but I was slightly better.

As we swam, the water birds squawked and squealed and either took off in front of us or just swan out of the way a short distance. They didn't seem overly worried about us being there and I realised they had probably rarely seen humans and that they therefore had few natural enemies and were more curious about us being there than worried.

Eventually I swam back to the beach, and allowed him to catch me as I walked through the shallows. He put his arms around me from behind and nuzzled my neck. I could feel his cock pushing against my bottom so I pushed back towards him. His hands cupped my breasts. He was breathing hard as he turned me around and kissed me then picked me up and carried me easily to the blanket and laid me down.

I looked around me through half closed eyes.

"This must be the most beautiful place I have ever made love in," I whispered into his ear.

"And you are the most beautiful woman I have ever made love to," he breathed. I groaned and pushed my hips up towards him.

He seemed to be desperate for me and thrust and jerked his hips almost frantically. I tried to control him, but he seemed uncontrollable. It didn't last long until he let out a deep moan and I felt his whole body shudder. He collapsed on top of me, and I hugged him close. He was panting in my ear.

"Oh Clair," he said, "I love you so much. I love you more than I have ever loved any other woman."

I didn't say anything. He pushed himself up onto his elbows and looked at me.

"Do you love me?" he asked.

I sighed inwardly. What should I say? I thought he genuinely probably did love me or was it just lust, but I obviously didn't love him. I liked him, but how could I love a man who had kidnapped me and was just about to whore me out to rich businessmen? But what should I tell him? I wanted him on my side. I mustn't upset him.

"I like you, Moldie," I said, cautiously, "But it takes a lot longer for a woman to fall in love. Give me time. I may well fall in love with you but it's too soon."

He sighed. A big sigh.

"That's the best I can hope for," and rolled off me. We both walked to the lake to have a wash, and I said, "I'm feeling a bit peckish after all that exercise. What have you got to eat and drink in your rucksack?"

Moldie pulled out some sandwiches, some fruit, some biscuits, a bottle of Cadian white wine, of course, and two glasses. He filled the glasses and toasted us.

"To us," he said, "And to the success of our venture."

I thought that was a bit ripe. Our venture? Nevertheless, I toasted us anyway.

I had a question to ask him.

"Moldie," I said. "I've been thinking. Are you really telling the truth when you say that you have a number of rich businessmen who are willing to pay one hundred thousand dollars just to spend one night with me? It does seem a lot. I mean, for a few dollars they could probably spend the night with one of many prostitutes."

"That's true," he said. "But the prostitutes wouldn't be you, would they? Clair, there are hundreds, maybe thousands, of millionaires and multimillionaires in Abacadia, most in Snuka, the capital city, but many elsewhere. None in Effghania though."

He sounded wistful.

"Many of these men, and a few women, have so much money they don't know what to do with it. To them, spending one hundred thousand dollars is nothing. They won't even miss it. It's just pocket money."

"How do you contact them?" I asked, intrigued.

"We find potential vict.., er, clients by exploring Google and through the ODOE network and other means. Then we send them emails, mentioning your name. Any that respond, and lots do, we send an Effghani agent to talk to them, and explain what they would get and how much it would cost. Most of the men, and some of the women, were genuinely interested. Now you are here, we have re-contacted them. Some have paid already."

"Who do you mean by 'we'?" I asked.

"ODOE," he said. "We have some very clever people in our organisation."

I sighed.

Life has many strange twists and turns and my life had taken one of the strangest.

"What about my safety? Alone in a bedroom with a strange man."

"All the clients have been carefully vetted," he said, "And they will all be body searched before they meet you. Don't worry, you will be perfectly safe."

Which reassured me not a lot.

We stayed on the beach for an hour or so whilst we ate the sandwiches and finished the wine, had another gentle swim, got dressed, and then walked back to the Landrover where we found the gorillas waiting for us. They grinned as we approached and I ignored them.

Back at the hotel and I said, "Thank you for taking me to Lake Lucinda, Moldie. Do you think we could visit again?"

"I'll see what I can do," said Moldie.

He didn't sound very convinced.

Chapter 10 - Stig

The next evening was the first time that I was to be visited by a 'client', and Moldie spent all evening and all the next day time preparing me.

"His name is Stig de Silva, "he explained to me. "He's a businessman, a very, very successful businessman. He's only 32 and is Abacadia's youngest ever self-made millionaire. He designs and makes his own clothes for ladies. Not only does he want, well, you know, I think he also wants to talk to you about fashion and the clothes that posh ladies are wearing in Britain.

Reading between the lines, I actually think he may ask you to join him in his business. I think, but this is just a hunch, that he might ask you to be not only an advisor but also maybe an agent for him in England. I've brought you some stuff to read about him and his company. I do suggest you study it."

I was a bit taken aback. I was expecting to have to act like the Lady that I was and then bonk his brains out, but now here was something extra. Something extra that quite interested me. Really interested me. Anything that could help bring some money in for the family.

"Okay," I said, "Thank you."

"He is very keen to meet you." Moldie looked pleased. "And he has already paid. $100,000 in used notes. It was collected from him yesterday by one of our agents, and is already being spent. Next week I will take you out to see what we are doing. I'm sure you will be delighted."

"I'm sure I will be," I agreed.

Moldie left and I sat down to study the folders that he had left me. There were photos of Stig de Silva. He was quite good looking, which pleased me. I'm not overly fussy, but I do prefer handsome men, I must admit. He was clean-shaven, with jet-black hair. He had green, intelligent looking eyes. He looked friendly enough.

There was a brief biography about him. He actually went to

Oxford University where he read Business Studies and obtained a first class honours degree, so at least we had a common university education to talk about. His rise to wealth and success in Abacadia was meteoric and spectacular.

He had noticed that fashions in Abacadia were years behind the rest of the world. He had bought a huge quantity of ladies clothes at a knock down price from a warehouse in Oxfordshire before he left England. They were the previous year's fashions so he got them very cheap.

Back home in Abacadia, he had bought some low cost Abacadian ladies clothes and had mixed and matched the English and Abacadian, to make a new range of ladies clothes. All it took was one series of adverts on Abacadian television and he was made.

He called his business Abawest Designs, short for Abacadia and Western, and he was a millionaire before his 27th birthday. He was unmarried, though it appeared he had had a number of lovers and mistresses, all beautiful. He was a minor celebrity in Abacadia and many photos of him and his ladies were featured in the press.

I was actually looking forward to meeting him.

On a hunch, I walked through to the bedroom and looked more carefully at the dresses hanging in the cupboard. They were all Western designs, and none of them had been made by Stig's company. That was obvious. I tried to compare these dresses with Stig's I had been studying. Were they better, more fashionable? I wasn't sure. Stig's were different, but that was okay. I was intrigued by the idea of helping him, maybe even excited.

After lunch, at which Moldie joined me and answered some of my questions about Stig de Silva, Pebble appeared with the sole function of helping me get ready for his arrival. She helped me bathe, washed and dried my hair, and then helped me choose one of the dresses to wear.

Eventually we chose between us a knee length dress in dark green, with a light green belt. I twirled in front of the mirror and Pebble clapped her hands.

"You look beautiful," I think she said in Abacadian and I smiled at her.

She was right though. I did look beautiful.

Pebble then helped me put on some makeup. I decided to keep it simple, but allowed her to paint my nails for me and brush my hair so it shone. I slipped a pair of light sandals on my feet and I was ready.

I had learnt a little bit of Abacadian by now, and Pebble was helping me, in between fits of giggling, to learn a few more words.

Using the dictionary I managed to ask her, "What's the name of this hotel?"

She shook her head.

"It's not a hotel," she said. "It's an apartment block but you are the only occupant. What made you think it is an hotel?"

I think that's the gist of what she said.

It was my turn to shake my head.

"I just thought it was," I mumbled in English.

Bother. I had told Alice that it was a hotel, if she had got my message. I was constantly thinking about messages I could send to them. Now I would have to think of another. I was wondering if I could mention about Lake Lucinda. Tricky. Time to think of that later.

Moldie came up to see me.

"You look like a million dollars," he said, looking me up and down. "Ten million dollars."

"One hundred thousand dollars, you mean," I said, and he laughed.

"Moldie. May I ask you a couple of questions?"

He nodded.

"Of course. Anything."

"I was just wondering where we are, that's all."

He looked a bit confused.

"We're in Effghania."

"I mean, what's the name of the local town?"

I was wondering if he would tell me. I was testing how much he trusted me.

"The local town is called Redik," he answered without hesitation. "Would you like to visit?"

"Yes please. That would be nice. And what's the name of this hotel?"

He looked confused again.

"It's not a hotel, it's an apartment. It's owned by the people of Effghania, and this is the presidential suite. Why did you think it's a hotel?"

"You told me when I first arrived here," I said. "And the lovely food, it just feels like a hotel," I stuttered, a bit embarrassed.

"When you woke on that first day, I thought it would just be a lot simpler to say you were in a hotel. I thought you might be a bit confused. The food here is very good," he said. "We have our own cook. Properly trained. I'm sorry if I have confused you. Is there anything else you want to know?"

He was looking at me a bit strangely. On impulse, I kissed him on the cheek.

"No Moldie, thanks. Actually, I'm feeling a bit nervous. Any chance of a drink? Maybe a glass of wine?"

Immediately he said, "Of course, Clair."

He went to the drinks cabinet, took out a bottle of Cadian rosé.

And two glasses.

"To our success," he suggested, and this time I did clink glasses with him.

"To our success," I said, and he smiled.

His mobile phone rang. He answered.

"Stig de Silva is just arriving. I must go down and meet him."

He gave me a kiss and squeezed my arm.

"You'll be just fine," he said, and disappeared through the door.

I sat down and took a few big breaths.

"Come on," I told myself, over and over again. "You're Lady

Clair Hamilton. You can do this. You can do anything. This is no big deal. You just have to make love to an attractive man. And convince him that you could help him with his business."

I heard footsteps approaching outside and then there was a knock on the door.

I took a big breath and said, "Come in," and Moldie walked in followed by Stig de Silva. He was exactly like his photographs, and slightly taller than I expected.

Moldie introduced us.

"Stig de Silva, this is Lady Clair Hamilton," and I held out my hand.

He took it and lifted it to his lips, kissing the back of my fingers. You've been watching too many romantic movies, I thought.

"Good afternoon," I said, in my most ladylike voice. "It's a pleasure to meet you. Would you like a cup of tea?"

Moldie had suggested this would be a good way to break the ice. Everyone knows English Ladies like their tea.

He said he would, and I politely asked Moldie if he would bring us some tea and biscuits. Off he went, and I asked Stig "Did you have a good journey here?"

He looked surprised. "Don't you know how I got here?"

"Eh, no," I said, "Moldie organises all that. I just let him get on with it."

He smiled ruefully.

"A taxi was sent to my home in Snuka, and drove me to a local second rate airport. I got into a helicopter and flew for 40 minutes. I couldn't see out of any windows, then landed somewhere close and was driven here by car. I really have no idea where I am. It's a bit of an adventure really."

"I assume it will the same trip home tomorrow," I suggested, "Except in reverse, of course!"

We both laughed, though it was a very poor joke.

"So where are we?" he asked.

"I'm sorry, Stig. I can't tell you."

He chuckled and just then, Moldie brought in some tea and

biscuits. I told him I would pour and he left.

Stig and I seemed to hit it off immediately. I told him why I was there, describing how the government took all our money in death duties and how I thought this was a good way to earn lots of money very quickly before we lost Hamilton Hall but whether he believed me or not I couldn't tell.

I told him he was my first client and he chuckled.

"Maybe I could suggest another way for you to make some money," he said, "And you can give up this, eh, profession."

He then went on to give me a brief summary of his life, most of which I knew anyway, before getting on to his business. As Moldie guessed, he wanted me to help him with some new designs and be his agent in England.

"Moldie has shown me some of your designs already," I said, "And I really like them."

He was pleased about that.

"I'm not sure how much money you would make," he told me, "That would depend on how sales in England went.

"It sounds really good to me," I told him.

I was actually quite excited about it.

"Leave some of your new ideas with me and I'll study them and get back to you when I get home. I think we could work well together," which pleased him even more.

Pebble brought in some dinner. It was spare ribs with potato wedges, which Moldie knew Stig enjoyed. He'd asked him beforehand.

Stig opened a bottle of Cadian wine, and we ate and drank and talked about anything and everything except the other reason why we were there together. Pudding and coffee followed then he looked in the drinks cabinet and suggested Scotch whiskey on the rocks. We toasted our new business venture, and then I suggested it was time for bed.

He had the decency to look a bit embarrassed.

"I've been in love with you, Clair", he said, "Since I was a teenager, and dreamt about this moment, and now that moment is about to come true. I'm suddenly feeling a bit nervous."

I leant over and took his hand.

"I'm a bit nervous as well," I told him. "I've never done this sort of thing before. I'm hoping I'll be good enough for you. You are paying a lot of money for it."

This seemed to relax him, and I took his hand and led him to the sofa. I pushed him down and sat on his lap. I gently kissed him, and stroked his hair, and he put his arms around me and hugged me and started kissing me back and he was a good kisser. I gently broke away, and started undoing the buttons of his shirt. I put my hand inside his shirt, and stroked his chest.

His hands were all over me now. He cupped my breasts through my dress then stroked my neck and slowly undid the zip, which ran all the way to the small of my back. He pushed the dress off my shoulders and down to my waist, then unfastened my bra and took it off. He gently fondled my nipples and let out a low groan, then bent down and took one then the other in his mouth and gently nibbled. It was nice and I shuddered.

I stood up and let the dress fall to the ground. I was only wearing a very small pair of panties, and he leant forward and pulled them down. I was totally naked now, and he just looked and moaned some more.

"You can touch if you like," I told him and he ran his hands over my bottom and hips and then through my neatly trimmed pussy hair.

"Oh my dear," he stuttered, "You are even more beautiful than I imagined," and I smiled, and said thank you.

"You've still got your clothes on," I told him. "Stand up and I'll help you take them off."

Seconds later he was also naked, and his manhood stood up proudly. It was a good size. I pushed him back onto the sofa and took it into my mouth. All men like that, and he was no exception. I sucked and licked and stroked until I heard him start to pant, then stopped and climbed on top of him. We both let out a sigh as he slipped easily inside me.

"Nice?" I asked him and he grinned up at me and said, "Very,

very nice. The best."

I bounced up and down a few times and that was all it took before he climaxed with a shudder. He hugged me tight, and started to apologise for coming so quickly. I told him not to be silly and anyway, we've got all night and we can take our time next time.

"Come on, let's go and share a nice bubble bath," I said, leading him to the bathroom.

"I enjoyed that bit in the film," he said, and I checked. What film, I thought, but had the sense not to say it out loud.

"Good," I said. "What other bits did you enjoy."

"Well, I enjoyed all of it, of course, though I must admit the lake looked cold."

So Moldie had filmed me in the bath and down by Lake Lucinda. It must have been the gorillas. No wonder they smirked when we returned.

"What about the rest?" I asked. "Was I any good?"

"I could hardly believe a woman could be so sexy as you in bed," he said, "But now I know that you are!"

He chuckled.

"You are so lovely."

I smiled but I was thinking. So, Moldie had filmed me in the bath and by the lake and in bed with him, and he must have made a short film of it and sent the film to potential clients. The crafty devil. I would ask him to show it to me tomorrow.

"I never did see the final film," I told Stig. "How long did it last?"

"Oh, about three minutes," he said, "And I loved every second of it! I've watched it a dozen times or more already, and I only received it yesterday."

So I was right. I wondered what Moldie would say. Surely he wouldn't deny it.

The bath was now full, hot and bubbly, and we both got in and I splashed him and he splashed me and we acted like two naughty children before getting out and drying each other and walking to the bed. I studied the bedroom but couldn't see any hidden cameras. I knew now that they were there and that Moldie was probably watching us.

"Let him watch," I thought, "It's far too late for false modesty now."

Stig was ready again, and this time he made love to me properly. He was very good at it, kind and gentle, and I came and so did he again, and we fell asleep in each others arms with me thinking how I would get the truth out of Moldie the next day.

Stig made love to me again in the morning and once again it was very enjoyable. Over breakfast, which was brought to us by Pebble, we further discussed his business proposition, then Moldie arrived and I said goodbye to Stig and Moldie showed him out of the door. I wondered if I would ever meet him again and hoped I would.

"Probably," I thought to myself. "I'll make sure I do."

I went for a shower and then Moldie returned, and I told him to sit down at the table whilst we had a coffee.

"Well," he asked me, how did it go?"

"I think you know how it went Moldie, don't you?"

"What do you mean?"

He looked suspicious.

"I'm going to ask you some questions, Moldie, and I want you to be totally honest when you answer. Do you think you can do that for me Moldie? Be totally honest."

I smiled at him sweetly.

"Well, yes, of course," he answered, though he did look a bit concerned. I think he knew what I was about to say.

"Have you been filming me in the bath, by the lake and in the bedroom?" I asked him.

"Oh. Right. Eh……"

"Moldie. Answer me. Tell me the truth," I ordered.

"Yes," he said, simply.

"And did you make a short three minute film which you emailed to potential clients?"

"Yes," he answered again, looking very sheepish.

"Show me a copy," I ordered him and he immediately left the

room and returned two minutes later carrying his laptop. He showed me a film exactly as I had predicted. He looked extremely embarrassed but I told him not too be.

"I'm not angry with you," I said. "I can't blame you. Don't worry about it," and he looked relieved.

I must admit, I was very impressed with how wonderful I looked on the film. If it had been anybody else and not me, I would definitely have fancied myself, whether I had been a man or a woman or even a chimpanzee.

I did look gorgeous.

I kissed him on the cheek.

"Any more secrets you want to tell me?" I asked but he told me there weren't any.

I didn't believe him but, so what?

Chapter 11 - The Film

Theo let out a funny squeak. He'd spent all evening on the internet. He was trying to find out anything he could about Abacadia or Effghania or Redik or even our mother.

"Oh my God," he said. "Ooooh myyyy Goooooooooood," and he sat back in his chair.

I went over to look at the computer screen.

"Oh my God," I said.

On the screen was our dear mother, having a bath. Naked, of course.

"I'll start from the beginning," said Theo, "Though I don't think I want to watch this."

"Hang on," I put up a hand. "I'll call Pauline. I think we should all watch this together."

When she arrived, Theo started the film from the beginning. It was only three minutes long, but that was long enough. It started with a film of mother in a long posh dress. She seemed to be at some important function somewhere in England. She was laughing and smiling and looked at her best.

'Lady Clair Hamilton,' said a voice, in good but accented English. 'Is she the most beautiful and most desirable woman in the world? Would you like to see her undressing? Of course you would. Watch.'

The film showed her in what appeared to be a posh hotel bedroom. She was wearing the same clothes she had been wearing when she had been kidnapped, so obviously very recently. She undressed, and then, naked, walked across the room and through a door. Another camera view showed her entering a bathroom, where she got into a very bubbly bath.

'Isn't she gorgeous?' said the voice. 'What a body.

Would you like to see some more of her? Of course you would.'

Now the film changed to an outside location. The camera was panning over a very picturesque lake, surrounded by hills and woodland. The water looked very blue and very calm. The sun was shining.

Then mother came into view. She was walking beside the lake, hand in hand with a man, who was carrying a rucksack.   They stopped by a small beach, and the man pulled out a very small red bikini. He said something, and mother appeared to laugh. Then she turned from him, facing the lake and the camera, and undressed. She seemed to be laughing and ran naked into the water. The man also undressed and ran in after her. They started swimming.

'Perfection,' said the voice. 'I bet you're wondering what she's like as a lover. Let's find out.'

"I don't think I want to watch anymore," said Theo, but he stayed.

Mother and the man walked out of the lake, he picked her up, laid her on a blanket, and started making love to her.

"Oh my God," said Pauline. "I wonder where that is. At least we know she's safe and well. She seems to be enjoying herself."

The man climbed off, and the two of them had a picnic. The voice said, 'Would you like to see a bit more? Of course you would.'

The film went back to the bathroom, where the man and mother shared a shower. Then to the bedroom, where the man and mother shared the bed. I stared in horror as my own mother acted like a wanton prostitute, making love to him in every conceivable position.

'Good, isn't she?' said the voice. 'Very, very good. I bet you're thinking, I wish that was me with her. Well, it could be. She's here in Abacadia, and, for a small fee, you can spend the evening and all night with her.

The visit includes dinner and breakfast with drinks, and can be yours for the small sum of just $100,000.'

There was an internet link to click onto.

"This is a once in a lifetime opportunity to spend a night with one of the worlds' most beautiful and desirable women. If you don't take this chance, you will regret it for the rest of your life."

The film ended. We sat in silence, dumb struck.

At last I spoke.

"Our mother has been kidnapped to be pimped! I can't believe it. Why?"

"I think I can explain," said Theo. "Look."

He opened a new web page. It looked like it was from a newspaper.

"The newspaper is called the Abacadian Drum. It's a sort of gossipy celebrity daily newspaper and is very popular in Abacadia. The equivalent of our Sun or Mirror. And look who is their number one pin up."

We looked. It was mother. As Theo flipped through various pages, there were dozens of pictures of her, and, although none of us could speak Abacadian, it was fairly obvious the articles were about her.

"I've managed to translate a couple of the articles," said Theo. "It seems that mother is their number one fantasy sex symbol. They like the fact that she is a genuine English Lady, the fact that she does so much good for charities, and the fact that she is so pretty. They love her in Abacadia."

"Somebody has realised they can use her to make a lot of money by charging men to spend the night with her," I said. "Have you tried clicking onto the link Theo?"

"I have. Nothing happens. I think you would have to be in Abacadia for it to work."

We sat in silence and contemplated what we had just seen.

Eventually Pauline said, "Could anybody else in Britain see that?"

"They could," said Theo, "But highly unlikely. I would say the chances are almost zero. I think that the film would have been sent as an email to various selected clients in Abacadia. I used the experience and knowledge of some of my fellow computer nerds at university to help me, but they don't know why I was asking them. I pretended I was looking for some Abacadian porn. We keep it a secret when we are looking for porn!"

I quickly looked at him, but his face was a mask. He wasn't my little kid brother anymore. He was a young man and I kept forgetting.

"I suppose we ought to tell the Inspector Hector," I sighed.

Our opinion of the good inspector was waning. He didn't appear to have really done anything to help find her.

"Do we want to?" asked Pauline, "We will have to show him the film. Do we want anyone else to see it? Will he keep it a secret? If it gets onto the British web, it could become viral. It would almost certainly become viral, more like. We don't want that."

"If we don't tell him, we'll have to go it on our own," I said, "And what can we do?"

"Would we be breaking the law if we didn't tell him?" asked Theo. "Withholding vital information."

"The most important thing is to save mother," I said. "Is it better if we tell him or not?"

Silence.

"Shall we sleep on it?" I suggested.

My mind was in a turmoil during the night and I didn't sleep very well. The film kept haunting me.

In the morning we met up over breakfast.

"I wonder who the man is?" pondered Pauline, "You know, mother's lover."

"You mean her rapist," I suggested, but the others disagreed.

"That was no rape," said Pauline, with utter certainty. "She was going along quite happily and enjoying herself. She's not that old, you know!"

I sighed.

"She did look very attractive on that film," I said. "Sometimes it's hard to imagine that older people enjoy sex."

"She's only 48," said Pauline. "Not so old. I still wonder who the man is."

"I stayed up quite late last night trying to find out ," said Theo. "I started off by looking at photographs of the Abacadian government, and he wasn't any of them, definitely. Then I tried to find some pictures of anyone to do with Effghania, but there isn't much information about the place. I did eventually find some photo's and I think I might have found our man in a couple of them."

He turned the laptop to face us, and showed us a couple of images. They weren't very good.

"I suppose that could be him," I said dubiously, pointing at one of them. "Do we know his name?"

"Nope," said Theo, "But I have emailed copies to some of my mates at university and hoping they can come up with something. Don't worry, I haven't told them any of the details."

"Would the police be able to identify him?" I asked.

Theo answered again.

"Maybe, if they can be bothered. Just leave it with me for a couple of days and see what I can come up with. We can always tell the good Inspector later."

I didn't take long before Theo got back to us. Just

an hour.

"I have some much clearer images of the man," he said, "And it is definitely the same bloke who was with mother by the lake and in the hotel, but no news on his name, I'm afraid. My friends at university are still working on the problem. If anybody can find anything, then they can.

However, we have found out something else. There is an organisation in Effghania called ODOE, which stands for Organisation for the Development of Effghania. We haven't found out much about them, but it seems they are non-profit making who try and help the local people by repairing houses and supplying food. I was wondering if they may be behind this kidnapping."

At least we had some sort of starting point, possibly.

Chapter 12 - Introducing Bim Dram

My next client was the following evening. Again Moldie provided me with a folder about him. His name was Lef Pamu, and he was a lawyer. A very successful middle aged lawyer. He was not very tall, shorter than my five feet and eight inches, stocky with a slight belly, with lank mouse brown hair. He was probably the most dull and boring man I have ever met. His face was dull and boring, his hair was dull and boring, his clothes were dull and boring and his personality was even duller. And boring.

He had paid the money for one reason and one reason only and that was for the sex. He obviously adored me and he never left me alone. We had sex in this position and we had sex in that position. We did it this way and we did it that way. We did it in every single way that his kinky mind could think of.

He was fascinated by my pussy. I know I have a nice pussy, I have even heard men describe it as beautiful, but Lef Pamu was fascinated by it. He just wouldn't leave it alone, and eventually I got a bit annoyed with his devotion to it, though I made sure he didn't realise. He had, after all, paid $100,000 for the pleasure of my beautiful pussy.

He wanted to shave me. He begged me to let him shave away my lovely pussy hairs. He even offered to pay a lot of extra money to shave me but I refused.

"English ladies do not have shaven pussies," I explained to him. "I will do anything else you ask, but not that. Sorry."

He shrugged, obviously disappointed. I think it must have been a dream of his. Oh well. Can't please all the people all of the time.

I just let him get on with whatever else he wanted to get on with, though when he eventually left after almost 18 hours of non stop bonking and pussy admiring and no sleep, I was feeling rather tired and my pussy was rather sore.

When I said he was rather dull and rather boring what I really meant was, he was unbelievably dull and unbelievably boring. I was glad to see the back of him.

"Did you enjoy watching that?" I asked Moldie. "You should have plenty of new material for your next film about me!"

This was said very much tongue in cheek, and Moldie knew it, but he played along.

"I don't know what you are talking about," he said, grinning. "Don't worry, you've got until tomorrow afternoon to recover, that's 30 hours away!"

I groaned, but accepted my fate.

"Who have you got next lined up for me?" I asked him. "Somebody less energetic, I hope."

"Indeed," said Moldie. "He is."

I was immediately suspicious. "What do you mean by that?"

"Your client tomorrow is called Mud Oneye. He is general in the Abacadian army and he wants just one thing of you. He wants to stick his cock up your bottom."

I gasped. I had never had anal sex. My dear husband had tried once but it had hurt and he didn't seem that bothered to carry on.

"I hope you haven't agreed to him," I said in horror.

"Of course." Moldie was grinning again. "He has already paid. Is there a problem?"

"Yes there is. I don't do anal. Give him his money back and find me someone normal."

"I'm sorry Clair, but you have to. He has paid. What's your problem? According to the latest statistics, almost half of all women have tried anal. It's not that special and not that uncommon."

I suddenly realised.

"You want to get me ready for him, don't you?"

"The thought did cross my mind," he said, and I sighed.

"Tonight, then," I said, and he looked rather smug and pleased with himself.

After lunch, Moldie and I spent some time talking about the Abacadian army.

"The army officers, like the government," explained Moldie,

"Are all Jakalamnian. Remember, they don't like Effghania and Effghanians so make sure you don't let on that you are here in Redik. If he asks, just say it's a secret and wink. He will understand that."

I was a bit worried that, being a soldier, he might be a bit rough and raw, but Moldie told me not to worry.

"I have some film of him," and I watched on his lap top.

Mud Oneye was quite famous, it appeared, in Abacadia. Educated at Sandhurst in England, he was above average intelligence for the average soldier and came from long line of soldiers. He was a big man, and hardworking and with these attributes, on his return to Abacadia soon progressed through the army ranks.

He had made many appearances on Abacadian TV and spoke fluently and well, with a deep kindly voice. It made me feel a tad strange watching him and realising that the following evening he would be here with me.

That evening, Moldie joined me in bed and he had a jar of Vaseline with him.

I watched him undo the lid, and sighed. I told myself to relax, I reminded myself of all the money I was earning to help the poor people of Effghania, and I let him get on with it.

He was very gentle with me, and it wasn't as bad as I thought it would be, but I still didn't really enjoy the experience.

Moldie enjoyed it though. I think another of his fantasies involving me had come true.

"Not so bad, was it?" he asked me, when he had finished and recovered.

I admitted that it wasn't so bad, no, but pointed out to him that he had been extremely gentle. Mud Oneye might be a vicious brute.

"He seems like a gentle and kind man, but I'll talk to him before he meets you," promised Moldie but I wasn't looking forward to it.

Mud Oneye turned out to be a big man, with a small-ish cock, for which I, and my bottom, were eternally grateful. He was rather full of himself, but, despite that, I found him quite interesting. I have never been a great fan of soldiers and armies and fighting but Mud gave his point of view and gave it well. He explained how much he enjoyed being a good soldier, and was proud of doing his job to the best of his ability. He explained the camaraderie, and the friendship he experienced and felt for his fellow compatriots was something he really enjoyed.

He told about the excitement of being on patrol and the heart stopping terror he had felt when he had been shot at, and more than a few times.

"I thought that Abacadia was supposed to be a peaceful country, where weapons and shooting were frowned upon," I suggested to Mud.

"That's what the cuffing government preach," he answered, "but in reality, there is always cuffing fighting going on somewhere, usually against cuffing Effghania. Not a lot, but some."

He was very keen on the word cuffing which he seemed to use all the cuffing time.

"Have you ever actually shot and killed anyone?" I asked him in chilled fascination.

"I have shot a couple of cuffing men," he replied, "but as far as I know, I have never actually cuffing killed a man. They are, after all, fellow cuffing Abacadians and cuffing human beings."

I asked him when he was next going on patrol and he told me the following week. When I asked him where he would be, he looked slightly suspicious so I changed the subject and told him if he ever visited Britain again, he should visit me in Worcestershire and he liked that idea.

I thought to myself that Moldie would be quite interested in what Mud was saying. Mud obviously had no idea that he was actually in Effghania and, as I had promised Moldie, I wasn't about to tell him.

When we actually got down to the sex, everything was fine. We did all the normal things that normal men and women do together and then only later did his little daydream involving my bottom come true.

"Please be gentle with me," I begged him, when he suggested it. "I am not very experienced at that sort of thing."

"When you say that, do you mean you have cuffing never done it before or that you haven't done it cuffing much?"

"I haven't done it very much," I told him. "I don't mind you doing it, just be gentle please," and he was gentle and I realised how lucky I had been with the clients. None of them so far had been bad, even the lawyer, Lef Pamu, wasn't particularly rough. I had known worse lovers in my past.

Moldie was very pleased with me next morning after Mud had left.

"Well done with all the questions about the army," he said. "That will really please the Effghanian council. Thank you. By the way, how's your bottom?"

Moldie and I were now getting into a routine, and both of us seemed contented. If you had suggested to me just 2 weeks earlier that in 2 weeks time my life would have revolved around a different lover every other night, I would have been horrified, but now I had just accepted the situation. To be honest, there was not much else I could do. Saying that, I decided it was time to send another message home, and I suggested this to Moldie.

"This time, please, could you get an answer from them, just to satisfy me that everything is okay at home and they are not worrying too much about me?"

Moldie said he would see what he could do. I changed the subject.

"Can we go out somewhere soon, please? I am getting a tad fed up with this apartment and you did promise me a trip into Redik to see how my money is helping the local people."

"I did promise you that, didn't I?" he agreed. "You have another client tomorrow night, then a couple of nights off. How about in three days time?"

I agreed that would be nice, and composed a note for the family, which Moldie recorded for me and I assumed, sent off to Worcestershire.

In the message I included, 'Concerning the whist drive, try letting Adrian Williams skype the others for a session next Thursday.'

I was hoping they would guess I would be in Redik that day, though whether they could get there was a totally different matter. I still don't know if they had even got any of my messages let alone understood them.

So my final client before I had a trip into Redik was with a chap called Bim Dram. Moldie actually warned me about him.

"He is a member of the Abacadian government," he told me. "There are some rumours going about that he is a bit dodgy. They are just rumours."

"What sort of rumours?" I asked nervously.

"It has been suggested that he is corrupt, but that suggestion has been made about virtually all the Abacadian government. He is also rumoured to have beaten up his wife. But don't worry, I'll make sure nothing happens to you."

"That's very reassuring," I said sarcastically, as I studied various documents about him.

Bim Dram arrived. He was tall, well built, extremely handsome, and exuded wealth and success. He was very full of himself, thought he was God's gift to the world. I tried not to take an instant dislike to the man, but it was difficult. It took some good acting from me to hide my true feelings.

We started chatting over a cup of tea and he told me about being an Abacadian MP. The government sounded less like an elected responsible government and more like a dictatorship.

He was the Minister for Home Affairs and proud of the work he did.

"What exactly are you responsible for?" I asked him, with genuine interest.

"I am the minister responsible for the maintenance of internal security and domestic policy. Police and secret service, M in James Bond films. I am also in charge of business, education, energy, healthcare, law enforcement, money and taxes, natural resources, social welfare, and personal rights and freedoms."

I gasped.

"That's quite a portfolio," I said. "How on earth do you find time to look after all that lot?"

"Delegation," he said, with a smirk. "Everybody else does the work, I just shout and scream and get out my big whip if things go wrong. Things don't go wrong very often."

"Is that a real whip or a hypothetical one?" I asked in fascination.

He smiled.

"Both."

"What do you do for Effghania?" I asked him.

Moldie and I had discussed whether we should ask him about Effghania and had decided that I should. It was the sort of question I would be expected to ask, what with me being such a thoughtful and caring person and being well known for my charity work.

"Effghania is well looked after," he boasted, without a trace of dishonesty. "The area is treated exactly like the rest of Abacadia. Don't worry your pretty little head about them. In fact, because they are a relatively poor region they get more help per person than any other part of Abacadia. They are considered a special case," he continued to bullshit me.

I didn't believe a word he said.

In bed, if he had been half as good a lover as he thought he was, he would have been the greatest lover in the history of time. I'm not a real expert, well, not then I wasn't, a bit more of an expert now, on the greatest lovers of all time, but I would have thought a good male lover would have been endowed with some sort of even vaguely medium sized penis, even a larger than average probably.

Bim Dram's penis was more on the little side. Somewhere between little and tiny I would describe it as. The smallest penis I had ever known in my romantic life, even when erected. So small, I almost asked the worst question a woman can ask a man.

Is it in yet?

But I didn't.

I faked my orgasm that night. I thought it was probably the diplomatic thing to do. I was glad when he eventually left almost at lunch time. I had been feeling uneasy when he was there, and I told Moldie so.

"He didn't seem quite right in the head," I said. "A couple of sandwiches short of a picnic. A Japanese maple short of a good Bonsai tree collection."

"Never mind," said Moldie, "He's gone and you now have a couple of nights off. I promised to take you to Redik. We'll go tomorrow, spend the day away and have lunch in a restaurant. Does that sound good?"

Chapter 13 - Uncle Flambert

We spent most of our free time trying to come up with a plan to rescue mother from Abacadia. One of our main problems was whether we could go it alone, or whether we should involve Inspector Hector and the police.

It was a tricky because none of us liked or trusted Inspector Hector. His stupid name didn't help but it was his pessimism which really bugged us.

Pauline decided to be on the side of the police. Not because she wanted to but to make the arguments fairer. Devil's Advocate, whilst Theo and I argued against her and him.

"You start the debate, Theo," I said.

"Inspector Hector is a useless fucking twat," he suggested.

"I agree," said Pauline. "Let's not tell him anything."

She always was a big success in the school debating society.

So, with that thorough and comprehensive debate, we decided to go it alone. But where to start?

"We need help," I stated. "We have plenty of contacts. Who should we ask?"

"Let's decide on the facts first," suggested Pauline, always the practical one.

"I'll make notes," said Theo, always the organised one.

"And I'll be chair-mouth," I said, always the bossy one. "Now then, what actual facts do we have?"

"We know that mother disappeared on 23rd June," said Pauline, "Fact. And we think she has been kidnapped. We think she has been taken to the town of Redik in Abacadia where she is being held by members of ODOE and used as a high class prostitute."

"Blimey," I said, "You don't hold back, do you Pauline."

"Facts is facts," she said. "There is no point in denying anything."

"I suppose you're right. But," it was my turn to be clever, "Is it fact that she actually is in Abacadia or is it just supposition?"

It was Theo's turn to join in.

"I think it's fact," he said, "Remember the film of mother? Of course you do. Well, remember the lake? At the beginning, there was a few seconds of film of an actual lake and surroundings."

Of course we remembered. It was indented into our memories. Images we would never forget.

Theo continued.

"I have used Google earth to study all the lakes in the vicinity of Redik and one of them fits exactly to the one in the film. It's called Lake Lucinda and I think it is now fact that mother was at Lake Lucinda in Abacadia. Look. I'll show you."

He turned the laptop to face us and showed us the quick view of the film and then a quick view of Google earth, and there was no doubt about it, they were the same.

"So, she is definitely in Abacadia," I said, "What next?"

"It's obvious," said Pauline, "We rescue her."

"Or do we?" asked Theo. "She doesn't seem to be in any immediate danger. Contraire. She seems from the film and the phone messages to actually be enjoying herself. Maybe she wants to be left alone. Maybe she doesn't want to be rescued."

Pauline and I looked at him in amazement.

"You are joking." I was shocked. "She's being used

as a prostitute!"

"I'm playing Devil's Advocate," said Theo, "Just trying to put another point of view. I thought that was what we were supposed to be doing."

I sighed.

"You're right, of course, but do you really believe that?"

"Do you?" countered Theo, speaking to both of us, and we looked at each other.

"If only we could actually talk to her," I said.

"I've been thinking about that and I've come to a conclusion about it."

Theo looked gloomy.

"The answer is no."

"Okay," I said, "Let's assume for the moment that she does want rescuing, how do we do that?"

"Someone would have to go to Abacadia."

Pauline was obviously thinking out loud.

"But who? I'm not so sure the three of us would manage it on our own."

"I agree," I mused. "There is no way that we could manage on our own. We wouldn't even know where to start. So, we have to find someone who will come with us."

"Or go on their own."

Pauline wrinkled her brow.

"But I think I would like to visit Abacadia. It sounds an interesting place."

Further discussions followed and quite quickly we decided that we needed advice and help. We were so obviously completely out of our depth.

"Who do we know who could help and will be discrete? Mum and Dad know, knew, loads and loads of influential people. Surely one of them can help."

I looked at my kid brother and sister.

"Surely."

"What sort of person do we need?"

Theo said, "Army?"

"Do you think there might be shooting?"

I was worried.

"No, of course not. Tut, girls. A soldier would have the skills needed to rescue someone. They're trained for that sort of thing, especially someone who is, say, a member or an ex-member of, say, the SAS."

Immediately Pauline and I both knew where his thoughts were going.

"Uncle Flambert," said Pauline, and I chuckled.

Uncle Flambert was not a real uncle. He was a friend of Granddad Gael, Mum's father, and as he had been a regular visitor to Hamilton Hall, we grew up with him being around and always called him uncle.

He had also been a senior official in the SAS. He was an old man now, in his late seventies, I reckoned. We hadn't seen much of him since Dad had died, but I was sure he would help. He had a soft spot for us.

"I'll give him a ring," I said, and did.

"Alice!"

His voice had lost none of it's parade ground authority.

"Wonderful to hear from you. How are you? How's the family? How's your mother? Now then, she was a sweet young thing when she was younger. Now, she's a sweet middle aged thing, what ho!" and he chuckled.

"Actually, Uncle Flambert, she's in a spot of bother and we were wondering if we could pop round to see you for some advice."

Instantaneously his attitude changed.

"In a spot of bother, hey? Want Uncle Flambert's advice. Right, when can you visit? Today? Why not come round for lunch? All three of you? That's grand. Say, twelve for twelve thirty? I'll get cook onto it immediately. It'll be nice to have some company!"

We turned up promptly at noon in my beloved Morris Minor 1000. We had decided, unanimously, to tell Uncle Flambert everything. If we couldn't trust Uncle Flambert, then there was no one in the whole world who we could trust.

He lived in a small cottage at the end of a private narrow unmade lane. Built in the 18th century, the cottage had originally been two small semi-detached cottages but had been converted into one many, many years ago. There was a good sized garden, in which the three of us had played when we were younger. It brought back many happy memories.

Uncle Flambert had been a member of the SAS for many years, firstly as a soldier but then, when he was forced to retire from active duty, as an administrator. As far as we knew, although now retired altogether, he kept in touch with many of his old mates.

If anyone could help us, then he could.

He held us all at arms length, one by one, studying us, before embracing us and kissing us on the cheeks, except Theo, whom he gave a huge handshake, before embracing him.

"I remember you as a snotty nosed little urchin," he happily told Theo, "Whose favourite pastime was dropping slugs and worms down the backs of your sisters knickers. I hope you don't do that anymore."

"Only when they annoy me," laughed Theo, "And now it's usually down the front of their blouses," and Uncle Flambert laughed and slapped his back.

"That's my boy, that's my boy!"

We each had a small port before lunch, and mother wasn't mentioned. We talked about our soap business and Theo's university course, and Uncle Flambert's love of his pet ferrets, and politics and religion, you know, the usual stuff, over lunch, which was roast pheasant and was delicious.

It was during coffee that Uncle Flambert asked, "So, your mother is in a spot of bother, is she? Pray tell."

So, we told him everything and he listened in silence.

At the finish he said, "Poor, poor Clair. What a dreadful thing to happen to such a wonderful woman. But....she is strong, very strong willed, and she will survive. If anyone can come through unscathed, she can."

His eyes were unfocused and he was obviously thinking of mother. After a few seconds he continued.

"Right, so what do you want me to do?"

"We want your advice. We're thinking we'd like to go to Abacadia to rescue her but don't know where to start."

"Hmm," he said, "Go to Abacadia to rescue her, hey? I can see why you need some help. Well, you came to the right person. Me."

He leant back in his chair, and thought.

"Often it is good to visit foreign realms pretending to be tourists, and take it from there rather than entering the country illegally. I think that would probably be better in this case. Were all three of you thinking of going?"

We all shrugged.

"We're not really sure."

"Okay," he said, talking slowly, "Let me give you some initial thoughts. When going on holiday, usually people go as couples. Man and woman. A couple looks less inconspicuous than, say, two young pretty ladies on their own or even two young pretty ladies and one young man. With two men by your sides, you are much less likely to be hassled, especially if the men are mean and tough looking."

We all nodded. We could see the sense in that.

"Also," Flambert continued, "It might be a good idea

to have someone at home to coordinate things through the internet, but also in case there are any phone calls. I would be willing to do this, but, to be honest, I'm not very good at computing. Actually, I'm pretty hopeless.

So what I am suggesting is this. And this is just a first suggestion, remember. Theo, you stay here with me and we can act as a sort of mission control. I'll find two tough reliable men to go with you two ladies. What do you think?"

We looked at each other and shrugged and nodded. It was a plan and as we didn't have any plan at all, it was the best plan we had.

I asked Theo, "How would you feel about staying at home on your own?"

Theo shrugged again.

"I'll do whatever needs doing to rescue mother," he said. "You two go away on your holiday with two tough reliable men and I'll stay here and keep my nose to the grindstone."

I turned to Uncle Flambert.

"We all agree with your plan."

"Okay and I think I know the men who can help," he said. "They're called Sam and Stu. They are both about 30, and retired from the SAS a couple of years ago.

Actually," he chuckled, "They didn't actually retire. They were kicked out. They had, eh, another job which the, eh, MOD didn't approve of. Shall we leave it at that?"

"Oh," I said and he carried on hurriedly.

"But believe me, they are a couple of really good fellows. Top rate chaps."

"Would they be willing to come with us?" I asked, feeling a pang of excitement. "There may be a touch of danger."

"I think they would be much more willing if there

was a mountain of danger. Would you like to visit them?"

We all nodded and Flambert made a phone call.

"They're both at home at the moment," so we all climbed into Flambert's car, a Rolls Royce Silver Cloud, of which he was immensely proud, and off we drove.

"Sam and Stu live together in a small cottage in Shropshire," he explained, "So only a forty five minute drive."

"Are they, you know?" I asked, but Flambert shook his head.

"No, they are definitely not homosexual, just good mates, and that is not the reason why they were chucked out of the SAS."

"Just wondering," I said.

Flambert asked us about money.

"How much are you going to offer to pay them?"

That was something else we hadn't thought about. We really were totally inept organisers.

He saw our further confusion.

"I understand you are a bit short of money since your father died. But you have got a little bit of cash stored away, yes? Well, let me sort that out. Sam and Stu aren't short of a penny or two and I'm sure they'll do the job for the excitement. But there are expenses. Will you leave that all to me? You will? Good."

We eventually arrived at their cottage, which was at the edge of a village near a pub and was small and quaint with flowering honeysuckle growing either side of the front door and exactly what a cottage shared by two former SAS men should not look like. Inside was the same. Neat and clean and tidy and quaint.

Sam and Stu met us by the front door. They were both big men, over six feet, and they looked mean and tough and hard. Clean shaven, with short hair cuts.

Handsome in a rugged sort of way but not the sort of blokes anyone with any sense would mess with.

They were both delighted to see Flambert and were very polite to us three. They took us through to their small but neatly presented back garden and sat us down on rustic metal chairs around a rustic metal table.

"Tea and cake everyone?" asked Sam.

His voice was very West Country, the sort of voice that should be sitting on the back of a tractor. He was obviously the leader of the two of them, but he came back with a tray containing a large pot of tea, with dainty flower patterned tea cups and a delicious looking strawberry cheesecake.

We discussed the weather and the state of the England rugby team before Flambert brought up the subject of the meeting.

"These three delightful young people have a serious problem and would like to know if you two vaguely capable middle aged wasters would be willing to help them."

"Tell us about it," said Sam, and Flambert told them about the kidnapping but not about the prostitution.

"They want to go to Abacadia to rescue her," explained Flambert, "But need some help."

Sam and Stu exchanged glances, and nodded at each other.

"We are temporarily at a lose end," said Sam. "When do we leave?"

"First," said Flambert, "Let's go through everything we know. Alice, why don't you do that?" so I did.

Sam and Stu listened intently, asking no questions. When I had finished, Uncle Flambert said, "Do you know anyone who lives in Abacadia?"

"Not off the top of my head," said Sam." Can we check on that Stu?"

"I'll get onto it," said Stu, and he disappeared into another room.

"It would probably help," suggested Flambert, "If you went as two couples. How do you feel about that, Sam?"

Sam looked at me and nodded.

"Sounds good to me."

"Pretend couples," I added hastily, noticing the look in Sam's eyes.

Sam grinned.

"Pretend couples," he agreed. "Can I be your pretend boyfriend Alice?"

I stuck my tongue out at him, but smiled anyway.

"Right," he said, being serious again. "First things first, and have you both got passports?"

We nodded.

"Do we need visas?"

We shrugged.

"What injections do we need?"

We shrugged again.

"What about money? Do they accept sterling?"

"We know none of these things," I said, feeling rather foolish. "Sorry."

"No problem. I'll get Stu to check and let you know. What's the weather like there at the moment? What language do they speak? Is English widely spoken? Religion? Is there any specific type of dress code?"

We knew the answer to none of these questions and Sam sighed dramatically.

"Stu will check for us and let you know. Speak of the devil, here he is."

Stu raised his eyebrows but Sam said, "I'll tell you later. Have you found out anything?"

"Dave Gulldred lives in Abacadia," Stu said. "He's married with kids and lives on a ranch not far from the capital city, Snuka. He's the only one I can find."

"I remember Dave," said Sam, "He was a good guy."

"I think you should explain who he is," said Flambert.

"Oh, right," said Sam. "Dave was a former member of the SAS. We have a sort of old boys organisation and have an unwritten law to help each other. I'm sure if we phoned him he would agree to help us."

"Go for it," I said.

"Let's decide when we're going," suggested Sam.

"As soon as we possibly can," I suggested. "Surely.

"I think I agree with you," said Sam. "Time is of the essence. It shouldn't take us long to organise what we can here in England. But let's speak to Dave Gulldred first. Stu, have you got a phone number for him?"

Stu nodded, and so Sam phoned up Dave in Abacadia. It took a while to get through, but eventually he said, "Dave, this is Sam Johnson from Hereford. How are you?"

"Sam." Dave sounded shocked. Sam had put him on loud speaker.

"Good to hear your voice. I'm fine."

There was a click, then Dave said, "My phone is bugged but I've over ridden it. I'll switch it back on in a second. Don't say anything suspicious and don't mention SAS."

There was another click then Dave said, "Hello, hello, are you still there?"

"Yes, hello Dave. I can hear you again. Are you and the family well?"

"We're all great. And you? It's been a long time."

"I'm good. Look Dave, can we keep this phone call short. It's costing me a lot of money. I'm thinking of visiting Abacadia for a holiday next week and thought it might be nice to pop in and say hello."

"That sounds great," said Dave, "I'll be here. Phone me when you get in the country."

Sam hung up and looked at Stu. He raised an eyebrow.

"Telephone bugged, hey. But Dave always was an electronic wizard. I bet the first thing he did was to check for bugs in his phone and all over the house. Do you remember that time in Belfast?......" and the two of them started reminiscing before Uncle Flambert interrupted with a cough.

"Plenty of time for reminiscing later. Let's get back to planning."

Sam took charge and decided what was to be done and who was to do it.

Theo was to send all the information we had to Stu's laptop, but we couldn't bring ourselves to send The Film. That was personal.

He was also going to request some time off from his job at the printers, Print-U-Like, in Kidderminster, and move in to Uncle Flambert's house.

Pauline and I were to pack overnight bags and try and sort out everything that we could about the soap business and get ready to leave at a moment's notice.

Sam and Stu would do everything else.

Chapter 14 - Redik and Cupp

The next day, after breakfast, Moldie and I left the apartment for the short 10 minute drive into the centre of Redik, and I gazed around me with interest. The town was generally rather run down. Moldie told me over 150,000 people lived there, but the facilities for so many were rather lacking. Most of the shops seemed to be closed but none were shuttered up. I saw none of the common stores that we had in Britain. I thought they were totally international but not, it appears, in Redik.

There were far more market stalls than there were shops. Many sold food, fruit and vegetables, mostly, and some had clothes and shoes, but I didn't see any selling gifts or luxury items. I saw one hotel, which looked rather run down, and I hoped the children didn't think I was being kept there, if they had managed to unravel my secret messages.

There were very few cars or vehicles of any type, moving or parked. One or two clapped out vans sputtered their slow way by and, Moldie told me, there was only one petrol station in the town.

I saw lots and lots of beggars.

It was a sad town.

Moldie started telling me about the work that had been done in the last few days, most of it thanks to the money I had earned through my carnal activities.

"Many buildings were damaged in the earthquake last year. We have started repairing those which weren't completely wrecked, starting with houses. We are trying to make them habitable and we are giving them to homeless families. We have made sure that each house has the basics of beds and blankets and chairs. Some of them have electricity, but not many. That is one of the priority jobs, to provide electricity to everyone. Even the empty shops have people in them, though they have been told they must leave if the shop owners return to re-open their shops."

"What about running water?"

"All the water main pipes were damaged in the earthquake, and we have had many problems getting them replaced or repaired. They are very expensive, and difficult to get hold of but, thanks to your money, new plastic pipes should be arriving from India very soon. Meanwhile, we have managed to cobble together a few standpipes, one for each region of the town, and the women queue up to get water everyday. Look, I'll show you."

We drove on for a couple of minutes then around a corner I saw a long queue of women, all carrying buckets or bowls or any type of container that could carry water.

"How long do they have to queue for?"

"Two hours, three hours. I know it's not perfect, but for the time being, it's the best we can do. At least they know they are getting fresh water. They can go upstream to the river, where the water is also fresh, but that is about one and a half miles, quite a long way to carry heavy containers of water."

"Where does this water come from?" I asked, pointing to the standpipe.

"From the river. About two miles upstream."

He shrugged.

"I know it's not perfect but it's the best we can do for now. We've had no outbreaks of cholera, which is what we dread above anything else."

I squeezed his arm.

"I think you're doing very well," I told him.

I saw what looked like yet another beggar so asked him about them.

"They are mostly single men," he explained. "They all have somewhere to sleep. I will show you where in a few minutes, and they are all fed proper meals from food stations we have set up. The food is provided by you, thank you very much!"

I considered my surroundings more carefully, studying the beggars especially. I saw that they all did look quite well fed, and wore proper clothes, even though some of the clothes looked old and patched and threadbare. I also noticed that although everywhere was run down, there was no litter or rubbish to be seen.

"This is all very impressive, Moldie," I told him. And I really meant it.

"Do you have much trouble with theft and violence, that sort of thing?"

"Very little," said Moldie. "And I think that is because everybody is in the same sort of situation. Nobody really has anything so nobody has anything to really get jealous about. A bit like the stories you heard during the Second World War in England. For the time being, at least, everybody seems to club together and help each other. I think it's when you have 'haves' and 'have nots' that envy sets in and that leads to violence. For the time being, fingers crossed, we have few problems."

He smiled at me.

"Enough about that. Let's have some lunch and then I'll take you to see the outlying areas," he told me and drove me to a small café. It was called 'Loaves and Fishes' and was very clean and tidy and welcoming.

"It's regularly checked for cleanliness and hygiene," explained Moldie, "As are all the food outlets in Effghania. You may recognise the food. The cook is the same cook who cooks for you in the apartment."

"Can I meet him," I asked.

Moldie grinned, and a young and very pretty white lady appeared. I stood up and shook hands.

"This is Eileen Edwards," said Moldie. "Lady Clair Hamilton."

"I really do enjoy your food," I said to her, "You are a wonderful cook."

She smiled, curtsied, and blushed bright red and to my amazement, replied in a broad, broad Welsh accent.

"Thank you," she said, curtseying again. "You are very kind."

"Eileen won BBC Wales Young Chef of the Year competition two years ago," explained Moldie. "I met her when I was in Cardiff and suggested she come here for a couple of years to cook for the people of Effghania, and she agreed."

Eileen smiled shyly.

"Are you enjoying working here?" I asked her.

"I feel I am helping people who are a bit down on their luck," she said, "And gaining a lot of experience," and returned to the kitchen.

"This café is just a small part of her work," said Moldie. "She is also training up local Effghanian women to cook healthy and nutritious meals, and teaching them all about hygiene and cleanliness. She also cooks for us occasionally, as you know. She really is truly wonderful and we feel very lucky to have her here. We will be sorry when she leaves but hopefully those she has trained will be able to take over."

The food she prepared for us was a lovely rich stew, delicious, and when we had finished, Moldie drove us out of town to the area he had taken me on my first day in Effghania.

Things had changed, as Moldie explained.

"We have bought five trucks with your money which daily bring in food and supplies from northern Abacadia. The trucks go to five different areas and the food is distributed fairly amongst the people. They now have two healthy meals a day. We have also supplied clothing and shelters for them and canvas beds. Soon everyone should have a roof of some sort over their heads and a bed to sleep in and a blanket and a pillow."

Moldie was talking with real excitement and passion in his voice.

"And we are opening new classrooms, in marquees and tents at the moment but we are hoping to build proper school rooms in the near future.

We have bought a number of larger tents which we are setting up as first aid centres as well as updating the hospital tent you saw earlier and have hired doctors and nurses from Abacadia and abroad. We also stockpiled some drugs and other medical supplies."

"I thought the Abacadians hated you?" I asked.

"Not all of them," he answered, "Many of them are our friends and sympathisers. We also have an American television crew visiting next week and hopefully our plight will be passed on to the rest of the world."

I was very impressed by everything I had seen and everything Moldie had told me and told him so.

"All this," said Moldie, squeezing my hand, and looking pleased, "Is due to you. On behalf of all my people, I thank you from the bottom of my heart."

I was really was very, very impressed and told him so and promised to carry on bringing in the money. Which pleased him even more.

Redik was a sad town, but getting better.

I spent part of that evening studying the designs of Stig de Silva's, my first client. He specialised in ladies dresses and blouses and skirts. Many of the designs seemed rather crude and old fashioned to me, but a few of them had real promise. He liked clingy dresses that showed off a ladies figure. I thought they would look good on me. I wondered if maybe I could model them for him. If I sent him my measurements, he could make some for me, and bring them to me here in the apartment. Or maybe I would wait until I got home, if I ever got home, and suggest it to him then. I wouldn't mention it to Moldie.

I also spent twenty minutes on the running machine. I was determined to keep in shape. The sex would help, of course, but twenty minutes each day on the running machine would help more.

After my day off, I had to get ready for my next client. His name, Moldie told me, was Cupp. Just Cupp. He was an eccentric English gentleman, who, it appeared, inherited a shed load of money many years previously and had spent most of it on women and drink and drugs. But before it had all gone he came to his senses and had moved to Abacadia and started Abacadia's first lap dancing club, called 'Cupp of Life'.

Gentleman's clubs like that were supposed to be illegal, but rather cleverly, Cupp had started the business in partnership with the Abacadian Deputy Prime Minister. This meant he was left well alone by the police and other interfering parties, and the 'Cupp of Life Gentleman's Club' had thrived.

Cupp was, once again, a very wealthy man, who had paid the bonk fee in used notes without any quibbles, Moldie told me.

"We have checked him out," said Moldie, "And he seems relatively normal. He appears to run the club just like another business. A very successful business but just a business. The only kinky thing he has requested is a bit of bondage."

I let out a big, big sigh.

"Oh bothersome bouncing battleships," I declared. That was one of my father's favourite swearwords. Swear phrases.

"Is that a major problem?" asked Moldie.

I sighed again.

"No," I said, resignedly. "It's not a problem," but I did wonder about the weirdness of men. Too many of them seemed to want something extra in bed. Straightforward sex wasn't good enough.

I had indulged in a bit of bondage in my younger youthfulness but that was about thirty years before. I vaguely remembered enjoying it, but in those days I was up for anything in bed. So, nothing had really changed!

"Don't worry," said Moldie with a chuckle, "I'll keep an eye on you!"

When Cupp arrived, he was the epitome of a typical eccentric English gentleman. He was, it seemed to me, in his mid fifties, tall and thin, with a long, strong looking face and a neatly clipped moustache. In the middle of the Abacadian summer he wore a tweed suit and a bowtie. His face was a deep red colour.

"Good afternoon, Lady Hamilton," he said in a posh middle-England accent. "How absolutely delightful to meet you. My father and yours often went shooting together, you know. He often used to speak about your mother. I think he secretly fancied her. Ha, ha."

I really wasn't sure about him. He was too over-the-top. It was obviously an act to impress the rich Abacadians who used his club. I decided that I wouldn't put him on my Christmas card list.

Despite my misgivings, we got on well enough, chatting about this and that and reminiscing about England.

"Sometimes I miss the old place," he told me, sounding wistful, "But then I remember the weather and what a good time I am having here, and I miss it less."

I asked him why he called himself Cupp.

He whispered in my ear.

"Secret," he whispered, "If I tell you?"

"Of course," I said, intrigued.

"My real name is Cuthbert Uppingbell. Cupp is easier."

I laughed.

"I like the name Cuthbert," I said. "I called my first pet hamster Cuthbert," and he chuckled.

The sex at first was predictable. Missionary.

However, he was well into his bondage and after the missionary, he tied me up using leather bondage straps he had brought with him and had sex with me in many various positions. He had numerous vibrators and used them on me as well, and, as usual in those days, I came and came.

When I wasn't coming, I just thought about all the money he was paying to play out his fantasies and realised who was the fool. I didn't get upset, I didn't feel humiliated, it didn't worry me, I just let him get on with his pleasure and thought of how his money would help all the poor Effghanians I had seen the previous day.

But as I lay there, I did wonder what Moldie was thinking. He was so obviously madly in love with me. He must have felt a bit jealous. Was he getting ideas from Cupp? Was he wanking himself blind? I thought I would ask him and watch him squirm. That made me smile, which made Cupp chuckle.

"You're enjoying it. I knew you would," and I agreed with him that I was enjoying it.

Before he untied me, he said, "I'll only untie you if you make me a promise. Do you agree?"

Oh God, I thought to myself. What does he want now?

"What do you want me to do?" I asked cautiously.

"I want you to do the same to me as I've done to you. I want you to tie me up and do as I ask!"

I breathed a sigh of relief.

"Of course. I'll do whatever you want me to."

So he untied me, and I stretched and rubbed my wrists and ankles and had a drink of wine, which was on the bedside table. He also had a sip. He was looking rather flushed and very excited and I couldn't help myself.

I grinned at him, and he grinned back. I was pretty sure he was having the best time of his life.

"What do you want me to do?" I asked him.

I expected him to lie on his back but instead he lay on his front. He spread his arms and legs out and said, in a funny little whinny voice, "Mistress, please don't tie me up, please, I beg you, don't tie me up."

I understood. He wanted me to play dominatrix. I smiled to myself and shook my head in slight disbelief. I tied his wrists and ankles to the four bed posts as told and he tried to pull himself free but couldn't.

"Please mistress," he whined, "Don't look in my bag and don't take out the whip because there isn't a whip in my bag."

I chuckled, and rooted around in his bag. Amongst the remaining handcuffs and vibrators I found a whip. It was very expensive looking and I wondered if they used it at his club. I took it out and flexed it. He had twisted his head and was watching me.

"Pleased don't hit me with the whip," he begged. "Especially across my buttocks. I would hate you to whip me across my buttocks."

Whish! The whip stung his arse and he shrieked and tried to move his bottom but the bonds held him still.

"No more," he moaned, "Please, no more."

I whacked him again, and he screamed and again and again and he moaned and writhed and his arse was criss crossed with whip marks.

"Please don't move to my back," he begged and then later,

"Not the backs of my legs," and then "Not my feet."

By the time I had finished he must have been in agony and the whole back of his body, from his toes to his neck, was covered in whip marks. I lifted his head by his hair and looked at his face, and tears of pain were running down his cheeks.

"Are you alright?" I was genuinely concerned, but he just nodded.

"Oh yes," he said. "Now please untie me."

I untied him, and he rolled over onto his back. He groaned in obvious pain as his back touched the bed. It must have really hurt, but he stretched out his arms and legs and whispered, "Please don't tie me up again."

So I tied him up again, and he lay there groaning and wriggling, and his cock was twitching as if it had a life of it's own.

"Please don't tease me with your hands and your tongue and your pussy," he begged, and I grinned. Weird, I thought. Touched as a fruit pie, but, he was the one paying, so I did as I was asked not to do.

I started running my hands all over his body, starting with his face and working downwards, but avoiding his cock, until I reached his feet. He groaned and moaned, begging me to stop. I tickled his feet and sucked his big toe and he writhed and wriggled against his bonds and moaned and called me a sadistic bitch and I was really enjoying myself. It was the most fun I had had for many a long year.

I moved back to his face. His eyes were closed. I kissed him on his mouth, slipping my tongue into his mouth and he pushed his tongue into my mouth. I kissed his face and stuck my tongue into his ear. He tried to move his head but I held his hair, stopping him. I moved my tongue down his body, following the journey my hands had recently made. My tongue gently touched his cock, which was continually twitching and jerking.

I moved my bottom so it was just inches from his face. He was seriously moaning and groaning now.

Then I rolled off the bed, and stood up.

"I'm bored with this," I told him. "I'm going to take a shower," and started to walk towards the bathroom.

"What? What are you doing?" He genuinely sounded alarmed. "Come back. You haven't finished. I've paid for this! You must come back. Please!"

His voice was desperate.

I stopped. I'd been teasing him, of course.

"Beg me," I ordered, and I saw him breathe a big sigh of relief as he realised I'd been teasing.

"Please mistress, please come back, I beg you, please."

"Have you been a naughty boy?"

I picked up the whip.

"Well, have you?"

"Yes. Yes I have. I've been a very naughty boy. Please mistress, please."

So I reluctantly walked back to him, and this time actually sat on his face and it took just half a dozen strokes of my hand before he came with a huge moan.

I sat up and realised that I had probably fulfilled the fantasies of yet another of Abacadia's honourable citizens and, although he was definitely touched, he was touched and harmless.

And happy.

We made love again in the morning but it was gentle and normal and nice. I had rubbed some salve that he had brought with him onto his back and bottom and feet but he still walked stiffly and obviously in some sort of pain.

Later, when he had left, and Moldie and I were having our now traditional lunch together, I asked him, "Moldie, were you watching last night and this morning?"

"Of course," he said, not looking in the least embarrassed. "I had to keep a check that he wasn't hurting you."

He grinned.

"Oh," I said. "Of course. Were you masturbating?"

I asked the question very casually, and this time he did look embarrassed. The grin disappeared. It was obvious that he had been.

"Don't worry," I said. "You're a man. Of course you were wanking. It wouldn't have been normal if you hadn't been. I just hope you're not getting any ideas of you tying me up. You would have to pay for that pleasure!"

I smiled sweetly at him, but he didn't look too pleased.

"Can we change the subject?" he suggested, so we did.

"Tomorrow the client is arriving at lunch time," he told me, and I raised an eyebrow.

Moldie smiled.

"I think you'll actually like what I am about to tell you." .

"I doubt it," I replied, "But carry on."

"His name is Danger Goodness, and he is a well known film director here in Abacadia."

"You mean he makes porn films?" I suggested, sarcastically. "I was wondering when it would come around to this."

"Actually, you're wrong," chuckled Moldie, "Though that is a good idea."

He pretended to make a note on an imaginary notepad.

I stuck my tongue out at him.

"He actually makes adverts for TV and cinema. He wants to come over and use you to advertise Cadian Wine."

"Oh," I replied, a tad shamefacedly. "Tell me more."

"He wants to bring a cameraman and a soundman, and two actors, a male and a female, and act out a little scene here in the apartment. From what I can gather, the lady is the gentleman's girlfriend, but he is secretly in love with you and your image. The two of them are sitting on the sofa when you walk in from the bedroom wearing one of your evening dresses.

He immediately stands up, with adoring admiration in his eyes. He fusses over you, kissing your hand and looking awestruck and his girlfriend thinks she is losing him. She takes a bottle of Cadian wine and a wine glass from her bag, and slowly pours some wine into the glass.

He looks around, and you can see he is torn between you and the wine. After a few seconds of indecision, he goes back to the girl and the wine. You shrug your shoulders and say 'I can't blame him. I would have done the same!' Do you think you can do that?"

I smiled. "I think so. And then they all leave, I assume."

"The actors and the film crew do. Danger will stay for the night."

He grinned again.

"Of course."

"How much is he paying you? I hope it is a bit extra."

"Indeed he is," said Moldie, happily. "$50,000 for the advert and $100,000 for the night with you. He says he can therefore write the whole lot off as a business expense."

"I should have guessed he'd want sex," I said sarcastically. "Fee foe, money is money. So, an earlier than usual start tomorrow, but that's fine. I didn't have anything planned for the afternoon anyway."

Chapter 15 - Couples

Sam and Stan did all the arranging for us. They got the visas in double quick time, 'We contacted a couple of people we know,' and arranged for our injections, which we had. They got some Abacadian money. One hundred pups to a fang, and there were about seven fangs to a pound. The notes were very colourful and gay, almost like children's money, with pictures of brightly coloured birds prominent.

All we had to do was pack our bags, and choose some clothes to wear.

"Basic everyday clothes, so that you will blend in with the locals. I've looked at photos of the Abacadian locals and many of the men and quite a few of the women wear western-style jeans and T-shirts."

Pauline, Theo and I drove to Uncle Flambert's cottage, arriving mid morning. Theo took all his computer stuff with him, and Flambert settled him into one of the spare bedrooms.

"Try and contact us as often as you can, but not so often that officialdom in Abacadia may get suspicious," said Flambert. "Sam and Stu will advise you."

Sam and Stu arrived at lunch time. Theo and Stu disappeared to Theo's bedroom and spent a couple of hours talking computing and swapping computer stuff.

Flambert and Sam and Pauline and I spent the time going over our plans for what we would do once we arrived in Abacadia.

We had some lunch and Uncle Flambert opened a bottle of Champagne and we toasted a successful trip.

"Here's to Clair returning home to Hamilton Hall in the very near future," suggested Flambert, and we all clinked glasses.

We said goodbye to Theo and Flambert, giving them both big hugs, and piled into Sam's car, a very unobtrusive and plain Ford hatchback, and drove to Gatwick airport.

"We must start acting as couple immediately," said Sam as we drove down the M4. "The sooner we start, the more natural it will appear in Abacadia. Acting natural is hugely important to keep away suspicion. We have no idea if we will be watched or spied on in Abacadia. Better to be safe than sorry."

I was sitting next to him in the front seat of the Ford, and he smiled at me.

"A bit of play acting," he said, "But important, I think."

We parked up at Gatwick and Sam carried my bag for me through the airport and we held hands and spent a fair amount of time holding hands, looking into each others eyes and gently kissing. It wasn't unpleasant.

Stu and Pauline did the same. Either she is an Oscar winning actress or she was enjoying herself as well.

The ten hour flight to Snuka, the capital city of Abacadia, was uneventful, though we changed planes at Rome. Sam and I got to know each other quite well, talking about this and that. I found him to be quite intelligent and quite interesting.

Hmmm, I thought, hmmm.

We arrived safely in Snuka at the Winston McMillan Airport. We were thoroughly searched at the airport, and warned by the officials not to visit Effghania. This was without us even mentioning we intended going there.

"We have always been intrigued by Abacadia," we told them, "And have come for a short holiday here."

"If you get into any trouble in Effghania," he

continued, as if we hadn't spoken, "You are on your own. The Abacadian government won't come to your rescue."

As we left the airport, I asked, "Who was Winston McMillan?"

"I believe he was the country's first prime minister after independence," said Sam. "Come on, let's go and hire a car."

We found a local car hire company and rented an oldish dull green Lada Samara, which Pauline immediately nicknamed 'Lady Sammy'. It was the most common car in Abacadia and the most common colour. Stu stole some number plates from a derelict and abandoned car, which was the same make and colour.

"If we are going anywhere dodgy," he explained, "We can swap the number plates. The authorities will find it harder to pin any mischief onto us. If there is any mischief."

Sam and Stu visited a local shop and bought some maps and used their spare time to plan the route to Redik and Lake Lucinda and plan an escape route from there just in case anything went wrong.

Sam booked us into a local hotel. Not too cheap and not too expensive. Non distinct. It was called The Coconut Soup Hotel, which seemed an odd name for a hotel to me, but we were in a foreign country and maybe it was perfectly normal for a hotel in Abacadia to be named after a starter.

Sam booked two double rooms, one for him and me and one for Pauline and Stu. We had discussed this.

"The art of pretending to be someone that you are not," explained Sam, "Is to always remain in character. We must always play the part of two couples in love who have come away on a romantic holiday together. And this includes sharing rooms in a

107

hotel I'm afraid. We don't know if anyone is watching us so we must assume they are."

"You are just a typical man," I said. "You just want to sleep with me."

I saw the look of disgust on his face and realised I had gone too far.

"I'm sorry. I didn't mean that. I was just trying to be clever and amusing."

I gave him a sort of sick smile and he smiled back.

"That's no problem. We all want the same thing. To rescue your mother," and I saw he was telling the truth and felt extremely guilty.

"I know you do," I said, humbly. "Come on, let's go and see what the room is like."

It was a small room with a small double bed, a small set of drawers and a small sink. Clean but plain. The shared bathroom was down the corridor. We unpacked, visited the bathroom and went downstairs to meet Stu and Pauline in the bar for a snack and a drink. We sat around a table and chatted about anything that came to mind, except why we were there.

"Walls have ears," explained Sam. "We don't know who is listening."

We called the waiter over and Sam asked for a mixture of snacks that we could share and a bottle of Cadian wine and four glasses. The snacks consisted mainly of spicy fruits and vegetables, with some coconut bread and chutneys. All very tasty, but spicy.

It soon became evident that the four of us were getting on very well. Sam and Stu were very good company, and had many stories to entertain us from their SAS days, though they made sure the words SAS were never used.

The bottle of wine didn't last long, and when Sam and Stu visited the bar buying some more drinks, I managed to have a word with Pauline in private.

"Are you going to, you know, with Stu?" I asked her.

"Are you with Sam?" she asked in return.

"I asked first," I said.

"Yes," she answered, simply and honestly. She then tried to defend her decision, but there was no need.

"He is very handsome and kind and a lot of fun," she said, "And it has been a long time since I slept with a bloke. And I will do anything within reason to rescue mother and sleeping with Stu is a small price to pay for rescuing her. Now you answer."

"Yes," I said. "Yes."

We retired to our bedrooms fairly early after saying goodnight to the others. It had been quite a long and tiring and stressful day.

As soon as we entered the bedroom, I said, "Sam do you want to make love to me tonight?"

He looked totally shocked and I had to smile. He stuttered, so I answered for him.

"I would like that, but maybe we could wait until the morning. It's been a long day and I am very tired. What do you think?"

He agreed. What else could he do? I went down the corridor to the bathroom and returned wearing a knee length nightie. He went to the bathroom and returned wearing boxer shorts. I groaned inwardly. What a body! So strong and muscular with no hint of fat and a lovely hairy chest.

Ooooh! Lovely!

He climbed into bed with me and I cuddled up into his arms. I kissed him on the cheek.

"Good night Sam," I said and he kissed the top of my head.

"Good night Alice."

In the morning I persuaded him to make love to me. It took a lot of doing.

Not!

He was gentle and loving and I was wondering if I could settle down with this man and I decided yes, I probably could.

Over breakfast, Pauline and I exchanged glances. I winked and she smiled and nodded and she winked and I smiled and nodded. So, I thought, we'd both got our oats. Excellent.

After breakfast, which consisted of savoury coconut pancakes filled with scrambled eggs, yet more chutney and coconut gravy, and was truly delicious, Sam phoned Dave Gulldred, and discovered he lived just a two hour drive from Snuka.

"Would you like to come for lunch?" Dave asked, and we agreed we would, thank you very much.

Pauline and I visited the toilet together and I asked her, "What was it like?"

"Great," she told me, not looking in the slightest bit embarrassed, "How about you?"

"Wonderful," and we laughed.

"Could you settle down with him?" she asked me and I told her that probably I could and she said the same about Stu.

We had a coffee in the bar and the waiter told us that it was locally grown and it was strong and tasted of coconut, slightly, and was different but kind of nice.

We piled into Lady Sammy and set off to visit Dave and Laura Gulldred. As we drove through the lovely countryside, Sam asked a question.

"Ladies," he said, "There is something which is worrying Stu and I. This whole thing about your mother's kidnapping. Something doesn't seem right and we think you are withholding something from us. If she's not being held for ransom, then why is she being held? If you are holding something back then it may jeopardise our chances of success."

110

I turned around and looked at Pauline sitting in the back seat next to Stu.

"Maybe we ought to tell them," I said, and she nodded.

"Maybe we should," so we did. We told them everything we knew.

"Please keep it a secret," I begged. "It would be awful if this all came out in Worcestershire. It would be so embarrassing for everyone."

"I can see why you wanted to keep it a secret but thank you for telling us and trusting us. We promise not to tell anyone else."

"We promise," said Stu, and I gave a big sigh of relief that we had told them.

"This may sound a bit pervy," said Sam, "But can we see a copy of the film. Every little bit of extra information might help."

Pauline and I looked at each other again, and nodded.

"Of course. The most important thing is to rescue mother. You'll have to ask Theo to send you a copy."

Sam turned Lady Sammy off the main road and we headed down a narrow tree lined un-made road. After a couple of hundred yards we turned a corner and saw Dave Gulldred's house in front of us.

It was rather nice. Two stories, built, I thought, in the Dutch style, with very steep red clay tiled roofs and columns either side of the front door. To one side was an immaculate lawn, gently sloping away from the house and down to a small lake.

Dave lived there with his wife, Laura, their six children, and two large Alsatian dogs who had big teeth and waggy tails. They seemed quite pleased to see us, but not over enthusiastic.

"Why don't we walk out onto the lawn," Dave suggested. "It is lovely out there."

We followed him into the garden and sat down around a table under a large umbrella.

"The phone is bugged and the house is bugged," he told us. "I suspected so when we first moved in. It didn't take me long to find them. It's because we are foreigners, I think, not for any other reasons. We are safe out here in the garden."

"Why have you retired to Abacadia," asked Sam.

"Just look around," said Dave. "Isn't this just the most beautiful place in the world?" and it was. Very green, with hills and trees beyond the lake, cows and horses and chickens.

"We own thirty acres of this. There are three villages on our land, and we feel like a Lord and a Lady. The people are so friendly. We pay the workers well. Well for here, a pittance compared to England, but they all seem very happy. The cost of living is so cheap."

"Are you not worried about crime?" I asked.

Laura laughed.

"I have never felt so safe in my entire life. There is virtually no crime here. We never lock the doors and let the children roam and play wherever they want. And we have the two dogs, Mopsy and Bucket. They are very protective of the children."

We watched as the children and the dogs played together and we could see how much the children loved the dogs and how much the dogs loved the children. They climbed on their backs and pulled their tails and when they inadvertently pulled their whiskers, the dogs growled and gently shook the children off, but always with their tails wagging.

"We are completely certain no harm will come to them," said Laura, and we believed her.

We talked a bit more about Abacadia. Dave and Laura made it sound like a wonderful place to live and

I started to feel a bit jealous. Then we talked about England and mutual acquaintances and Flambert was mentioned and stories swapped and there was much laughter until some food and soft drinks were brought out by a servant.

We ate lunch then Dave asked us why we were really there.

Sam told him, leaving out the reason why mother was really being held and suggesting ransom instead.

"I see," Dave said. "And you have come to rescue her?"

"That's the plan," answered Sam. "Any help or advice you can give us would be gratefully received."

Dave looked dubious.

"I'll do what I can."

"What do you know about Effghania?" Sam asked. "The airport officials told us it was a highly dangerous place, and if we went there and got into trouble, then no one would come to help us out."

"I do know that that is complete bollux," said Dave, with a chuckle. "Effghania is certainly the safest place in Abacadia, and possibly the safest place anywhere in the world. Effghanians are the most laid back and gentle people I know. That's their problem. They're pacifists. They don't believe in violence. That's why the Jakalamnian tribe have managed so easily to become the ruling party here. Stories about violence in Effghania are just government propaganda."

"So if we can find her," asked Sam, "And attempt to rescue her, are you saying that no one will try and stop us?"

"I didn't say that," said Dave. "ODOE keep preaching that they are totally non-violent but that doesn't mean that everybody in the organisation is like that. Just generally, Effghanians are gentle, peace-loving people."

"What do you know about the town of Redik?"

It was my turn to ask a question.

"We are fairly sure that that is where she is being held."

"To be honest," answered Dave, "I've never been there. I know very little about the place. I assume you've done all the research so you probably know more about the place than I do. Sorry."

"In one of her, Clair's, messages, she said was being held in a hotel. Do you know of any hotels in Redik? We've googled it but can't find any hotels mentioned. Do you know of any way we could find out? Do you know anybody who comes from Redik?"

Dave scratched his cheek.

"Let me get back to you on that one. Call me tomorrow."

"Have you ever been to Lake Lucinda. We have reason to believe she has been there, and we think there is a chance she might visit again."

"I can help you out there," said Dave, smiling at Laura. "We visited there just last year. It really is a most beautiful spot. We had a lovely day there with the kids. Swimming in the lake and eating a picnic on a little beach."

He told us what else he knew about the lake and surrounding area and even lent us a map.

"We need a cover story. Any suggestions?" asked Sam.

"There are quite a few birds around the area, and I seem to recall that the bird life around Lake Lucinda is especially diverse," said Dave, furrowing his brow. "I think it may be famous for its storks and herons though you would need to check on that. I'll lend you a couple of books. I would lend you some binoculars but I only have one set. It should be easy for you to buy some in Snuka. Bird spotting might be a good cover story."

"Good idea, Dave," said Sam. "Thank you."

Dave sighed.

"I'll do all I can to help, Sam, but to be honest, that's not a lot. If I get caught helping you, then I would be thrown into prison, and we would lose all this."

He swept his hand around encompassing all his land and the surrounding hills and trees.

"I can't take the risk. I have a wife and a family. I'm under surveillance as it is, not because I've done anything wrong, simply because I'm a foreigner here."

"Dave," said Sam, in a very sincere voice, "We're not asking you to do anything, just give us advice. I understand your position."

Dave sighed again.

"Okay. What else can I do?"

"Do you have any guns?" asked Sam.

"I thought you might ask that. Come with me," said Dave and the two of them disappeared around the corner of the house. The rest of us watched the children and dogs playing and I told Laura about the oddly named Coconut Soup Hotel.

Laura smiled and said, "They love coconut here in Abacadia and put it with virtually everything. Coconut curries, coconut stews, coconut milk, coffee, tea, cake. Coconut with everything. Okay if you like coconut."

Dave and Sam returned a few minutes later, and Dave had a bag over each shoulder.

"Rifles in this one," he said, "And walkie-talkies in this one. I'll show you the rifles later, but these are the walkie-talkies."

He opened the smaller of the two bags and took out two walkie-talkies. They looked ancient, quite large and bulky and solid.

"They have been well maintained," said Dave, "And

still work perfectly. They have a working distance of about five miles and the batteries should last about twelve hours or so before they need recharging."

He showed us how to use them, which was rather simple, and Stu grunted in satisfaction.

"Thanks mate," he said.

"They have a vibrating function as well," explained Dave, "In case you want complete silence when calling each other.

"As for the guns," he continued, "They are dart guns," and Sam and Stu raised their eyebrows.

Dave explained.

"A few years ago, the Abacadian government were alarmed by the amount of gun deaths in the country and decided to clamp down big time on the ownership of guns. There was a lot of opposition to the idea so, as a compromise, they asked a gun manufacturer to develop a cheap but accurate dart gun. They figured this would be some sort of compromise which would be acceptable to everyone. They also developed a new type of dart, small and cheap to produce, which would rarely kill but rather tranquilize the victim quickly. They also have the advantage of being almost silent.

Now almost everyone has these dart guns. If you shoot someone with a bullet, the penalty is a hefty jail sentence or even hanging, and the government here like their hangings, which are done in public. However, if you shoot someone with a dart gun, likely or not you will get off with a fine, even if you accidentally kill them.

So dart guns are popular, and now even most of the army use them."

I was impressed with the government's forward thinking and told Dave so.

"Many of the government's policies are rubbish," he said, "But this was a very good one. I have provided you with twenty darts. You can pay me for them if you use any, but they don't cost a lot. You can get more at any sports shop. You don't even need proof of your identity."

"There must be real guns in the country," asked Sam, and Dave nodded.

"Of course. The army have them, but don't use them for shooting at people, but, as I said, the punishment for using dart guns is almost nothing, so people use them instead."

Sam and Stu nodded.

"If you do manage to rescue Lady Clair, come back here as quick as you can," continued Dave. "You can shelter or hide in one of the villages. I have a hut available at all times, just in case of emergencies. The villagers won't tell."

We all thanked Dave and Laura, and headed off back to Snuka, promising to let them know what happened.

Chapter 16 - The Advertising Star

Next morning, Danger Goodness and four others turned up to make a wine advert. Danger was the nicest, politest man I had ever met, even nicer, if it's possible, than my late beloved Alfie. He always called me Lady Hamilton, or My Lady, always held a chair for me, and always opened the doors. That night in the bedroom he helped me undress, carefully folding up my clothes for me. In bed he always asked me in the politest possible way before he did anything to me. He was very concerned that I was always happy with whatever he was doing, and was genuinely anxious that I orgasmed.

Which I did.

Of course.

He told me a bit about himself. He had obtained a degree in practical film making and production from Snuka University. He passed with the highest marks in the university's brief history, and was immediately snapped up by the government to make promotional films.

It wasn't long before he became self-employed, selling his talents to the highest bidder, and becoming wealthy. He produced his first full length film, a romantic thriller, which was a box office hit, and since had made more than twenty highly acclaimed and profitable movies.

The previous year he had invested some of his money in buying outright the top wine company in Abacadia, Cadian Wines.

"The company has been struggling," he explained, "So I managed to buy it for a bargain knock down price. I think that with a decent advertising campaign and proper management, Cadian Wines can really succeed. The wines they have been producing are actually very good."

I nodded.

"I agree with you about that," I said. "I have been drinking them since I arrived in Abacadia. As you say, they are actually very good."

He nodded and smiled.

"So, that's why I'm here. This will be the first advert I have made for Cadian wines. I have been looking around for a good idea, and when I heard you were in the country, bingo, the answer to my problem."

"Well," I said, "I hope I can do justice to your faith in me."

Despite my misgivings, the filming for the advert went well. I didn't really have much to do, just look pretty, which I did, look sexy, which I did, and try and utter two lines of script. I did that as well. It wasn't difficult and Danger Goodness seemed very happy with everything.

They filmed it all a number of times. Half the adverts were filmed in English, the rest of the time in Abacadian. I had to learn my two lines in that language but it wasn't difficult and Danger seemed happy enough with my performance.

Pebble helped with the make-up for all of us 'actors' and seemed to really enjoy herself. A bit of glamour for her and some extra wages and a couple of free bottles of Cadian Wine. Later, I asked Moldie about her.

"She went to glamour school for a short while but had to leave due to lack of money. She is quite bright and good at everything she sets her mind to, it seems."

I got left a box of wine. One dozen bottles. Four red, four white and four rosé.

"If you behave yourself," I told Moldie the next day after Danger had left, "I might let you share a bottle, and if you misbehave, I might let you share two!"

A few days later, Danger Goodness contacted Moldie and said that he was really happy with the final advert and he was wondering if he could film a series with me as the celebrity character and Moldie said, "Yes, of course, Lady Hamilton would be delighted," and it just needed to be arranged.

An advertising star was being born.

The next morning, after Danger Goodness had left, Moldie and I shared a early lunch or a late breakfast. Bacon and eggs that day. Moldie was in a particularly good mood.

"Well done Clair, that went really well. I have a distinct feeling Mr Goodness will return to make more Cadian Wine adverts. More easy money. He is a very nice man, isn't he?"

"Yes," I smiled. "He is. I wish I could tell my children that I might become a famous advertising star. They would be impressed."

He looked at me. I could almost see his mind working.

"Of course you can send another message, but I'll ask if you can mention the adverts. I don't see why not."

I thanked him and said I would think of a message.

"Things are going well, aren't they, Moldie? You know, my days off really help me. I would love to visit another beauty spot. What do you think?"

"Of course," he said, sounding enthusiastic. I knew he loved my days off as much as I did. He got to make love to me.

"Anyway back to normality. Would you like to hear about tomorrows clients?"

He smiled.

I looked up from my breakfast.

"Clients?"

Moldie chuckled.

"Two of them. They call themselves John Smith and Tom Jones. They are Abacadian but for some reason unbeknown to me or anyone, they want to be called John Smith and Tom Jones. They want to have you at the same time. Three in a bed and the little one said rollover," he continued before I could answer.

I looked at him and once again sighed. All my love making till then had been with one man at a time. My friends at uni had boasted about taking on two or more men at once, and women, come to that, but it had never appealed to me. Sex had seemed to me to be a private thing but now, it appeared, I was to sleep with two men together. Oh well, what the hell, nothing ventured nothing gained.

I wasn't going to let Moldie know that I might actually have been looking forward to it so said instead, "I thought you loved me Moldie. Why do you want me to suffer?"

Moldie had the vague decency to look vaguely troubled.

"I've seen it on film," he said, talking about two men servicing a woman at once, "And the women seem to really enjoy it. I'm sure you won't suffer. Much."

I sighed. Again I sighed.

"Fair enough. Are they paying double?"

Moldie chuckled at that suggestion. The rotten bastard often chuckled at my expense, despite his protestations of love for me but wouldn't answer the question.

John Smith and Tom Jones turned out to be bi-sexual middle aged men who were just as happy to do to each other what they did to me and what I did to them. They were up for anything.

When it came to both of them enjoying me at the same time, they were very gentle with me. And it was a strange experience. A sort of slightly painful pleasure or a slightly pleasurable pain. They moved in unison inside me but, for once, I didn't come. Despite my recent botty experiences, anal sex didn't seem natural and right to me. Bottoms are for pushing stuff out not for pushing things in.

But I endured and they both seemed happy enough when they left next morning.

Over breakfast, after discussing the previous evenings events, and Moldie asking me what it had felt like, and me explaining that he didn't have a vagina so couldn't possibly understand, Moldie said that it would be okay for me to mention in my message to the children that I had made a short advert and that it may bring some money to the family.

"But you are not allowed to mention that it is for Cadian Wines," I'm afraid. "They think that that might give them an idea of where you are."

"Fair enough," I said. "I'll think of something and let you know this evening. And this time, Moldie, please could you try and get some sort of reply. I'm sure everything is okay at home but I would love to know."

"Okay. I can't see that being a problem."

"I have a day off soon. Have you thought of anywhere nice we can go?"

"In two days time," smiled Moldie, smiling. "I have thought of the most beautiful spot in the world. It's called Angel's Hair Waterfall. It's truly wonderful."

"I thought Lake Lucinda was the most beautiful spot in the world," I teased.

"It is very beautiful there," he conceded, "But Angel's Hair Falls is even nicer."

So that evening I tried to concoct another message. I needed to tell them I would be at Angel's Hair Waterfall on the 19th July without Moldie getting suspicious. How on earth was I to do that? I racked my brain.

The nickname for one of the girls that Alice was at school with was Angel. What was her name? Come on Clair, think. I went through the alphabet, thinking of names. Anne, Abigail, Audrey, Alex, etc. this often worked for me.

I got to J and immediately thought of Jackie. She was a stunner, long blond hair and a face like an angel. Now I needed something to make them think 19. Theo spent his 19th birthday in France. That was the best I could think of.

In the end I came up with 'Theo, is Jackie still playing whist and are you still taking her to France for your birthday? I miss you all and would love to hear some answers to my questions.'

It wasn't brilliant, I know, but it was all I could think of. I still didn't really know if Moldie was actually sending my messages, though I suspected he was. And of course I had no idea if the children were getting my secret messages. I wouldn't know until I got an answer.

Chapter 17 - The Angel's Hair Waterfalls

My next client was a man of the church. His name was Reverend Feely Thrussel, who was a priest from northern Abacadia. Where he got the money from I nor Moldie ever found out. Maybe it was stolen from his parishioners but we really don't know. Moldie could find out very little about him.

"He contacted us. How he found out about you, I don't know, but he's paid already and hasn't asked for anything special, so God knows what he will be like."

The Reverend Feely Thrussel actually spent a lot of the time trying to convert me into becoming a Born Again Christian, even when he was bonking me he tried, but with no luck. I was, and still am, a firm atheist.

He wanted me to talk dirty to him.

"Please," he begged. "Talk dirty. Tell me what you want me to do to you. Talk dirty."

What a weirdo, I thought, but if he wanted me to talk dirty then I would talk dirty and I reckoned I could talk as dirty as any woman.

Actually, thinking about it now, I'm a bit embarrassed to repeat what I said. I wasn't dirty, I was absolutely filthy. I blush now to think about it. I'm an English Lady, not a common hoe from the gutters. But Feely Thrussel seemed delighted with my utter trash and he told me what a good girl I was and how the Lord would love me forever.

He also prayed for me to have 'The most wonderful orgasms of her miserable sin filled life' as he was shagging me from behind, and, lo and behold, I came. Not the most wonderful but good, and he thanked the Lord for me for the pleasures He beheld and came himself shouting the Lords name.

A very strange experience.

"A very strange experience," I told Moldie the next day, and Moldie, who was religious, shrugged and agreed it was indeed a very strange experience.

"Tomorrow," he told me, "You have earned a break and I am taking you to my favourite beauty spot in Effghania. My favourite beauty spot in the whole world," he corrected himself. "It's a waterfall called The Angel's Hair that I mentioned yesterday. It's not very high but quite wide and falls into a large pool. It's surrounded by trees and is totally private and hardly anybody visits there these days. Almost certainly we will be the only ones there. We could go swimming," he suggested, and winked.

"I won't bother packing my swimsuit then," I said, and he grinned.

"And I won't bother packing mine either."

"Gorillas?" I asked.

"Unfortunately, yes." He shrugged. "Sorry, but the powers that be won't let us go unless those brutes come with us. But they'll keep their distance."

It was a two hour drive so we set off nice and early, and ate breakfast on the way. The countryside was truly memorable, and for some odd reason it reminded me of Mid Wales, around Llangollen. The trees were different species and grew in small clumps, many were knurled and gnarled and misshapen, but the hills were Mid Wales-ish, and there were lots of streams and small waterfalls everywhere.

We passed two or three small villages but once we were a few miles from Redik, we actually saw no traffic at all

"The name of the hills translates to The Hills of the Fairy Streams," Moldie told me. "Locals claim they have seen fairies playing in many of the streams. Obviously there are no such things as fairies. They probably saw fish jumping. But the streams are pretty."

Like we did with our visit to Lake Lucinda, Moldie parked the Landrover a short walk away from the actual waterfall. The gorillas stayed whilst Moldie and I walked.

"Will they be filming us?" I asked Moldie, with a huge amount of sarcasm in my voice.

"No," he said, with a huge amount of humility in his voice. "We only filmed it last time to make the recruiting video. I promise you, no more filming. We will be totally on our own."

I looked at him. To be honest, I didn't care one way or another. I'd been filmed so often in the nude and bonking this and that, that I just didn't care anymore.

Moldie picked up the bag containing the picnic and a bottle of Cadian wine that Danger Goodness had given us and we walked hand in hand to the waterfall. I turned and waved at the gorillas, and smiled sweetly. They just glowered as they always glowered.

The walk wasn't far but it was delightful. A twisting path led through an ancient woodland with wondrous contorted and twisted old trees with exposed roots, moss covered rocks with butterflies fluttering. It was slightly uphill and I was slightly out of breath as we crested a small rise and turned a corner in the path to a view of stunning beauty.

The waterfall was directly in front of us. It wasn't so high, 20-30 feet maybe, and twice as wide. The river cascaded over the lip in a steady flow, all white and sparkling in the sunshine, with a crackling waterfall sound.

It dropped into a small lake, or a large pond, which, away from the falls, was calm and blue and reflected the falls perfectly. A large tree grew away from the bank near the falls, seemingly to sprout straight from the water itself. Some rushes grew in one corner of the pond, and a kingfisher flew low over the surface. The lake disappeared around a corner to my left to where, I assumed, the water flowed away down a small river.

More trees totally surrounded the lake, reaching to the edge, with branches hanging out and actually touching the surface of the water in places. I was sure I saw a large brown fish swimming in the shadows.

In my wildest dreams I could never have imagined somewhere so wonderful.

I held Moldie's hand. I could sense his eyes on me, watching my reaction. I could feel tears in the corners of my eyes.

"Moldie," I said, squeezing his hand, "This is the most perfect place in the whole world. It must be. It's, it's ………wonderful. Thank you, thank you so much for bringing me here," and I turned and kissed him and now tears really were flowing down my cheeks. He gently wiped them away, and smiled at me.

"Isn't it! I never tire of coming here. Come on, there's a lovely grassy spot over there. Let's go and unpack the goodies that Pebble has prepared for us, or maybe you'd like a swim?"

I laughed.

"A swim sounds good."

We found the spot, took out the bottle of wine and placed it in the lake to cool. Then we undressed and walked hand in hand and naked into the lake. The water was pleasantly cool in the hot mid-day sun.

"This lake is called the Angels Puddle," Moldie told me as we slowly swan towards the middle, hardly breaking the surface and disturbing the calm.

We swam to the falls themselves and ducked through them. At the back was a small overhang with a ledge to one side. We sat there, holding hands again, with our feet dangling into the water, and looked through the falling water to the lake and forest beyond. The sun reflecting off the waterfall produced a vivid, bright rainbow.

It truly was one of the most memorable moments of my life.

Moldie started telling me a bit more about Angel's Hair Falls.

"I first came here about 10 years ago," he told me. "I was helping some Effghanian who live, used to live, in a village a couple of miles away. The whole village was suffering from a viral illness and I helped get them to a doctor. One of the elders told me about this place, and I drove over here one day and immediately fell in love.

I have been back 3 or 4 times but always on my own. I haven't told a soul about it apart from you."

I squeezed his hand.

"Thank you for bringing me here," I said, and really truly meant it.

He smiled back at me.

"Once," he continued, "I came here for a week, sleeping in a tent and explored the surrounding area. There's a sort of animal path, I think, which you can use to scramble up above the falls. We can go for a short walk up there after lunch, if you like, though we can't go too far. We don't really have the time."

"That sounds lovely. How come the whole world doesn't know about this place?" I asked him. "It must be the most beautiful romantic place. I could stay here forever."

Moldie smiled, obviously delighted that I loved the falls and lake as much as he obviously did.

"It's in Effghania," he explained, "The Abacadian government don't want to promote anywhere in Effghania. But, the world's loss is our gain," and he suddenly pushed me back into the water and dived in over my head and swam away with a strong overhand crawl. I chased after him and grabbed his ankle, duck diving and pulling him below the water.

He reached for me but I was too quick and swam off underwater. The water was crystal clear and I could see fish swimming nearby. What a place. What a wonderful, wonderful place.

I surfaced and looked around me but couldn't see the so called gorillas and I was glad about that. It was as if Moldie and I were the only two people alive in the world. We swam to the side and climbed out and, of course, we made love and then got dressed and had a picnic and some wine.

After lunch we climbed the narrow animal track that Moldie had mentioned up around the falls to the river above, and carried on for half a mile or so following the river. It gurgled and bubbled over many rocks and small pools and there were 3 more smaller waterfalls and rapids, though none to compare with the Angel's Hair falls. The sun shone through the tops of the trees and it was a lovely walk.

Paradise must be like this I thought to myself and it was possibly the happiest few hours of my entire life.

As Moldie drove back to Redik two hours later, I sat next to him in the front of the Land Rover and I wondered about him.

He was my kidnapper but he was a good man. A very good man. Everything he did seemed to be to help his people, the poor, unhappy people that he cared for. Was I falling in love with him? I wasn't sure, but I did like him.

Oh well, we'd just have to wait and see what happened.

Back in the apartment, and Moldie opened the fridge to get out a drink, when he tutted.

"I left that bottle of wine in the Angel's Puddle," he said. "Oh well, there's plenty more where that came from."

Old Man Manders was my next client the next day. He was an old man and his name was Manders. Very, very rich and very, very old and very, very wrinkly. He was so completely the opposite from Moldie.

I struggled being with him, I must admit. It was hard to be sexy with him. He was so old. He was nice enough. I can't deny that but he was just so old. As I was making love to him I closed my eyes and tried to imagine it was Moldie making love to me, and that helped a bit.

Old Man Manders offered me marriage.

"I am a multi millionaire," he said, "And haven't got that long to live. If you marry me, when I go, it will all be yours. My first wife died a few years ago and I have no children. All you would have to do is have sex with me twice a week."

I was vaguely interested until he mentioned the twice weekly sex then I lost interest.

Actually, I'd rather not talk about Old Man Manders.

Even Moldie was rather disgusted.

"I couldn't watch that," he said. "He was so old. Were you tempted by his marriage proposal?"

"I most definitely was not," I assured him.

"Shame," he said. "We could have had him bopped off and the money could have come to ODOE."

I looked at him, horrified but then saw he was teasing.

"ODOE don't do violence," he said. "Have another piece of toast. Oh, and by the way, we have had an answer from your son, Theo. Here, I have a copy for you."

My heart gave a flutter as I read it and I had to make a real physical effort to stop my hands shaking.

'Mum. We have been so worried about you,' the message said, 'but we're so glad you're okay. Thanks for all the messages. The whist drives are going well. I am still taking Jackie to France. How did you guess? Do you have any idea what your kidnappers want and have they said when they will release you? We wish we could talk to you and hope to see you soon. We all miss you and love you so much. Theo.'

I tried to hide my excitement by sighing.

"I do miss them all," I said to Moldie. "Is there no chance of me talking to them?"

He shook his head.

"Sorry. Not just yet. Soon maybe. Tell me Clair, what is a whist drive? I've never heard of such a thing. It seems very popular with your charity group."

My thoughts were on the message, and it took me a second or two to realise what he had asked.

"Oh," I said, trying not too look alarmed. "It's, eh, a bit like bridge but without the bidding at the start. Sometimes called poor man's bridge. As you say, it is very popular."

"What has it got to do with charity?" he asked, and I wondered if there was any suspicion or was he just genuinely interested.

"There are, um, normally 30-40 people at a whist drive," I said, making it up as I went along, "And they all pay £10 each, so we do make quite a lot of money. They play in couples and the winning couple usually get a, uh, free meal at a local pub or restaurant who have sponsored the evening. It's a fun evening, but also quite skilful," I explained, and he seemed to accept my make believe, and I silently sighed a big sigh of silent relief.

I studied the message carefully after he had gone, making sure I didn't show too much excitement. There was a chance he might be watching on one of the many hidden cameras.

They had written 'I am still taking Jackie to France. How did you guess?' So they understood my messages and must know I was in Abacadia and had visited Angel Falls.

'Hope to see you soon.' Did that mean that they were going to attempt to rescue me?

Why was the message from Theo, and not Alice or Pauline? That made me suspicious. Why?

My mind was in a turmoil. Where were they? What was happening? I wished I could talk to them. But at least the message had given me some hope. All I could do was wait.

Then I realised that there was no real way that they could find out where I actually was. I didn't know the name of the apartment or the street it was on. Dare I ask Moldie the name of the street? Would it make him suspicious? When would he allow me to send another message?

As I lay in bed that night, another thought crossed my mind.

Did I want to be rescued?

I had settled into a routine. The work, if you could call it work, wasn't so bad. I actually enjoyed most if it. And I was getting on really well with Moldie. But most of all, I was earning a lot of money to help the poor Effghanians. It took me a long time to get to sleep that night. I wished Moldie was lying next to me.

That was the first time I had had that thought. Suddenly I was lonely and I started weeping silently. I scolded myself.

"Come on," I said quietly, "You're Lady Clair Hamilton. Pull yourself together. You can get through this. Be strong."

Chapter 18 - Brave Doggut village

As soon as we arrived back at the Coconut Soup Hotel in Snuka, we all met up in Stu and Pauline's room and Stu switched on his laptop and contacted Theo again on skype. He told him that things were going fine here, and that we had been to visit some old friends, and asked if he had anything to report.

"We have had another secret message from mother," Theo told us.

He read out the message and said, "It came yesterday so I have had time to look for her secret message. The whole message was rather cryptic but I think I have got it right. Mother is much cleverer than she looks, for an elderly person."

There was a touch of awe in his voice.

"Basically, she said that she was visiting a local beauty spot called Angel's Hair waterfall, but, unfortunately, that was a couple of days ago. She had recorded the message on the 16th and had included that days football results but it was only sent yesterday. I'm not sure why there was such a delay.

At least we know she is still alive and well. I'll let you know if there are any more messages."

I spoke to Theo and asked him to email us a copy of The Film.

"Sam thinks it might help with mother's rescue," I explained after Theo hesitated for a second.

Theo sighed, and sent a copy. Sam and Stu studied it.

"You say that's Lake Lucinda?" Sam asked. "If that man takes her there again, it shouldn't be too much of a problem to rescue her if we got there first. Let's hope he does take her back."

We got out the map of Abacadia that Sam had bought and found Angel's Hair waterfall on it.

"It's on our way," I noticed. "Well, not too much of a diversion. Why don't we visit it on the way down to Redik? That's what proper tourists would do, wouldn't they. and we are supposed to be tourists."

Sam phoned Dave to see if he had found out anything about a hotel in Redik.

"Hello, Dave," he said, cheerfully. "It was lovely to see you and Laura yesterday."

The first bit of the conversation was just in case anyone was listening. Trying to act normal.

"It was part of our SAS training," explained Sam.

Dave replied equally cheerfully.

"It was good to see you as well. Alice and Pauline seem nice girls."

"They are," said Sam.

There was a click and Dave said, "There is one hotel in Redik. It's rather run down. I think it is highly unlikely from what you have told me that she is being held there"

There was another click, then both Sam and Dave said in unison, "Hello, hello. Are you there?"

"Bloody phones," said Dave. "Often go wrong."

They chatted for a couple of more minutes about meeting up again, then Sam hung up.

"You heard what he said," he said. "I wonder if Clair was mistaken about being kept in a hotel, or maybe you misread her message."

"Possibly," I said, "But we were fairly sure about it."

Next day we all walked to the centre of Snuka to do some shopping. The city centre reminded me a bit of Cardiff, though not so big, with wide streets and narrow pavements. Lots of traffic, many buses and bicycles, and almost all of them tooting their horns almost incessantly.

There was one posh new shopping centre, made mostly of glass, with many escalators and lifts, and all the usual shops. We stopped at a rather elegant and obviously fashionable coffee shop, called The Coconut Coffee Shack, and had a rather delicious cup of coconut coffee.

"I think a coffee shop like this would do rather well in Worcester," suggested Pauline, and we laughed, but she did have a point.

The men went off shopping without us and when we met up later they had bought two pairs of binoculars, for our 'bird watching'.

"They're not great quality," said Stu, "But they should do."

Us girls bought bread and cheese and other goodies to make enough picnics to keep us going for a few days.

We spent the evening in the Coconut Soup Hotel bar, as we had the night before, and tried some of their famous coconut soup, after which the hotel had been given it's name. The best soup I had ever tasted, second to none. I was beginning to like Abacadia.

The following day we set off for a leisurely drive to Redik in Lady Sammy. The countryside for most of the journey was beautiful. It reminded me a bit of the Derbyshire Dales, though the trees were different, and the wildlife we saw, mostly birds but some monkeys and a small herd of small deer, were more exotic. We saw many streams and waterfalls, and everything was so, so green.

Beautiful.

We stopped off at a couple of touristy spots, on the way, including a temple and a traditional Abacadian village, where we were given a traditional meal and entertained by a traditional musical group and singers and traditional dancing. We stayed in cheap accommodation, whatever we could find, including one night in a traditional mud hut, sleeping on traditional mattresses filled with straw and listening to wild animals snuffling outside.

We were slowly heading for Redik, desperately hoping another message would come from mother via Theo and Flambert, who we contacted every other day, but none did.

We eventually arrived at The Angel's Hair waterfall. It truly was a delightfully picturesque spot and we all put on our swimming costumes and went for a swim, ending up on a ledge behind the waterfall itself.

"It's strange to think," mulled Alice, "That mother was here just a few days ago, possibly sitting on this very ledge with her lover."

"I bet they went swimming in the nude," commented Sam, grinning.

"Trust you to think of that," I said, and the others all chuckled.

"I wonder what she's doing at this moment?" I mused.

Later, when we were having a picnic, Stu put his hand into the water and, with a chuckle, pulled out a half drunk bottle of Cadian wine.

"This must be theirs," he said. "They must have been occupied doing something else to leave it behind," and we all laughed, even us girls.

"You are so rude," I said to him.

After Angel's Hair Falls we headed towards Redik. We discussed what we were going to do there. Would anyone get suspicious of two white couples driving around in an old Lada Samara and asking questions? We could ask if there was an hotel that we could stay at. No one would get suspicious about that. But we would still be very noticeable and it would surely come to the attention of any local officials that were there. We wanted to stay in the background. Hidden totally if possible.

So we stopped at a village just a few miles north of Redik and asked if there was somewhere nearby which had some spare beds. There was always somebody who would put us up for the night for a few pounds and this village was no exception.

The village was called Brave Doggut, and named after an old Effghanian called Doggut who, many years ago, had saved the life of a child who was being attacked by a monkey. A big wild male monkey. But still only a monkey.

We asked if we could speak to the village elder, who was also called Doggut. He was the great grandson of the original Doggut. And he spoke English.

"When I young man I live in Australia for while," he told us.

"I work down gold mine," he said proudly.

We told him that we were in Abacadia on holiday and that we thought it was a beautiful country.

Then we told him that we had heard that a friend of ours was in the area, and we wanted to surprise her one day by suddenly just turning up. He thought this was a great wheeze.

"Ha," he chuckled. "The look on her face to see you when she thinks you in England. Ha."

He had a thought.

"A lot of work being done in Redik," he said. "Hospital tents being put up and trucks arrive daily full of food for poor people. Rumour is money donated by rich beautiful English widow."

We looked at each other. Could that be mother he was talking about? Surely it must be. More proof that she was nearby.

"That could well be our friend," I said. "We think she is staying in a hotel in Redik but we don't know which one. Is there a way we could find out?"

"Granddaughter work in Redik," said Doggut without hesitation. "I tell her find out for you tomorrow. You stay here until then?"

We said we could and he moved a family out of a hut so we had somewhere to sleep and we gave the family some money, which pleased them overly. We spent the day relaxing and chatting to Doggut and answering his innumerable questions about England.

"Have you met Queen Elizabeth?" he asked and started singing a version of God Save the Queen which included some slightly dubious lyrics, to our amusement.

That evening Doggut invited us to drink some locally brewed beer and share a pot of goat stew with him, sitting outside his hut.

"This granddaughter."

He introduced a young lady dressed in a smart two piece suit.

"Her name Tedwina. She work in shop in Redik."

He smiled at her fondly.

"She speak little bit English. If she try harder as young girl she speak English well as me but she too interested in chasing after boys."

She looked at him and snorted.

"They chase after me," she said.

"Tell good people what you found out," Doggut told her, grinning.

"There just one hotels in Redik," Tedwina said. "My friend work there as cleaner. There no white people staying at moment and certain no woman. Just Abacadian business mans.

But two days before now a beautiful white lady seen driving around Redik in old car. A handsome man driving and two large men in back seat. They hairy and very ugly. That might be your friend?"

It must have been mother, I thought, and that evening we had my thoughts confirmed. Sam skyped Theo who had a message for us.

"The message was 'I hope the whist drives are going well. Tell Lucy to hold the fourth round in the Lakeside Pavilion.'

I'm pretty sure that means that she will be at Lake Lucinda again on Thursday 4th August, which is in 3 days time," said Theo.

"The man on the phone asked me if I had a message to send to mother, as she was worried about us and wanted to know if we were well and carrying on with her charity work.

I had prepared a message to send to her, just in case the opportunity arose. I asked him to tell her we were fine and thank her for the messages, saying we were glad she was well and we had acted on her requests for the whist drives. I finished by saying that we hope to see her soon. I'm pretty sure she will realise that someone will be at Lake Lucinda."

"That's good timing for us," said Sam. "We can have a steady tourists drive down there, arriving on Wednesday. We'll then have a day to prepare our plans for her rescue."

Chapter 19 - Four Virgins

My next so-called client were actually many clients and didn't earn any money at all. Moldie explained.

"There are many, many people who help ODOE," he said. "The work is all voluntary and they work very hard. Long hours of physical work in difficult situations. They care for the sick and injured, the elderly and the dying.

The ODOE senior officials thought it would be a very good idea if some of them were to meet you for tea and cake. They all worship you. They would be very happy to spend time with you."

"Is that it?" I asked. "Just tea and cake and chit chat?"

"Not exactly," he said.

He was grinning again.

"We thought of bringing sixteen helpers to see you. Four of them are young men. They are extremely good workers and we thought that tea and cake would be a bit dull for them. They would probably prefer sex. Say, half an hour each? What do you think?"

I groaned.

"Whatever."

So the next day sixteen Effghanians trooped into my room. Moldie had brought in some extra chairs and stools and they all sat facing me and Moldie. They were all dressed in their very finest clothes. It was obviously a very big deal for them to meet me, a 'beautiful and god like celebrity'.

Moldie had given me a folder explaining who they all were with photos of them all. He suggested I learnt their names but I found that very difficult. The names were all so odd and I knew I would never remember them all. There was a lady called Lattice, another called Friendship and yet another called Helpful. The old men's names included River, Stone and, very oddly, Field. The four younger men who were obviously those who wanted the sex as payment were called Beckham, Giggs,

Scholes and Neville.

And the faces on the photos all looked the same to me.

In the end, we agreed to have the photos on the table in front of me to consider as I talked to them. Any problems and Moldie would be there to help me out.

Before they all came in, I asked Moldie, "Do they know that I earn all this money and how I earn it?"

"Yes," he said. "We have made sure they all know. And they think you are absolutely wonderful for doing it."

"They're not disgusted?"

"On the contrary," said Moldie, seriously. "They think it is a perfectly natural way to earn money. They can see all the good work your money is doing and love you because of it. The people coming to see you are true Effghanians. They love their country and they love their people and they love you."

Actually, the afternoon went really well. The reason Moldie had chosen those particular sixteen to visit with me was because they were sixteen of the best workers. It was so obvious that they all cared deeply about their people and the work they did, even the four young men. They told me about their work with such passion that I was carried along with their enthusiasm. Moldie helped with the translation, and explained some of their actions.

This was obviously one of the reasons Moldie had brought them to see me. Not just to encourage them, but to encourage me also, and it worked. What I was doing seemed so little for such massive rewards and I decided to carry on with my good work.

Not that I had any choice really.

After about four happy hours, the older visitors left, leaving me with the four young men and Moldie. They had drawn lots on the order they would go to bed with me. Whilst one was bonking, the other three would wait in the living room and watch television and chat with Moldie.

Before we started, Moldie walked through to the bedroom with me.

"Best to change out of your posh frock now," he said. "Here, let me help you. I think I should tell you that the four men who are visiting you are all virgins, so try and make it good for them."

I looked at him and felt my heart flutter. Four virgins, hey. I'd make it good for them. I'd make it so they would never forget the night they lost their virginity with the beautiful and Godlike Lady Clair Hamilton.

I kicked Moldie out of the bedroom.

"I'll come for them in a few minutes, after I've showered."

Twenty minutes later I walked into the living room wearing a very sexy nightie and all four of them gasped. Even Moldie smiled as he looked at their reactions.

"Whose first?" I asked, in my slowly developing Abacadian, and one of them stood up nervously. They were all nervous, despite their slightly cocky attitudes.

The first one was Beckham. In the bedroom, I sat him down on the bed and kissed him gently. He responded shyly, which excited me. I told him to stand up and undressed him. He stood unmoving. He was so nervous, I could tell, and needed relaxing.

I led him through to the bathroom and removed my nightie. He groaned as he saw my naked body and only then did he become erect. I made him stand in the bath and washed him all over, but when I started washing his erection, he came immediately. I looked at his face to see he was crying.

"Don't cry," I said, cuddling him to me.

"I'm sorry," he said, over and over as he sobbed. He obviously thought he had let me down by coming so quickly.

"Don't worry," I said, in my appalling Abacadian. "We'll try again in ten minutes."

At least I hope that's what I said.

I dried him and he dried me and I led him back to the bedroom, and climbed naked under the covers with him, and cuddled him some more.

I tried to chat to him, asking him about his work and family. I discovered, I think, that his parents lived nearby, as did his 6 older brothers and sisters but, being the youngest, he was the only volunteer. The other's were all farmers. His family supported Manchester United, he said, as did, it seemed, most of Effghania.

He soon relaxed and he soon stiffened again and this time I climbed on top and took his virginity and we made love properly and he came a second time in the missionary position with my arms around his neck.

I kissed him goodbye and the left the bedroom, closing the door behind him whilst I headed for the shower once again. Moldie told me later that the other three crowded around him, asking what it was like, and he had told them it was the best, the very, very best and that I was wonderful, which was, of course, absolutely the truth.

So Giggs, Scholes and Neville all came in to see me one by one, entering my bedroom as shy virgins and leaving as very happy young men.

Moldie was delighted.

"That went fantastically well," he exclaimed after they had all left. "All four of them will go back to their friends and tell them about you. It will encourage them to work even harder and we are sure to get more volunteers, especially if I tell them that this will be a regular occurrence."

He looked at me.

"If that's okay with you Clair?"

I nodded.

"I enjoyed myself," I said. "How many women can say they have taken the virginity of four young men in one evening? I may be the first."

"Something different tomorrow," said Moldie, changing the subject, and this time his grin threatened to split his cheeks open.

"Good or bad?" I asked.

"Good for me," he grinned. "I'll enjoy this one."

"Tell me," I said, "Before I slap you very hard indeed."

"Her name is Sparkling Eyebrows. She is a lesbian porn star

and wants to come with a couple of cameramen and make a lesbian porn film of her and you together."

He really was enjoying himself. Tears of joy were actually trickling down his cheeks in anticipation.

What next, I thought to myself. Is Moldie arranging my clients for his own pleasure? Then I shuddered and Moldie stopped chuckling long enough to speak.

"We have managed to get her to sign a contract that we will also get 20% of any profit she makes from the film. If it is a big success, and she thinks it will be, we could make quite a lot of money from this. She is a famous porn star in this country, so I've been told, and you are the most famous celebrity."

He was actually rubbing his hands together in anticipation of all the money I could make for him by acting in a lesbian porn film.

And he got to watch.

"I've got my laptop," he said. "I'll show you some film of her."

Sparkling Eyebrows was a blonde large breasted attractive youngish lady. I could see why she was popular with Abacadian men. She was indulging in a lesbian session with a younger brunette and seemed to be thoroughly enjoying herself. Moldie was grinning as he watched.

I sighed. I'd never tried Lesbianism. I'd had chances but it didn't appeal to me. I preferred men, preferably manly hairy men with big muscles and big cocks but now, it seemed, I was to participate in some lady love. Oh well, if you've never tried something, don't knock it until you do. I might actually enjoy it!

So the next day, Sparkling Eyebrows turned up at my apartment with two cameramen who were women and a sound man who was also a woman. They were filming and recording as they walked in.

Sparky, as she preferred to be called, looked exactly as she had in her film. What I wasn't expecting though, was a broad Derbyshire accent.

"Ay up, me duck," she greeted me. "How ya diddlin?"

I actually liked her, liked her a lot. Talk about down to earth, she should have been a coal miner!

She was born Annie Green in a little village half way between Derby and Nottingham called Breaston. Her dad had been a farmer and she had helped him catch and kill chickens as a child. She had been kicked out of school for smoking and being generally a pain in the butt and had drifted into prostitution and eventually pornography, at which she was, her words, 'extremely good.'

She quickly realised she preferred women to men and had specialised in lesbian scenes, though she still occasionally went with a man.

"Just for a change," she explained. "Sometimes I just get the urge to have a cock inside me again. So I do!"

Someone she had been acting with, she couldn't remember who, had mentioned to her how the porn industry was starting to flourish in Abacadia so, on a whim, she had come out here, took the name Sparkling Eyebrows, of which she was absurdly proud, and started making and starring in her own films, filmed in her apartment in Snuka.

The films became hugely popular and she became quite wealthy. She had seen my promotional video and contacted Moldie and here she was.

I was tempted to tell her the truth about why I was there, but instead told her about my money problems and she told me that if we make a really good film, then the both of us could make a lot of money from it.

"Leave the finances to Moldie," I told her. "I trust him completely."

After tea and cake she told me what she wanted from me in the film. She was actually very professional and I was impressed. She also put me totally at my ease and I lost my nervousness and almost started looking forward to it.

"The crew are filming everything that happens," she told me, "And we will edit it all together at the end. We are thinking of calling the film simply 'A lesbian evening with Lady Clair Hamilton'. We think that just having your name on the title will really help the sales. So, just try and enjoy and be your normal self."

So all evening and the following morning I became a lesbian and sort of eventually sort of slightly started to enjoy it a little bit sort of but, to be honest, not a lot. I didn't think I would ever try it again but it was an experience, I suppose.

Sparky seemed delighted with me.

"We should both make a lot of money from this," she said, with a twinkle in her eye. "Let me know if you want to act in another one of my films? I could bring along a man or two if you like."

I said I would let her know, and she went off with her ladies and Moldie came in for lunch. He couldn't keep the grin off his face.

"I enjoyed that," he gloated. "Very much. I will remember that for the rest of my life."

"Pervert."

But I didn't really think that.

The next day I was visited by another actor who was, it seemed, quite famous in Abacadia. All the famous celebrities were visiting me. Wasn't I a lucky girl?

His film name was The Golden Stud, Gold to his friends. I assumed, when Moldie first told me, that he was another porn star but no, he was a straight actor. He just had a porn star name.

When I first met him, I thought that he really did fancy himself. I must admit he was rather good looking, but no more handsome than Moldie. He seemed to think I was extremely lucky just to be in his company. For him to actually have sex with me was a total privilege. For me!

Actually, when I got to know him a bit better, underneath his borish exterior he wasn't so bad and I quite enjoyed his company.

I asked him why he chose the name The Golden Stud, and he said that an American name meant he had a better chance of becoming a success in the western world, and he liked the name

The Golden Stud.

"Do you not like my name?" he asked.

"It's a fine name," I told him, "I was just wondering."

He told me all about the Abacadian film industry, which was flourishing, it seemed, and he was one of it's biggest stars. He told me about some of the films he had been in and I had to admit I had never heard of any of them.

"Maybe you'd like to watch one of them with me," he suggested, almost humbly. "I have brought one with me. It's called 'House of the Rising Gun' and I play a role similar to James Bond. I think it's just about my best role. Would you like a look?"

I told him I would be delighted so he put the DVD in the player and we settled down on the sofa together with a bottle of Cadian red wine and watched the film. It was had obviously filmed in Abacadian but had been dubbed into English, I thought. The dubbing was extremely good, especially Gold's.

"I filmed all my bits twice," he explained, "Once speaking Abacadian and once speaking English, to make it more available to the American audience. Some of the others didn't speak English so they have been dubbed and I don't think the dubbers have done such a bad job."

We watched the film through to the end, with Gold sometimes telling me about aspects of the filming which he thought might interest me.

"That stuntman, there, actually broke his arm in this scene. Watch, there, you can actually see it snap, just there," or "Before this love scene the actress, Cool Waters, suggested we do it for real, so we did. At this moment I was actually inside her and her pretend orgasms, here, were actually real orgasms, or so she told me later."

At the end of the film, which I had enjoyed, he took me in his arms and gently undressed me and we made love on the sofa, which was nice. He had obviously had plenty of experience with plenty of leading ladies and knew how to treat a proper lady like me.

Before he left the next morning he said, "Lady Clair, I have really enjoyed my time with you, thank you."

I was touched by that and told him I had also enjoyed being with him and he looked pleased.

On a moment of impulse, or so it seemed to me, but probably wasn't, he suddenly said, "Lady Clair, I was wondering if maybe you might be interested in appearing in one of my upcoming films. The one I have in mind would have you playing the part of a posh English Lady, so, basically, you just have to play yourself. Maybe we could even film some of the action at Hamilton Hall. Would you be interested?"

I was a bit taken back. Me? A film star? Little old me.

"Are you serious?" I asked him and he said he was and I said, "Crikey, I'd love to," and he said that he would get in touch with me in a couple of months time.

Which would be nice.

The following day, Moldie had so kindly agreed to let me have a day off. We spent the day visiting Redik again. He was very keen to show me all the changes that had been made since my last visit two weeks previously, and changes there were aplenty.

For a start, most of the town now had electricity, and ODOE had organised regular rubbish and refuse collections, so the town was even cleaner than it was before. I saw many people painting and repairing many of the buildings, so the centre looked a lot smarter.

"They are all local people," explained Moldie, "And they are paid a basic wage."

Many more shops were open.

"We helped them buy their original stock, but now it's up to them to make a success."

A large hall had been turned into a hospital and there were doctors and nurses who were now being paid.

There were more cars and vans and trucks and motorbikes driving around than there were before, I noticed.

Moldie explained.

"We have managed to get a more regular supply of petrol.

146

Before, petrol was strictly rationed to those who needed it and they needed a permit, but now anyone can buy petrol, though it is still rationed. Hopefully, soon, we will be able to end the rationing, but not quite yet."

As we drove around the town, I was looking everywhere, hoping, but not expecting, to see Alice or Pauline or Theo or somebody else from England. I saw nobody. Moldie was watching me so I pretended I was even more interested in the going's on than I was.

I was disappointed that there was nobody there but I kept remembering the message.

'Hope to see you soon,' it said.

I was now starting to miss my family. The temporary confused thought I had had about whether I wanted to be rescued or not had cleared itself.

I did want to be rescued.

And as soon as possible.

That evening, Moldie said to me, "I've got a short film I would like you to see, if you don't mind?"

I shrugged and he pulled out his laptop. He switched it on and we settled down to watch, with the inevitable glass of Cadian wine each.

It was an American International News Service report all about Effghania.

"It was filmed last week," Moldie explained. "It hasn't been shown on the television yet but I have been sent an advanced copy. See what you think."

The film was a typical news report. There were shots of many parts of Redik, concentrating on all the good work that was being done. An American voice-over explained that the money had been donated by a rich foreign business man, and I chuckled at that.

Then at the end there was an appeal to send more money and a phone number to donate.

"Hopefully, when this film is shown in America and Britain and elsewhere, lots more money will come and help us. The money will go straight to a bank account here in Redik which belongs to ODOE. The Jakalamnian government will try and steal some of it but with the Americans on our side, hopefully most of it will come to us."

I was impressed and pleased for Moldie. All his hard work was beginning to come to fruition. But, and I pointed this out to him in the nicest possible way, I was the catalyst. Without me, very little would have happened, despite ODOE.

He agreed, thanked me and kissed me on the cheek. Then he suddenly looked serious.

"I have some bad news," he said. "A previous client is returning."

"Oh. As long as it's not that strange Bim Dram!"

Moldie pulled a funny face.

"Oh no," I said, dismayed. "It is him, isn't it? Why have you allowed him to come back? He was just weird and a bit scary."

"I'm sorry but he is an MP, a member of the cabinet, a very rich and powerful politician and in charge of the police and the army. He implied that if we didn't allow him back he would arrest us all, including you, so we had to agree. I'm sorry. And he has paid."

I sighed.

"Botherations. Please keep an eye on him, won't you?"

"Of course we will," assured Moldie. "Everything will be fine, I promise."

"His penis is even smaller than yours," I told him, and he chuckled.

"So I noticed. Even smaller than mine."

Chapter 20 - Bim Dram, again

So I had to spend another night with Bim Dram. I tried very, very hard to please him and keep him happy. I got the impression there was a huge amount of violence hidden just beneath the surface of his peculiar personality and I wanted to keep it at bay.

So I moaned and my faked orgasms were the best ever and I knew I had fooled him into thinking he was a brilliant lover.

"How long have you been in Abacadia," he asked me and when I answered, "How long do you think you will be staying here?"

I told him I didn't know and he asked me if I spend my whole time in this apartment and I told him occasionally I allowed Moldie to take me out and he asked me where we went and, like a fool, and to please him, I mentioned that we sometimes visited a local beauty spot.

Then he said, "Lady Clair, I am very fond of you and I was wondering if you would consider coming to live with me. I am willing to pay you $1,000,000 if you move into my house in Snuka and live with me for one year."

I was astonished and horrified by his offer. Another man wanting me to live with him, this time as a mistress not a wife. Or was he asking me to marry him. I asked him.

"Are you proposing to me?" I asked. "Do you want to marry me?"

Now it was his turn to be astonished.

"Eh, well, no. I thought we could just live together first. See how we get on."

I remembered what Moldie had said about him being potentially a bit nuts so rather diplomatically answered, "Thank you very much for your offer, Bim. It's all a bit sudden. Please may I have time to think about it?"

I expected Bim to react badly even to my gentle answer, but he didn't. He just shrugged his shoulder and said, "The offer will always remain open, Clair. I promise I will look after you and treat you like the lady that you are."

When he had gone, I asked Moldie what he thought. He shook his head.

"I must admit, I wasn't expecting that. You weren't tempted were you? No, of course not. I do hope that he will take your no as a final answer and that is the end of him."

But neither of us seemed convinced.

Bim Dram questioning me about visiting local beauty spots had given me the urge to return to Lake Lucinda, so I asked Moldie if it could be arranged.

"I don't see why not. You certainly deserve another trip there. You are working very hard for us, and things are going better than we ever thought they would. I have arranged three more clients for you, then we could go the day after that if you like."

"On Thursday you mean," I said, and Moldie said that he did in fact mean Thursday. I said thank you and I meant it.

"I just need to clear it with the committee, but I'm sure they will say yes."

"Meanwhile," I asked him, "I haven't sent a message home for a while. Could I?"

Of course he agreed and I composed a message which included the line 'I hope the whist drives are going well. Tell Lucy to hold the fourth round in the Lakeside Pavilion.'

I was really hoping that Moldie wouldn't cotton on and that the children would understand. They seemed to have decoded the previous ones, if my understanding of the message I got from them was anything to go by.

Back to work though, and next came another middle aged man, but this one was different. His name was Ton Malo and he was known as LonelyTon Malo. Once again, he was a successful business man, owning and managing the second largest minicab business in Abacadia. The reason he was LonelyTon was because he had no real friends and no wife or girlfriend, despite his wealth, and this was because he was extremely ugly.

As a young man he had contracted not only elephantitis but

also another tropical disease called blotcherism which had left his face badly misshapen and covered with blotches and marks all over. His chin was large and lopsided and one of his eyes was missing. He also had many teeth missing and many of those that were left were black or discoloured. Patches of hair had dropped from his head.

He was an unbelievably ugly man and I did genuinely feel sorry for him as he told me about his young adult life and how it affected him.

"I looked perfectly normal before," he explained as he showed me some photos of himself as a teenager. I saw a cheerful young man staring happily at the camera, with a pretty girl sitting on his shoulders and a silly grin on his face.

"The doctors think I caught the disease after swimming in a river near my home. It seems that a chemical factory just upstream from there had accidentally or on purpose dumped some dangerous waste into the river, which had flowed straight down to me. I wasn't the only person affected but probably the worst. Lots of fish and other wildlife had been killed but it never made much of a story in the newspapers. I think there was some bribing done to keep it out.

"Anyway, I spent many months in hospital, but it seems there was no cure and I was stuck with this face. The disease wasn't, isn't, infectious. Not at all. Despite that, girls just wouldn't come near me. I eventually found a blind lady who went out with me for a while but she could hear people talking about us. Beauty and the beast they used to say. She left me.

'I'm sorry Ton,' she said, 'But I can't bear to hear all the cruel remarks', and she was gone.

Since then, 22 years ago, I haven't had a girlfriend of any sort. I've spent all my time building up my minicab business, which is very successful, but I would give it all away just to have a wife who loved me.

I've admired you for years and thought that this was a good opportunity to meet you. I thought you would see past my ugliness and, well ...."

I did see past his ugliness. I saw a kind, gentle, unlucky man. A man who was desperate for love and was willing to pay anything to find it. So I looked past his ugliness by closing my eyes a lot and turning the lights off and I gave him some love. I know it was only for a few hours, but it was the best I could do.

But more than that, I think I gave him some hope and confidence. He wrote to me about 18 months later to say he had found a lady in his life. He enclosed a photo of the two of them. She wasn't a stunner, I must admit, but she had a kindly face and a nice figure, and Ton said that the two of them were very happy together and were looking to settle down somewhere and start a family.

A happy ending is always nice.

The next client was not good. Things didn't go so smoothly. Moldie said he vetted every client before they came to see me, but, after this one, I wondered how good his vetting research really was. The man's name was Rahul Amin and he looked, well, shifty, and not so pleasant. Dubious, maybe, with twitching eyes that couldn't keep still. Undeniably rich, I could tell by his clothes and the confident way he carried himself, but there was something about him which made me nervous.

Anyway, we chatted and drank tea but he didn't seem at all relaxed and didn't like it when I suggested we shared a bath or a shower. Was he upset that I was making the decisions?

We showered together anyway, but it was a sort of clumsy experience, despite my efforts at romance. Then to bed, but he soon started to get rough with me. He held me down, and hurt my wrists and when I complained he slapped me. I knew Moldie would be watching and wondered how much longer he would let this go on.

Then Rahul Amin held me by the throat whilst bonking me, starting to choke me, and I tried to struggle but he was much stronger and I couldn't really do much.

Just then the bedroom door burst open and Moldie and the two guards rushed into the bedroom. Before Rahul Amin had a chance to retaliate, Moldie shot him in the middle of his back with a dart gun. Rahul Amin tried to reach the dart but before he could pull it out, he collapsed on top of me, unconscious.

The guards pulled him off me whilst Moldie checked I was okay and held me close.

I was panting, gasping for breath, but I knew he hadn't really done any serious damage to me, and I soon recovered.

Moldie was so apologetic, and helped me put on a dressing gown.

"Clair, my darling," he said, "I'm so, so sorry," but I told him not to worry.

"You came in plenty of time," I told him, "Which is more than can be said for Rahul Amin."

Moldie didn't laugh.

"We check up on all your clients," he told me for the umpteenth time. "We never realised he was so violent and touched. We just thought he was a successful businessman. I'm so sorry, Clair."

"What will you do with him now?" I asked, almost totally recovered.

"He won't get a refund, that's for sure. We'll dress him, put him in the back of a car, and drop him near Snuka somewhere."

He started to check the man's pockets, and pulled out a wallet.

"He has plenty of money here," and Moldie swore, not a common occurrence.

"Snapping crocodiles," which to Moldie was swearing, "He has thousands and thousands of Fang," (Fang was the local currency, about seven Fang to the pound, roughly).

"Actually," he said, excitedly, "Over fifty thousand Fang. Now why does he need all this money, and what will he use it for? Something dubious, no doubt, and I can think of a much better use for this money. This money will pay to repair dozens of homes in Redik. A much better use, don't you think?" and I told him I agreed with him.

"I'll leave him a few Fang so he can get home, and a note explaining what has happened and what will happen to him if he tries such a stunt again."

The four of us, including the two guards, who had had, I noticed, a good ogle at my naked body, then proceeded to dress Rahul Amin and then they grabbed a wrist each and dragged him unceremoniously from the apartment.

And I was glad to see him go.

For the rest of the evening, and all the next day, Moldie couldn't do enough for me and treated me like royalty, which was nice but even so the day after that I was visited by a man and his wife. Mr and Mrs Frog, they were called. I never did find out their first names. I'm not even sure if they had first names. I'm not even sure if they were married.

They were middle aged and did not have, shall we say, classical film star faces and figures. Rotund is a word which could be used to politely describe their shapes. Bubbly personalities though. Happy people. Happy with each other's humpty dumpy bodies. Happy with their lives.

They were really into orgies and group sex. They delighted in telling me all the things they had got up to in the past. I think they were trying to shock me but by then I was well past the stage where anything to do with sex could shock me.

They lived for group sex and due to their winning the Abacadian state lottery a couple of years previously, they could indulge all they liked.,

They told me all this over dinner, which, I noticed, was somewhat larger than normal. Moldie told me later that they had specifically asked for large, large portions of everything which they gobbled down with a gusto.

The three of us spent most of the night in the king sized bed gobbling everything else with gusto. His cock and my pussy and his cock and her pussy and my pussy and her pussy and his cock were all gobbled with gusto. Every combination of 2 pussies, 1 cock, 3 mouths and 4 titties were tried.

They called his cock Timmy the Tadpole and every time one of them said Timmy the Tadpole they both giggled. It was rather sweet really.

'May I kiss Timmy the Tadpole, giggle, would Timmy the Tadpole like to visit the big hairy cave, giggle, oh no Timmy the Tadpole has been sick, giggle giggle slurp slurp.'

Strange.

And I loved it.

The next day, after they had left and before Moldie came in for breakfast, I lay in the bath surrounded by bubbles and wondered about myself.

I had always enjoyed sex but now I was worried I was becoming addicted to it. I was really enjoying myself and somehow I felt that I shouldn't be. Surely it was wrong what I was doing? I was, for the time being, a prostitute. A high class prostitute earning lots and lots of money for sure, but still a prostitute.

When, or if, I ever escaped from here, would I miss it? Probably. Would I be able to go back to being Lady Clair Hamilton, upright citizen and stalwart of the community, raising money for charity, mother of three grown up children, mistress of Hamilton Hall?

I didn't know. I just didn't know. I would just have to wait and see what happened.

Chapter 21 - Lake Lucinda

We left Brave Doggut village the next day, after giving Doggut a gift of a smart imitation ivory-handled knife, with which he was thrilled.

"I hope you find friend," he said, smiling. "There always space for you in Brave Doggut."

We headed off for Lake Lucinda, taking yet another steady touristy drive. On the way down we studied the books that Dave had lent us, learning the names and photos of some of the birds we might see around Lake Lucinda. We then tested each other until we were fairly certain we could pass as bird watchers. At least to somebody who wasn't a bird watcher. We may have problems with a twitcher but reckoned we probably wouldn't bump into an Effghanian twitcher that day.

We arrived in the vicinity of Lake Lucinda in the afternoon of the 3rd July, the day before the day that mother had suggested in her message to Theo that she might be there.

Sam took charge, as usual.

"We are about a mile from the lake," he said, studying the map with Stu. "We'll park Lady Sammy here, under the trees, so she is hidden from casual observers. Then we'll set up the tents. Then we'll go for an explore."

We found an old track which led into some woods. It was overgrown and had evidently not been used for a number of years, and Stu drove Lady Sammy slowly until she was hidden from view from the road. The boys then spent a few minutes removing any tyre or other marks from the ground, even bending up squashed blades of grass, so that there was virtually no indication that a car had been driven that way. We found a small clearing and Sam and I then put up our tent whilst Stu and Pauline put up the other one nearby.

"We still have a few hours of daylight left," said Sam. "I suggest we have an explore. We have no idea if anyone else is here, so we need to be very careful and cautious."

Pauline and I nodded, and gave pretend salutes.

"Aye aye captain," I said, and Pauline grinned, but Sam looked serious.

"You must do exactly what Stu or I tell you to do," he said, patiently. "This is a serious matter. Your mother's freedom is at stake and we don't want anything to go wrong just because of you two clowns pissing about. Do you understand?"

We had never seen him so serious. We put on our most serious faces and nodded seriously.

"Sorry Sam," I said, humbly. "We will do exactly as we are told."

"Good," he said, and led the way through the trees, followed by me then Pauline with Stu at the rear. We walked slowly up a narrow track, probably made by animals, climbing gently until we reached the brow of a small hill. Sam waved his hand and we all stopped.

Sam crept forward on his hands and knees and peered over the edge, then indicated for us to do the same. We lay down and I saw Lake Lucinda in front of us. I recognised it from the short video and from Theo's Google earth. The water was calm and a deep blue and reflected the sky and the surrounding hills. It was a lovely spot.

The first thing we noticed was the bird life. There seemed to be hundreds of waterfowl almost covering the lake, some with short necks and some with long necks. They were every colour under the rainbow from pure white to jet black and everything inbetween.

Thanks to Dave's book and the studying on the trip down, I was able to recognise many of them but only a small proportion.

The lake looked smaller in real life than it did on the video. It was vaguely square in shape, and probably only 300 yards across. I could see two small streams flowing into the lake off to my left and on the far side opposite us there appeared to be a larger stream or small river flowing out of the lake.

To the left of the river there seemed to be a small beach. I nudged Alice.

"Is that the beach that we saw on the film?" I whispered. "Where mother and the man went swimming and, well, you know."

She nodded.

"I think so. It looks like it. The film was probably taken from that small rise over there," she said pointing.

Both Sam and Stu studied the area for a few minutes with their binoculars, making sure, I noticed, that the lenses were always in shadow, presumably to stop any reflections which may have been seen by somebody.

"I can't see anybody," said Sam quietly, "But that doesn't mean there's nobody there. An army could be hidden in these woods. I think we should split up and head around the lake in opposite directions. You two go that way," he indicated an anticlockwise direction, "And Alice and I will go this way."

He positioned the binoculars and said, "Stu, see that small river, on the far side, just beyond that small beach," Stu nodded, "We'll try and meet up there," and Stu nodded again.

"Right ho."

"Check your walkie talkie," said Sam, and they both checked and everything seemed in order. The ringer was switched off and set instead to vibrate.

"Good luck," said Sam, and we set off in opposite directions, with me following closely behind him. We moved slowly but steadily, always keeping below the skyline and stopping every few minutes to listen. We heard nothing but the occasional bird song and the odd tree creaking.

After a few minutes we approached a larger clearing, and once again we went down on our hands and knees and crawled to the edge of the trees. We peeked carefully between two tree trunks and saw two tents pitched on the far side of the clearing between two small streams.

"I wonder who they belong to?" whispered Sam.

"Mother and her lover?" I asked, but he shook his head.

"I wouldn't have thought so. Even if they had some minders with them, they wouldn't put the tents so close together. They are probably either nothing to do with your mum or like us, they are up to no good."

"They haven't made much effort to hide them," I whispered to Sam.

"They wouldn't be seen from a road," whispered back Sam. "I don't suppose they would be expecting anyone else to be here. If some tourists turned up, then they wouldn't become suspicious if they saw them here. Can you see the occupants anywhere? Two tents probably means four people."

He took the binoculars out from under this jacket where he had been keeping them, so they wouldn't snag on anything as we crept through the trees. He studied the clearing and the surrounding area but obviously saw nothing because he whispered, "Come on, follow me. Let's see if we can find out who they are."

We carried on through the woods, skirting the

clearing and passing between the tents on our left and the lake to our right. Sam was walking very warily, placing each foot carefully and stopping every few seconds. I tried to put my feet exactly where Sam had put his.

After a few minutes we saw another tent hidden in the trees ahead of us and to the left. Sam took out the binoculars again. He held them to his eyes then chuckled, and passed them to me.

I looked at the tent and also chuckled. I could see through the opening and saw two black men, naked and in each others arms. They were enjoying themselves.

"Six men," whispered Sam. "Well, four men and those two. Come on, let's see if we can find the others."

We carried on another 100 yards or so until we came to the edge of the woods and had a clear view over the north side of the lake and the dirt road which disappeared into the distance towards Redik. I spotted four men sitting on the headland which overlooked the cove. I nudged Sam and pointed. He grunted and took out the bino's.

"Two of them seem to be relaxing," he said. "The other two are staring up the road. I assume they are on the lookout for someone coming, and that someone must be Clair and her mate. I need to speak to Stu."

He pulled out the walkie-talkie which he had also been keeping in an inside pocket of this jacket, and pressed the contact button. Within five seconds the thing vibrated and he held down the transmit switch and spoke quietly into it.

"Stu. The small headland above the beach. Can you see it?"

"Not yet. It should come into view within about ten minutes."

"There are four men on the headland. Two seem to be looking vaguely towards the lake. The other two away from the lake, probably looking up the road for somebody approaching. Have a careful look then return to the tents. Be careful."

"I'll be extra careful. I'll have a look then we will return to the tents. Roger and out."

Sam handed the binoculars to me to me and told me to study the men and the area.

"What do you think they are doing there?" he asked me.

I thought about it.

"Two of them are looking up the road, waiting for mother or anyone else to appear. I assume that is the road to Redik."

Sam nodded.

"When they arrive, I am thinking that they will park their vehicle over there," I pointed off to the left, "And that mother and the man will walk up past the headland, to the cove and beach where they swam in the film. If anyone is left with the vehicle, then the two gays in the tent will look after them. These four will attempt to kidnap mother either there on the headland or down by the beach."

I looked at him, and he smiled and nodded.

"Very good," he whispered. "I agree with you. Now we need to make a plan of our own."

He took the binoculars and spent quite a time studying the men and the surrounding area.

"Right," he said. "This is what I suggest we do ...."

Forty minutes later, and we were back at the tent. Stu and Alice were waiting for us.

"Anything to report?" asked Sam.

"We saw nothing of interest on that side of the lake," answered Stu. "From the edge of the trees we

could clearly see the four men on the headland. We
didn't approach any closer, but just returned here."

Chapter 22 - Kidnapped, Again

I was looking forward to visiting Lake Lucinda again. It had been 28 days and 11 clients since we visited before and in that time I had only had a few hours at Angel's Hair waterfall. My visits to Redik I considered more like business than pleasure. I had earned over a million dollars for Moldie and Effghania and I reckoned I had earned another days holiday and relaxation.

I was wondering if my latest message had been received and understood, and whether anyone would be there. Was it too soon? How on earth could they possibly be there? Had they told the police? My emotions kept soaring and then plummeting. I told myself not to expect anything, but I had my fingers crossed. And my toes. Every part of my body I could cross, I did.

"Do we really need to take the gorillas with us?" I asked Moldie. "I'm not going anywhere and nothing's going to happen to us?"

"I'm sorry, Clair, but it is a precondition. We have to take them with us."

"Whose decision is that?" I asked him but he refused to tell me.   He did seem rather secretive about his superiors or whoever he was responding to.

"I was just wondering," I asked, "Do they carry guns?"

He looked at me suspiciously, but then shrugged. He was probably wondering why I asked but then decided it was just me being inquisitive.

"No. As far as I know, no one in Effghania has any guns. It is against our religion. We are not a violent people. There may be some, of course, but none that I have ever heard about. Why?"

"Just wondering," I said.

Moldie drove in the same Landrover taking the same route as before, and we parked in the same place. There was no sign of anyone, and Moldie and I left the gorillas by the Landrover and walked hand in hand to the same little cove we had last time. It was just as beautiful as I remembered, and I was feeling a mixture of happiness and trepidation. I tried to keep looking around me without raising Moldie's suspicion, but saw nothing.

We did exactly as we did before, stripping off and going for a swim, except this time the swimming was much more relaxed, and we slowly swam together, further out into the lake, disturbing the birds before heading back for the shore. We walked back to the rucksack and the blanket, and were drying ourselves when Moldie went "Ow. I've been stung on my bottom," and at that moment I also felt something hit my bottom.

"So have I," I said, and immediately started to feel sleepy. I collapsed towards Moldie but he was also collapsing and the last thing I remember is lying down on the blanket in his arms and wondering if Alice was there.

Later, I managed to find out what had happened. Bim Dram had great delight in telling me, and I have cobbled together his boasts to produce the following........

It seems that Bim Dram was a man who was not used to not getting his own way, and wanted me for his own. My rejection of his kind offer to look after me for a year for $1,000,000 had annoyed him and he decided to do something about it.

On his second visit to me, when he had offered to take me away, he had a pretty good idea I would refuse, and had decided that he would kidnap me instead. He reckoned it would be difficult but not impossible to kidnap me from my apartment block, but much easier to catch me at Lake Lucinda. When I mentioned that we sometimes visited a local beauty spot he figured I meant Lake Lucinda.

He had discovered it was Lake Lucinda by studying the short film he had been sent originally by Moldie to entice him to visit me. He had isolated the panoramic view of the lake that Moldie had included, and quickly discovered that it was Lake Lucinda, and he had also identified the cove that we had visited the time before. How he did all this he did not tell me, but then again, he had the whole of Abacadian intelligence to help him, so it probably wasn't difficult.

He was an Abacadian MP, a member of the cabinet, a man of importance and influence and he had many contacts, and some of these contacts were in the army. He 'borrowed' 6 soldiers, all especially trained, and had sent them with orders to kidnap me at Lake Lucinda. They were specifically told, no shooting. He didn't want anyone killed, and especially I was not to be hurt.

"If Lady Clair is hurt or molested in anyway," he had told the soldiers, "Then I will personally hurt you 100 times worse," and he had issued them with dart guns.

He didn't know, of course, when Moldie and I would be visiting so he had sent the six men down there with tents and supplies enough for a month. They had found a hidden place to park the two vehicles just a few hundred yards from the lake edge and had pitched the tents nearby. They were not in army dress. Bim Dram didn't want anyone to know that the army was involved so they were in casual civilian clothes.

The six men couldn't believe their luck to be given this easy and undemanding assignment. They treated it more like a holiday, but after four days of doing almost nothing, there was a falling out. Two of them moved their tent to another place. The four remaining laughed about it. They guessed the other two were gay and the falling out was just an excuse to be on their own.

The leader did manage to keep two of them on a lookout at all times, and after six days of doing nothing, he got a radio call from them to say a Landrover was on its way towards the lake. He had organised a plan, which they had practised and gone over a couple of times, and now he brought it into action.

Two of the men had hurried through the woodlands along hidden paths until they had reached a spot overlooking the cove and the beach. The two lookouts had hurried back through the trees half way between the cove and a spot where they reckoned the Landrover would be parked and hid themselves on top of a small headland. From there they could see the Landrover parking area and the cove, and the others could see them. The leader and another had stayed hidden by the potential parking place, and they were ready.

They saw the Landrover arrive, and park up as expected. They saw Moldie and I get out and walk hand in hand towards the cove, leaving the gorillas behind. As soon as we were out of sight, the gorillas pulled out from their bag what looked like a cine camera and the leader grinned to himself. The gorillas followed Moldie and me, keeping out of sight, and headed towards the small headland.

The two army men there saw them coming and made sure they were hidden. The two gorillas were completely intent on getting to the top so they could see me, Lady Clair, swimming in the nude again and film me, as Moldie ordered, even though he had promised that there would be no more filming of me. Bim Dram's soldiers just shot them in the back of their necks with the dart guns from fairly close range and they collapsed without a sound.

The soldiers gave a thumbs up to the leader, who grinned again. They then looked back towards the cove and saw Moldie and me get undressed and go swimming. They saw us walk up onto the beach and then collapse, and this time radioed the leader. Everything was going as planned.

The two who had shot Moldie and me then cautiously walked onto the beach, but, seeing no danger, had approached us. They had rolled me onto my back to study my naked body, and laughed and signalled to their comrades on the headland, who laughed back. Bim Dram had taken great pleasure in telling me that news. Then they had packed up all our belongings into Moldie's rucksack, including the blanket, and one of them had taken a number of photos of Moldie with a camera he had produced out of his pocket. This was so he could be identified later. They had had no orders to take Moldie with them.

He then picked up the rucksack, whilst the other picked me up and started carrying me back towards the Landrover.

It had all been as easy as that.

Chapter 23 - Two Silly Girls

The boys wouldn't let us light a fire that evening, but we had some hot water left in a flask and ate sandwiches for supper, with a cup of tea and some fruit for pudding.

Sam quietly told Stu and Pauline about the plan he had suggested to me at the lakeside earlier. Stu made one or two suggestions but otherwise agreed.

"What happens if the plan goes wrong?" asked Pauline, and Sam suggested a couple of backup plans.

"Hopefully we won't need those," he said. "I don't think your mother will arrive particularly early. It's an hours drive or more from Redik but we need to be in place when they get here, so an early start in the morning.

"Who do you think the others are?" I asked, but nobody had any idea.

"Are they there to keep an eye on mother when she arrives tomorrow?" I pondered.

"Or kidnap her," suggested Alice.

That night we took it in turns to keep lookout, in pairs, but we had a quiet night. I heard a few night animals and birds and there were a million billion insects buzzing and flying around, but nothing from our camping friends.

In the morning we got up just before dawn and ate some biscuits and cake for breakfast and some coconut juice, then gathered a few things together and walked slowly and carefully back towards the lake. We returned to the same place where we had been the day before and had seen the others. There was no sight nor sign of them this time.

"You two girls stay here," ordered Sam, pointing to

some trees, "Whilst Stu and I go and see what is happening."

They disappeared around a corner. Pauline and I looked at each other.

"Come on," she said, "I want to see mother. If we keep hidden we'll be alright," and off she went.

I thought I'd better go with her, and followed her as she took a narrow path gently uphill until we came to a spot where we could clearly see the lake.

We sat with our backs against two tree trunks, making sure we were in shadow and waited and whispered and waited some more. After an absolute age, which was probably about two hours, we both heard the distinct noise of a car engine in the distance. It was coming closer. We strained our ears and eyes but the engine shut down and then there was silence.

"That must be mother, surely," said Pauline, and we waited a bit more. Pauline suddenly grabbed my arm and pointed.

I looked to where she was pointing to see a man and a woman walking towards the headland at the far side of the lake, coming from our left. They were a long way off but I was pretty sure that the woman was mother. I gasped. Pauline gasped. I wished we had some binoculars with us.

They disappeared behind the headland and reappeared walking towards the beach, holding hands. We saw the man drop the bag he was carrying and spread a blanket on ground.

We watched as they took off their clothes and went swimming. They splashed and laughed like a couple of young lovers. A few of the water birds took flight but most just slowly swam out of the way.

I dragged my eyes away from mother and looked back towards the headland. Two new men were lying down there. Their position meant they would be all but hidden from the beach. One of them had what looked like a cine camera and was obviously filming what he saw. I nudged Pauline, who also looked at them.

They were quite away a way but I'm pretty sure I saw one of them touch his neck, then the other, and they didn't move again.

"Stu must have shot them with a dart gun," I suggested, and Pauline nodded, excitement showing in her eyes.

I looked back to the beach, and watched as mother and the man walked out of the water and lay down on the blanket. From the corner of my eye I saw two men at the edge of the trees behind them, and they both had guns. I saw my mother touch her bottom, and the two of them collapsed into each others arms and lay still.

We both gasped.

"Oh my God, they've shot her," said Pauline.

She stood up and forgetting Sam's orders to keep well hidden, started shouting, "Mother, mother."

I tried to pull her down, but both of us were crying and we hung onto each other and wept.

We watched as the two men cautiously approached mother and the man, and rolled her onto her back. Even from this distance I could see they were smiling, probably laughing. One of them picked up all their belongings, including the blanket, and shoved them back into the bag. He took out a camera and took some photos of mother's friend, then his companion easily picked mother up in his arms and carried her away. They left the man where he was, lying naked on the beach.

We were both so intent on watching and my eyes were so full of tears that neither of us noticed two men sneaking up on us. That was until I heard a click behind me. I turned around to find two black men pointing guns at us. I wasn't sure but I think they may have been the two men I saw enjoying themselves in the tent the day before.

They were both dressed in open neck blue shirts and black trousers. They were wearing baseball caps, one brown and one green, and were clean shaven with what appeared to be very short hair cuts. They were grinning.

Brown Cap said something in Abacadian, I assumed, but we both dumbly shook our heads. He grinned again, then said "Don't do silly thing," in a heavily accented English, "And nobody get hurt. These not dart guns, they loaded with real bullets. Don't do silly thing, I beg, and keep quiet. No noises, please," he repeated."

Pauline started to stand up but he shook his head and signalled her to remain seated and she flopped down again.

He pulled a walkie-talkie from inside his jacket and switched it on, and when someone answered, spoke in what was, I guessed Abacadian. I heard him say the word Flakey and wondered if that was his name.

He switched off the walkie-talkie, put it inside his jacket, and grinned again. He never seemed to stop grinning. All the time, his mate had his gun pointing at us. It was very steady and very menacing. Pauline and I looked at each other but didn't move or say anything.

I was very scared. We both were.

"You come with us," said Brown Cap and indicated with the point of his gun for us to walk down the path that Pauline and I had walked up a couple of hours earlier, and led eventually towards the tents.

Sam will be so angry with us, I thought, as I trudged along. Just like two silly little girls, can't keep down and out of sight and can't keep their traps shut.

We turned a corner, and there suddenly in front of us were Sam and Stu pointing their own guns at two other men, possibly two of the four we had seen on the headland the day before. The men were on their knees and Stu appeared to be just about to tie their hands behind their backs with some string whilst Sam covered them with his gun. Stu's gun was on the ground next to him.

He stood up when he saw us and looked at Sam, who lowered his gun.

"Don't hurt them," said Sam, and he threw his gun onto the floor and backed away. Stu went to join him. They both put their hands on their heads.

"We won't try anything. Just don't hurt the women."

"That good," said Brown Cap behind us, indicating to the two men who, until a few seconds previously, had been captives, to pick up the guns from the ground.

"I not know who you are. Expect here try and rescue woman on beach. Me right?"

Sam and Stu remained silent.

Brown Cap put the nuzzle of his gun against the side of Pauline's cheek with enough force to make her squeak.

"Answer me."

"Yes," said Sam, wearily. "We are here to try and rescue the woman."

Brown Cap laughed.

"You fail. Now, you lie down, hands behind back."

With four guns pointing at them, Sam and Stu had no option. They lay down. One of the others pulled some plastic ties out of his pocket and used them to fasten Sam and Stu's hands behind their backs. As soon as this was done, I could sense the four men relax.

They talked amongst themselves. I had no idea what they were saying but I heard the word Flakey again. Brown Cap did most of the talking. I imagined they were deciding what to do about us. I crossed my fingers and hoped they would let us go.

Brown Cap seemed to come to a decision.

"I need take photo of you all. Men, stand up."

Sam and Stu struggled to their feet.

"You women stand next," and Pauline and I moved over and stood one either side. Still grinning, Brown Cap took out his phone and took 4-5 photos of the four of us. He checked they had come out alright then said to Sam, "We tie you men together then we go. Take girls. No harm them. Few minutes we drive in cars. Women return. Untie you. Us gone long way by then," and he laughed and the others laughed with him.

He indicated for Sam and Stu to lie down back to back then one of the others used another tie to fasten their wrists to each other. They were now helpless until we returned to undo them.

One of the men ran his hands all over their clothes and pulled out their walkie-talkies. He showed them to the others, who laughed.

"Very old," said Brown Cap, "But work good yes?"

They didn't find anything else even when another of them took great delight in searching Pauline and me. That morning, Sam had put all our valuables in a bag and hidden it near the tents.

Brown Cap indicated for Pauline and I to follow one of the men down the path. I looked despairingly at Sam who shrugged and said, "Don't worry. Everything will be fine. Just do as they say."

There was nothing we could do but follow them and hope they wouldn't hurt us. Brown Cap came last. The guns were over their shoulders now and they were in very good moods. They talked continually, laughing often.

We walked to the tents. On the way we passed a

172

Landrover. It must have been the vehicle mother and her man arrived in, I reckoned. Two other men, dressed similarly to our captors, were taking down the tents. They jumped up when they heard us approaching and started asking questions. They laughed when Brown Cap answered.

I looked around for mother. There was no sign of her. I reached out and touched Brown Cap's arm.

"Please," I said, "Where is the woman?"

He looked at me, grinned again, and took my arm. He led me over to one of the two cars parked nearby and indicated for me to look into the back. Pauline walked with me.

Mother was lying on the back seat, on her side, covered with a blanket. She wasn't moving.

I gasped.

"Is she ....?"

Brown Cap laughed.

"She sleep. You know her? She your sister? Her pretty like you pretty," and laughed again.

I felt overwhelming relief as I looked at her and noticed her gently breathing. She groaned softly.

"What are you doing with her?"

"We take her away. No harm come. You not worry."

"Where are you taking her?" but he shook his head.

He looked at me and seemed to have some sympathy in his eyes.

"You wait there. We go soon then you go to boyfriends."

He moved away from the cars, and in the distance I saw him lift the bonnet of the Landrover. I thought I saw him remove something from the engine, then watched as the other men loaded the tents and all the rest of their belongings into the boots of the cars.

All six men climbed into the cars, three in each. Brown Cap got into the front seat of mothers car. A man got in the back and I saw him lift mother up so she was leaning against him.

Brown Cap leant out of the window.

"Not worry. No harm come to woman."

He laughed and waved and the two cars drove off quickly heading along the road towards Snuka.

Pauline and I watched them go.

"Come on," I said with a sigh, "Let's go and untie the boys."

Chapter 24 - Prisoner

For the second time in a few weeks, I awoke from a deep sleep to find my hands tied. Behind my back this time. I was obviously in some sort of vehicle which was being driven along a bumpy road. I was half sitting up and half lying. I tried not to groan, but I couldn't help myself. I sensed a face near mine, and opened my eyes to see a man grinning at me. It was him who I had been leaning against. He helped me into a sitting position.

"Hello Lady Clair," he said in Abacadian.

I kept quiet and closed my eyes again. My head hurt. I felt drowsy and sick.

"Oh God," I thought to myself, "What now?" and suddenly I missed Moldie desperately. I tried to remember what had happened. I remembered being on the beach by Lake Lucinda, Moldie crying out he had been stung, then a sting in my bottom, then nothing.

What had happened? I couldn't think properly. I felt sick and tired. I felt rotten.

Then I thought of my children. I was hoping they would have been at the lake, but there had been no sign of them. I felt a tremendous sense of disappointment and loneliness. I suddenly realised that the man was speaking to me, but I pretended I didn't understand him, and said nothing.

One of them then spoke in broken English, which was heavily accented, but he made himself clear. He was sitting in the front seat, and was twisting round to look at me. He was wearing a brown base ball cap.

"You kidnapped, Lady Clair, and now we take you to new master. You do as you told, nothing happen to you. Are you okay? It is long journey."

I then realised I only had a blanket around me, the blanket that Moldie and I were just about to make love on by the lake. I bet they made sure they got a good eyeful of me. At least they seemed to be leaving me alone now.

I asked for a drink and a bottle was raised to my lips. It was coca cola, still surprisingly cold, and I drank as much as they would let me.

I looked around me. I was in the back seat of a saloon car. A man was sitting next to me, and there were 2 men in the front. Brown Cap in the passenger seat and a driver. The driver was looking at me in the mirror and grinning.

I looked out of the window. We were travelling through hilly countryside, almost mountains, and I realised from my very basic knowledge of Abacadia that we must be travelling north, probably to the capital, Snuka. Why would they be taking me to Snuka? Then it dawned on me. Bim Dram. It must be him. He wanted me to go and live with him so desperately, and I had refused him. So he had kidnapped me.

I remembered what he was like. Not an evil man but not a kind man either. Very intelligent. I wondered what he wanted me for then answered my own stupid question. I could look forward to lots and lots of sex but now with just one man all the time. Him. At least that's what I thought.

I closed my eyes and felt despair overcome me. I thought of my home in England, Hamilton Hall, and my three children, Alice, Pauline and Theo. I thought of the four of us having a picnic on the back lawn on a warm summers day and then my best friend, Marjory Hackett, came to mind. I hadn't thought of Marjory since I had first been kidnapped.

'I should be back home in Worcestershire,' I thought to myself, 'Not sitting in the back seat of an old car, with my hands tied, guarded by 3 soldiers and on my way to be the love slave of a mega rich member of parliament. A fiction writer couldn't make this up.'

I sighed and half smiled to myself. I shook my head.

I was Lady Clair Hamilton. I'd be alright. I'd survive.

The journey seemed to go on forever, but was probably only about 4 hours. Eventually I had leant against the man sitting next to me, and he had chuckled and put his arm around me. I could smell tobacco and smoke and sweat on his clothes. I tried to relax. I tried to think but my thoughts kept returning to Moldie and my children. I think I may have dozed.

As we drove through the outskirts of what I assumed was Snuka, I sat up and the man next to me put a large floppy hat onto my head.

"So people not see you," said the English speaking one wearing the brown cap.

We were driving through a poor area of the city. The houses looked old with peeling paint and the gardens uncared for. The road was full of pot holes, and there was sewage in some of the gutters. And this is the capital city, I thought to myself.

We passed through to another district. It seemed to be a business quarter, with 'The Bank of Abacadia' prominent. There were numerous shops, most of which I recognised including, of course, McDonalds. It was all so very different from Redik.

Eventually we drove down a leafy lane which led into a much smarter part of town. We turned right into a posh tree lined avenue. I tried to spot the name of the road but didn't. The houses along this road were larger and the gardens well kept, with perfectly manicured lawns and flower beds. Many had high walls and security gates.

We drove up to one such gate. The driver pressed a button in a wall, spoke to someone through an intercom and, after a few seconds, the gates slowly opened. We drove through and along a short drive and up to the front door of a small mansion. I was helped out of the car, my hands still tied, and the blanket 'accidentally' dropped from my shoulders leaving me once again naked. I looked at the men, straight in the eyes, and one of them shrugged, picked it up and put it over my shoulders again. He grinned, and shepherded me up some steps and through the front door.

I found myself in a large entrance hall with expensive looking paintings on the walls and a wide staircase in front of me. At that moment, a man appeared at the top of the stairway and started slowly to walk down. It was, as I had guessed, Bim Dram. He was smiling. He nodded and the blanket was slipped from my shoulders and yet again I was totally nude.

I lifted my chin and looked straight at him. I smiled back.

"Hello Bim," I said. "I thought it would be you. How are you? Would you mind telling these thugs to untie me? If it's not too much bother!"

He nodded again, and I felt my hands being untied. I rubbed my wrists.

"What do you want of me, or is that a silly question?"

He beckoned me up towards him, and I slowly climbed the stairway with as much dignity as I could. I knew the other men were watching me, but I didn't look back. Bim Dram held out his hand, I took it, and he led me up to the top of the stairs.

He looked at the men in his hall and smiled.

"Well done," he said. "Well done all of you. Flakey, please bring me a report. Tomorrow will be fine. You can all have the rest of the day off then report back to your unit tomorrow. Well done and thank you."

Bim walked me along a short corridor and through a door. It was obviously the master bedroom, I thought. The bed, which dominated the room, was a magnificent four poster. That was all I had time to notice before he pushed me roughly onto the bed and started to undress.

"Did they hurt you?" he suddenly asked me.

"No."

"Did they touch you?"

"No."

He nodded in satisfaction, and started to climb onto the bed. I held up my hand.

"I need the toilet," and climbed off the other side, and went through the other door. I heard him grunting behind me. The bathroom was very plush. There was no lock on the door.

I thought as I tinkled. Bim Dram seemed very angry. Was he angry with me or just angry? I remembered the times we had spent together in my room in Redik. He wasn't that angry then. A bit dominating but that was all. Maybe he was having a bad time at work.

I had to play things carefully. I wasn't overly worried. I was Lady Clair Hamilton and I could cope with any situation I told myself. I must show him I was still an English Lady, but without getting him angry. Or angrier.

I flushed the toilet and switched on the shower. Dram came into the bathroom.

I held out my hand.

"Come," I said, "Let's share a shower together."

"No," he growled, "You do as I say," and grabbed my wrist. He switched off the shower and dragged me to the bed and once again pushed me onto my back. He knelt between my thighs and held both my wrists above my head. His face was very close to mine.

"Two hundred thousand dollars I paid for your little pussy," he whispered. "I want my money's worth," and he moved forward and started to rape me.

So that was the problem, I thought, as he thrust up and down. Although he was a multi, multi millionaire, he was upset about having to pay so much to have me. Time to use all my lady-like skills to keep him from hurting me.

I wrapped my legs around his bottom and started moaning.

"Mmmmm," I said. "That's nice."

I started to move my hips. I was looking straight at his face and saw the surprise there. He was trying to humiliate me and I was trying not to let him. He thrust harder but he wasn't hurting me with his tiny little penis and suddenly I started to enjoy myself.

He was still holding my wrists otherwise I would have put my arms around his neck, pulled him to me and kissed him. Surprisingly I could feel myself approaching orgasm, and started to moan. He was moaning as well and we came exactly together. He was panting. I was panting.

"Oh my God," I said. "That was fantastic. The best ever."

That was a bit of a lie. Possibly not the best ever. My husband Alfie, bless him, was the most wonderful lover I had ever had. He had learnt how to please me over time and did it wonderfully, but I had enjoyed this 'rape' by Bim Dram.

He was still holding my wrists.

"You're hurting my wrists, Bim," I said, and he immediately let go. A minor victory to me. I pulled his face down and kissed him. I could see confusion on his face. He had probably been dreaming of humiliating me, and it hadn't worked. I mustn't get too cocky though. He was still in control. I had to play things carefully.

"How about that shower now?" I suggested. "We're both a bit sweaty after that."

He nodded and rolled off me. I took his hand and led him to the bathroom.

The shower cubicle was huge, plenty large enough for both of us, and the water poured out. Hot and steamy. I washed him all over, even washed his hair for him, but he didn't touch me, just let me do all the washing.

As we showered together, I wondered if I should question him about what was going to happen to me but decided to keep quiet. Plenty of time for that later, I reckoned.

After the shower, during which he never spoke a word, he got dressed. I crawled into bed and pulled the duvet up to my chin. If he didn't say anything, I would speak but I would wait for him to talk first.

He was now fully dressed. He brushed his hair in front of a mirror, then turned and looked at me.

"I must go to work," he said brusquely. "There is an evening session at parliament and I am expected to vote. I will return later.

 You must be hungry. Some food will be brought in for you in a few minutes, along with a bottle of wine. The television remote is over there," pointing. "There are some books and magazines in that cupboard," pointing again. "The door is locked for now, as are the windows, and there is a guard outside in the corridor."

On impulse, he came over to me and kissed me on my cheek. He looked at me for a few seconds, then turned and walked out of the door. I heard a key turn and sighed. A prisoner again.

I heard his footsteps disappearing along the corridor, then I got out of bed. Whatever happens, I mustn't start feeling sorry for myself. There was a silk dressing gown hanging on the back of the door, and I put it on. It was far too big for me. Certainly one of Bim's.

I walked over to the window, and looked out. The view was over the front of the house. There was a perfect lawn and a high wall. Over to the right I could just see the gate that we had driven through. Beyond the wall and the gate was the tree lined avenue we had driven along earlier, I assumed. I could see one or two cars driving past the gate. On the far side of the road were more posh houses.

I tried the windows. They opened about 6 inches and then were held by a chain. I examined the chains. They were rather stout and riveted to the window and the wall. Unlikely I could get out of there but if I could, it was only a 10-12 foot drop to the lawn. I could handle that.

I also noticed some wires on the window frame. I examined them and reckoned that if you opened the windows too much an alarm would go off.

Then I remembered the room in the apartment in Redik and how the windows there were also fastened so they could only open six inches. I didn't think they had been alarmed. They might have been. I didn't know.

Did nobody trust me not to try and escape? In the apartment they even filmed me continually. That made me wonder if there were any cameras in Bim's bedroom. I wouldn't put it past him.

I looked carefully around the rooms. It didn't take me long to discover three of them. Two in the bedroom, one at the top of the posts in of the bed and the other hidden behind a picture. There was one in the bathroom disguised as a sprinkler.

There may have been others, maybe hidden behind a mirror or somewhere else, but I couldn't find them. I was fairly certain, though, that there were none directed towards the windows.

What good that was I wasn't sure but it gave me a smidgen of hope.

Chapter 25 - What next?

Pauline and I ran back up to where Sam and Stu had been left. They hadn't moved but turned their heads to look at us as we approached.

"Are you two okay?" asked Sam, relief obvious on his face.

"We're fine, they never touched us," I said. "We saw mother. She was in the back of a car. She looked to be sleeping. She was shot by a dart gun. They have driven away with her. We must go after them."

"Alice," said Sam gently. "Calm down. You need to release Stu and me first. You need scissors to do that. There are some in my rucksack. It's still where I left it hidden by the tents."

"I'll go," said Pauline, and ran off down the path towards the tent.

"Bring the whole bag," Sam shouted after her.

"We must go after them," I said to Sam, in desperation. "They were heading towards Snuka. If we leave soon, surely we can catch them up. They've got mother."

"Calm down, Alice," he replied. "We can't do anything until Stu and I have been cut free. And what about the man they left on the beach. I think the effects of the dart gun will run out soon. The chances of catching up with your mother will be very slim. I think it's much more important we question the man on the beach."

I stared at him but it slowly dawned on me he was right. I swore.

"Don't worry," said Sam gently, "We'll get her back. I promise. I hope Pauline doesn't take long. The plastic cuffs are cutting into my wrists," and immediately I was concerned about his and Stu's wrists and stopped worrying about mother, which was his general idea.

"Are you alright Stu?" I asked. He said he was.

"There's also two men hidden by the headland," said Sam. "They arrived with your mum in a Landrover. We saw them shot with darts by the kidnappers. They dragged them into some bushes and dumped them there. They had a film camera with them, and I assume they were there to film your mother and her man getting on with whatever. We must decide what to do with them as well."

We discussed who the six kidnappers might be. Sam and Stu both thought they must be soldiers from the Abacadian army.

"They all seemed calm and professional. They didn't panic when we captured them and did exactly as they were told. Their hair cuts were also a bit of a giveaway. I wonder who employed them. They were obviously here for one reason, to kidnap your mother and make sure she is unharmed. Maybe beach man can help."

He asked me how Pauline and I had been captured. Rather shame faced, I told him how we had seen mother shot and had stood up and shouted in horror.

"Suddenly there were two men behind us with guns," I said.

"I'm sorry Sam," I added. "So sorry."

Eventually Pauline arrived with Sam's rucksack. She brought out the scissors and, after a bit of difficulty managed to cut Sam's plastic cuffs. He rubbed his wrists then released Stu, who also rubbed his wrists.

"I put in some shorts and a tee shirt, for the bloke on the beach," said Pauline. "I hope you don't mind, Stu. Alice and I saw the kidnappers go off with all his clothes."

"Good thinking," said Sam and grabbed the bag and

we set off around the lake to the beach.

"Come on, let's go and see who he is."

As we crossed the small headland, Sam and Stu disappeared into some trees, and returned dragging two unconscious men. They were both big, ugly looking brutes and snoring gently.

They laid them in the shade, and ripped off the shirt sleeves from one of them. They used the sleeves to tie the men's hands behind their backs, then tied their shoe laces together but with a tree in between their knees, totally immobilising them.

"We'll come back for them later," said Sam.

We carried on down to the beach. The man there was lying on his side.

"Is he alive?" I asked.

Sam rolled him over onto his back and the man groaned in his sleep.

"It's the same man who was in the films," said Pauline. "We never did find out his name."

"He's quite good-looking," I said, and Pauline chuckled.

"He is, especially where you're looking!" and I stuck my tongue out at her.

"Let's get some clothes on him."

Stu chucked over the shorts and tee shirt from the rucksack and Pauline and I dressed him, giggling like a couple of school girls as we pulled the shorts up over his waving penis.

"If they are the same darts as we have," said Sam, watching and laughing, "He should be asleep for about another hour or so. We will question him when he wakes. There's nothing we can do till then, so let's have some lunch and talk."

We were just finishing eating when the man groaned again, and started to wake up.

"Shouldn't we tie him up?" I suggested, "In case he

gets violent."

Sam and Stu exchanged glances.

"No need," said Sam. "There's two of us, and he'll be in no state to do anything for a while. Besides, we need him on our side. There's a good chance he'll know who the men are and where your mum's being taken."

The man shook his head and tried to sit up. I went over to help him, and offered him a drink of water, which he gratefully accepted. He looked around.

"Don't worry," I said to him, "We're on your side. I'm Lady Clair's oldest daughter, Alice, and this is my sister Pauline. These are Sam and Stu, good friends of ours."

"What happened?" he said, groggily. "Where's Lady Clair?"

I recognised that voice. He was definitely the man on the film. Mother's lover.

"She's been kidnapped," I said, "By six men. She was shot with a dart gun, the same as you, and they've taken her away."

He looked shocked. He put his head in his hands. He was shaking.

"I never should have brought her here."

He looked up.

"Who were the men?"

"We were hoping you might be able to tell us," I said, gently.

He shook his head.

"I don't know. It could be anyone."

"Let's start at the beginning," I suggested. "Who are you?"

He looked a bit cagey.

"You haven't got much option, mate," said Sam. "If you want her back, then you have to help us. Now then, what's your name?"

So he told us he was Moldie Bedlam and we learnt the whole disgusting story. He seemed to leave nothing out, and I tried to imagine what my mother would be thinking through it all.

Suddenly he asked, "How did you know she would be here? I told no one, not even the committee."

"She left secret messages in the recordings you sent us," I explained, and he grinned. He looked quite handsome when he grinned, I thought.

"She's a clever one, that Lady Clair," he said. "She always got exactly what she wanted. I knew she was playing with me to get her own way, but I had to admire her."

Then he looked serious again.

"Thinking about it, I think I know exactly whose taken her and I think I know exactly where she's been taken."

He looked at each of us in turn.

"It's almost certainly a man called Bim Dram. He's a politician. He has slept with Lady Clair twice, the only client who's done that. He asked her to leave Redik and go and live with him in Snuka. He offered her a million dollars to stay with him for one year. She refused. He's not a very nice man, ruthless and ambitious."

"So, where will she be?" I asked. "Do you think she'll be hurt?"

"I wouldn't have thought so," said Moldie. "She's far too clever to allow herself to be hurt. She'll play along with him as much as she can get away with. I should imagine she's being held at his house in Snuka. I know where it is. I've driven past it."

"Who do you think the men where?" asked Sam. "Army? They were very professional."

"Probably," said Moldie. "Bim Dram can virtually do what he likes, within reason. Recruiting half a dozen soldiers would be no problem."

He took another drink of water and looked very sorry for himself.

"What shall we do now?" I wondered aloud.

"The first thing is to go and get the car," said Stu.

"That reminds me," I said. "The Landrover is still here. The one that mother and Moldie arrived it, but I saw one of the kidnappers lift the bonnet and take out part of the engine, I think. He put the part into his pocket."

"Probably the rotor arm," said Sam. "We'll check it before we leave. It shouldn't be too difficult to get hold of another one, even here in Abacadia."

Stu stood up.

"I'll go and get the car. I suppose I might as well take down the tents and pack them into the boot."

He looked at Sam who nodded, and off he went.

Pauline shouted after him.

"Wait for me Stu. I'll come with you," and she trotted off after him.

"May I make a suggestion?" asked Moldie after Stu and Pauline had disappeared around the headland, and before waiting for an answer carried on, "Why don't we drive back to the apartment in Redik that Lady Clair, your mother, has been using? We need a base and that seems as good as anywhere for now. We can look at maps and discuss what to do next. I will provide food and wine for you. What do you think?"

Sam looked surprised.

"You are assuming quite a lot, aren't you? What makes you think we will take you along with us and why on earth should we trust you?"

"I love Clair," he answered simply, and I could see he was telling the truth.

"I love her more than you could know. I can help you. I am Abacadian. I can help you. Without me, your job to rescue her would be a lot harder. As for trusting me, well, I'll just have to prove myself, won't I?"

Then he had a thought.

"What has happened to the two gorillas? They should have been minding the Landrover."

"Gorillas?" I asked.

"That's what Clair called them. Two ugly looking brutes."

"They're tied up under some trees just over there."

Sam pointed to the headland.

"They were shot by dart guns by two of the men, but we tied them up. Is it safe to release them?"

"Why are they at the headland?" wondered Moldie. "They were told to remain by the Landrover."

"They were filming you and mother," I said, "Like they did before."

Moldie stared at me.

"You know about that? How?"

"Our very clever brother found a copy of The Film on the internet. He's a computer student at university."

"Oh. I see."

Moldie pulled a funny face and said, "I was just trying to earn some money for my people."

He shrugged.

"What about the gorillas? Is it safe to release them?" asked Sam again.

Moldie nodded.

"Yes. They'll do as I tell them. Especially as they were caught filming again. Where is the camera?"

"The soldiers took it," said Sam. "Come on, let's go and untie them."

We walked up to the headland. The gorillas were conscious by now but still lying on their sides. They seemed to be suffering and stared at us as we approached. No emotions crossed either of their ugly faces, even when they recognised Moldie.

Moldie spoke to them in Abacadian.

"They don't speak English," he explained, "Though I am sure they understand a bit. I'm telling them what's happened. What are you going to do with them?"

"I've thought about that," said Sam. "We still have some food left. We could leave them food and one of the tents. Somebody could return from Redik tomorrow or the day after with the missing Landrover part to take them back."

Moldie nodded and spoke to the gorillas, who also nodded. Then he knelt down and untied them, and offered them some water. They drank noisily. They were probably quite thirsty by now.

We all walked over to the Landrover, the gorillas lagging sulkily behind. Sam checked under the bonnet.

"Thought so. They've taken the rotor arm. I can't see anything else missing. It should start easily once a new arm is inserted."

He showed the gorillas, who nodded.

"Even they should be able to do that," chuckled Sam.

A few minutes later Stu and Pauline returned in Lady Sammy.

"Sorry we took so long. We had to pack up the tent and all our belongings."

Sam explained the plan and Stu and Pauline nodded. They unloaded one of the tents and most of the food, and Moldie talked to the gorillas again, who nodded.

"I've told them to come and see me when they get back to Redik. I'll probably still employ them. They are a bit stupid but loyal."

He shook his head.

"Brawn, not brains."

So the five of us clambered into Lady Sammy. Sam drove, as usual, and I sat next to him. Moldie sat in the back in the middle between Pauline and Stu.

We drove to Redik and on the way Moldie explained to us about ODOE and how all the money that mother had earned was being used.

"She has made a tremendous difference to the local people," he said. "Her money has changed their lives."

Moldie directed us to a small apartment block, about a mile outside the town.

"This," explained Moldie, "Is where your mother has, eh, lived for the last few weeks."

He coughed, and at least had the courtesy to look slightly embarrassed.

Sam parked the car and we entered through a back door. Sam and Stu took everything slowly and carefully, checking every doorway before going through. We climbed up one set of stairs before walking down a short corridor and stopping in front of a door.

Moldie unlocked it. Sam and Stu, dart guns ready, looked at each other, nodded, then burst into the room, but it was empty and we all relaxed again.

We recognised the apartment from the film. It was a strange feeling for me, knowing that mother had been there just that morning. I looked at the bed, and shook my head as I considered all the lovers she had entertained in and on it.

Moldie brought us some food and drink and his laptop. As we ate and drank, he showed us a film of mother and Bim Dram in this very apartment, including the bit where he actually asked her to go and live in Snuka with him.

"You filmed everything?" I asked Moldie.

He grinned. A sort of sickly, self conscious grin.

"Just about everything," he said. "We thought we might be able to use it later somehow to get more money for our people."

"Blackmail, you mean?" said Pauline, and Moldie

just shrugged.

"Whatever it takes. We just want money to help our people. Every penny your mother earned is going into helping our people, and I mean every penny."

He was trying to justify what he had done, and I sighed.

"What else have you got about Bim Dram?" I asked.

He played with the computer for a few seconds then showed us what he had found.

"This is from ODOE," he said. "This is his house and the area where he lives. We have film and photographs and details of every politician and influential person in Abacadia. You never know when it will come in handy."

"The men took a few photographs of the four of us at Lake Lucinda," said Sam. "This Bim Dram has probably seen them by now. He will probably work it out that the girls are Clair's daughters, or he might learn from her."

He looked at us then at Moldie.

"Do you think he will come looking for us?"

"I've no idea," said Moldie, looking worried. "I don't know that much about the bloke. He may do, he may not, I really don't know."

"We must assume then," said Sam, "That he will be looking for us. Does he know where this apartment is?"

"Probably."

Moldie thought for a second.

"He's been here twice but we tried to keep the location a secret," and he told us how the clients were flown in by a helicopter with no windows.

"But he is a rich and powerful member of the government and he could easily, probably, almost certainly, find out."

"We must assume he does know," said Sam. "We

need to get to Snuka and we need a safe place to stay. Any suggestions Moldie?"

"I'm not sure if we would be safe staying here even one night, "he answered. "I think we should leave for Snuka as soon as it gets dark, and drive there keeping off the main roads. There are plenty of minor back roads we can use. If he is looking for us, he couldn't cover all of them.

Once we get to Snuka, there is an Effghanian businessman who lives there. He lets members of ODOE use his house whenever he is away from home. I think he is overseas at the moment, so we could probably stay there. It won't take me long to find out."

A couple of short phone calls later, and he nodded.

"The house is empty. A cleaner goes in once a week. I've just spoken to her and she will leave a key for us hidden in the garden. The owner isn't coming back for a few weeks, so, basically, we can stay there as long as we like."

Sam and Stu were studying a map of Abacadia. Moldie joined them. They pointed out a route to Snuka and Moldie suggested a slightly different road and they soon agreed. We were going to leave as soon as it got dark.

"It's about 250 miles and should take about 6-7 hours along those back roads in the dark," said Moldie.

He made another couple of phone calls.

"A mechanic and his mate will drive out to Lake Lucinda tomorrow, with a spare rotor and a tow rope, just in case they can't get it to start."

He walked to the bedroom.

"I need to chose some clothes for Clair," he said. "Maybe you two ladies would like to help me?"

We looked in the wardrobes and discovered a number of beautiful dresses hanging.

"They were all made to measure, especially for her,"

said Moldie, with a sigh. "She did look so lovely in them. I think she actually enjoyed wearing them. I know she did. I'll keep them safe here, just in case she ever wants them. I could always send them off to England for her."

He gave us a sad smile, then brightened as he opened a cupboard.

"Here are her shoes and nighties."

He handed a couple of nighties for Pauline and I to look at. We held them in front of us and looked in the mirror.

"She looked even better in those," he said with a small laugh. "This is her favourite though. This is the one she wore when she was on her own."

He held up a cream cotton knee length nightie.

"I think we should take this one for her."

He pulled out a small overnight bag and pushed it in. Pauline and I pulled out some underwear, very expensive and sexy underwear, and packed those. We chose two pairs of shoes. A pair of light boots and something slightly smarter and they went into the bag. A pair of jeans and a pair of shorts were also packed.

In one drawer we found some trousers and a blouse.

"Those were the clothes she was wearing when she was, eh, um, well, captured," said Moldie. "They have been washed."

We left those.

We looked in the bathroom. We recognised it from the film. It was full of all her favourite perfumes and soaps and shampoos. We picked out one or two of each and packed those also.

We had one last look around. Under the bed we found a small suitcase. In it was a small note book. It was full of mother's writings and we realised she must have been keeping a diary. That would make interesting reading.

"She has thoughts of making it into a best selling novel," said Moldle. "Put it in the bag. You can fill in the gaps for her."

Back in the living room, and Sam and Stu had been talking.

"We've been going through our various options," said Sam. "We can't do much planning until we get settled in in the house in Snuka. We have thought of visiting Dave and Laura but there's not much point until we have something to tell or suggest to them.

We've also considered visiting the British Embassy but we think it's better leaving that as a last resort, or at least until we are sure she is being held by Bim Dram. If they contact him, he might just deny it and hide her away somewhere, or even kill her. He's a very powerful man here in Abacadia and the Embassy would probably be very reluctant to accuse him of kidnap without definite and conclusive proof.

We think we should do some snooping first and maybe contact them later."

"Do you really think he might kill her?" I asked horrified.

"No, of course not," said Sam, rather quickly. "But we always have to look at every alternative. Is everything packed?" he asked, changing the subject.

"Almost," said Moldie. "I have a few bottles of Cadian wine downstairs. One of her clients presented her with a crate. She did an advert for him, promoting the stuff. I think she mentioned that in one of her messages. There are five bottles left. We may as well take them with us. I'll bring some food for the journey as well, and fill your flasks with hot water.

If it's okay with you, I'll take the car and get her filled up with petrol. There's only one station in Redik and petrol is rationed at the moment but they know me and will allow me to fill up the tank and there

194

won't be any filling stations on the way."

Sam and Stu looked at each other. I knew what they were thinking. Can we trust him? I think they realised they had to trust him, so Sam nodded.

"That's fine Moldie. There are some petrol cans in the boot. Make sure they are full as well. Do you need any money?"

He shook his head and said "Thank you. Thank you for trusting me," and disappeared through the door.

Sam and Stu looked at each other and shrugged.

"I hope we are doing the right thing."

I suggested we all have a shower. It had been a few days since we had washed properly and we were probably beginning to smell.

Pauline went first and Stu asked her if she would like him to help her wash her hair and she said that would be nice, thank you, and the two of them disappeared to the bathroom, with Stu looking back over his shoulder and giving us a wink.

"That's disgusting," said Sam, shaking his head. "Fancy the two of them sharing a shower. Outrageous. It shouldn't be allowed."

"I agree," I said. "Totally wrong. We wouldn't do a thing like that, would we?"

"Wouldn't even think of it," he said, trying not to grin.

But we did!

Chapter 26 - Mkubwa

Bim Dram returned in the early evening. I was sitting up in bed, reading a magazine. His first words surprised me.

"So, war is it?"

I seriously had no idea what he was talking about.

"I seriously have no idea what you are talking about," I told him.

"I want to humiliate you, and you don't want me to. War."

"Why on earth do you want to humiliate me?" I asked him, but I knew the answer. Because he had to pay so much money to have me, and I had rejected his very kind offer to live with him, here, in this house in Snuka. He didn't like paying for sex and he didn't like anyone refusing him. So, out of revenge, he wanted to humiliate me.

But he was right in another way. I wouldn't let him humiliate me. I wondered what he had in mind for me. As if he could read my thoughts, he said, "I have a friend who would like to visit with you."

He pushed a button and I heard a bell ring in the distance. A few seconds later there was a tap on the door.

"Come in," called Bim and a huge black man walked into the room.

"This is Lady Clair Hamilton," he told the man.

"This is Mkubwa," he told me. "Mkubwa is from Kenya and his name means big, or large, or massive or enormous. He is in the Guinness book of sexual records. He is accredited with having the largest erect penis in the world and in a few minutes time, he's going to shove it deep into your tight little pussy. I'm going to watch and film it. How do you feel about that?"

I wasn't going to let Bim know what I felt about anything. I kept a straight face and said, "That sounds nice," and Bim laughed.

"I don't think Mkubwa has ever had his cock described as nice before."

He turned to Mkubwa and said, "Maybe you would like to show Lady Clair why you won the title."

Mkubwa grunted and started to undress. He was a beautiful man, with firm black muscles and a firm flat stomach. When he took down his boxer shorts, I tried not to gasp, but I could hardly help myself. His penis hung down almost to his knees. It truly was massive. It looked like an elephants trunk.

I felt myself tremble. I couldn't take my eyes off it.

Bim chuckled.

"I'll let you choose how you go about it," he told me.

He went and sat down in a comfy chair. He took out a film camera. I sighed. I was going to be filmed having sex. Again. Yet again. I must now be the worlds most prolific porn star. Definitely the most prolific unpaid porn star.

I pulled down the bed covers. I was naked, of course. I seemed to spend a lot of my time naked. I reached out for Mkubwa's hand, and pulled him down onto the bed. I pushed him down onto his back, and reached for his cock. As I stroked it, I felt it stiffen and enlarge. It got bigger and bigger. And bigger. Both my hands could only just reach around it and it was about three hands long. Closer to four.

I still couldn't take my eyes from it. It seemed to have a life of its own, twitching and throbbing. I looked at Bim, who was busily filming me and grinning. I grinned back, and, still looking Bim straight in the eye, opened my mouth as wide as I could and took Mkubwa's cock into my mouth. Well, the tip. That was all I could get in. I reckoned it wouldn't take long before I got lockjaw.

After a couple of minutes, I sat up and climbed onto Mkubwa's tummy, facing away from his chest and facing Bim. I lifted up my bottom and felt for him. I positioned it against me, and, looking at Bim all the time, slowly lowered myself onto it. Very slowly indeed. I could feel myself being stretched and spread, and I groaned. Bim had stopped grinning and was watching and filming intently.

I lowered myself a bit more onto him, and I had to close my

eyes. The feeling was amazing. I could feel it pushing against the very insides of me. I felt down between my legs and there was still many inches left over. There was no way I could take all of it.

I gingerly started moving up and down and rocking from side to side. Mkubwa, luckily, remained still. If he started thrusting, he could really have hurt me. I was sure he knew this, which is why he stayed still.

I climbed off him and knelt down at the edge of the bed, pushing my bottom into the air, again looking at Bim. I grinned at him.

"This is very nice," I said.

Mkubwa stood behind me, and I could feel the tip pushing against me. I pushed back and in it slid. It felt even bigger than before and I encouraged him to move. He did, slowly at first, but quicker and quicker until he came with a grunt. He withdrew, turned me round and kissed me on the lips.

I looked at Bim again. There was a strange expression on his face.

"Thank you Mkubwa," he said, "You can go now."

Mkubwa got dressed, and as he left, Bim handed him an envelope which obviously contained some money. Mkubwa grunted, and nodded and left, closing the door behind him. He hadn't uttered a single word the whole time he had been there.

Bim looked at me again and said, "Go to the bathroom and get yourself cleaned up,"

Whilst I did so, I wondered about Bim Dram and Mkubwa. Was it coincidence that Mkubwa had been in Snuka and Bim had known exactly where he was or had he arranged to have him flown here from Kenya or wherever he had been? It was too much of a coincidence. Bim must have searched him out and paid him to come here. And that would have taken time. A few days at the least, maybe longer. So Bim had been planning to kidnap me for a while and had wanted to try and humiliate me.

Men, I thought. Bloody men and their stupid sexual daydreams. I shook my head. Over the last few weeks I had got used to Moldie and his ideas. He just wanted to help people but Bim's dreams were all for his own personal gratification. I hoped that he was now satisfied and would start treating me properly.

Then I thought of Mkubwa's huge cock and then I thought of Bim's tiny penis and smiled. Then I actually laughed and wondered what Bim had been thinking as he watched.

Little and large.

I laughed again, and suddenly felt sorry for Bim. Then I didn't feel sorry for him at all as I figured he was a ruthless bastard and had kidnapped me then I felt sorry for him again.

Men, bloody men.

Keep calm, Clair, I told myself. Keep calm and just play along with his silly games. Everything will turn out fine.

On my return to the bedroom, he held up his dressing gown and I slipped it on. He indicated for me to sit down in a comfy chair next to his.

He took a deep breath.

"I wish to apologise," he said, hesitantly, and not looking at me, "For the way I have been treating you."

I felt my eyebrows rising.

"I have been trying to humiliate you because you would not succumb to my advances last time we met. I realise now that this is wrong of me. You are an English Lady, and do not deserve such treatment. I am known to be ruthless and possibly corrupt in many of my dealings, but I am not known for my harsh treatment of women. I promise that from now on I will treat you correctly and with the dignity that you deserve."

I remembered what Moldie had told me, about the rumour that he beat up his wife. Maybe it was true and maybe it wasn't. I didn't know. I decided not to mention the rumour! Not then.

He now turned and looked at me. What did he want me to say? Surely he didn't expect me to say, "That's okay mate. No worries. I forgive you completely," but I had to say something.

I didn't want to anger him, so I said, "That's very noble of you, Bim. I'm glad to hear you feel remorse. Let's see how things go from now on, shall we?" and he nodded.

"Okay," he said, and I held out my hand in a peace offering and he kissed the back of my fingers.

"Would you like a glass of wine?"

I nodded.

"Yes please," and he walked over to a cupboard which I knew contained a fridge, took out a half finished bottle of Cadian rosé, picked up two glasses and brought them back to me. He filled them up, handed one to me, held his up his own glass, and said, "Cheers!"

I had to smile, whilst shaking my head.

"Cheers, Bim, cheers."

"Oh, by the way," he suddenly told me grinning. "When my men kidnapped you at Lake Lucinda, there were other people there. We think they were there to try and rescue you."

I gasped and gaped at him. My mind was in a turmoil. Who were they? Could they have been from my family? Did they get my messages?

Bim answered without me asking the questions out loud.

"My men took some photographs of them. Look. I have one to show you."

His face was one huge smug grin as he pulled a large photograph from his jacket pocket and handed it to me.

It was a photo of Alice and Pauline and two men who I didn't know but vaguely recognised from somewhere maybe. They were in some woods and in the background was a lake. Obviously Lake Lucinda. The men had their hands behind their backs, probably tied.

I looked at Bim, who smiled.

"They are your daughters, aren't they? Who are the two men? We haven't been able to find out."

I shook my head.

"What's happened to them? Are they alright?"

"As far as I know, they're perfectly okay. We left them there. Unhurt. As I said earlier, I don't hurt women. They are your daughters, aren't they?"

I nodded. My mind was whirling. So, they had definitely

worked out my messages. They had come to rescue me. And they were here in Abacadia.

"I thought so," said Bim. "Who are the men?"

I shook my head.

"I don't know. I truly don't know."

He chuckled.

"I believe you. Probably just a couple of bums they hired for a bit of muscle. It doesn't matter. They don't know you are here, and even if they did, they wouldn't dare attempt to rescue you."

He chuckled.

"I suppose they might somehow find out you are here. I wonder what they would do if they did? I wonder if they would try and visit me. I would just deny it of course. Then I would move you somewhere else. I do own other properties. Or I could send you somewhere where nobody could find you. Or maybe I would sell you. I could get a good price. I would easily get back my $200,000."

He chuckled again.

"Maybe I should do that anyway, after I have finished with you."

He looked at me.

"Would you like that, Lady Clair, would you like to be sold on from person to person, like a pet?"

"I thought you were going to treat me with respect and dignity, Bim?" I said, and he held up his hands again.

"Only teasing, my lady," he said with overdone sincerity. "Only teasing."

I smiled, though underneath I was a bit worried. I wouldn't put it past him. At least whilst I was here I was fairly safe from harm and Bim and I could settle down to some sort of harmless routine. Better the devil you know.

What could I do to make myself indispensable to him? I thought. Take an interest in his work? Maybe I could talk about some of the influential people I knew in England. Suggest I introduce him to them. A trip back to England with him, but now I was fantasizing.

He surprised me then.

"Would you like to dance? I enjoy dancing."

"Eh, yes. Yes, if you like. I also enjoy dancing."

There was a CD player in one of the cupboards. He switched it on and put in a CD. I was wondering what sort of music he would put on. It was a slow, romantic song. He held out his arms, and I joined him. He held me close as we slowly danced around the bedroom. He danced well, with nice rhythm and I actually quite enjoyed it.

When the music finished, he bowed and kissed my hand.

"Thank you Lady Clair. We must do that more often. Now, I must go to work. I'll see you later."

He turned and went, leaving me standing in the middle of the room in his dressing gown.

Chapter 27 - Uncle Jak's House

We left for Snuka in Lady Sammy that evening. It was a bit of a squash, Sam and Stu were quite big men, though Moldie and Pauline and I were fairly slim, so we decided to swap seats every hour or so. We also decided to take it in turns driving, even us girls would take a turn. The person in the passenger seat had the job of navigator.

Once we were out of Redik and onto the side roads, we didn't see another car for hours. The roads were mostly dirt roads, often quite overgrown with weeds, and twice we had to stop to move a fallen rock or a fallen branch. We drove steadily. There was no great rush and we couldn't risk an accident.

Those in the back tried to sleep. Pauline and I dozed a bit, but Sam and Stu fell asleep almost immediately. We could tell by their gently snoring. They were probably used to catnapping where and whenever. They had probably trained themselves.

When it was my turn to drive for an hour or so, Moldie was sitting next to me and we chatted constantly and I quickly found out what made him tick and I could understand why mother may have fallen for him and gladly gone along with his plans.

"To be honest," said Moldie, "She didn't have much option. I didn't really give her an alternative. We were so desperate to earn some money to help our people. She helped us more than we thought possible. It was a desperate plan and some of the committee were against it. I wish you could see all the good that has come from her help. You would be amazed,"

Moldie told me about the projects ODOE had planned and were carrying out, and I was impressed.

Very impressed.

"When your mother gets back to England," he said, "We are hoping she will continue to help us."

"I'm sure she will," I told him.

The journey was uneventful, which pleased us. If we could have seen anything, I'm sure the views would have been spectacular, but it was pitch black. We hardly saw another light for the whole of the six hour journey.

Moldie was driving as we arrived at Snuka, and he drove us straight to the ODOE safe house. It was in one of the more pleasant suburbs of Snuka. The houses, which were mainly bungalows, looked in the light of the street lamps to be in good condition with neatly kept front gardens. There was nobody about.

Moldie pulled into the drive of one of them. It looked very much like all the others. He got out of the car, leaving the engine running, and went around the side of the building, returning seconds later. He put a key into the garage door and lifted it up and over, then drove the car into the garage and switched off the engine. He pulled the garage door closed before switching on a light.

"We're here," he said, stating the obvious, and we all climbed out of Lady Sammy, stretching our aching backs and legs. Moldie took another key and opened a door which led us straight into a kitchen. We followed Moldie through into a tidy living room which was plainly decorated with a three seater sofa and two comfy chairs, and an old fashioned television in the corner.

"Cup of tea?" suggested Moldie. "The cleaner said she would leave some milk in the fridge."

We all nodded, and just ten minutes later were all supping hot tea from flowery mugs and eating chocolate biscuits.

It was 3.45 am, and, as usual, Sam took charge.

"Sleep," he said, and we all agreed. "When we get up, we can discuss a plan of action."

"There are three bedrooms," said Moldie. "One has a double bed and the others have twin beds. Who wants the double bed?"

"You have it," I said.

I slept surprisingly well in my single bed, with Sam sleeping in the other bed. I was expecting to lie awake worrying about mother but I was exhausted and fell asleep almost instantly. Sam woke me in the morning with yet another cup of tea, and when I eventually made it to the dining room, the others were already there eating cereal and fruit.

Sam asked how safe was this safe house.

"It's been used by ODOE for a number of years now," explained Moldie, "But is actually owned by an Effghanian businessman. He runs a publishing house, and spends a lot of time overseas. He often lets people use it when he is away, so there will be nothing unusual about us being here."

"We all need to act naturally," said Sam. "Two couples on holiday. But what about you Moldie? Do the neighbours know you?"

"I haven't been here often. They may have seen me before, but I wouldn't have thought that they would think anything suspicious seeing me here again."

"Have they talked to you? We need a story to tell everyone why we are here? Obviously on holiday, but why here, in this house?"

In the end we decided that the house belonged to a family friend who was away on business.

"What's the businessman's name?" Sam asked Moldie.

"Jak Treetrunk."

"You Abacadians do have strange names," giggled

Pauline.

Moldie looked hurt.

"We think you English have funny names as well. Why is Treetrunk any odder than Churchill or Westwood or Underhill? I had a friend in England whose last name was Clutterbug."

We all laughed.

"You're quite right, of course," I said. "What was the name we heard by Lake Lucinda? The soldier with the brown cap."

"Flakey, I think," laughed Pauline, and Moldie gasped.

"Did you say Flakey?" and Pauline nodded.

"Why?"

"What was he like? This Flakey?"

Moldie was looking at us rather intensely.

"A youngish man, quite good looking. Actually he looked a bit like you. Don't you think, Alice?"

I suddenly had a thought and looking at the expression on Moldie's face confirmed it.

"Is he related to you, Moldie?"

"Sounds like my kid brother," said Moldie. "I've never heard of anyone else called Flakey. It must be him and you say he looked a bit like me. I haven't seen him for fourteen years. He was kidnapped by the army, along with my other two brothers and my three younger sisters. I haven't heard a thing since. I didn't even know if they were still alive. I would have thought he might have recognised me."

"I don't think he saw you," I said, looking at Pauline, who nodded. "You were on the beach and he was in the woods, capturing us."

Moldie sighed and chuckled.

Pauline said, "I must admit Moldie, he did seem quite nice."

"Thank you," said Moldie, smiling.

"And he seemed quite happy being a soldier," I added.

"Anyway," said Sam, "Let's get back to the planning."

We all nodded and I said, "So, this house belongs to our Uncle Jak who has offered it to us. We just need to act like tourists and don't do anything that brings attention to us."

"You've got the idea," agreed Sam.

"They took some photos of us at Lake Lucinda," said Stu. "Do you think Bim Dram will be looking for us? Would he send copies to local police and other informers who work for him?"

We all looked at Moldie, who shook his head.

"I don't know," he said. "He might but I would guess he probably wouldn't."

"Even so," said Sam, looking thoughtful, "We mustn't take the chance. We need to disguise ourselves."

"I can get hold of some theatrical beards," said Moldie. "That should work until you grow real beards. And if you wear karatam hats, they are very popular, and you should fit in with the crowds."

"We could dye our hair and have it cut shorter," I suggested, and although Pauline didn't seem keen on the idea, she loved her long blonde hair, she reluctantly agreed.

Moldie arranged for a discrete mobile hairdresser to visit, and bought some new clothes for the four of us, and, the next day, when everything was finished, we did look quite different.

Moldie, who was also growing a beard, looked at us and said, "Yes. Good. You still look like tourists but you do look very different from yesterday. That's good."

So for the next two days, the four of us acted like tourists. We visited three different temples and two museums. We went shopping in the floating market and visited the 400 year old fort which had been built by the Dutch when they ruled Abacadia. We had picnic lunches in the botanical gardens and admired the aviaries, recognising a few of the birds thanks to our swotting up for Lake Lucinda.

And we drove past Bim Dram's house four times.

Stu and Pauline had been shopping at one of the numerous markets, and had bought some large flags and a coloured spoiler which would bolt on to the back of Lady Sammy, and some rolls of bright sticky tape.

"We may have to drive past Bim Dram's house a number of times," Stu explained. "If anyone there sees the same car going by more than 2-3 times, they may get suspicious. But if you add something really outlandish, like the flags or the go faster stripes, what people tend to see are the flags and the stripes. They don't notice the car so much. And we can take it in turns driving and swap number plates."

And this is what we did. On the first morning, all five of us were sitting in Lady Sammy. We were all wearing base ball caps and Pauline and I had our hair up, tucked into the caps. We all wore dark, plain jackets.

Moldie, who was navigating, was sitting in the front. We drove through the centre of the town, and then turned up a tree lined avenue. Houses either side were rather posh. It was called Queen Victoria Avenue.

"How come you know about this?" I asked Moldie.

"It was part of my brain washing training by ODOE," he said. "The idea was to make us realise how unfair life is. Most Effghanians live on a few fang a week."

Fangs were the local currency. One hundred pups to a fang. Seven fang to a pound, roughly.

"The folk who live here live off thousands of fangs a week. Effghanians have almost nothing, these people have almost everything. So we all piled into a minibus and they drove us up this street, pointing out who lives in which house and how much money they earn and what cars they drive and where they go on holiday and lots more."

"Did it work?"

"Did what work?" asked Moldie.

"Did it brain wash you?" I asked.

"It did," he replied.

By the time that pointless conversation had finished, we had passed a number of houses and Moldie said, "This is Bim Dram's house just around the corner."

We all craned our necks as we drove by and saw a smallish two storey mansion behind a high wall and a higher security gate.

"He also owns another mansion, in the country, about thirty miles away," explained Moldie. "He stays there when parliament is on holiday, but I know he is here at the moment. It was mentioned in the papers yesterday."

"I wonder if Clair's in there with him?" wondered Stu.

"If she is, I wonder which room she's in," wondered Sam.

"How will we find out?" wondered Pauline.

"I have been thinking about that and I think I can help," said Moldie. "He is bound to have servants working in the house. Definitely a cleaner, but maybe also a cook, a gardener and security. Lots of servants in Snuka are Effghanians. There is a good chance that at least one of the servants in Bim Dram's house is an Effghanian. Servants have a sort of network and I'm sure I can find out if Clair is there and if so, which room she's in. I'm also pretty sure I could even get a message to her."

We all turned and stared at him in amazement and

Sam almost crashed.

Moldie looked smug and said, "I'll get onto it this afternoon," and when we got back to the house, he disappeared.

Later that day, Sam and I drove by Bim Dram's house, with me driving and my hair let down. We had changed our clothes and now wore gaily coloured shirts and large sunglasses. We had fastened a couple of flags to Lady Sammy's front bumper and drove by with the windows down and loud, cheerful music playing. We were laughing and smiling as we drove by but still craned our eyes for any clues on the layout of the house and also the garden, though all we could see was a glimpse through the large gates.

That evening we went out for a meal and a small drink at a local trendy bar called, oddly, Wine Not. Despite the name, the food was good, not too expensive, and the Cadian wine very drinkable. Sam only allowed one bottle between us.

"No drinking on the job," he said. "One glass each. We need clear heads. But if we didn't drink, that would look suspicious. So one bottle between us."

Moldie didn't return that night, and we didn't see him until the following evening. By then, as well as the touristy sight-seeing things, we had also managed two more drives up Queen Victoria Avenue and past Bim Dram's house. We altered the appearance of Lady Sammy each time. When Pauline and Stu drove by, we had covered her in flags, and again the two of them wore sunglasses but with floppy hats.

When Sam and Stu drove by, all the flags had been removed and bold go faster stripes were added. We had even changed the number plates.

The boys had removed their false beards and replaced them with thick stick-on moustaches, which made them look much younger and wasn't that unusual. Many young men had moustaches in Snuka. It seemed to be the trend.

"I could almost fancy you with a moustache, Mr Sam," I told him. "It makes you look a bit like a modern Errol Flynn."

We continually discussed Bim Dram's house and mother's rescue.

"Scaling the walls into the garden would be easy," they both agreed. "We can take a lightweight folding aluminium ladder."

"If we can get her out of the house, then getting her over the wall should be easy as well," they also agreed.

"We need to find out more about the garden and the layout of the house," said Sam. "Most importantly, we need to find out which room she is in."

"I wonder how long Moldie will be?"

Pauline spoke.

"Sam," she said. "Do you trust him? I mean really trust him."

"That's a good question. Yes, I think I do. He does seem like a genuinely decent bloke, and I think he is really deeply in love with your mother. Yes. I think I do trust him. What about you?"

Pauline wasn't so sure.

"Not after what he's put mother through," she said.

But I was sure by this time, and, I think, so was Stu.

"I agree with Sam," he said. "I think we have to trust him really. Without him, rescuing your mum will be much more difficult."

"Do you think they may have dogs?" wondered Pauline. "You know, in Bim Drams garden."

"I've been wondering about that as well. There's only one way to find out," stated Sam. "Stu and I need to go and have a look. Tonight."

Stu nodded, but just then Moldie returned and he

was in good spirits.

"Good news," he said, proudly. "I have discovered that there is a young Effghanian lady called Flower who works as a maid in Bim Dram's house. Her job is to clean and wash.

I have talked to her. She has seen Clair and cleans her room everyday. She is unhurt and seems in good spirits. Her room is on the first floor and is the last room on the right looking from the front. She says she thinks that Bim Dram visits her regularly."

Both Pauline and I sighed.

"Thank goodness for that."

Sam said confidently, "Now we know that, I think we can rescue her easily. We just need a way to find out when she is on her own in her room."

"I've thought about that," said Moldie. "Flower has agreed to take a message to Lady Clair. I read in a book once that a spy would leave one curtain drawn and one curtain open when there was danger about. She could do that, but the opposite. Leave one curtain open and one curtain closed when she is on her own. We should be able to see it from the road."

"Good idea," agreed Sam.

"Does Flower speak English?" I asked her. "I assume we won't be giving her a note."

"She speaks very good English, but only if she has to. She pretends she only speaks Abacadian. That way people often talk about things they wouldn't talk about if they knew she was listening. She is actually quite clever. Very reliable. A good girl. But Clair has been learning Abacadian and speaks a little bit now."

I chuckled.

"Good for you, mum," I said.

Sam then told Moldie all our news.

"Stu and I were thinking of sneaking into the garden to have a look, possibly tonight. But we are worried about dogs roaming. Do you know if he has guard dogs?"

Moldie said he didn't know but if we could wait a day, he was sure he could find out.

"I could also get some plans of the house and the garden for you," he said. "If they would help."

Sam said it would.

"Also, ask if there is a guard in the house, and if the windows open wide or are alarmed."

"Okay. Is there anything else I can do?" asked Moldie. "Anything you need?"

Sam had drawn up a list.

"Most of the stuff we need we can buy from the local shops," he explained. "But two dart guns would be a help. We had ours taken from us at Lake Lucinda."

"No problem," Moldie said, without raising an eyebrow. "I'll have them for you by tomorrow evening."

I asked Moldie about his brother Flaky.

He sighed.

"I don't know. Look, I'm so pleased to find out that he is still alive, but I had a good idea he was probably in the army anyway, and I haven't been able to find him in the last fourteen years. Bim Dram could have got the six soldiers from any unit in the army. I'm not really any better off finding him. But I will think about it."

"Good luck," I said, genuinely feeling sorry for him.

Sam decided to put off the midnight visit to Bim Dram's house for a couple of days, to give them a chance to get all the stuff they needed and wait for Flower to report back with answers to his questions.

Not far away from the house in Snuka was an area known as the Food Quarter. Here there were a large number of cafes and restaurants and market stalls which all specialised in food. Whatever type of food you wanted, you could get it in the Food Quarter.

Moldie had offered to visit and buy the evening meal.

"What would you like?" he asked and I shrugged, but Pauline answered.

"Typical Abacadian fare," she said. "Why come all this way and eat English food, or Indian or Chinese? We can get those at home. Half the fun of going abroad it to try the different food and drink. So I suggest we have a typical Abacadian meal."

We all agreed with that, and Moldie nodded.

"Your wish is my command," he said, "Though I must tell you, Indian and Chinese food here is very, very different from Indian and Chinese food in England, but Abacadian food it will be. Does anyone want to come with me?"

We told him that that was an excellent idea and we all went with him and had a lovely time wandering around. The choice of different foods was amazing but it was the different smells and aromas which astonished and fascinated me.

Eventually, with Moldie's help, we chose a starter of a fruit called wood apple, in which you scooped out the insides, then a main of three different types of curry, and a pudding of local cake cooked with treacle. All extremely tasty and I wondered once again about opening an Abacadian restaurant in England. It was an idea.

Chapter 28 - Flower

After Mkubwa, and his failure to humiliate me, Bim started acting slightly more humanely. He still wanted to have lots and lots of sex with me, but that was fine. I did as he asked and kept him happy and gentle.

He wouldn't let me leave the room though, even when I begged him.

"Please, Bim," I begged. "It's so boring being here all day. Please, even just a walk around the garden. The guard could come with me," but he refused.

"Someone might see you," he said, "And we wouldn't want that, would we?"

He said he would take me out when he had some spare time and did I believe him? Yes and no! I would have to help him decide that taking me out would be what he wanted. I was sure my womanly charms would succeed once again.

He also refused to give me a nightie to wear.

"I like you to be naked in bed next to me," he said, "And during the day you can wear my dressing gown. Why would you need a nightie?"

So my days were dull. Bim would make love to me in the morning, make love to me in the evening and sleep next to naked me in the luxurious double bed. Occasionally he would come back at lunch time and make love to me then. He did seem to have an unlimited sexual energy. It took all my skills to make every session a good session for him. I didn't want him getting bored with me. God knows what would happen then.

Between him leaving me in the morning and returning in the evening, usually I was on my own. And life was dull.

I tried to keep busy. I wished there was a running machine like there was in the apartment. I would ask Bim. I was sure he would get one for me. However, I did discover a music channel on the television and danced along to the songs, which all seemed to be British or American. It made me hot and sweaty and helped to keep me sane.

The TV had a BBC World News channel, which I watched and enabled me to catch up on what was happening back home and world wide. There was no mention of an attractive middle aged lady from Worcestershire being kidnapped.

Everyday, a maid came in to clean the room. She was fairly young, probably in her mid twenties, but rather plain looking. She had bright eyes but a face which seemed to show little emotion.

With my rudimentary but improving knowledge of Abacadian, I managed to chat to her. She didn't say a lot but I did discover she was called Flower. I asked her what was her favourite flower but she just looked at me as if to say 'Nobody has asked me that before.'

I asked her where she came from and when she answered Snuka, for some reason I didn't believe her, but didn't push the point. If she didn't want to tell me then she didn't have to.

On the fifth day of my time with Bim Dram, Flower appeared nervous. I could tell as soon as she walked in. Her whole attitude was different. She wouldn't make eye to eye contact.

I decided to wait and see why. She kept glancing at me as she went about her work. I waited, sitting in the comfy chair and pretended to read a book.

Eventually she walked over to the windows and whilst dusting there, looked at me. She jerked her head with the universal sign that she wanted me to join her by the windows. She obviously knew about the cameras and had worked out a position where we couldn't be seen. Why had she done that?

I casually stood up and sauntered over to her, and pretended to look out of the window. She moved her mouth towards my ear.

"Moldie Bedlam has a message for you", she said, in perfect English, though accented. "He has Alice and Pauline with him. They want to rescue you. They know you are in this room. They need to know when you are on your own. Draw one curtain only when you are on your own. I will speak again soon."

She walked into the bathroom and I stared after her. My heart gave a flutter and I tried to control my breathing. They had found me. How? Moldie! He must have guessed that Bim was behind the kidnapping. How did he discover Flower worked here? She must be Effghanian.

I was trembling with excitement.

I wondered when they would come to rescue me. I wondered how they would rescue me. I reckoned Flower would let me know. I mustn't compromise her position. I would wait until she spoke to me again.

And I mustn't give any hint to Bim Dram that anything was happening. It would be difficult not to show excitement but I was Lady Clair Hamilton, I could do it.

It was only then that I suddenly realised she spoke perfect English. Until then we had only conversed in dubious Abacadian. I looked at her with new respect. Maybe she was a lot cleverer than she seemed.

Everyday after that first day, Flower spoke to me. Most of the time it was in Abacadian, for the cameras and any microphones that may be hidden, and I tried to talk to her about her home life and childhood and Snuka and the outside world. I think Bim would expect me to do this and if I didn't, he might get suspicious. That is, if he was taking any interest in me at all. I might have been totally over reacting, but no harm was done.

Sometimes Flower would whisper to me in English, and then I knew the message was from Moldie and my daughters.

"Moldie is making his plans," she said one day. "It will be soon."

Another day, she said, "Plans for your rescue are complete. They are waiting until you are alone overnight."

I tried to remain calm whenever Bim was with me.

Once he said to me, "Are you alright, Clair? You seem a bit on edge."

"I'm bored, Bim," I told him. "It's not so bad when you are here, but during the day I am on my own, and I'm not used to being on my own. At least before, I was always planning for my next client, but here, I have nothing to plan, nothing to do. I'm bored Bim."

He did have the decency to look slightly concerned and thoughtful.

"I think you are right," he said. "You need something to keep you occupied. I'll think about it."

"A trip to the shops would be nice," I suggested, but he chuckled at that.

"Not at the moment, but maybe we could go away for a couple of days, to a local beauty spot. One of my favourite places is called Angel's Hair Waterfalls. It is extremely lovely. I think you would like it there."

When I laughed, he looked at me and I hurriedly said,

"Do you want to take me there because you think I have the hair of an angel, Bim?" and shook my head so my hair glistened in the lamplight.

He laughed as well.

"That's right Clair," he said. "You are just like an angel."

He chuckled and kissed me.

And life went on.

Then one evening as we lay in bed drinking wine and chatting, Bim suddenly said, "Clair, you may have heard rumours that I am an evil man, and that I beat my ex-wife."

He looked at me and raised his eyebrows.

What should I say? A cautious approach was needed. I remembered what Moldie had told me.

"I have heard that," I said. "But you hear all sorts of rumours about well known people. Some are true, some are made up."

"That rumour about me was made up," he said, looking straight into my eyes. "Made up by her when I wanted a divorce after catching her in bed with a fellow MP. I beat him up and slapped her a couple of times, nothing much, but I was very angry, as you can imagine."

He was still looking straight at me, almost begging me to believe him, I think, and, to be honest, I did believe him. Why else would he tell me?

"I'm sure you were, Bim," I said, "But didn't you get into trouble for beating up the MP. Even members of the government can't go around beating up people."

"It was all hushed up. None of us wanted it to become public. He is still an MP, and quite a good one. I haven't forgiven him but we talk civilly to each other, at least when we are in public. My ex wasn't happy when I told her I wanted a divorce and she made up the stories about me hitting her to try and get a better divorce settlement. The judge sided with me, but, as you know, the saying is no smoke without fire, and the false allegations stuck. I am not wife beater, Clair, I promise you."

Best for me to be understanding, I thought, so stroked his cheek and said, "I believe you, Bim," and, still staring straight into my eyes, he said,

"Good. I'm glad about that."

I wondered why he was telling me all this. Probably he had nobody he could really talk to, to really express his feelings, until now. Maybe I had got the wrong impression of him. Maybe he wasn't so bad after all.

"I'm also a very good MP."

He was in an extremely talkative mood.

"I know I am, which is why I am a member of the government and Minister for Home Affairs. I genuinely do care about Abacadia and the people, and do everything I can to help them."

"What about the big whip?"

He looked confused.

"What big whip? What do you mean?"

"You told me when we first met that you use a big whip to get people to do what you wanted."

He smiled and laughed.

"I remember. Sometimes you have to bully people to get things done," he chuckled. "That's what I meant. There is no big whip, I promise."

"What about Effghania?" I asked him. "From what I have heard, things aren't so good down there."

"What have you heard?"

He sounded suspicious.

"There has been a drought and an earthquake in the last couple of years and people are going hungry and have nowhere to live," I said.

"Who told you that?"

He sounded even more suspicious.

"I am a charity worker in England," I told him. "One of the best and we have a sort of network, passing on information and news to one another. I can't remember who told me that. Is it true and what are you doing about it?"

I thought he was going to get angry with me, but instead, he sighed.

"I'm not doing enough," he admitted, "Abacadia is quite a poor country, and there is not a lot of government money to do everything that needs doing, so we have to prioritise and, unfortunately, Effghania comes near the bottom of the list. Sorry."

"That's not what you told me the first time we met," I reminded him. "You told me Effghania was a special case."

He chuckled.

"I did," he admitted, "And I apologise. I didn't know you then and was trying to impress you. Now you know the truth."

I pondered what he had said and wondered if I could influence him in any way to help Effghania more. Now I was getting to know him better, he didn't actually seem such a bad guy. I decided to question him some more about my kidnapping.

"Bim," I said, "Do you think it is right for you to keep me locked up here? Shouldn't you let me go. I promise not to tell anyone what you have done."

He looked away.

"I can't," he muttered. "I love you so much and can't bear the thought of you sleeping with anyone else. I just have to have you all for myself."

He turned around and held my shoulders.

"That offer I made you, about you living with me for one

year. It is still on," he said. "Stay with me for one year, and I will give you one million dollars. Then I will let you go, I promise."

I was taken aback. I had forgotten about that offer. I had assumed it was just an empty promise to get me to live with him. Now I wasn't so sure.

"Within one year, I am sure you will learn to love me like I love you," he explained further, "And then you'll stay with me of your own free will. You may even marry me," he said, half smiling.

I touched his hand again, and said, "Thank you Bim. Thank you for the offer. I will certainly think about it," and he smiled.

And I did think about it. I thought about him. He was turning out to be alright after all, and I was sure I could influence him hugely especially if I was his wife, to help the people of Effghania. Fall in love with him? Hmm, unlikely, I reckoned.

Then I thought of Hamilton Hall and Worcestershire and my family and knew I couldn't do it. I had to go home.

Life went on but three days later, in the morning, before he left for work, Bim told me that he wouldn't be returning that night.

"I have to visit Effghania," he said. "There is an American news crew visiting and they have asked me to give some interviews for them first thing in the morning. Something to do with the early morning light being in the right direction so I have decided to stay overnight. I need to look at the work that has been going on there before they arrive. I'll be back tomorrow evening."

He was silent for a moment.

"I've been thinking about what you have been saying about Effghania and you are right. I really do need to help them more. I promise to have a proper think about it."

I touched his arm.

"Thank you Bim," and kissed him on the cheek.

"Whilst I am away, don't you go and do anything you shouldn't be doing."

I almost said, "Can I come with you Bim?" but stopped myself and instead I laughed.

"As if," I said, but already my mind was ticking over.

When later that morning, Flower came to do her daily cleaning, I called her over to the window. She carried on cleaning but slowly walked over to me.

"Tonight, Bim Dram won't be here. He will be in Effghania. I will be in the bedroom on my own. Can you get a message to Moldie and tell him?"

She nodded.

"I can," and continued with her cleaning.

"Tell them I have no clothes with me," I told her and she nodded again.

"I will. Remember to leave one curtain open," she reminded me and this time I nodded.

I tried to keep calm. I talked myself into believing that they would come that night then decided they wouldn't. I wondered how they would attempt it, then decided it would all go horribly wrong. Then I thought what if they forgot some clothes for me then I thought I could wear Bim Dram's dressing gown and the thought of me escaping wearing his dressing gown made me smile.

Chapter 29 - Preparation

Over the next three days we attempted to get everything ready for the rescue attempt. We went shopping and bought some clothes. We bought a light aluminium ladder and a small duvet and some black paint and a paint brush. We bought some card and a black marker pen and a small spot torch.

We painted the duvet and the ladder black.

The three men went off in Lady Sammy twice, to check over all their plans then double check them all.

And eventually Sam seemed satisfied.

"I'm satisfied," he said. "But it would be nice if Stu and I could actually get into the garden beforehand but I'm not sure if that's a good idea anymore. If we were detected, then Bim Dram would surely guess we were there to rescue her, and would almost certainly either move her somewhere else or lock her up overnight or something even worse. I think we should just trust to luck one night and hope for the best."

Stu nodded.

"Careful planning should reduce the need for luck," he said.

"So," continued Sam, "I don't think we can do any more to ensure her rescue. We just need the right time. It would be so much easier if she was on her own in the bedroom overnight. Moldie, can you find out from Flower if Bim Dram ever spends nights away from home?"

We were sending daily messages to mother now via Flower. Messages of reassurance, but we didn't want to jeopardise Flower's position. We kept them simple. 'It won't be long,' and 'As soon as you are on your own overnight,' etc.

Moldie also questioned Flower about the house.

"Are there any dogs in the garden?"

"I've never seen any, no."

"Are there any outside security lights or alarms?"

"Don't know. I'll try and find out."

"Are the windows double glazed?"

"No."

"Are the windows alarmed?"

"Yes. They can only open 6 inches."

"Are there any guards in the house overnight?"

"I think so," she said, "But they sleep in the bedroom next to Clair's, and only when Bim Dram is not at home. So if he goes away for a night and leaves Clair on her own, there will probably be a guard in the room next door."

"That's good to know," said Sam. "It means we are forewarned. Utter silence is needed, but we would have been utterly silent anyway."

I was concerned for Flower.

"If, I mean when, mother is rescued, won't Bim Dram guess that Flower had something to do with it? What will he do to her?"

"That is a good question," said Moldie. "Once your mother is rescued, Flower will not be able to return to his house. Her job will be done there. She's a clever girl, that one, and we'll find another job for her. Don't worry about her, she will be rewarded and well looked after."

The discussions went on as to what we could do with mother when she was rescued.

"What are the options?" I asked.

"The ultimate aim is to get her back to England," said Sam, and we all nodded. "The safest way is on a normal commercial flight. She hasn't got her passport, though, but, if there's no hurry, we can get Theo to post it here for us. It will take a few days. We can just continue as tourists."

We all nodded. Seemed logical to us.

"We should have thought to bring it with us," said Pauline.

I shrugged, "We can't think of everything."

"So," continued Sam, "We need to keep her safe and out of harms way for anything up to two weeks whilst we wait for the passport to arrive, or maybe even longer. There are a number of options that I can think of, though I am open to suggestions.

1 - She could stay here.

2 - She could stay with Dave Gulldred.

3 - She could go back to the apartment in Redik.

4 - She could go somewhere else, either here in Snuka or somewhere else.

Then," he continued, "If she goes off somewhere else, does she go on her own, or does someone go with her?"

He looked at us.

"Where would she be safest? Do you think Bim Dram would come looking for her?" I wondered out loud.

"You've met him, Moldie," said Sam. "What do you think? Would he come looking for Clair?"

"He might." Moldie looked thoughtful. "He is a very proud man and loves to get his own way. If we rescue Clair, sorry, when we rescue Clair, he will be extremely annoyed. I also think he is genuinely fond of her and would want her back. And he has the resources to do something."

Moldie sighed and looked at us all.

"On the other hand, he is also very ambitious. From what I can gather, his aim is to become Prime Minister of Abacadia. If his kidnapping of Clair became public knowledge, then he could kiss that ambition goodbye."

He suddenly grinned.

"I think he could well be susceptible to a little

blackmail. Clair's safety for our silence."

Sam didn't grin.

"You think that, but we can't be sure. You can never tell with proud men. I think we could try the blackmail but also keep her hidden."

The rest of us nodded.

"Where?" asked Pauline. "Probably safest with Dave and Laura. I'm sure Dave said they had a hut somewhere in a village where we could take her, didn't he?"

"Yes, I can remember him saying that," I agreed with her.

"We need to talk to them," said Sam. "Why don't you, Pauline, and Stu go and visit them and find out the situation?"

"Okay," said Stu, looking at Pauline and smiling. "I'll phone and arrange it for tomorrow if I can."

"Tell them that there will only be two people stopping," said Sam.

He looked at Moldie.

"You and Clair. Us four will stop here and continue being tourists. Do you all agree?"

We all did. Moldie looked pleased with the idea of stopping in a mud hut with mother for up to two weeks.

"We'll keep in contact daily through mobile phones. Can you arrange two phones for us, Moldie?"

"I've got mine," he replied, "And I can easily get hold of another. No problem."

"Good," said Sam. "But, if need be, what about the apartment in Redik."

He looked at Moldie.

"Would she be safe there?"

Moldie shook his head.

"I wouldn't have thought so. Bim Dram might not know exactly where the apartment is in Redik, but as we discussed when we were there, I'm sure he could soon find out. If he is going to search for her, I don't think the apartment would be particularly safe. It would be safer here, I think."

"We would have to keep her hidden, though," said Sam. "After being locked up for the past few weeks, I don't think she would like that."

He avoided looking at Moldie.

"Let's leave that decision until you two return from visiting the   Gulldreds."

The next day, Stu and Pauline went to visit Dave and Laura, Moldie went about his business and to talk to Flower whilst Sam and I carried on with doing touristy things.

"Do you really think the police or secret service are watching us?" I asked Sam, as we sat on a blanket by the river, having a picnic.

"No," he said, "I don't think so. Stu and I have been keeping our eyes peeled, and haven't seen anything suspicious, and we have been trained at the SAS for exactly this sort of thing. But better to be safe than sorry."

He smiled at me.

"Things are going well," he said. "Try not to worry about your mum. We'll get her back to England."

That evening Stu and Pauline told us about their visit to Dave and Laura.

"They're not thrilled about the idea of two people staying, despite what they said when we visited them, but they have agreed. We went to look at the place. It's a mud hut in a small village of mud huts. The beds are straw and there is no electricity, but it is comfy enough. The villagers would feed them. They would have to wear traditional village clothes and Clair would have to hide her long blonde hair under a hat, or get it cut."

Stu and Pauline told us all this between them. We all looked at Moldie.

"Sounds like paradise to me," he said, grinning. "I'll buy some traditional clothes for us to wear. It's the least I can do."

He had brought another mobile phone with him, which he gave to Stu.

"My number is already entered," said Moldie. "It's pay as you go, and it's been rented with a false name and it can't be traced back to me."

The waiting to hear from mother was rather nerve racking, especially for Pauline and me, who weren't used to such things, but Sam and Stu remained calm enough.

"There's nothing we can do at the moment, so just relax," they said.

Easier said than done.

Two evenings later, and Moldie returned looking excited.

"I've had a message from Flower," he said. "Bim Dram is in Effghania at the moment and won't be returning until tomorrow. Lady Clair will be on her own all night. I think we should make the rescue attempt tonight. We might not get a better opportunity."

"I agree," said Sam. "Everything is ready. Tonight will be the night. Is there any chance of getting a message to her?"

"No," said Moldie. "I think it would be too risky. I'm sure she'll be expecting us and ready. She's very bright. She has no clothes with her so don't forget to take them with you."

Sam and Stu gave him a look to say 'as if' then went over their plans with us.

"We will attempt it in middle of the night. Three o'clock is when the human body is at it's lowest ebb, when the guards and the household will be least receptive.

We will wear these clothes."

He took some black clothes from a sack. Black polo neck shirt, black trousers, black socks and shoes and gloves and black balaclavas with just two small holes for eyes.

"Moldie will drive Lady Sammy and drop us off two streets away from Bim's place. We will walk to Bim Dram's house, always keeping in the shadows. Once we have reached the house, we will put this ladder against the wall at the spot we have chosen, climb over the wall and pull the ladder up and over behind us."

Stu showed us the ladder. It was aluminium, very light, and painted black.

"It expands to ten feet long," explained Sam, and Stu showed us how.

"When it is collapsed, it will easily fit in Lady Sammy, but when expanded will reach to the window sill of Clair's room.

There is broken glass embedded into the top of the wall. We will lay this small black duvet," he showed us the small black duvet, "On top of the wall to make sure we are not cut by the glass.

Once we are in the garden, we will carry the ladder to a place just below Clair's window, keeping in the dark shadows at all times. Stu will hold the ladder against the house wall whilst I climb up it.

I will make contact with Clair by gently tapping on the window. When she responds and comes to the window, I will hold up this piece of card, which I will illuminate with this small spot torch."

He pulled a small piece of white card from a black rucksack and showed it to us.

'My name is Sam,' it read. 'I am a friend of Alice and Pauline and Moldie. Stu is at the bottom of this ladder.

Keep away from the window.'

He showed us the small spot torch, switching it on and off.

"I will push this plunger against the window."

He showed us a sink plunger which he had painted black.

"I will then attempt to cut the bottom glass pane out of the window frame using this glass cutter."

He held it up to show us.

"I've been practising with it and it seems to work very well. When the pane has been totally removed from the frame, I will lower it gently onto the carpet of Clair's bedroom using the plunger.

I will then pass her this bag containing these clothes and tell her to quickly and quietly put them on."

He showed us a small black canvas bag, and pulled out some black trainers, black tracksuit bottoms, a black tracksuit top, black gloves and a black balaclava.

"I got everything size medium," he said.

"I will place the small duvet on top of the window frame, just in case there are some jagged edges from the cut.

Once she is dressed," he continued, "I will help her through the window and she will follow me down the ladder. At this moment, Stu will send a pre-prepared text message to Moldie, who will be waiting on the next street, and who will send a pre-prepared text reply.

When Clair and I reach the bottom of the ladder, Stu will collapse it. We will take it with us. We will sneak back to the same place in the garden wall as before. Stu will then send Moldie another text, and we will use the ladder to climb over the wall, using the duvet and pulling the ladder up behind us as before.

Once in the street, we will walk to a spot fifty yards or so away from the wall. It is directly in between two street lamps, and relatively dark. Hopefully, thanks to Stu's text messages, Moldie should arrive at exactly the same moment.

We have calculated that the whole operation, from Moldie dropping us off to picking us up, should take about 45 minutes. In Lady Sammy we will remove our balaclavas and Moldie will drive us back here."

"What happens if anything goes wrong?" I asked.

"We have made contingency plans," said Sam. "Both of us will carry loaded dart guns with spare darts. If we get spotted in the garden, there is an alternative place we have discovered to climb the wall, even if we don't have the ladder. There is an overhanging branch we can use.

If we work together, all three of us should be able to get over the wall quite quickly and easily. Your mum is quite athletic, I believe."

I nodded.

"She is indeed," and Moldie chuckled.

We all looked at him and he smiled. We all knew exactly what he was thinking.

Sam continued.

"In the rucksacks we will be carrying brightly coloured T-shirts and baseball caps, which we can put on over the black tops. We will split up. Clair and I will act as a couple, holding hands, and we'll meet up with Stu at another prearranged meeting place, where Moldie will pick us up in Lady Sammy. We will keep in contact through text messages. Don't worry, Alice, I think we have it all covered."

I was very impressed. I actually thought that maybe we would be able to rescue her.

We tried to get some sleep that evening but I don't think any of us actually did. At 2.30, we all got up. Sam and Stu were both dressed from their necks to their feet in black. Black balaclavas were stuffed into their pockets. They kissed us goodbye, and, on impulse, I kissed Moldie on the cheek.

"Bring mother back to us, safe and sound," I whispered in his ear, and he grinned at me. It was a sickly half grin. He was obviously nervous. He wasn't used to this sort of thing.

"I'll bring her back safe and sound," he said, trying to sound confident. The three of them climbed into Lady Sammy with Sam and Stu in the back and drove off down the road.

Chapter 30 - Camping

Dim Dram surprised me by coming home at lunch time. At first I assumed he just wanted more sex, but that was okay, as long as he left again for Effghania, but then he dismayed me.

"I've been thinking what you said, Clair," he said. "About taking you out somewhere. As I told you, I'm off to Redik this afternoon to give an interview to an American TV crew tomorrow morning, but that shouldn't take long. I've arranged to have the rest of the day off, and then also the next day as well.

I've arranged for us to go to Angel's Hair Falls. I'm sure you'll like it there. We'll have to sleep in a tent, but I'm sure you won't mind that."

Bim was really excited but my mind was in a turmoil. I was going to be rescued that night but now it seemed that maybe I wouldn't be. I tried to keep a straight face but something must have shown because Bim said,

"What's wrong Clair? Don't you want to go away with me?"

I thought quickly and said, "Bim, I have nothing to wear."

"Don't worry, I have bought some clothes for you," and passed me a bag. He was grinning. I looked inside and pulled out a good quality medium length blue dress, some underwear, a pair of trainers, and a swimming costume. There was also a thin jumper.

"Take a towel and washing stuff from here, whatever you think you might need," he told me.

"When are we going? In the morning?"

"No, this afternoon. The soldiers will take you down there this evening, and set up the camp and I will meet you after lunch tomorrow. Obviously you can't be seen with me so everything will be done in secret."

"How long will we be staying for?"

"You will be there for two nights, but just one night for me, I'm afraid. I have to get back in the evening for a parliamentary vote."

My mind wandered. I had to get a message to Flower. She had already been that day and almost certainly wouldn't return. Would she come back tomorrow when Moldie and the others discovered that I wasn't in the room? Maybe I could leave a message. Just in time, my mind flicked back to what he was saying.

"Oh Bim," I said, pretending a false enthusiasm, "That's not very long. Can't you have more time off?"

He shook his head and looked sorrowful.

"I'm sorry Clair. It took quite a bit of arranging just to have this short time off. But we'll have a lovely time, I promise you. Get some stuff together. The guards will be here soon."

He kissed me, gently but with passion, and then he was gone. I heard him lock the door behind me. He may be looking forward to going away camping with me, but he still remembered to lock the door.

I dressed in the clothes he had brought me, and they fitted quite well and I looked in the mirror and reckoned I looked quite nice in them. I went into the bathroom and brushed my hair and would have liked to have put on some make up but there wasn't any.

I packed some soap and a flannel and toothpaste and toothbrush and a towel into a small overnight bag and then looked around me to try and find some way of leaving a message for Flower.

I looked at the shampoos and the soaps and the perfumes. I racked my brains. How can I tell Flower that I was going to Angel's Hair Falls?

Last time I went there the message I had sent had included me asking Theo if he was taking Jackie to France. If I could just do something that would make Alice and Pauline think of Jackie or France or even J and F then I thought they would cotton on. Possibly.

Eventually, I got some of the shampoos and laid them in the bath to make the letter J and some more on the floor to make the letter F. That was the best I could do. I had to make sure that no one went into the bathroom in case they got suspicious so took my overnight bag into the bedroom and closed the door.

I sat in the comfy chair and as I waited for something to happen, felt despair overcoming me once again.

"Come on," I told myself. "You are Lady Clair Hamilton. You will come through this. You will escape, just not tonight."

There was a knock on the door half an hour or so later.

I said, "Come in," and the door unlocked and two men walked in. I recognised them immediately as two of the men/soldiers who had kidnapped me from Lake Lucinda. One of them was Brown Cap, who I thought had been in charge of the other five last time and assumed he would be in charge again and was still wearing the same Brown Cap. Did he ever take it off?

They were both wearing casual clothes, jeans and T-shirt and trainers. They carried no weapons and no indication that they belonged to the army.

Brown Cap smiled and said, "Good afternoon, Lady Clair," and I remembered he spoke quite good English, which would be a help. "We come take you Angel Fall. Minister Dram orders. You ready?"

I nodded and picked up the overnight bag, and handed it to Brown Cap who passed it on to the other one. I was blowed if I was going to carry it. We went through the door, Brown Cap first, then me then the other one.

There was another man in the passageway, presumably the guard that Bim had told me was always there, and Brown Cap spoke to him in Abacadian. I think he told him he could go home now.

We went down the main staircase and through the front door. A car was in the drive and I recognised it as the same car which had brought me there from Lake Lucinda. It was nice to be outside, even for the short walk from the front door to the car.

My overnight bag was put into the boot and I was told to climb into the back. A man got in either side of me and Brown Cap climbed into the passenger seat.

On an impulse I touched him on the shoulder and said,

"Why don't you come and sit in the back, next to me. We could talk on the way. It will pass the time. Please."

He shrugged and said why not, and swapped seats with one of the guards, and we set off on our journey to Angel Falls.

I asked him what his name was and he told me it was Flakey. I asked him where he came from and he told me a story about growing up on a farm in Effghania, with three brothers and three sisters, and it sounded familiar. Then he told me that one day some soldiers arrived and raped all his sisters and his mother and took him and his brothers away and made them join the army. The brothers were separated but he occasionally saw them and they were all fine. He never saw his mother or his sisters again, but believed they worked as prostitutes, though maybe his mother was a cook somewhere. He wasn't sure.

He enjoyed the army and was quite good at it, he told me, and it wasn't long until he was promoted to become a sergeant. He was good at that also and often did special duties for Bim Dram. One of the duties was to kidnap Clair from Lake Lucinda.

"He give us order that no one killed, Lady, and you not touched in any way. He make that point number of times."

He grinned.

"That such an easy job, Lady," he continued. "Only strange thing your sisters there, with two men," and he told me how they had captured Alice and Pauline and then the two men.

"It like taking rubber bone from puppy," he said. "Easy Lady," and he laughed.

"How were my sisters?" I asked him, deciding not to tell him that they were my daughters.

"They pretty like you, Lady, but not happy we take you away in car. Men not happy also," and he laughed. "I think them sisters lovers."

I wondered who the men were. Had they come from England with the girls or had they met them here in Abacadia.

"Were the men from Abacadia?" I asked him, but he shook his head.

236

"I think they English, Lady," and I wondered again who they were.

"Please don't call me Lady," I asked him. "My name is Clair. Please call me Clair and I will call you Flakey," and he laughed but, after some embarrassment, agreed.

He must be one of Moldie's brothers, I reckoned. It was too much of a coincidence that his story was the same as Moldie's. Should I tell him that I knew Moldie? Probably not, at least for the time being.

I wondered if I could get some more information from him about his and Moldie's brothers and sisters and maybe also his mother.

"That was a terrible story you told me about being kidnapped from your family home when you were younger," I said. "How often do you get to see your brothers?"

"Oh, only occasion," he said. "Last time saw littlest brother two months in Snuka. He well. Him sergeant like me. Different unit though. Good man. Get on well."

"Why do you think your mother is working as a cook?" I asked him.

"I heard somewhere," he replied, thinking. "Can't remember when. Someone tell me she work for top restaurant. Her good cook. I know. I eat her food as child. Always nice."

"Have you never tried to find her?"

It seemed odd to me that he wouldn't have tried.

He shrugged.

"Maybe one day."

"Does it bother you that all your sisters are working as prostitutes?"

He shrugged again.

"It job that women do. Well paid. Easy work. Stay in bed all day, lie on back," and he laughed.

I didn't think it was so funny. Not after what I had been up to for the past few weeks.

After a four hour drive, which seemed to pass surprisingly quickly due to my talks with Flakey, we arrived at Angel's Hair

Falls and the men immediately set up three tents. Two were close together, but the other was a short distance away. I would sleep in that one tonight on my own, but with Bim the following night.

Flakey produced a length of thin but strong looking chain and, with an apologetic shrug, fastened one end to my ankle. The other end was fastened to a stake which was hammered into the ground.

The chain was thin, not heavy, and caused me little discomfort, but Flakey still apologised, and explained how they were orders and if he let me escape then he would possibly be shot, or, at the very least, put into jail and kicked out of the army.

One of the guards lit a fire and made some tea and heated up some food which they had brought with them, a rich stew, which was nice and I told them so.

One of the guards grinned when Flakey translated what I had said.

"He made stew," he told me. "His name Duck, and he do all cooking and he pleased you enjoy," and Duck grinned some more when I smiled at him.

So far things were going well.

We chatted for a few minutes about Abacadian food, which, they told me, was usually spicier than the stew Duck had made for us, then I asked Flakey if I could visit the falls for a swim.

"Yes, Clair," he said, "But two of us with you all time. Sorry."

They removed the chain from my ankle and I went into the tent to change into the swimming costume. It was bright red, one piece, and fitted nicely. It showed off my figure and the men all grinned when I came out. I put on the trainers, picked up the towel and headed for the falls, and all four of them followed me.

"I thought just two of you were coming with me," I said, but Flakey just grinned.

"You just want to stare at me in my swimming costume," I teased them and they grinned some more.

We arrived at the Angel's puddle, and it was just as beautiful as I remembered. I took off the trainers.

"Are any of you coming in with me?" but none of them could swim.

I dived in and swam for half an hour, remembering the last time I had visited. I remembered how Moldie had said we had left a bottle of Cadian wine where we had the picnic and checked but it was gone and I wondered if Alice and Pauline had been there and found it.

It was now getting dark, so I climbed out, dried myself on the big fluffy towel I had brought with me, and we walked back to the tents. I changed back into my clothes, the chain was put back onto my ankle, with a shrug from Flakey, and some more food was produced. After we had eaten, Flakey brought out a bottle of something, and five small glasses and poured some into each. The drink tasted like coconut flavoured rum and was very strong. It took a bit of getting used to but I drank it at the same rate as the men, which impressed them.

One of the soldiers, his name was Pot, produced a home-made reed flute and started to play some Abacadian tunes, and the others started to sing along. They all knew the words. The tunes were upbeat and I hummed along. Then, on an impulse, I stood up and started to dance, and the others laughed and clapped along, then Flakey got up and danced with me and for the next hour or so they took it in turns to dance with me and there was much, much laughter and we had a wonderful time.

Flakey told me the names of the others and I tried to talk to them in Abacadian, which produced much laughter as Flakey told me what I had actually said. Sometimes I did it on purpose, just to make them laugh.

Eventually it was bedtime, and I kissed all the men lightly on their cheeks, which made them giggle.

"One of us has to stay awake all night," Flakey told me, "So you don't need to worry about wild animals."

Bim hadn't supplied me with a nightie or pyjamas, so I slept in the jumper and pants. I had been provided with a blow up double mattress and a duvet and a pillow. All that drink made me sleep well and I woke up with quite a hangover, but a short swim in the puddle helped to wake me up and clear my head.

Breakfast consisted of maize cereal and coconut juice, then we went for a walk in the local woods. The chain was still around one of my ankles and the other end was held by one of the guards.

Flakey apologised about that but he needn't have bothered. I knew he was just following orders.

Thoughts of trying to escape did cross my mind, but I reckoned it would be almost impossible. Flakey and the guards were being very thorough, and even if I did get away from them and run, I would have very little start before they discovered me gone and would surely soon catch up with me.

I was slowly getting Bim Dram's trust, and an attempt at escape would only make him angry.

And I knew that as soon as I got back to his home in Snuka there would be an attempt at rescue from Alice and Pauline and Moldie, so I contented myself on enjoying the beautiful countryside and the freedom to stretch my legs after being cooped up in Bim's bedroom for the past couple of weeks.

Bim turned up as Flakey was considering lunch, driving himself in a posh new Range Rover. He seemed genuinely very pleased to see me, smiling with a big broad grin.

"Hello Clair," he said, "Are you enjoying yourself?"

I thought to myself 'Should I put my arms around his neck and give him a big kiss in front of his men?' but then decided I shouldn't as it would really embarrass him so I did it anyway and it did embarrass him and I turned to see the men grinning but they looked serious when Bim glared at them. I just smiled sweetly and said,

"I've missed you."

He smiled again. He really did care for me, probably actually did love me. Hmmm.

"Why don't you go and put on your swimming costume," he suggested, whilst I have a quick word with Flakey."

I pointed at the chain, and he told Flakey to take it off.

"I'm sorry about that," he said.

Five minutes later and the two of us were walking towards the Falls together, me in my costume and he in his swimming trunks. As soon as we were out of sight of the guards, he held my hand and said,

"That was very naughty of you, Clair, to kiss me in front of the others like that. Were you trying to embarrass me?"

"As if," I said smiling up at him.

We turned the corner and arrived at the Angel's Hair Falls.

"Isn't it just the most beautiful place in Abacadia?" he said, "Possibly the whole world."

I nodded.

"It is the most wonderful place I have ever been to," I agreed with him. "Everything is just perfect here."

We dived in and swam together. Bim wasn't such a good swimmer, and when I splashed him and swam away, he couldn't catch me. I could see he was starting to get annoyed, the last thing I wanted, so I let him grab me, and we kissed then swam back to the side and climbed out. We dried ourselves, then he undressed me and himself and we made love in exactly the same place the Moldie had made love to me a few weeks previously. I smiled at the memory and Bim thought I was smiling at him, and he smiled back.

We got dressed into our costumes again and wandered back to the tents, Bim only letting go of my hand as we reached the final turn. Duck had produced another wonderful stew, and the six of us sat around the campfire and ate. Bim had brought a case of local beer with him and we drank one each. I don't normally drink beer, preferring wine, but I enjoyed that one.

After lunch, Bim and I retired to our tent for a snooze then went for a walk together, before returning for dinner. Another stew.

I wondered if I dare tell Bim about the previous evening, and the music and the dancing. Would the troops get into trouble? Bim was in a very good mood, slightly drunk I thought, but very chilled out so I said, "Did I see a flute earlier. Do one of you play?" and Bim said,

"That's right. Pot plays. I've heard you before. Come on Pot, let's have some music," and Pot started to play the tunes from the previous evening and I grabbed Bim's hand and pulled him up and I said, "You're a good dancer, Bim, dance with me and show these common soldiers how to really dance," and we danced together and the others clapped and cheered and everyone relaxed.

We went for another swim later, in the dark, using a torch to find our way and again I remembered Moldie and wondered where they were and what they were up to. Although I actually was having a good time with Bim and he was treating me perfectly, I still wanted to escape and be with my family and get home to Hamilton Hall.

'It will happen soon,' I kept telling myself.

The next morning, lying in bed in Bim's arms, I told him what a wonderful time I was having and could we stay a bit longer but he shook his head.

"I'm sorry Clair, but I have to get back to Snuka this afternoon."

"Couldn't I stay here on my own, I mean, with the guards, of course, just for a bit longer," but again he shook his head.

"Sorry, Clair, no."

"Bim, please don't take me back to that dreary bedroom," I said, and immediately regretted saying that. Escape plans from the bedroom had been made, I hoped, and I could endure a few more days there if it meant I would be rescued.

He lay in silence for a while, obviously thinking.

"Parliament ends in a few days for a summer break," he eventually said. "I normally spend some of my time at my country home. It's called Heavenly Winds, because it overlooks a large lake and, as you can probably guess, and the cool breeze from the lake makes the place cool and delightful.

"You can stay there, I suppose. Yes, I'll send you there and you can wait for me. You'll enjoy it. There's plenty of rooms and gardens for you to explore and lots of servants to look after you. I'll tell them to treat you like royalty."

After we had made love, of course, and after we had had breakfast, he got on his phone and made some calls and told me that it had all been arranged. Then he talked to Flakey and told him what was happening.

"This is what I have organised," he said to me. "I will drive to Redik after we have had another swim and a quick lunch, then fly by helicopter to Snuka. Flakey and the others will pack up the tents and everything here and then the five of you will drive to my country home. They know where it is, they've been there many times. I've told the staff there to expect you. I'll join you as soon as I can, probably in four or five days. Does that sound like a good plan?"

I smiled at him and said,

"That sounds wonderful Bim. Thank you," and kissed him on the cheek, but underneath I was thinking 'Bugger. Bugger. Bugger. Will I ever be rescued?'

After a last swim and lunch, Bim left, waving and tooting his horn, then the others started to take down the tents. It wouldn't take them long, I could see.

I thought about leaving a message for Alice. If they came here the signs of the tent and the fire would be obvious. I needed a way to let them know where I was going next.

I told Flakey I was going into the adjacent woods for a toilet visit, and he just nodded, and I walked off alone. Since Bim Dram had visited, they hadn't bothered putting the chain back on.

I found a small open space just a few yards away, and left a message on the ground using pebbles and small twigs which I pushed into the earth. If anybody was coming here, it would be in the next day or so, I reckoned, so the message didn't have to last long.

The message I left read 'Gone to country house, C'.

I was hoping Moldie would know where Bim's country house was. If not, then he could surely find out through ODOE.

When everything was packed away into the boot, and the fire put out and everything cleaned up tidily, which impressed me, we all got into the car, with me in the middle at the back again, and set off for Bim Dram's country home, a six hour drive, I was told by Flakey.

After an hour or so, I saw a car driving by in the opposite direction. It was a mucky green colour, similar to hundred's of other cars I had seen in Abacadia, but in this one I was sure I saw two men and two women with long blonde hair. Could it have been Alice and Pauline and the two men they had recruited to help them? I turned my head to watch them disappear.

Bugger.

Chapter 31 - Disappointment

Pauline and I watched Sam, Stu and Moldie drive away down the road. There was no point in us trying to sleep, so we made a cup of tea and sat in the kitchen and talked. We talked about the three men.

"You seem to be getting on very well with Stu," I suggested to Pauline.

"It's not a crime," she answered. "And anyway, you and Sam are just as friendly. What do you reckon, a double wedding?" and I had to laugh.

"A bit early for that," I chuckled. "Though they are both very nice. Sam makes me feel, well, he's, so, you know, competent. When I'm with him, I always feel that everything will be fine, that no harm will ever come to me. Even at Lake Lucinda I knew that I would be okay."

"I feel exactly the same when I'm with Stu. When there's just the two of us, when Sam's not around, he's a lot more chatty and outgoing. I think I'm falling in love with him."

I smiled. "Me too, with Sam. What do you think of Moldie?"

"I'm not sure," Pauline replied. "He also seems very nice. If I didn't know that he is the man who kidnapped mother and pimped her out then I think I could actually quite like him. But he did it, and now I'm not sure what to think."

"How old do you think he is?" I mused.

"Early thirties," suggested Pauline. "He's a lot younger than mother."

"He seems to be madly in love with her," I suggested, "And he has implied that mother is actually very fond of him. Do you think that could be possible?"

"Stranger things have happened. I wonder how they're getting on?"

We were silent for a few seconds as we wondered, then I wondered something else.

"It must feel something like this when men go off to war. They always say the waiting is the worse part."

Less than an hour later, and we heard a car approaching the house. It slowed and through a gap in the curtains, we saw it was Lady Sammy. We watched her pull into the drive and disappear into the garage. We hurried through to the kitchen and through a door and into the garage, and saw Sam and Stu and Moldie climb out. There was no sign of mother.

Both Pauline and I gasped.

"Where's mother," we said in unison.

"She wasn't there," said Sam, and he explained how he had climbed up the ladder and tapped on the window but the curtains were both open and he had shone his torch in but there was no sight or sound of her.

"I thought about cutting the window and climbing in but decided against it. I was certain she wasn't there. We must hope that Flower can find something out tomorrow."

I was so disappointed. It was such a massive let down. I was so certain that she would be rescued but she wasn't. I looked at Pauline and there were tears running down her cheeks, and that set me off and I started crying as well.

Sam and Stu came and cuddled us, and I clung to Sam.

"It's not fair," I said. "It's just not fair. She should be here with us now."

Moldie left early in the morning to catch Flower before she left for work. We never asked him where he met her and he never volunteered to tell us.

We all waited for Moldie to return with news from Flower. It seemed forever but eventually he did but it was early afternoon.

"Flower says she thinks Clair didn't sleep in the room last night. The bed was made up and the curtains were still both open, and there were some shampoo and toothbrush and toothpaste missing from the bathroom.

But, and this is the odd thing, she had laid out some bottles to read the letter J in the bath and the letter F on the floor. Flower put them back on the shelves before she left. It's a mystery to me. Do you know why she left J and F like that?"

We all shook our heads.

"It's definitely a message," Pauline said.

"Let's look at the previous messages," suggested Stu. "Maybe that will give us a clue."

It didn't take long for us to work it out.

"Look," said Stu. "This message on seventh of June. 'Theo, is Jackie still playing whist and are you still taking her to France for your birthday? I miss you all and would love to hear some answers to my questions.'

Jackie was known as Angel because of her lovely hair and the reference to France was the date, the 19th. She would be at Angel's Hair Falls on the 19th. The J and the F must mean Jackie and France and she must have gone with Bim Dram to Angel's Hair Falls."

He looked at us, and we all nodded.

Moldie chuckled.

"So that's how she did it! Do you actually have whist drives in Worcestershire?"

Pauline also chuckled.

"No. That's the clue she gave us to let us know where to look."

Moldie just shook his head.

Sam took charge.

"So what do we do now? Do we drive to the falls or do we wait until she returns?"

"Flower says she may be able to find out a bit more information," said Moldie.

"How?" asked Sam.

"The guard who has been looking after Clair really fancies her. She reckons if she sleeps with him then he'll tell her everything he knows."

Sam and Stu chuckled but Pauline and I shook our heads.

"Bloody men and their sex drive."

"I think," said Moldie, "That I should also be able to find out when Bim Dram is next expected in parliament. If he's there tomorrow, then they'll be back tonight or first thing tomorrow morning."

Sam made a decision.

"If we leave right now for Angel Falls and they leave this evening, then in all likelihood they'll have left before we get there. If they're staying a bit longer, then we can drive down overnight and think about rescuing her tomorrow morning. We'll wait until we hear from Flower and Moldie and then make the final decision. Does everyone agree?"

We all agreed with him.

The next day Moldie disappeared first thing in the morning and returned just after lunch.

"ODOE have told me that Bim Dram is supposed to be in parliament tomorrow but certainly has to be there in the evening because there is an important parliamentary vote which he can't miss. Flower has found out from the, er, well, you know how, that the er, guard has been told to return to duty tomorrow night. So, in all probability, Clair will be back here in Snuka in his bedroom tomorrow night."

"Okay," said Sam, "I think therefore that we

shouldn't got to Angel Falls but wait until she comes back. If we do go there, and attempt a rescue, there will be very little forward planning and guards, maybe 6 again, and a good chance it might go wrong, and that means Bim Dram will be forewarned. The plan to rescue her from the bedroom seems a much better bet to me."

We all agreed with him, and waited for mother's return to Snuka. However, the next day, that plan went up the spout, when Moldie returned at lunch time with another message from Flower.

"She tells me that she has, er, um, communicated with the, er, guard again. He has been told that he won't be needed for night guard duty for a while and can return to his unit."

"So," said Sam, "You're thinking that if he's not there then Clair won't be sleeping in the bedroom?"

Moldie nodded.

"That's what I'm thinking."

"If that's the case, where do you think she might be?"

We all looked at Moldie who shrugged.

"He could have taken her anywhere."

It was back to square one.

Chapter 32 - Heavenly Winds

We drove straight to Heavenly Winds, Bim Dram's country residence, arriving in the early evening. We were driving through thick forest and the first indication that we were anywhere near the place was when we came upon a guard hut and a barrier. The barrier looked somewhat substantial and was about five feet high, and there was a very strong and secure looking fence leading either side of the road. The gate was at the end of about one hundred yards of straight road, presumably so that the guards could see anyone coming in plenty of time to shoot the tyres out, or whatever they were supposed to do.

We drove slowly up to the barrier and stopped. Two guards had appeared at the door of the hut, but they obviously recognised the car as they were very relaxed, but still had dart guns over their shoulders.

Flakey, who was driving, opened the drivers door and got out. The guards grinned.

"Hey, Flakey, our brother, you come for another holiday, you idle lump of hippopotamus dunk."

Flakey grinned back.

"Harbs. You son of a warthog whore, are you still rutting with your mother," and the two guards roared with laughter and they all high-fived each other.

"Who have you got here," asked Harbs, peering at me as I climbed out of the car to stretch my legs. The three in the back of the car were also climbing out, and the friendly insults continued.

I've always thought blokes were strange that way. The friendlier they got towards somebody, the more they insulted them. And ruder.

'This is my best mate in the whole world. His name's Dave. He's a right fucking wanker!'

Blokes. A strange breed of creatures.

"This is Lady Clair Hamilton," said Flakey. "Lady Clair is a very good friend of our lordship Bim."

And everyone laughed again. Very good friend obviously meant, in their world, lover. I smiled. What else could I do? Actually, I thought to myself, there was something I could do. In my slowly improving Abacadian I think I then said,

"Flakey speaks like a goat and sleeps with a cow."

Everyone looked at me in astonishment so I made a rude sign. It was something I had seen many Abacadians do and involved both hands and my mouth, and I pointed at Flakey.

This was too much for all six of them, and they actually collapsed with laughter. Their legs gave way and they held onto the car or the barrier or even rolled on the ground, hooting and shouting with a sound that sounded like agony. Their hands slapped the earth and they were so helpless with mirth that I considered jumping into the drivers seat and driving away, but Flakey had the car keys in his hand, otherwise I might have.

I watched on in amazement. These men were handpicked by Bim, I assumed, and would surely be considered the best of the best, but here they were, made utterly helpless by a few words and actions from a middle aged English lady. Weird.

They slowly recovered so I said, I think,

"Harbs, how is your trouser snake," and that set them off again, and one of the men who had accompanied me to Angel's Hair Falls was actually physically sick with laughter. I think another wet himself. If Bim Dram had seen them, they would all have been sacked on the spot.

Eventually, they recovered, all of them with tears trickling down their cheeks, and one by one came and high fived me. I had made some friends, and I needed all the friends I could find.

We all climbed back into the car, the barrier was lifted and we carried on along the road to Bim Dram's country residence.

"How far does the fence go either side of that barrier?" I asked Flakey, who looked at me suspiciously, then shrugged and said,

"Not far, just few yards. Why?"

"Just looking for a way to escape Flakey," and he chuckled.

"You quite a lady, Clair," he said. "You make us all laugh by barrier. Say Harbs had worm in pants very funny," and he laughed again.

"I thought I had said snake in pants," I told him and he laughed again, almost losing control of the car. He told the others what I had said and they laughed as well.

"You very funny lady."

My first impression of Bim's land was one of simple but expensive. The drive from the barrier was about a mile long through thick jungle, curving slightly uphill. We rounded a slight bend and I had my first glimpse of the house. It was, to my utter amazement, thatched. To be honest, I really didn't expect to see a thatched building of any kind in Abacadia, but here was one. Right in front of my eyes.

Even odder, it was black and white. The walls were painted white, and all the beams, real or false, I wasn't sure at that moment, were painted black. It had four chimney pots with smoke coming out of two of them, and fancy Georgian style window frames.

It looked like it had been transferred brick by brick and beam by beam directly from Stratford upon Avon.

Flakey drove the car to the front door, where I was met by the head butler, who bowed to me and introduced himself as Jeeves. He was a tall man, well over six feet, strongly built, clean shaven, of course, and he wore a black bowler hat, a black tie, a black suit and black, immaculately polished shoes.

"I chose the name after my favourite series of books," he told me when I asked him.

He showed me around the house, which was very impressive.

"Politician Bim bought it three years ago and has made many alterations," Jeeves explained, in perfect English, as he took me to each of the sixteen rooms and showed me the bedroom where I would sleep, on my own to start with but with Bim Dram when he turned up. Once again it had a huge double four poster bed and an en-suite luxury bathroom, but the stand out feature was a huge floor to ceiling window.

I stood by the window and looked out. A lake lapped almost up to the house and I was looking right over it. I saw thousands of water birds, and, I thought, some hippopotami. I spotted a couple of boats tied up to a small jetty nearby. In the distance beyond the lake, which was much larger than Lake Lucinda, were hills and woodlands. It was a truly spectacular view.

Jeeves showed me how the windows opened out onto a wide balcony, with tables and chairs and I imagined having meals there.

"The windows will be locked at night," he said, almost apologetically.

He opened a couple of the fitted cupboards, and I found them full of ladies clothes. They were of good quality and of many colours, and looked to me like clothes chosen by a man. I sighed, but at least Bim was trying to please me.

Then I had a thought. When did they have time to get all these clothes for me? Bim only told me that morning that I would be coming here. Or had he bought the clothes earlier in anticipation of bringing me here. I decided to ask Jeeves.

"Jeeves," I asked, "How long have you known that I would be arriving here today?"

"Politician Bim told us about two weeks ago," he said. "Why?"

"It must have taken you ages to buy all these lovely clothes for me."

He chuckled.

"I didn't buy those Lady Clair," he said. "I think one of his staff from his Snuka home did that. Do you like them?"

"Was the member of staff a man?"

"Well, yes, I believe, actually, it was a man. How can you tell?"

"Believe me, Jeeves, I know. A woman would have chosen differently, but to answer your question, they look fine, thank you," and he smiled.

So, I thought, Bim had known for ages that he would be bringing me here today, like he had known beforehand that I would be kidnapped and taken to his house in Snuka. His little charade this morning in the tent was just that, play acting. The bugger. I wondered why he did it. Probably so that I couldn't plan anything for the future, to keep me on my toes.

Then I wondered what he had planned for me next. He said we would be here for two weeks. Was he telling the truth about that? I metaphorically shrugged. I'd soon find out.

Jeeves then showed me around the grounds and out buildings. These included a kidney shaped swimming pool, a tennis court, servant's quarters and stables, and I counted a number of horses and ponies. I looked forward to riding once again. It had been a while since I last rode.

Flakey and the other guards followed at a discreet distance and I realised that although this was a lovely place, it was still a prison for me and this was confirmed by the fact that there were half a dozen kennels filled with half a dozen large and very ferocious looking dogs.

"They are let out at night to help guard the grounds," said Jeeves. "They are trained to bite people."

He raised an eyebrow at me, and said, "Please don't get bitten, Lady Clair."

I looked at the dogs and they stared back at me, unblinking. They were huge, with large mouths and teeth and I agreed with him. I didn't want to be bitten by them. I would stay indoors at night.

"How far away is the nearest town," I asked Jeeves.

He raised his eyebrows again.

"It's about twenty miles, Lady Clair," he said, "And there is only one road away from the house, and that road has a permanently manned guard house, which you drove through earlier. Otherwise the house is surrounded by almost impenetrable jungle."

He was giving me a not so subtle hint that it would be pointless for me to try and escape.

I wandered over to the stables and had a closer look at the horses and ponies.

"Can I go out pony riding Jeeves?"

He nodded.

"Of course, my Lady, but unfortunately somebody must always be with you. There are various trails cut through the jungle, and the one down alongside the lake is particularly delightful. I thoroughly recommend it."

We walked back into the house and Jeeves informed me that dinner would be served in exactly one hour, and would I like to bathe and get changed?

So I bathed and got changed and tried on four of Bim's dresses before I found one that wasn't garish and wandered down to the dining room. The table was huge and could sit about twenty people and today it was set for just one. I sat and Jeeves served me my five course dinner, full of all my favourite foods, and a bottle of my favourite Cadian wine. Everything about it was perfect, even the portions, which were on the small size but exactly right for me, except for the fact that I was on my own. It was so weird and I decided that until Bim arrived, I would not eat there again. I would find somewhere else to eat, maybe my room, on the balcony, overlooking the lake. Anywhere but in this dining room.

Bim phoned just as I was finishing the real coffee and after Jeeves had spoken to him, he passed the phone to me. He asked me if I had settled in, and what I thought of his house, and if I was being looked after, and had I any plans for tomorrow. I told him I would really like to go pony trekking and he said that would be fine and the stable lad, Gort, would show me some of the trails though unfortunately two of the guards would have to go with me.

"I will probably be with you in about four or five days," he told me. "I will count the days and hours."

So for the next few days I had a wonderful time. I swam regularly, I watched the sun set over the lake, which was fantastic, and played tennis with one of the guards. Gort took me for a horse ride each afternoon, and as Jeeves said, the ride beside the lake was particularly special.

It had been a while since I had been on a horse, but riding a horse was like riding a bicycle. You never forget how, and I soon got in the rhythm. I was riding a small placid pony called Bundy, and Gort and two guards were on larger horses. They all rode well.

"Part of army training," explained Flakey.

The trails were cut straight from the jungle, but had been planned with care and thought, winding up and around hills so that suddenly there were spectacular views over the surrounding countryside, which, as far as I could see, was just jungle, with a river in the distance and a couple of small lakes.

We saw many animals on the rides, which initially surprised me, but when I thought about it, I realised it was wild, wild land with very few people and of course there would be animals about.

There was a troop of monkeys, about the size of small children, but with tails which seemed to be twice as long as their bodies, who screamed abuse at us when they saw us riding by and even threw coconuts at us but stopped when they saw us riding away.

There were grey squirrels, which looked like those I knew in the grounds of Hamilton Hall, but were larger and didn't have such bushy tails.

I saw a small porcupine, with white tips to it's quills and a few hares in the distance. I realised that many of the animals were similar, if not identical, to many animals we had in England, and probably other parts of the world. I wondered what the local equivalent to the fox was, and Flakey told me it was a type of jackal, which looked like a smaller and slimmer wolf, and were always seen in pairs.

"Do they attack humans?" I asked Flakey, but he shook his head.

"Never heard of it, them scared of people."

We saw a small herd of small deer, brown with white speckles and very timid, but I also saw goats and sheep and some domesticated water buffalo.

"Are there any dangerous animals?"

"Leopards, of course, but they don't cause trouble. Occasionally take goat or lamb but they not bother us. They see and hear us long time before we see them and go into hiding. Don't worry about them."

"It's actually quite safe then?" and Flakey agreed.

There were plenty of birds including pelicans and herons and storks and parrots and lots of colourful pigeons. I saw something that looked like a small eagle or maybe it was a falcon or a buzzard, and a kingfisher that looked like a robin but with a blue chest.

But it was the ride down by the main lake that was the best. We rode initially along a ridge overlooking the lake, then down to the lakeside, where we had a picnic that Jeeves had packed for us. I sat and stared at the small boats and my mind flitted from the beauty of the scene to the thought of using the boats for escape.

"What's at the bottom of the lake?" I asked, and Flakey looked confused.

"Mud?"

I laughed.

"No, I mean, is there a stream or a river where the water flows away?"

He pointed to the far distance.

"Right over there, Lady, small dam and water flows in stream. Small stream, I jump over it. You jump over it, easily.

There went my idea of sailing across the lake and carrying on down a river to freedom.

"Could I go for a sail in one of the boats?" I asked Flakey, and he shrugged.

"I ask for you," and he asked and I could and I did.

It was a four man yacht, with two crew and me and one of the guards who knew a bit about sailing, which was good because I knew nothing, but it wasn't difficult and it was very pleasant out on the lake.

This is a lovely place to come for a holiday, I decided, but I might get bored if I lived here all the time, not being allowed to leave.

Twice I saw a helicopter land in an open area one hundred yards or so away from the house, but I didn't see anyone get in or out.

That made me think again about Bim Dram's proposal of living with him for one year for one million dollars. He did have a lot to offer, and he was very good looking, and powerful, but I longed for Hamilton Hall.

And he did have a very small penis.

At night though I did get lonely. My mind wandered to Moldie and my children and I lay awake thinking of them and Hamilton Hall. When Bim arrived I knew my sleep would improve. I always slept better with a man beside me, as long as he didn't snore.

I started to spend time each day in the kitchen. There were three women working there. The youngest, called Parrot, was in charge and had been trained at one of the top hotels in Snuka before Bim Dram took her to work here at Heavenly Winds. She was rather pretty, which I assumed was one of the reasons Bim chose her, but rather bossy I thought. I didn't like her very much.

The other two ladies were more elderly, more my age, and were short and chubby, with happy faces that were always smiling. They were called Waving Grass and Sid, strange names, oh well, and I liked them both immediately. All three had a room each in the servants quarters. They returned to Snuka two days a week each, to see their families and buy provisions for the house.

I like cooking. I always have done and I hadn't cooked for weeks now. First Moldie then Bim had provided all my meals and I asked Parrot if I could help in the kitchen and she agreed, after looking at Flakey, who nodded, but I don't think she was really happy about the idea.

So I spent a couple of hours everyday in the kitchen, helping to prepare food, doing exactly as Parrot told me, and really enjoying myself. Chatting to the others really improved my Abacadian and I was getting quite fluent. I told them I was staying as a guest of Bim Dram, we were old friends, and was waiting for him to arrive for the parliamentary break.

It came as a bit of a shock to me when, on the third day, Waving Grass and I were in the kitchen alone, preparing lunch. The other two had gone to the garden to pick some fresh herbs. Waving Grass called me over to show me how to prepare some peppers . I was leaning close to her when she said, in perfect English, "I work for ODOE. I am a friend of Flower and Moldie. Tomorrow I will visit Moldie. Do you have a message for him?"

I was dumbfounded but thinking about it later, I shouldn't have been. ODOE had spies and employees everywhere, it seemed. I needed to think fast.

"Can you take a written message?"

"I'm not supposed to but just this once, yes, I think I can."

"I'll write one out and give it to you tomorrow."

"Leave it under the mixed spice jar this evening. That won't be used."

She carried on explaining about preparing the peppers in Abacadian and just at that moment Parrot and Sid reappeared.

"In England we chop them this way," I said, in Abacadian, I think, "But I think your way of preparing peppers is better."

When I left the kitchen a few minutes later, I walked up to my room and thought about what sort of message I could send. I didn't know then how often Waving Grass would return home, so I asked Jeeves who told me once a week for two days. This time, then, would be the only time I could send a message before Bim Dram arrived to stay for his summer parliamentary break.

Then I realised that Moldie and the others had actually worked out and knew that I was staying at Bim's country estate. How had they done that? The more I leant about ODOE the more impressed I became.

I asked Jeeves if I could have the use of a paper and a pen, and he looked at me suspiciously.

"I am a bit bored without Bim here. Before I met Bim, I was writing a story about my stay in Abacadia," I told him, "And thought I might carry on with it. It would help me get through the evenings, and help me sleep at night. I would let Bim read everything, of course," and Jeeves relented and gave me a children's exercise book and a pencil.

I sat down and carefully ripped out the middle sheet of paper from the book and composed a letter to Moldie and Alice and Pauline. I told them I was well and being properly looked after. I told them where my bedroom was and everything about the house and gardens that I had learnt. I told them about the security measures Bim had installed and Jeeves had told me.

I told them about the things I got up to, tennis, swimming, horse riding, cooking, but I made no mention of Waving Grass. They would know about her, obviously, and mentioning her name could put her in danger.

I told them that I was on my own at the moment but that Bim Dram would be arriving to join me in two or three days. Then I told them about ideas I had had to escape.

By car - Either steal a car and drive straight through the barrier, but I had been told it was very sturdy, and would stop a normal car or hide in a car, in the boot or back foot well, but had been told that every car was examined by the guards at the barrier, and even more thoroughly now I was there. Bim was still worried, it seemed, about me trying to escape.

By horse - Six horses in the stables, would be easy to ride away on one, but always guards with me and they were competent riders, but not as good as me. Could probably leap the barrier, maybe, though it would be touch and go. I wasn't sure how good they were at leaping.

There were various trails around the grounds but even at their furthest extremities from the house, I wasn't sure how close one was to freedom. Maybe Moldie could find out. Google Earth, possibly, I thought.

By boat - There were a number of boats on the lake, some motor some sail. It may be possible to steal one and travel to the other side of the lake, but what then? I told them about the dam and the small stream. Would be away from the house but would then need a plan from the lake.

By helicopter - I had seen it land twice. Wasn't sure of the make but not large, maybe a four seater. I was sure ODOE could find out the make and find someone who could fly one.

By foot - The jungle looks incredibly thick, almost impenetrable, but there must be a path or trail through them somewhere, used by thieves and robbers or even animal trails. But could we find them?

I couldn't get all this on one piece of paper so had to carefully remove the new inside page, and gently folded the staples back down so it wasn't obvious the pages had been removed.

I told them that I expected Bim to join me in three or four days and that he intended to stay at Heavenly Winds for almost two weeks. I finished the letter by repeating that I was well and healthy, and told them how much I missed them all and I was looking forward to be rescued. I hoped they were all well, and wished them all my love.

I re-read the letter, twice, and I couldn't think of anything else to add.

I carefully folded the letter and hid it down the side of my knickers, then started writing the story of my time in Abacadia ever since I had been captured by Bim. Jeeves would inevitably tell him about my request for the notebook and pencil and he would expect me to write something, so I wrote. I made sure I didn't mention Bim's name, and didn't write anything too controversial. I didn't want to upset him when he read my notes, as I knew he would.

I remembered the notes I had written in the flat in Redik and wondered what had happened to them. Did Moldie have them with him? I was sure he would keep them safe for me.

Later that afternoon, I was back in the kitchen, and, as usual, asking Parrot, the head of the kitchens, about the meal they were preparing that evening. It was a dish of steamed rice with curried prawns and lentils, but the curry was very different from anything I had ever tasted before, and I was genuinely intrigued. My mind wondered if I could get some of these recipes together and produce an Abacadian cookbook. It was a thought.

I caught Waving Grass's eye and looked down at my hand, and she gave a slight nod. At the first opportunity, I walked over to her to see how she was preparing the prawns, and deliberately mispronounced the Abacadian word for prawn, deliberately using the word for worm instead, much to the amusement of the others. Waving Grass laughed and 'accidentally' bumped against me. Our hands touched and she took the letter and pushed it into a pocket in her dress, and we carried on as if nothing had happened. The others didn't suspect a thing, and I breathed a sigh of relief and continued helping with the meal.

Chapter 33 - Scouting

The only topic of conversation was, 'What could have happened to mother?'

We talked and talked and came up with a number of theories, all of them just theories, with no evidence to back them up.

The worst, worst case was that she could be dead. Either Bim Dram murdered her, or she was killed trying to escape, but those theories were too horrible to contemplate so we ignored them.

Then we thought that maybe Bim Dram had got bored with mother, and had sold her on to somebody else, but we didn't really believe that. He seemed to be genuinely fond of her, infatuated, possibly he even loved her, and mother was too clever to allow herself to be sold on to somebody else who might not treat her so well.

Then the two of them might have gone to another holiday destination, like Lake Lucinda, for instance.

"There are dozens of lovely spots in Abacadia," explained Moldie, "For them to visit."

If that was the case, then all we could do was wait until they returned to Snuka. It would be almost impossible to find out where they had gone.

However, the most likely scenario, we thought, was that Bim would have taken her to his country home.

"Next week parliament goes into recess for a couple of weeks," explained Moldie, "A sort of early summer holiday for the poor hardworking overpaid bureaucrats to recharge their batteries. Bim often goes there during recesses. If I was a betting man, which I'm not, I would bet on Clair being there."

"Where is this country residence?" asked Sam, and

Moldie got out a map of Abacadia, and showed us.

"It's about eighty miles from here," said Moldie, "Heading southeast from Snuka. The place is called Heavenly Winds, because it overlooks a large lake, and the cool winds from the lake make the climate almost perfect. Otherwise it is surrounded by dense jungle, almost impenetrable, I have heard. There is just one road into the place, and there is a constant armed guard patrol at the border of his property. Here, let me show you some photographs."

He got out his laptop, and we studied photographs of Heavenly Winds. We were amazed. It was black and white with a thatched roof and looked like something straight out of Stratford upon Avon.

"Don't let appearances fool you," warned Moldie. "It is well guarded with proper security measures. I know someone who knows someone who knows someone else who did the security for him. It won't be as easy to rescue her from there as it may be from his Snuka home on Victoria Avenue."

"Could we drive up and have a look?" asked Pauline, but Moldie shook his head.

"Too risky at the moment," he said. "I'm pretty sure ODOE has someone working there. Let me see if I can find out about that and make contact first," and Sam nodded.

"Meanwhile," he said, "Let's find out all we can about Heavenly Winds. Do you have Google Earth on this laptop, Moldie?"

We studied the images on Google Earth.

"What's this?" asked Sam, pointing to an open area, a clearing in the jungle it looked like, about one hundred yards from the house, with a path connecting.

"Helicopter landing area," said Moldie, and Sam and Stu perked up. They could both fly a number of types of helicopters.

"Do you know what type of helicopter he has?" asked Stu, but Moldie had no idea.

"I'll try and find out," he said.

I asked a question.

"There seem to be a number of trails through his land," I suggested, pointing. "What are they for?"

"Bim loves to go horse riding, so he had these trails cut out of the virgin jungle, I believe," answered Moldie. "He has stables for about six or seven horses."

"Mother loves horse riding," I said, "And she's quite good at it."

"Worth keeping in mind when we're planning a rescue," said Sam.

"If she's there," said Pauline, with a shrug. "If she's there."

Next day Moldie disappeared to wherever he disappeared to and returned later that afternoon.

"I have news," he said. "There is a young lady working in the kitchens at Heavenly Winds. Her name is Lufu, but, for some odd reason, she prefers to be called Waving Grass. "

He shrugged his shoulders as if to say he couldn't possibly understand why somebody would rather be called Waving Grass rather than Lufu.

"She reports occasionally to ODOE, often when she visits her family here in Snuka, and she should be visiting soon. I have arranged to meet her."

"Could we phone?" asked Sam, impatient at the wait, but Moldie shook his head.

"There is no mobile signal there. Bim does all his correspondence via satellite phone. You'll just have to be patient, I'm afraid."

So we remained patient, but carried on with some sight seeing, to stay in character, just in case anyone official was watching us, though we didn't think anyone was.

Two days later Moldie returned from wherever he went to say,

"ODOE has received a message from Waving Grass." he told us. "She is definitely working in the kitchen of Heavenly Winds, and she has confirmed that Clair is at the home. Actually, that's not exactly true. The message is four days old, and the staff at Heavenly Winds were told to prepare for the visit of a lady, who would be arriving in a couple of days and staying for about two weeks. She was to be treated like royalty they were told. Bim Dram is not there. Waving Grass hasn't seen him for quite a few weeks."

"It must be mother," said Pauline. "Who else could it be?" and we all agreed.

"Right," said Sam, in a very business-like fashion. It excited me when he became business-like and I looked at him proudly. He must have sensed I was looking at him because he turned to me and asked me what I was grinning at, and then grinned himself.

"We'll rescue the beautiful princess from the hands of the wicked ogre," he said, "Don't worry," and I wasn't worried and knew she would soon be rescued.

"The helicopter, by the way," added Moldie, "Is a Bell 407," and both Sam and Stu whistled.

"Six seater," said Stu. "We can both fly those. Pretty straight forward. And a six seater. We could all fit into a Bell 407," and the two of them looked at each other.

"Is it there at the moment?" but no one knew.

"I'll try and find out from ODOE," said Moldie, "But unlikely, I fear."

We started making some plans on how to rescue mother, and eventually decided we would drive to the local area, and drop Sam and Stu somewhere nearby so they could have a scout around. The other three would drive to one of the many local lakes and pretend to do some bird watching and have a picnic.

266

"Moldie, can you tell us more about the security measures in place?" and Moldie told us all he could remember. In the gardens were movement sensitive cameras and lights, bolts and alarms on all the windows and doors, and large vicious dogs roaming the area at night.

"Four permanent guards, with dart guns," I think he said.

"What about the drive?"

Moldie screwed up this face while he tried to remember what he had heard.

"Two permanent guards by the barrier, and permanent security lights, I think. Then a couple of cameras between there and the house, I seem to recall, but to be honest, I'm not entirely sure about that."

"Okay," said Sam, "Thanks."

The next day we all dressed up as tourists, again, and set off for Heavenly Winds, which we reckoned should take us about two hours driving. We found a place where we could drop off the boys. An old track, now overgrown, led off into the jungle, but there was plenty of room to reverse in, ready for a quick getaway.

The spot was not too far away from the house, but not too close either. About three miles away, normally less than half an hour jog trot for Sam and Stu, but with the thick jungle, it would take them a lot longer.

We dropped them off mid morning, with the intention of picking them up an hour before dark that evening, at about seven o'clock. It they weren't there, then we would come back at this time, eleven o'clock, the next morning and then seven in the evening again. If they weren't there then, we would wait from them at the house in Snuka.

"Can't you use the walkie-talkie to let us know?" I

asked, but Sam shook his head.

"We will only use the walkie-talkies as a last resort. You never know who might be monitoring. And anyway, the range is great and it might not reach. But don't worry," he said, kissing me. "We'll see you this evening."

Sam and Stu watched us drive away then trotted along the road towards the house. They were in disguise. Even though it was a hot day, they wore thin balaclavas which hid almost all their faces and sun glasses. They had darkened their faces so they looked more like the locals.

They knew no one was expecting them or any trouble so they went at a good pace, trusting their ears and instinct to warn them of any approaching vehicles. Only one vehicle passed by, heading away from the house, and they hid in the jungle until it was gone. It was a small locally made car they didn't recognise, with three occupants, a man driving and two women. Servants they reckoned, probably going to a nearby town or village to buy supplies.

They had pretty good idea when they would be nearing the barrier, so, after a few minutes, they proceeded with much more caution. Around a bend they saw the barrier, a hundred yards or so ahead. There seemed to be no one there but then they saw movement in the hut, and one of the guards came out for a pee. He looked casually around but Sam and Stu were well hidden.

They examined the barrier carefully through their binoculars, always making sure the lenses were in shadow so as not to give away their presence through a reflected sun beam.

"The barrier seems rather stout," said Stu, gloomily. "I'm not sure our car would be able to crash through it. We may end up with a smashed and useless Lady Sammy if we tried that," and Sam agreed.

"I wonder what the control is to open it," wondered Stu. "Probably a button in the hut, though it might need a key. I also wonder how far the fences proceed either side."

A high fence was fastened to each end of the barrier and it

disappeared into the jungle. Moldie hadn't mentioned the fences and there had been no indication in the plans and photo's they had seen.

They did know from the plans, however, that the road turned to the right a few yards past the barrier and so they headed off into the jungle to the right also. They soon realised it would be hard work. The trees grew close together and in between were many other plants, including roots and vines and giant ferns and brambles. Sam and Stu had to fight their way for almost every inch of progress.

There were a couple of open spaces, but they were swamps, and impossible to wade through. Sam tried. Stu held his hand whilst he gingerly stepped forward into the water, but his foot just kept going down and Stu had to haul him out. They both swore.

Within a few minutes they were sweating profusely, and they had only progressed about two hundred yards. They still had over a mile to go.

They sat on a fallen tree trunk and had a drink of water and talked.

"This," said Sam, "Is a bit of a problem."

Stu agreed.

"A bit. It's going to take us hours to get there at this rate, and then what?"

"I think we need to get past the barrier and then double back onto the road," said Sam. "Come on, let's push on a bit further. Maybe the jungle will thin out as we go uphill."

A few minutes later and they came to the fence. The ground had been cleared either side of it for about ten yards, but they could see no cameras looking their way.

"Does this fence go all around the house," wondered Sam.

"It would have to be a very long fence," said Stu. "Four or five miles, at a guess, and through this jungle, up and down hills. Unlikely, I would have thought. Let's go and have a look."

They followed the fence for only a few yards, then it finished just around a corner and they saw why it finished there. It finished at the edge of a large and very dangerous looking swamp, and Sam swore.

"Bugger. I can't see anyway past there."

They looked at the fence again.

"It may be touch sensitive if we tried to climb the fence or cut a hole through it," said Stu. "Maybe we could dig a hole underneath it?"

They checked the area carefully, using their binoculars, and could see no indication of cameras, so got down on their knees and looked at the earth below the fence.

"The fence only goes flush with the ground," said Stu. "Look, it hasn't been countersunk. And the earth near the swamp is quite soft. I think we could easily dig underneath it."

They got to work, digging, using two pieces of bark they had found, and soon had a small hole. Sam wriggled his way through, and Stu passed him the two backpacks. Then he carefully brushed away any signs on the ground they had made, before slipping through the hole himself.

They used a couple of branches and some large leaves to lay on top of the tunnel on both sides of the fence until they were sure the tunnel wouldn't be noticed with a casual glance. They made a clear sign of the location of the hole by laying a couple of branches on the ground, pointing the way. They would not be noticed by a casual observer either, they were sure.

They headed back to the drive, as they thought it would be easier sneaking up at the side of the road than through the middle of the jungle. When they reached the drive, they left a rock on the road side as an indicator as to where they should leave the track for their return. Then they carefully removed any sign that anybody left the jungle there.

They figured that if they were careful, they should be able to spot the two drive cameras that Moldie thought might be there before the cameras detected them and they could make a detour around them, which is what they did, always leaving indicators.

Eventually, after almost two hours of careful sneaking, they arrived at the patch of open ground they had spotted on Google Earth and where the helicopter was supposed to land. There was a path from there to the house, which they took before they got their first view of the house across the garden.

They found two good places a short distance apart to observe what was going on and settled down with their binoculars. They had done this many times in the past and could communicate with each other with hand signals.

Almost immediately they both saw Clair in an upper room, which they assumed was a bedroom. They saw her get changed out of what looked like a bathing costume, before putting on a dressing gown and walking out onto a balcony. Sam considered signalling her there and then but they had no escape plan prepared yet, so decided to stay hidden. If she knew they were there, almost certainly she would react in such a way as to alert the staff that something wasn't quite right and the element of surprise would be lost. Better to wait until they had a proper worked out and thorough plan.

They watched Clair eat her lunch. She seemed healthy and well. She disappeared into the room and they waited for a few minutes, then signalled to each other, and went their separate ways.

Sam went to check on the stables, always keeping under cover and taking extreme care. At the stables he saw a young man, obviously the stable boy, and counted six horses, he thought. He wondered if they could steal some horses and ride down the drive, jump the barrier and ride away, but he knew they would be seen and chased by car, and could they jump the barrier anyway? It was quite high.

He looked around a bit more before he returned to the meeting place he had arranged with Stu.

Stu had been checking out the garages where he found two cars, one of them a four wheel drive Range Rover, but he realised even that car could never force its way through the jungle. They would have to drive down the drive and the barrier would stand firm, he reckoned, if they tried to ram it. He could easily start the Range Rover, even without the keys, that wouldn't be a problem, but could they use it to escape? The barrier would have to be opened when the car approached. That meant they would have to split up, one of them to rescue Clair, probably Sam, whilst he, Stu, overpowered the barrier guards.

He told Sam of his plan, and they both decided it could work. But when should they attempt it? Now or later that day or come back tomorrow? They had everything with them that they needed in their rucksacks. Dart guns and extra darts, rope to tie the guards and tape to put over their mouths, and, most importantly, walkie-talkies.

"It will take me at least an hour to get back to the barrier," whispered Stu, "Assuming nothing goes wrong."

"I would have to rescue Clair from the house. I think we should make sure that that is possible before you leave. We will only have the element of surprise once."

As they made their plans, everything changed as they heard the distinctive sound of a helicopter and they both instinctively looked up and saw it in the distance. They saw members of the household, including Clair, rush from the house to the landing area to greet it, and they ducked back into the jungle. Just two minutes later and everyone returned, including Bim Dram and Clair, and Sam swore under his breath.

"That's going to make things a lot more difficult," he thought. "He's brought another five guards with him, and they will be on high alert now he is here."

His thoughts went back to the helicopter and whether they could steal it but those were dashed when almost immediately it took off and disappeared over the jungle.

The time to leave to enable them to reach the rendezvous deadline with Moldie and the girls had passed and they would have to spend the night somewhere else. Not a problem but stop here or somewhere in the jungle? What to do? He thought about what Moldie had told them about the security measures here at Heavenly Winds. The security on the doors and windows overnight meant it was highly unlikely that an experienced and accomplished cat burglar could get in, let alone a bulky and occasionally clumsy former soldier.

But even getting to a door or window may be difficult. How many guards did Moldie think they had on duty overnight? Was it two or three? That wouldn't be much of a problem, but then there were motion sensitive lights, and he had no idea where they were. He studied the house again but could see no sign of them.

But then the main problem, of course, were the dogs. Half a dozen or so of the viscous beasts roaming free around the garden in the dark horrified him. They had better night vision, were quicker and had a superb sense of smell.

272

He made up his mind and told Stu, who nodded.

"I agree," he said, "And I think we should aim to get to the far side of the barrier before dark."

This time Sam nodded, and, with a last glance at the house, slipped off into the jungle. They carefully retraced their steps exactly, spotting easily the markers they had left to indicate where they should detour into the jungle, and reached the fence in half the time it had taken them for the inward journey. They found the tunnel, slipped through, and covered it up again, just in case. They snuck past the barrier and the guards and reached the rendezvous point just as it was becoming totally dark.

They found a spot nearby, just a few yards away, but totally hidden from the road, and made themselves comfortable. They had something to eat, making sure to leave no litter, and scrambled someway away to go to the toilet, which they did in a freshly dug hole which they then carefully covered up.

Then it was time for sleep, taking it in turns. They had done this before a number of times and Stu always slept first, as he did this time. They had almost twelve hours until they were to meet Moldie and the girls, so Sam woke Stu after five and a half hours, and then took his turn to sleep.

Stu woke him an hour before the meeting time, and, after toilet and a drink of water, made their way to the pick up spot. A few minutes before eleven, one of the walkie-talkies buzzed. That meant that if he had a reply, Moldie would be there in ten minutes. They replied and ten minutes later heard a car approaching. It reversed into the side track, and Sam and Stu climbed in. Moldie was on his own, and explained that they weren't sure if Clair would be with them, so the girls had stayed at home.

Sam told him what had happened on the journey back to the Snuka house and Moldie agreed they had done the right thing. .

Pauline and I heard the car coming down the road and walked to the garage to meet them. We had prayed that mother was in the car but we weren't that surprised to find that she wasn't there but very happy to see that Sam and Stu were uninjured and perfectly

fine.

"I'll get straight off," said Moldie, "To see if there is any news from Waving Grass, and you tell the girls what happened over lunch."

We listened whilst we cooked and were both interested to hear that they had seen mother and she looked fit and healthy.

"What do we do now?" I asked.

"We think and we talk and we come up with a plan," said Sam. "Let's wait until Moldie returns."

Moldie was very excited when he did return later that afternoon, with a huge grin on his handsome face.

"Come on Moldie," I urged, "What's tickling you?" and he looked confused.

"Nothing is tickling me, but I do have a letter from Clair," and he held it up.

"Let's have a look, what does it say," I demanded and made a grab for it, but he held it behind his back and pushed me gently away.

"Be patient Alice darling. Now, if you would all like to sit down," he was talking to us as if he was talking to small children, "I will read it out loud to you all. Would you like that, my children?"

"Just bloody get on with it," said Pauline, "Before I smack you Moldie."

He grinned and we all sat around the dining room table and Moldie read us mother's letter. I could see it was written in her small, neat handwriting, and, as usual, there would have been no spelling mistakes and the punctuation would have been perfect. Mother was like that. Even when she sent text messages, everything had to be exact and correct.

We listened to her letter.

"She seems quite happy," said Pauline. "Almost like she's on holiday."

"What else can she do?" asked Moldie, "But enjoy

herself."

"She says she will be there for almost another two weeks," said Sam. "That gives us time to make a foolproof plan. No need to rush into anything hasty. Let's try and get ready for action in three days," and we all nodded.

Moldie said, "And in three days, we should hear from Waving Grass again."

"That's right," said Sam. "She might have some more news for us. We'll wait until we hear from Waving Grass then pounce."

Chapter 34 - Four days of happiness

On the sixth evening, Bim Dram arrived in his helicopter. We all heard it arriving and all the staff, including me, rushed over to the landing pasture to greet him. A servant opened the helicopter door for him and he jumped out, instinctively ducking his head under the still rotating blades. He was all smiles and shook hands and said a few words with everyone and had small presents which he pulled out of a shoulder-bag and personally gave to each person. They grinned back happily. I could see that they all loved him.

When he got to me I said, "Hello Bim, where's my present?" and he gave me a kiss on the cheek and a small box.

"Open it when we get inside," he said.

I did open the present when we got inside, and it was a pearl necklace. Very nice indeed, I thought to myself, but not fantastic. I didn't tell Bim that, of course.

"It's very nice," I told him. "Thank you Bim," and I kissed him. Keep him sweet, I kept telling myself.

"Would you like a cup of tea?" I asked him and he said a cup of tea would be nice but taking me to the bedroom and undressing me and lying on top of me and moving up and down for a few minutes would be better and he grabbed my hand and dragged me upstairs. It took him less than ten minutes from the time the helicopter landed until the time we were both naked and lying in bed together. I was surprised it took him so long, the randy old goat.

Just twenty minutes later and he picked up the internal telephone and a few minutes later dinner was served by Jeeves on the balcony overlooking the lake. We were both wearing dressing gowns. Bim didn't seem to mind that it was obvious what we had been doing. Proud, more like, and Jeeves winked at me when his back was turned to Bim, and I winked back.

He made love to me twice more that night and in the morning, and I wondered about the sexual appetites of men, especially that of a man of Bim's age. He was older than me, I discovered, just over fifty.

After breakfast we went horse riding. Bim didn't ask me, but that was fine, and we went on our own. I rode my usual horse, Bundy, and Bim rode a big gray called Martian. Bim was a keen and competent rider, and as we rode along the trails side by side, he explained how the trails had come about.

"Before I bought this place, I made sure that I could create these trails. I loved this land from the moment I first saw it but I wouldn't have bought it if I couldn't have made these trails. I got a professional landscaper to map them with the main aim of making them interesting. I wanted lots of twists and turns and ups and downs and many surprising views, with one or two jumps if I felt in the mood. And I think he has done a wonderful job. I love riding around here."

All I could do was agree with him.

"We sold the trees that we cut down to make the trails," he explained, "And the price we got for the timber paid for all the work, so they were produced for nothing. And doing something for nothing is always close to a politician's heart," and we both chuckled.

He stopped at the top of a small hill, and we both looked at the view.

"Wonderful," he said. "This is probably my favourite spot," and we both climbed off and let the horses graze. He pulled a blanket from one of the saddle bags and laid it on the ground, and then I couldn't believe it when he suggested we made love yet again. I sighed but obliged.

When we had finished he took a picnic from the saddle bags and the obligatory bottle of Cadian wine and we ate and drank and talked. He started to tell me about his work in parliament.

"I listened to what you said about Effghania and I have been trying to get more aid to them, but it's difficult. Most of the MP's are Jakalmanian and, as you are probably aware, they don't like Effghania much. But I've had promises of support from a few of them, so things should improve a bit."

"Thank you for trying, Bim," I said, and kissed him.

Over the next four days we went horse riding regularly but also played tennis and went swimming everyday. He was a better tennis player but I was a better swimmer.

We ate every meal on the balcony and Bim was pleased that I was spending time in the kitchen helping the ladies prepare the food, and he took particular pleasure in eating any meals I had made myself. He had parliamentary work to do, he always had, he told me, and managed plenty of this when I was cooking.

In the kitchen I managed a few short conversations with Waving Grass. She told me that she had left my letter with ODOE who promised to give it to Moldie, so he certainly would have read it by now but as there was no way we could contact them until she returned home again, in three days time, there was nothing either of us could do about that.

Then Bim surprised me once again.

In an apologetic voice he said, "Clair, darling."

(He had never called me darling before, and that made me suspicious)

"I have something to tell you and I do actually feel quite guilty about it. I have to lend you to a fellow politician."

"What?"

I was a bit startled. I hadn't expected that.

"I am terribly sorry to have to do this to you," he continued, "But I have a problem. It is to do with money and also a favour I owe him. He supported me in an important parliamentary debate, and also lent me a lot of money. He is powerful and influential, and could ruin my career and also hinder or even stop me from doing a lot of the work I have promised you I would do in Effghania. Your name came up in conversation. He told me that he had received an email and had booked to sleep with you this week but now obviously that opportunity has gone. Anyway, Clair, to cut a long story short, I have agreed to lend you to him for a week."

I was a bit shocked. I thought he really cared for me, even loved me, and he had told me he couldn't bear the thought of anyone else with me, but obviously his job in parliament was more important.

Then I remembered how ruthless he was and suddenly I wasn't surprised at all.

I sighed. There was no point in causing a fuss.

"When am I going away?"

"Tomorrow," he said.

"We haven't spent much time together here," I said, "And I'm enjoying myself with you."

He kissed me, and apologised.

"As I said, I'm really sorry. I'll make it up to you, I promise and I also promise to bring you back here for a proper visit in the future."

"May I ask you a favour Bim?"

He shrugged.

"You can ask."

"Please will you promise me that you won't let him hurt me."

Bim chuckled.

"I promise. I truly promise. He most certainly will not hurt you. Worship you, more like."

"What is the name of this politician?" I asked him, but he wouldn't tell me, just chuckled some more.

"You'll find out when you meet him."

"Will he be coming here?"

I needed to know so that I could get a message to Alice and Pauline.

"Oh no. You'll go to his yacht," and that is all he would tell me.

I told Waving Grass next time I saw her, which was later that same day, in the kitchen.

"A politician with boat for one week leaving tomorrow," she said. "I tell ODOE as soon as I can."

Chapter 35 - Rum Hearty

The following afternoon I was handcuffed to Flakey, who was one of two guards who, it seemed, would accompany me on my journey. The other was Pot, who had played the flute at Angel's Hair Falls a couple of weeks earlier. I was led to the pasture where the helicopter had landed and I was bundled inside. I had no spare clothes or make up or washeries, just the clothes I was wearing.

"They will be provided," said Bim when I mentioned it to him.

He stood and waved goodbye to me with, I thought, a sad, resigned expression on his face.

The helicopter took off and I looked out of the window. I thought I saw a car parked under some trees in the distance but I wasn't sure. Why would there be a car hidden in some trees?

We flew for about forty minutes over hilly, almost mountainous countryside, then I saw a long narrow lake. It disappeared into the distance looking more like a wide river than a narrow lake. I saw a number of islands of differing sizes and a couple of rivers, but whether they were flowing in or out I couldn't tell.

As we descended I spotted a number of boats on the water and then I saw what I assumed was the yacht we were heading for. It looked tiny but as we got closer, the yacht got bigger and I realised it was actually quite big and obviously very expensive.

We landed on the outskirts of a small town and I was driven to a small jetty, where I was helped into a small motorboat, which took us over to the yacht. I saw the yacht's name written on the side, and read out 'Heloise'. A nice name. I wondered what it meant.

We parked the motorboat next to a ladder and Pot climbed up, then the handcuffs were taken off me and I followed him up. It was only a short climb and I soon scrambled over the side onto the deck. I had expected to see the MP, whoever he was, waiting for me but there was just a member of the crew who welcomed me.

Flakey scrambled up the ladder behind me, and the motorboat sped away. He was grinning and I was not surprised. A few days on a luxury yacht with the minimum of effort required to keep an eye on me. Talk about another comfy assignment.

I was taken to a small cabin by the crew member and met by a pretty young maid, who spoke English. Her name, she told me, was Dragonfly, and she called me Clair Lady. She told me she was the cook on board but her job for the next hour was to help me get ready to meet the boss.

"He want you to look your best, Clair Lady," she explained.

She helped me shower and washed my hair in a very posh bathroom then helped me choose a dress from a wardrobe. There were a number of dresses and, I noticed, all knee length, rather than the full length that Moldie had chosen from me.

Eventually I chose a sleeveless dark blue dress, with white lace around the collar. It fitted quite well, not perfectly but near enough and showed off my figure very nicely. I looked good in it.

"I chose dress for you, Clair Lady," said Dragonfly. "You like," and I told her it was lovely.

Then she brushed my hair until it shone and I applied a little bit of makeup. I asked her many questions but her answers were very discreet and I didn't really learn anything. Eventually she led me along a short corridor to the main cabin, to meet the boss.

I recognised him immediately, and was a bit shocked. I didn't expect him. It was Rum Hearty, who was the Prime Minister of Abacadia and I had seen him in numerous newspaper articles and regularly on Abacadian television. In my wildest imaginations I didn't expect it to be him.

He stood up when he saw me enter, and stuck out his hand, and kissed the back of mine.

"Thank you for visiting me, Lady Clair," he said with a huge smile and offered me a seat in a comfy chair opposite him.

He was a real gentleman. Softly spoken, with a quick smile. Tall and slender with grey at the temples, a good looking man. Aged, I knew, forty four, so younger than me.

He apologised for bringing me here under arrest. He explained how he had always admired me and really fancied me and Bim Dram owed him a big favour which he knew might never be repaid so thought up the idea of borrowing me for a while.

"I really hope you don't mind," he said. "Would you like a drink? We have a number of bottles of Cadian wine, which, I believe, you are quite fond of?"

Dragonfly, the maid, brought out a bottle of white Cadian wine in an ice bucket and Rum Hearty thanked her and poured us out a glass each.

"Cheers," he said, and we clinked glasses.

"I hope you enjoy your stay here on my humble yacht. Whilst you are here, I promise to treat you like royalty. You will be my honoured guest."

Which was nice.

I asked him what was the name of the lake and where were we, and he looked surprised.

"I thought you would know," he said, "But I suppose not. It's called Lake Bongadina and it is in the far east side of Abacadia. It's our largest lake, over 300 miles long, but, as you have seen, it is long and thin, only a mile or so wide most of the way. We're at the southern end, which is, I reckon, the prettiest part of the lake. I bought this yacht a few years ago and regularly fly here. It helps me relax and allows me to get on with much of my parliamentary work in peace and quiet."

We chatted easily about many things, but not about Bim Dram, then I asked him if he was married and he looked very sad and I vaguely remembered something and regretted asking the question.

"I was," he said. "Her name was Heloise, which means Sunshine in Abacadian. She had the sweetest nature of anyone I have ever known. Everybody loved her, as did I but she died. I named this yacht in her memory."

"I'm so sorry," I said, and I was. I knew how he felt. I felt the same after my beloved Alfie died, but now the memory had dimmed and was now more a dull occasional ache than the heart wrenching pain it had once been.

"Has she been gone long?"

He sighed.

"Two years and eleven days," he said.

He looked at his watch.

"And two hours and twenty five minutes."

He sighed.

"She went into hospital for a routine operation to have her appendix removed and she was given infected blood. She contracted AIDS, and just withered away. Despite the best efforts of the best doctors in our best hospital, she just withered away and died. It was unbearable to watch," and then I remembered hearing about it somewhere on the news or somehow.

"I am truly sorry," I said, and squeezed his hand, and he gave me a sad smile.

"I know you are. Thank you."

"I didn't know there was AIDS in Abacadia," I asked, wondering now about all the different men I had slept with over the last few weeks. I had assumed Moldie had had them all checked out before they came to me, but then again, maybe not. His main concern was the money I brought in.

"'There isn't," he said. "Well, not really. We have isolated cases but we have had a propaganda campaign and there isn't an epidemic or anything like that. Just one or two cases, as there are in the rest of the world. She was given blood using an infected needle. The doctor who did it was tried and is now in prison serving a jail sentence. A long jail sentence."

I squeezed his hand again.

"It's hard to lose a loved one. My husband died five years ago and I still miss him. I do feel for you."

"Since she died," he continued after returning the squeeze,

"I haven't slept with a woman. I just haven't had the desire. But now you are here and you remind me so much of Heloise. You are beautiful like she was, and you have a true kind heart also. I have always admired you. When I received an email and a film a few weeks ago, I was tempted to visit you, but didn't. Then when Bim Dram told me about you, well, I was tempted again, and this time, here you are.

I was hoping you might be able to help me get over Heloise. Not forget her, of course, but get back to living a normal life. A man needs a woman from time to time, don't you think?"

I agreed that most men did in fact need a woman from time to time and truly felt sorry for him.

"So you know what had happened to me over the last few weeks?"

"I have a pretty good idea," he said. "As I said, I got the email that was sent out, the one with a film attached, and, well, here you are."

"I really would like to go home to England," I said. "Can you help?" but he shook his head.

"That might upset Bim Dram, and, although you might not think it, he really is a good man and a good politician and I need him on my side, but I will talk to him. No promises."

He made love to me that evening in a luxurious double bed and I could tell that he really enjoyed himself. It was obvious that he had been dreaming about the moment but he was gentle and caring and we both had a good time.

I stayed on the yacht, which sailed slowly around the lake, for five days, making love twelve times, some sort of record. Lake Bongadina, as Rum Hearty had explained to me, was never very wide and at all times I could see both banks. Or cliffs, more like. Both banks for much of their length were rugged cliffs with odd Bonsai type trees perched on top and small coves and bays with beaches dotted here and there. In the distance I could see a range of mountains, with, it looked to me, snow on their summits.

There were many small islands and we sailed around and in

between them. Some were almost flat and some were rugged and craggy but they all looked interesting. It really was a rather fascinating lake.

Rum talked to me for some of the time, pointing out various land marks and interesting features around the lake and also telling me about the problems he faced as Prime Minister, but he had much work to do so I was left to my own devices for a few hours every day to do as I liked. I swam in the lake, in a decent swimming costume, red, again, and sunbathed and read, many books which had been provided for me, but always I was under the eyes of the guards, and always there was a dart gun handy.

Flakey and Pot were keen to try some fishing and were delighted when they discovered some angling equipment on board. One of the crew helped and advised them and they spent a few hours everyday fishing, much to their immense pleasure. I watched with amusement as they caught various small fish and they clapped and danced with delight as they were reeled in.

Then one day they caught a much bigger fish. It was, the crew member told them, a giant catfish, and they really struggled to try and bring it on board. It must have been over 10 feet long and probably weighed 20 stone or more. I could see it slowly swimming about beneath the yacht and even Rum Hearty came out of his cabin to have a look.

Eventually it was obvious to all that they would be unable to bring it up on board so they cut the line as close to the fish as they could and watched it slowly swim away.

In the evenings Rum and I had dinner together, the food was delicious, Rum was a perfect host, and once again I found myself enjoying myself and wondered about the direction my life had taken me. Sailing around a large lake in a far off country as the guest and lover of the Prime Minister. Never in my wildest dreams could I have come up with such a scenario.

One evening I asked Pot, the musical guard, if he could get out his flute and play some Abacadian tunes. Rum was delighted and knew many of the words, though the words he sung were slightly different from those sung by Flakey and the rest of the crew. Eventually I coaxed him into having a dance with me, and, as it seemed with all Abacadians, he was a good dancer. We partied until late in the evening, with all the staff joining in with the singing and dancing and Rum smiled and laughed, as we all did.

"Last night was the most relaxed I've felt since Heloise died," he told me over breakfast the next morning. "Thank you."

Twice we stopped beside two different small islands, and we got off the yacht and went for a walk and a picnic and a swim in the lake.

"I actually own these islands," Rum told me. "I keep them as nature reserves and I'm very proud of them. I have imported two indigenous but rare types of snake with an aim of preserving them. Don't worry though," he added, as he saw a look of alarm cross my face, "They're not poisonous."

On the sixth evening, Rum told me, reluctantly, I reckoned, that the following afternoon we had to return to Snuka.

"Bim Dram wants you sent to his house there," he said, and I realised that my time away from that dreaded bedroom was over, at least for a while and that depressed me a bit.

Rum was at his most charming that evening. The meal was magnificent, as was the wine, and he entertained me with stories from his past. Eventually it was bed time, and the love making was gentle and loving, and again in the morning.

Rum devoted the whole day to me, though by the time we had got up and had breakfast, it was almost lunch time. He anchored the yacht beside yet another small island which he owned and we both went swimming. Rum asked the crew to come swimming with us. Flakey and Pot couldn't swim and stayed on board the yacht, but the other's all joined in. We sat on a little beach and drank some wine, and then, sadly, it was time to leave.

Rum had organised for the maid, Dragonfly, to pack up all the lovely clothes he had bought me, and he gave me those as a farewell present and I gave him a big sloppy kiss as a thank you.

I took one last look around the deck of Heloise, suspecting I would never return, and followed Rum down the ladder and into the motorboat. Flakey, the guard, had suggested he put handcuffs on me, but Rum waved him away.

"Don't be ridiculous," he said, but then gave Flakey a smile and a pat on his shoulder. "I know you're only doing your job, but she'll be fine with me."

Even so, I noticed he held my hand, smiling, whilst we walked from the motorboat to the car and then from the car to the helicopter. Better safe than sorry, it seemed. I was too valuable to lose.

We landed at a small private heliport near the centre of Snuka. Before we got out of the helicopter, but after Flakey and Pot had exited, he took me in his arms for the last time and kissed me gently.

"Thank you Clair. Having you on 'Heloise' with me has made a huge difference to my way of thinking. I think I have overcome the loss of my late wife, and although I will never forget her, now I can get on with living again. Thank you."

Two cars were waiting for us. Rum disappeared into his chauffeur driven limousine whilst Flakey held my hand as he led me to Bim Dram's car, and I was driven back once more to his house and that dreaded, dreary bedroom.

Chapter 36 - Lake Bongadina

For three days we concentrated on getting everything ready to rescue Mother from Heavenly Winds. We discussed various ideas and eventually came up with the following as the best probable way for success.

Sam and Stu would return at first light in the morning and follow their original route around the barrier, under the fence, through the jungle, up the drive and around the cameras until they reached the gardens.

They would go straight to the garages and check if there were any cars parked. They would make sure that both cars could be started and driven away at a moments notice if necessary.

For their plan to work, they needed a captive. Not Bim, but a member of the household, preferably male, but possibly Waving Grass. They didn't want to use her. She was a valued member of ODOE and if they used her, then suspicion would fall on her that she assisted with Clair's rescue and she would have to leave Bim's employment and ODOE and Moldie didn't want that. So, after getting the cars ready, the next thing would be to find a male member of staff who could drive and who they could kidnap themselves.

The next part involved a bit of guess work, but calculated guessing. Mind you, a lot of the plan seemed to involve a lot of guesswork, but Sam and Stu seemed confident so Alice and I just went along with their plans.

"We'll improvise and make it up as we go along," explained Sam. "Don't worry. We're good at this sort of thing."

Moldie had discovered from his ODOE friends that

Bim Dram loved horse riding, and so did mother. We therefore guessed that the two of them would go riding together regularly, probably everyday, and probably on their own. There would be no need for guards. It would be almost impossible for mother to escape and it seemed she probably wouldn't want to. Not at the moment, anyway.

Sam and Stu would wait until Bim and mother rode off, noticing which trail they took. The trails were all circular so almost certainly Sam and Stu would know which way they would return. They would head along the trail in the reverse direction and find an ambush spot. Not too close to the house.

When Mother and Bim rode up, they wouldn't hesitate but just shoot Bim with a dart gun. Give him no warning, just shoot him. Then take Clair to the house and put her into the car. Grab the hostage, threaten them and make them drive to the barrier, hiding under a blanket in the back, and order the guards to open it. If they did, then just drive through. If they refused then jump out and shoot them with dart guns. Try and open the barrier ourselves but if not then climb over it and run along the road, where Moldie and the girls would be waiting in Lady Sammy.

That was the plan. Sam and Stu seemed happy enough. Pauline and I discussed it on our own and were not so happy, but we had no experience of these matters whilst Sam and Stu were former SAS. What did we know?

The next day, after this dubious plan was finalised, Moldie returned after lunch with a message from Waving Grass.

"She says," he told the rest of us in a neutral voice, "That mother has left Heavenly Winds and gone to stay with a politician who owns a boat. She will stay there for one week. That's all she knows but she has definitely gone," and Sam swore, quite rudely. I couldn't blame him. All the plans we had so carefully made were torn up and chucked away.

"Are you absolutely sure," he asked Moldie.

"That's what Waving Grass said, and she's always been very reliable. All we can do is assume she is right," he said.

Sam swore again.

Two minutes later, after he had calmed down, we put our heads together and tried to work out where she could have been taken. We all looked at Moldie who shrugged.

"I have no idea which of the politicians own a boat," he said, and sighed. "Not many, I wouldn't think. I'm assuming we're talking about something quite big. Well, large enough to live on and large boats cost a lot of money. Abacadian MP's don't get paid a lot of money. Only cabinet ministers or MP's with private riches could own one, I reckon and there can't be many of those."

Sam was still angry and said rather bitterly,

"You should have made enquiries whilst visiting your friends," he grumbled and Moldie grinned and held up a piece of paper.

"I did," he said, "And these are the four MP's who ODOE think own such a boat," and Sam also grinned and had the common sense and good nature to look remorseful.

"Sorry Moldie. A bit pissed off."

Moldie waved a vague hand and showed us the list.

"Of the four MP's, one is abroad in Australia on a business trip, and another is a definite homosexual, so I think we can discount them. The other two are, we think, on their boats. One of them keeps his yacht in the Mediterranean, so we think it's probably not that one. The other one is the most likely, we think."

"Where is it?" Sam asked.

"It's kept on Lake Bongadina, which is the largest lake in Abacadia, and is at the far eastern edge of the country. The owner likes to sail regularly around the lake, it seems, spending many of the parliamentary breaks there. If what Waving Grass says is correct, then I think your mother is probably there."

"Let's have a look at a map," said Sam, and Moldie spread one out on the dining room table.

"Here's Lake Bongadina, and here's where we are," and Sam muttered.

"It's a bloody long way. How long to drive there Moldie?"

Moldie shrugged.

"Nine hours?"

"Does anyone fancy a nine hour drive?" asked Sam, and sighed and swore again.

"Bloody hell."

"It's a jolly big lake," I suggested. "The yacht could be anywhere on it."

We studied the map. Lake Bongadina was very long and narrow, with a bend in the middle. It looked to be about three hundred miles from tip to tip and varied in width from about a mile or so to about twenty miles. There were a few towns and villages along on the shore.

"How would Clair get there?" Stu wondered. "Surely by helicopter. Where would that land?"

"Probably near one of the towns?" suggested Sam, and we studied the map a bit more.

"This is the largest town," said Moldie, pointing to a place called Karata. "Maybe we should head there and see if we can spot the yacht. The lake is not very wide and I think it shouldn't be that hard to find it."

That was a plan so we decided that unless somebody came up with something better, that was what we would do.

"Do we know the name of this MP?" I asked, and Moldie told us.

"Rum Hearty."

He was grinning and shaking his head.

I'd never heard of Rum Hearty.

"Who is he? Why are you grinning?"

"He's the Prime Minister of Abacadia," and I whistled.

"Oh! Do you know much about him?"

He showed us some photos of Rum Hearty. He looked harmless enough. Middle aged, fifty-ish, possibly in his late forties, with hair greying at the temples. Tall and slim.

"He's a decent man," said Moldie, " And a good Prime Minister. His wife, on whom he doted, died a couple of years ago, and the rumour is that he still hasn't really got over her loss. Maybe Clair is there to help him."

"What type of yacht does he own? Do you have any plans of it?"

Moldie pulled a sheet of paper from his pocket and spread it out, and also some photographs. We studied them. The yacht didn't seem so big. About thirty yards long, according to the details, so not small either, and could sleep eight people in four cabins, two double and two twin.

"Would he have guards with him," asked Sam, and Moldie nodded.

"He usually has three men and a woman with him who double up as crew and guards. I believe they are highly trained."

"Does the yacht have a name?" asked Pauline.

"Heloise," said Moldie, after studying his notes.

"That's a nice name."

"It means sunny in Abacadian," explained Moldie.

"That was the name of his wife, I remember, so I assume the yacht was named after her."

So we made plans to drive to Lake Bongadina. We decided we needed another car, for comfort and also as a backup in case anything went wrong. If we did rescue mother, six of us in one car for a nine hour journey would not be at all comfortable.

Moldie managed to get one for us from somewhere, another Lada Samara, which Pauline christened Sammy Two. We packed up everything we thought we needed in the two cars including food and tents and other camping necessities, and early the following day set off for Lake Bongadina.

It was not a good drive. The countryside, once we had got away from Snuka, became flat and rather dull, with a continuous view of jungle either side. It was hot and we took it in turns snoozing.

We stopped occasionally for toilet and stretching and regularly swapped drivers. The land started to rise as we approached the lake, with a few stunning views, and eventually we arrived at Lake Bongadina. We parked up beside the road and climbed out and looked across the lake. We could clearly see the other side in the distance but it disappeared from view to the left and right. It almost looked like a wide river and reminded me of Lake Windemere in the English Lake District. In the far distance were high mountains, with snow covered peaks. Very pretty.

There was no sign of the yacht so Sam suggested we drive to the main town of Karata, about twenty miles away, and we arrived there just as it was getting dark. We booked into a small guest house for the night, and visited a local bar for a meal and a drink. We found some locals who spoke English and explained to them that we were tourists and was it true that the Prime Minister was on his yacht nearby.

"He sailed from here just a few days ago," they told us proudly, "Heading south. The countryside is more beautiful to the south," so the next day we headed south and at about lunch time, saw the yacht 'Heloise' in the distance.

We parked on a small headland with good views over the lake and ate a picnic whilst studying the yacht through binoculars. We now had a set each, and I looked keenly, desperately hoping for a view of mother.

The yacht was a long way away, a couple of miles or more, and even through the binoculars, wasn't very clear. It was hard to make out any details. I thought I may have seen mother, but I wasn't sure. I was very disappointed.

The yacht sailed serenely onwards as we watched and after lunch we followed it in the car. We didn't need both cars that day, we reckoned, so had left Sammy Two in Karata. A road ran around the entire lake so we could follow the yacht forever, and eventually our luck held. It sailed closer to our side of the lake as it rounded a headland and we could all have a much better look.

We all saw mother at the same time. She walked up from below deck and was wearing a red one piece swimming costume. She looked extremely glamorous, I thought, and fit and well.

"Wow," said Sam, "Doesn't she look absolutely gorgeous," and got a punch from me for his observations.

"I was just wondering what you might look like in twenty years," he teased, and got another punch for his troubles.

But he was right, of course, she did look absolutely gorgeous. She sat down on one of the comfy looking loungers and pulled out a book and started to read.

She was wearing sunglasses and had her hair done up in a bun.

She sat and read and sipped at a drink of something, probably wine, possibly a spritzer, and seemed oblivious to the rest of the world. There was no sign of Rum Hearty.

Moldie sighed, and shook his head.

"So beautiful," he muttered.

I could see no one else on board, though obviously there must be someone sailing the boat, and then I spotted someone at the wheel or the tiller or whatever you call the steering device on such a yacht. I wondered what it would be like to own a yacht like that and started imagining Sam and me sailing on one together.

"What we need to find out," said Sam, breaking into my thoughts, "Is how many staff and guards are on board. So far I have only seen the driver and two others. They were probably guards, on board specifically to look after Clair. Has anyone seen anybody else?"

I immediately felt guilty. I hadn't spotted anyone apart from mother and the driver and vowed to keep a better lookout. But Pauline and Moldie hadn't spotted the guards either. We had all been staring at mother.

We watched until the yacht sailed out of clear visible range, then, as it was getting late, returned to our little guest house. We returned to the same bar as the night before, and the couple we had met were there again, and Sam started talking to them.

"We drove up the side of the lake," he said. "It must be one of the most beautiful lakes in the world," which pleased them. "We even spotted the Prime Ministers yacht, what did you say it was called?"

"Heloise," they said. "It means Sunny in Abacadian and was named after his late wife. She was lovely and it broke his heart when she died. We all felt so sorry for him. He's a lovely man."

"It sailed quite close to us when we were having a picnic on the headland," continued Sam, "And we had a clear view but were wondering. We didn't see him and only saw one other person who was driving. There must be more crew than that, surely?"

"Normally," said the locals, obviously happy to talk about their beloved Prime Minister, "He has only four crew with him, three men and a woman. They run the boat but also double up as guards to keep an eye on things. The woman, who's name is Dragonfly, also does the cooking and cleaning. She's a lovely girl."

"How do you know all this?" Pauline asked.

The local smiled.

"Dragonfly is our niece," she said.

"So basically he's on his own?"

It was my turn to ask a question.

The local sighed.

"Usually," she said. "It's so sad."

So nobody knew about mother being on board because if anyone knew, then surely it would be these locals whose niece worked on board.

We talked later in one of the bedrooms.

"Waving Grass told us that mother thought she would be onboard for a week. Seven days," said Sam. "Did we get the message on day two or day three?" but Moldie shook his head.

"Assume the worse," Sam continued, "And it was day three. That was yesterday, so tomorrow will be day five. We need to act quickly otherwise she will be whisked away from us once again. We need a plan."

"Will there be extra guards on board to keep an eye on mother?" pondered Stu, but we didn't know.

"So there are at least three male members of crew who act also as guards and are probably extremely well trained and dangerous," said Sam. "He is the Prime Minister and would surely only have the very best looking after him. Then there is Rum Hearty himself. If we get on board, he might put up some resistance and the last thing we want to do is injure him. There would be all hell to pay and absolutely no chance of escape. We would probably end up dangling on the end of a rope."

I shivered and Moldie nodded.

"Probably," he said.

"Problem number one, how do we get onto the yacht?"

"I'm sure we could hire a small boat," said Stu.

"I saw a 'boats for hire' advert in one of the shop windows," said Moldie. "I could check that out in the morning."

"Good," said Sam. "It would have to have a small motor to get us near the yacht, but for the last bit we would need total silence, so it would need a pair of oars. We need total surprise."

"I noticed a ladder on the side of the boat." I wanted to contribute to the conversation. "We could get on board by climbing up that."

"We?" said Sam, sounding astonished. "I'm sorry Alice, but you won't be coming with us. Just Moldie and Stu and me," and I sighed. It had been a good try.

"When?" asked Sam.

"It would have to be at night," said Stu, "To stand any chance of success," and we all nodded in agreement.

"Tomorrow night," said Sam, "To be sure she's still here. She may well leave the following day. That would be day seven."

In the morning Moldie went to find the boat hire place he had seen advertised, and the man had four motor boats available, with oars. When he asked for a trailer and a car with a tow bar, the man looked suspicious and asked him why.

"We want to explore the islands and coves at the picturesque southern end of the lake," he explained and the man laughed.

"You don't want to hire from me. You want to hire from my brother. He runs the other half of our business in the village of Shempa, in Shempa Bay, just where you want to go. Tell him I sent you. He will look after you and no need for trailer, hey."

We booked out of the guest house. We didn't expect to be returning, and set off with both cars towards Shempa village. On the way we needed to find out exactly where the yacht was and we found it much closer to Shempa than Karata. It was anchored alongside a small island, not so far from the shore, and we could clearly see, with our binoculars, Clair and Rum Hearty and three other men and a woman relaxing on a small beach. As we watched they ran into the sea to swim.

Then Moldie gasped and we looked at him to see he was staring at the yacht and not the beach. I turned my binoculars that way and saw the reason why he had gasped like that. Two men were sitting on the deck, obviously guards, and I recognised one of them. I was fairly sure it was Brown Cap, one of the men who had captured us at Lake Lucinda a few weeks previously. And I remembered his name was Flakey and that he was Moldie's brother and they hadn't seen each other for many years. I wondered what he was thinking and felt sorry for him.

"Come on," said Sam. "The boat hire place is just around the next bend. At least we know the yacht is still here with Clair on board."

As we climbed into the cars, I squeezed Moldie's hand, as did Pauline, to show that we understood what he was thinking, and he smiled weakly.

We managed to hire a motor boat without any problems in the village of Shempa.

"We want to hire it until tomorrow," Moldie told the man who ran the outfit. "We have always had the urge to row on this lake in the dark."

The man looked at us oddly, but shrugged his shoulders as if to say some people are mad, and asked for a larger deposit, so we paid him his larger deposit.

The boat was on a shingle beach and the man helped us push it into the water. He told Moldie how to start the outboard motor but it was all very simple and even I could have managed it.

We all climbed in and went for a short cruise, then switched off the engine and tried out the oars. Everything worked perfectly and Sam grunted with satisfaction.

"It'll do."

There was no sign of the yacht which had disappeared around the headland, but we weren't worried. It couldn't be far away.

We rode back to the shingle beach, pulled the boat out of the water, and explored the village. We found a small local café, ate a meal and waited for dark. As dusk was approaching we drove back to the headland and saw the yacht was anchored not far off the shore and Sam grunted again.

"Perfect," he said.

The three men got changed there, dressing entirely in black. Black boots, trousers and polo neck jumper and black gloves. As soon as they had launched the motorboat onto Lake Bongadina they would pull on black balaclavas, so only their eyes peeped through. They looked like bandits who were up to no good, and I suppose that that was what they were.

They cut the engine quite a long way from the yacht and very quietly rowed the last few hundred yards. The night was cloudy and in their dark clothes they were pretty certain no one would see them.

They glided slowly to the ladder dangling in the water, slowing the boat by gently back peddling and tied it to the ladder. Sam climbed the ladder first, followed by Moldie with Stu at the rear.

Moldie had mixed emotions. Partly he was absolutely terrified. He couldn't really believe he was illegally boarding the Prime Minister's yacht in the middle of the night. Partly he was excited at the prospect of seeing Clair again, and partly he was excited and worried about meeting his brother Flakey after all these years.

They climbed on board and very slowly and carefully explored the deck. It didn't take long. There was no one to be found.

"That's strange," thought Sam. "Surely with the Prime Minister on board they would have a lookout.?"

He began to have doubts.

From the plans Moldie had supplied they had a good idea of the layout of the yacht and Sam and Moldie went straight to the servants quarters whilst Stu kept guard on deck. Sam slowly and carefully pushed open a bedroom door to see two men asleep in twin beds. They were snoring lightly. To save time he just shot them both with darts, and they didn't make a sound.

In the next bedroom a man and a woman were asleep in a double bed. This must be the local's niece, Sam reckoned. He shot the man with a dart and woke the girl up with a hand over her mouth and a knife at her throat.

She struggled for a second and then went totally still as he pressed the side of the blade against her windpipe.

Moldie came over and spoke to her in Abacadian, but she shook her head and he looked amazed.

"What is it?" asked Sam.

"They've gone," replied Moldie. "Clair and Rum and the two guards left earlier this afternoon. They will probably be back in Snuka by now," and Sam sat down on the edge of the bed and swore, long and grossly.

"Ask her how she knows they've gone to Snuka," but the girl answered in English.

"My boss, the Prime Minister, told me ," she said proudly. "I am stay here on yacht and I am make sure it clean ready. He rent it out private in two week and I am to be cook."

"I want to go and check," and Sam dragged the girl with him. She put up no resistance but gasped when she saw the man lying next to her.

"He's sleeping," said Moldie. "He'll wake up in the morning."

He pushed open the door to the main cabin and it was empty and he swore again.

Bugger. Bugger, bugger, bugger. They had missed her again, by just a few hours. Again.

He whistled and went up onto deck, taking the girl with him. Stu had been hiding behind a pile of neatly bound ropes and magically appeared when he saw Sam. For a second he thought the girl was Clair but then saw she wasn't and looked at Sam.

"They left this afternoon, she says, and are probably now back in Snuka."

Stu also swore.

"What now?" he asked.

"There are three guards asleep in bed. I shot them with darts. And this girl. I think we should tie them up and bugger off. We can let the authorities know in the morning to come and release them. By then we should be well on our way back to Balhas."

Balhas was a town in Abacadia, but in a totally different direction from Snuka. He hoped the girl would remember him saying that and send the police or army in that direction.

"Can I quickly question her first?" asked Moldie.

"Sam nodded, "But keep it short."

They took her down to her bedroom and whilst Moldie talked to her, tied up the three men. Then they tied up the girl, and left.

They climbed down the ladder to the boat, switched on the motor, and headed back to Alice and Pauline.

Pauline and I were waiting in the car by the shore. We had the windows cracked but the doors locked. We waited in silence, with our own thoughts. My thoughts were please, please bring mother with you, though I also wondered how Moldie was feeling, meeting his brother after all these years.

We both heard the outboard motor at the same time but waited in the car as we had been told. Only when we saw three dark figures walking towards us, undeniably Sam and Stu and Moldie, did we get out and go to meet them. Mother wasn't there and I felt a great sadness sweep over me. I guessed what had happened. She'd got away again.

They climbed into Lady Sammy and as I drove the

301

short distance to Sammy Two Sam told us what had happened. They then got changed back into their travel clothes and we set off on the return nine hour journey to Snuka. We left a large gap between the two cars, and for part of the way took separate routes. Sam reckoned that in the morning, after they had phoned the local police station in Karata to tell them about the four captives on the yacht, the police would be looking for three men, and not a man and a woman or even two men and a woman. Hopefully they would be looking in totally the wrong direction, if they looked at all.

It was a long and despondent drive through the night, but we weren't stopped once, and eventually arrived at the house in Snuka and, after phoning the Karata police station, went to bed.

Two days later though, we received better news, when Moldie heard from Flower that mother was back in Bim Dram's house. Our original plan of rescuing her from there could once again be used.

We just needed to wait until she was on her own.

But her passport hadn't arrived. That was a concern. We phoned Theo to keep him up to date with what was happening and he told us he had posted it off to us over two weeks previously.

"It should have arrived by now," he said. "Uncle Flambert sends his best wishes."

No passport was a problem. We decided to wait a bit longer. Maybe it would turn up.

Chapter 37 - Rescued, Just

The days and nights in Bim Dram's bedroom continued as before but this time I was a lot more frustrated. Escape had been so close, but it hadn't happened and now I felt angry as well as bored and frustrated.

Bim, however, was absolutely charming. He still made love to me twice a day, which was okay, but he treated me more like an equal, rather than his personal mistress. We talked about Angel's Hair Falls and his country home. He didn't seem keen to talk about my time on Rum Hearty's yacht, but I told him all the details anyway. He knew I was teasing him, especially when I told him how wonderful Rum was, what a gentleman and how lucky Abacadia was to have such a competent Prime Minister.

When I told him how good Rum was in bed, he grumbled, looked jealous, tried to change the subject, laughed and made love to me, just to prove he was as good a lover as his boss.

Even with his very small penis.

Bim Dram, bless him, had even brought with him the small exercise book from Heavenly Winds in which I had been keeping notes about my stay there and he chuckled as he handed it over to me.

"It could make a good novel," he said. "I'm glad you kept my name out of it."

So I continued to write it up, putting in my experiences and thoughts, and that passed a bit of time.

Once Bim even took me shopping to an out-of-town-sort-of-retail-park-type-place. It was sort of touristy, with lots of small shops and cabins selling just about everything you could think of. He bought me a cute but cheap ladies watch and a huge bunch of flowers. How kind.

Two guards came with us, with their dart guns in full view, and Bim held my hand the whole time. He had to, as our wrists were handcuffed together. Heaven knows what the other shoppers thought of us.

Flower still came in everyday to clean for me. I had a little swear to myself when she told me that Moldie and the others had driven to lake Bongadina and they had boarded the boat just a few hours after I had left. At least they were still trying to rescue me and surely it would come soon!

She passed on messages of encouragement from Moldie and Alice and Pauline. The original plan of rescue was still there, they said. They were just waiting for another night when Bim Dram would be away. I just had to be patient.

Then the day arose. Bim had to go away on business somewhere and wouldn't be returning until the following evening he told me. For some reason, he wouldn't tell me where he was going. A more suspicious woman might have thought he was going to spend the night with a woman but I wasn't suspicious at all. Well, only a little bit.

I told Flower when she came in to clean that Bim wouldn't be there that night, and she, I assume, told Moldie and I wondered what would go wrong this time.

That evening, I was extremely tense and nervous. I had tried to read a book that Bim had left me. I had requested a romantic novel and he had brought me '50 Shades of Grey.' Ironic, I thought. I could write a sexier novel than that after the last few weeks!

I went to bed at my usual time, and turned off the lights. I then remembered to open one curtain, and leave one closed, to confirm I was on my own. I slept in the nude. Flower had told me previously that dark suitable clothes would be provided for me to slip into.

I tried to sleep but it was very difficult to drop off. I was far too nervous. I think I might have dozed for a few minutes then eventually did fall asleep.

I was awoken by a light tapping against the window. My nerves were so tense I almost jumped off the bed. I slid out of bed instead, pulled on the dressing gown, and tiptoed over to the window. There was a man there. I could just make out his outline against the lights of Snuka. It looked like he was wearing a black balaclava, with only his eyes showing. He looked sinister and scary.

He held his finger to his lips, and I nodded. He held up a thumb and winked at me, I think. He held up a piece of card, which he illuminated with a small torch.

'My name is Sam,' it read. 'I am a friend of Alice and Pauline and Moldie. Stu is at the bottom of this ladder. I have a bag of clothes for you to get dressed into.'

He pushed a small black bag through the small gap at the top of the window, and I grabbed it. He nodded and I took the contents out of the bag. I quickly put on a black tracksuit and black trainers and pulled a black balaclava over my head. There were also a pair of thin black gloves, and I put them on as well. They all fitted me, vaguely. I did, however, grab the small exercise book and rolled it up and shoved it into a pocket.

Sam signalled me to move away from the window so I sat on the bed. I thought I saw Sam put something that looked like a plunger up against the window. Then he got something else out of his pocket that looked like a knife. He held it against the edge of the glass at the bottom of the window and started moving it horizontally. It gave a high pitched screech, and I realised then that it was glass cutter. He intended to cut the glass completely out of the window. The plunger thing would stop it crashing to the ground.

I could just make out Sam as he continued cutting around the window. It took a few minutes but he eventually reached the bottom corner where he had started. I watched as he pushed with the plunger. He seemed to wiggle it slightly and then the glass moved and he slowly lowered it onto the bedroom floor.

I walked back to the window, and Sam took my hand. He whispered in my ear. He spoke with a broad west country accent, not dissimilar to the Worcestershire accent I had grown up with, and it gave me a sense of pleasure to hear him.

"Hold my hand and step carefully through the window. I am standing on a ladder."

He put what looked like a small black duvet on the window

ledge, presumably to stop me catching my clothes on any bits of glass. He thought of everything.

"Bring it with you," he whispered.

The hole in the window wasn't very big. I put one leg through it and Sam guided my foot onto the top rung of the ladder. My bottom went through next, then my other leg. Sam went down the ladder first, and I slowly followed with the duvet. I was feeling more excited than nervous. It was like something from a James Bond film.

Looking down, in the gloom I could just see Stu holding the ladder as Sam stepped onto the ground. I joined them, and Stu grinned at me and whispered, "Nice to meet you, Lady Clair."

The two of them carefully moved the ladder away from the house and slid it until it was half the size. Stu stooped down and picked up two rifles, I think. He put one over his shoulder and gave the other to Sam.

Sam whispered in my ear.

"Follow right behind us, keeping low. Step carefully. We're going to the wall to climb over," and he gave my arm a squeeze. It was even more like a James Bond film.

Stu picked up the front end of the ladder, and Sam followed with the back, and they carried it between them. They moved very slowly and I followed in their footsteps. Sam looked back to check I was following.

I was a bit nervous, obviously, but I felt more excited than worried. Sam and Stu seemed so professional and radiated confidence. I wondered who they were. Were they the two men in the photo Bim had shown me? Probably. I would soon find out.

We crossed the lawn to the wall and moved alongside it until we came to a place where some trees overhung. They leant the ladder up against the wall and Stu climbed up.

It was at that moment that the two dogs arrived. Dogs I knew nothing about and, I later found out, Sam and Stu also knew nothing about.

They came silently and swiftly and one attacked Sam and one attacked me. I was knocked flying, and landed on my front with the dog on my back. It's teeth were in my shoulder and it was shaking me violently, then suddenly it yelped and grunted and went still, and it's dead weight was on top of me. Stu had seen what was happening and had jumped down from the wall, landing next to me and the dog, and had slit it's throat with a sharp knife. The dog had died almost instantly. He pushed it off me then leapt over to Sam and the other dog. It was extremely dark. There was a small amount of light from the street lamps, but I think Sam had a hand on it's throat, and was desperately holding the slavering dog at arms length.

Stu also killed that dog by slitting it's throat, pushed it off Sam, then rushed back to me.

"Are you alright?" he asked, gently sitting me up, but my shoulder hurt. Badly. The pain was intense, and I gasped with it.

"My shoulder," I moaned, "It had it's teeth in my shoulder."

Stu took out his phone, which seemed an odd thing to do at that instant, but he was sending a pre-done text to Moldie to tell him something gone wrong and wait until he heard something else.

Sam was uninjured, but some guards had been alerted by the commotion, and suddenly the garden was flooded with light. I turned and saw four men running towards us from around the corner of the house. They appeared to be carrying guns, and shouted something in Abacadian. I think it was something like 'Stop,' but I wasn't sure.

"Shit," said Sam.

He grabbed me and he and Stu ran away from them, grabbing the ladder as they ran by. My shoulder was on fire but I ignored the pain and ran with them. They ran straight to a darker corner of the garden, and ducked behind a bush. We were now hidden from the running men, at least for a few seconds, and Stu shoved the ladder up against the garden wall and immediately climbed up, stopping at the top.

Sam had turned back and was firing a gun towards the men. It didn't go bang, more like whiz and I wondered what sort of gun it was that went whiz instead of bang. Then something clattered against the wall near to me, Sam fired again, then hissed at me to climb the ladder.

I tried but my shoulder felt like red hot needles were being sadistically plunged in and wiggled about. I tried not to make a noise but I couldn't help myself and moaned. I gritted my teeth and climbed the ladder and Stu leant down and grabbed my collar and half pulled and half helped me up the ladder. I almost passed out with the pain but then I was on top of the wall. Stu had taken off his jacked and I was sitting on that as he jumped down the other side of the wall.

"Jump," he hissed, "I'll catch you," and at that moment, I felt something hit me in my leg. I didn't know what it was. It was a dart from a dart gun I found out later. I jumped, I vaguely remember Stu catching me and then pain free darkness.

Chapter 38 - Together

Pauline and I watched Sam and Stu and Moldie drive away down the road. There was no point in us trying to sleep, so we made a cup of tea and sat in the kitchen and talked.

"Please, God," said Pauline, "Please let mother escape this time. Please."

Pauline wasn't religious, neither was I, but I knew exactly how she felt and I prayed also.

"Please bring mother to us, safe and sound."

Less than an hour later, and we heard a car approaching the house. It slowed and through a gap in the curtains, we saw it was Lady Sammy. We watched her pull into the drive and disappear into the garage. We hurried through to the kitchen and through a door and into the garage, and saw Sam and Stu and Moldie climb out and then gently lift mother out of the back seat. She was obviously unconscious, and her left shoulder was covered in blood. Lots of blood.

Pauline and I both gasped.

"She's been hit by a dart gun, and bitten by a dog," said Sam. "We need to treat her shoulder and then put her to bed so she can sleep it off. Come on, let's get her to the bathroom."

He gently picked her up in his arms and carried her through to the bathroom, where he sat her down on a stool.

"Moldie," he ordered. "Hold her still," which Moldie did.

Stu had taken a small medical bag out of his pack, which he always carried.

Sam looked at Pauline and me and said, in brisk tone, "Come on you two, snap out of it and help."

They didn't really need our help but they wanted us to 'snap out of it.' We were both in a state of shock, I think, but his harsh words made us come back to reality.

"What do you want us to do?" I asked.

"Get a bowl of warm water, and clean towels, then make everyone a cup of tea."

Pauline and I returned with some clean towels and a washing up bowl full of warm water and watched as Sam gently cut away mothers top with a pair of kitchen scissors. She wasn't wearing a bra and I noticed Moldie looking at her breasts longingly. Sam and Stu also had a quick glance, but that was all.

Her shoulder looked a bloody mess, and Sam carefully examined it with gentle, probing fingers but mother still groaned a couple of times.

"We're trained for this sort of thing in the SAS," explained Stu. "Sam has treated much worse injuries than this. Don't worry, he's rather good," and Sam grunted.

After about five minutes examination Sam grunted again.

"Well, I can't detect any broken bones," he said.

Stu took his place and also felt her shoulder and he concurred with Sam.

"I agree. She's been lucky."

"We have always backed each other up this way," said Sam. "One of us might find something the other has missed."

Sam then used one of the towels, which he had dampened with warm soapy water in the wash basin, to gently wash the wound. They both examined the cuts and teeth marks, then Sam gently squeezed them, one by one, to make them bleed.

I gasped. So much blood was oozing out but Stu explained.

"Bleeding helps to get rid of any infections. Dogs teeth can carry all sorts of nasty things. Lots of carnivorous animals teeth are the same. If a lion bites you, you are more likely to die from blood poisoning than from the actual bite."

I think he was talking to reassure us but it wasn't working.

"Moldie," asked Sam, "Is there rabies in Abacadia," and Pauline and I gasped again.

Moldie shook his head.

"I don't think so. I don't really know. I've never heard of it here. I can check, if you like."

"I doubt it is here," said Sam, "But yes please Moldie, could you check?" and he disappeared through to the living room.

"Don't worry," said Stu. He could see that both Pauline and I were horrified by the thought of mother having rabies. "There is a vaccine against rabies. If we think there is any chance of her being infected we will take her straight to hospital. It's not a major problem, I promise," but we still reached for each other's hands and squeezed.

Sam reached out his hand and Stu passed him a small bottle.

"Ethanol," he explained. "This will completely clean the wounds. It will sting rotten and, even unconscious, your mother might groan and move. Now, grab hold her other arm and keep her still."

Stu held her injured arm, whilst Pauline and I held the other, then, using some cotton wool, Sam washed the shoulder with ethanol, and mother did moan and she did struggle and it took all our strength to hold her still.

Sam carefully put the top back on the ethanol bottle, then Stu passed him a tube of cream.

"Antiseptic cream, savlon," and we nodded.

Sam spread the savlon over her shoulder, then took some bandages from his bag and gently wrapped them around.

"Do you two want to get her ready for bed. Wash her and put on her nightie. When she wakes up we'll give her some augmentin, which is another antibiotic, and some paracetamol. She's certain to be in some pain. Until then, we must let her sleep. If Moldie's example by Lake Lucinda is anything to go by, she should sleep for at least three hours. Now, get her into bed, and we'll make a cup of tea."

Sam picked mother up in his arms and carried her through to the bedroom, laid her gently down on the double bed and left the room.

Pauline and I undressed her, noticing how pale her skin looked, washed her, pulled her favourite nightie over her head, being very careful with her bad shoulder, and tucked her up into bed. We both kissed her forehead, then walked into the living room.

The boys were sitting around the table, and Stu poured us both a cup of tea from the pot.

"All done?" asked Sam, and we nodded.

"Good news," he continued. "Moldie has found out that there has been no reported cases of rabies anywhere in Abacadia for over twenty years and, thinking about it, there would be no way that Bim Dram would allow his dogs to have rabies, so I think we're one hundred percent safe about that," and I let out a sigh of relief.

"What now?" I asked, when I had finished my tea.

"Moldie will keep an eye on Clair for now. He will call us if he needs us. Otherwise, for the rest, sleep."

Chapter 39 - Goodbye Bim

I woke, shaking, from a nightmare. I was mouse, and a cat was playing with me. It had me in it's mouth and was shaking me from side to side. I moaned, and opened my eyes, and there was Moldie's face, just inches from me, and I sighed. Then I groaned, as a sharp pain shot through my left shoulder and down my arm. I looked down to see my shoulder was bandaged and I vaguely recalled what had happened. On top of the wall I had been hit by something, I was fairly sure about that.

Moldie was speaking to me.

"Clair, darling, try and sit up. You must take some tablets for the pain in your shoulder."

He helped me sit up, and despite myself, I moaned again. The pain was grim, and I could see anguish on his face. He put a pillow behind my back and I sat back wearily.

Here," he said, and put two pills into my hand. I put them in my mouth and he handed me a glass of water. I swallowed them, then he gave me two more pills and I swallowed them as well. I didn't question him, just swallowed.

"Oh, Moldie," I said, "It's so good to see you," and I reached for his hand with my good arm and squeezed. "Where are we?"

"We're in a safe house belonging to a friend in Snuka. Alice and Pauline are asleep in the next bedrooms, along with Sam and Stu."

"Sam and Stu?"

"Of course, you don't know them. They are former SAS soldiers and came out from England with the girls to rescue you. They're sleeping at the moment and I think we should let them sleep a bit longer. It was a long and stressful night for them."

"And for you," I said, but he shrugged.

"I'm okay. I'll catch up on my sleep later. Would you like a cup of tea," but I shook my head.

"Just tell me what happened. Oh Moldie, it's so good to be with you again," and he kissed me gently then told me the story of my rescue.

We talked quietly together for a while, then there was a tap on the door, and Alice and Pauline entered the room.

All three of us started crying and I think there were tears in Moldie's eyes as well. We hugged, gently, I told them my shoulder didn't hurt much, then the two men who had rescued me came into the room.

"These are Sam and Stu," said Alice, and I could tell immediately from the expressions on both my daughters faces that Sam and Stu were more than just friends, and I smiled to myself.

'Good for them,' I thought.

I thanked them for rescuing me, and they shrugged.

"All part of the service," said the one called Sam. "I would like to examine your shoulder please," he said, looking embarrassed. "You're going to have to take off your nightie. Sorry."

I smiled, as everyone turned their backs, including my daughters, and Moldie pulled it gently over my head. I groaned again, it really did hurt, then Moldie pulled the duvet up to my neck. I wondered why. They must have seen me partly naked when treating me.

"Okay," said Moldie, and they all turned around.

Sam took off the bandages and examined my shoulders. I could tell by his careful, gentle fingers that he knew what he was doing. He grunted in satisfaction.

"There's no infection," he said. "All being well, it should heal up completely, though you will probably have some small scars and it will be sore for a few days. Memento's of Abacadia. Moldie, have you given her the antibiotic pills and the paracetamols? Good. I'll reapply the bandage, to stop your clothes rubbing against it."

He rubbed on some savlon, I saw, then the bandage, and smiled.

"Good," he said, "I think we should all have something to eat, including you Clair, and then we have some talking to do. Come on Stu, let's get cooking," and they left the bedroom.

Moldie helped me put my nightie back on, and left to help with breakfast, then I looked at the girls.

"Are you, er, two couples?" and they blushed and I smiled.

"Tell me all about them."

After breakfast, well, brunch, really, it was almost noon, of sausages and bacon and eggs and bread and butter, Sam and Stu filled me in with the details of my rescue, finally getting to the part where I had been shot by the dart gun.

"You were scrambling over the top of the wall when you were hit," said Stu, and I nodded. I vaguely remembered.

"You just about had the awareness to jump down on the far side," he said, "And I caught you," but I couldn't remember that.

"I climbed the ladder and pulled it up behind me," said Sam. "There were darts flying all around me, but luckily I wasn't hit. One stuck in my pack," and he showed us the dart.

"I jumped down the other side, and Stu handed you over to me, so he could send a prearranged text to Moldie. We both ran, with you over my shoulder, obviously totally unconscious by now. We ran about quarter of a mile, then, thank goodness, saw Moldie driving towards us. We bundled you into the back of the car, chucked the ladder over a fence, and drove back here."

"I was shocked to see you," said Moldie. "You looked in a bad way, but you're okay now."

He put his hand on top of mine and squeezed and we smiled at each other.

"Thank you," I said, to everyone. "Thank you for rescuing me."

"Our pleasure." Sam grinned. "Any time you want rescuing, My Lady, just give us a call. Always at your service," and we all laughed. I liked him, and Stu, immediately.

"It was a blessing that you were unconscious," said Stu. "That saved you a lot of pain and I think it made rescuing you a lot easier."

Sam nodded.

"But, the more important question is, what do we do now? We have made plans, Clair, but we need to discuss them with you. Do you feel up to that?"

I nodded. I wasn't feeling brilliant, my head was thumping and my shoulder ached badly, but I was capable of serious discussion, I reckoned. At least for a while.

"Let's clear up the details of the rescue."

I could tell that Sam was the leader of the two of them. He seemed very capable, which gave me a pleasant confidence.

"Stu, what did we leave behind in Bim Dram's garden, and can any of it be traced back to us?"

Stu had a think.

"The ladder, obviously, but we were all wearing gloves, and it was wiped clean of fingerprints before we left. It is a fairly common ladder and could have been bought from a number of retailers. And it was chucked into a garden a few hundred yards away. It might not be found by now, or for quite a long time. So not a problem."

He had another think.

"The small painted black duvet, but again, there is no way they could find out anything from that."

Sam nodded and opened up the rucksack he had used on the rescue.

"I have the glass cutter, the spot torch and, most importantly, the piece of card with 'My name is Sam. I am a friend of Alice and Pauline and Moldie. Stu is at the bottom of this ladder. Keep away from the window,' written on it."

He held it up to show us.

"Leaving that behind could have caused problems, especially with Moldie's name on it."

He sighed.

"Anything else to worry about?"

"They may find some of Clair's blood on the top of the wall," suggested Stu, "But all that will tell them is that somebody has been injured, and they know that anyway. And if they could analyse the blood, they would only discover it was Clair's and they know she was there. I can't think of anything else."

"What about the car?" wondered Moldie. "I don't think there are any CCTV camera's in the area, though I may be wrong, but somebody somewhere may have noticed it."

"We were using the stolen number plates, so we'll swap them for the official ones before we go out again. Also, we will remove the go-faster stripes, give it a good wash, and then it should look like any other Lada Samara, and there are thousands of those in Snuka. I don't think the car should be a problem."

Moldie and Stu nodded then told me about plans they had made.

"Unfortunately, we don't have your passport with us. We have asked Theo to send it here, but it hasn't arrived. Until it does, we can't really leave the country. So this is what we have planned for you," and they told me about Dave and Laura Gulldred.

"That sounds fine," I said.

I was starting to feel a bit tired and faint, and I could see that Moldie was also having problems keeping his eyes open. Sam also knew.

"You two," he said, gesturing, "Need some sleep. Off you go to bed."

I kissed everyone, and Moldie and I disappeared into the bedroom. My arm really was very painful and Moldie had to help me get undressed, which he enjoyed and I pretended it hurt more than it did so he would enjoy himself helping me bit more. I then pretended I couldn't wash myself so he washed me, all over, which was nice. Then he had to help me put my nightie on, and I climbed into bed whilst Moldie had his wash. He returned wearing pyjamas and climbed in next to me.

I said, "I'm very tired and my arm hurts so much," and he said,

"So am I, but my arm doesn't hurt" and I cuddled up to him, gave him a quick kiss, and was almost asleep in his arms when he said,

"Thank you for allowing me to sleep with you. I was worried you might not, eh, want to."

"Of course I want to sleep with you Moldie. Now, shut up and actually go to sleep."

I woke up in exactly the same position. It was if neither of us had moved. Moldie was asleep . He was breathing lightly so I didn't move. Instead I just thought.

My thoughts roamed over my kidnapping and Bim Dram and my children and England and dogs teeth but always came back to Moldie. How did I feel about him? Whatever happened, I am sure he would be involved in my future.

When he woke, I was still in his arms. I saw him smile as he realised I was there and that smile made me realise how much he loved me. He kissed the top of my head and I knew what was on his mind, but I gently pushed him away.

"Not now," I said. "My shoulder hurts. Soon though."

Immediately he was contrite.

"I'm sorry Clair. I forgot. How is it?"

"Still sore, but getting better. A bit stiff. I need a shower, I think."

Moldie carefully took off the bandage, looked at my shoulder and said he thought it looked better than it had but he wasn't a doctor or a medic.

I went to the bathroom, and had a shower. Moldie felt obliged to help me. He felt so obliged that he actually got in the shower with me, to make sure 'that every square inch of you gets washed properly' he explained. He then helped me get dressed into some of the clothes that he had brought for me from Redik. A pair of jeans and a loose top. I thanked him. We left off the bandage until Sam had had a look.

Back in the bedroom Moldie grinned, and said, "I have something for you."

He went to a cupboard and pulled out a small package and gave it to me. I opened it, and knew that it had to be the notes I had been keeping in Redik.

My diary.

"Thank you," I said. "Have you read it?"

He shook his head.

"No," he said. "Of course I haven't."

"Promise."

"I promise I haven't read it."

He looked shocked that I should even suggest such a thing.

"I'm joking, Moldie. It doesn't matter if you do," I told him. "You can read it when I turn it into a best selling novel."

He looked really shocked at that, and I laughed.

"As if," I said.

Sam and Stu had rustled up a big breakfast for us all. The tastiest scrambled eggs I had ever tasted, and when we had finished, Sam and Stu examined my shoulder again.

"It's looking a bit better," said Sam. "I don't think an infection has set in, and we're lucky about that. Dogs can have all sorts of nasty things stuck to their teeth which can badly infect a bite wound, but you seem okay, Clair. If it's not too sore, I think we should leave the bandage off, at least for a while, to let some air get to it."

Whilst they examined my shoulder we talked some more.

"The first thing we have to do," said Alice, "Is contact Theo and let him know you are safe."

"Yes," agreed Pauline, "He'll be so worried."

"I'll do that," said Moldie.

He took his mobile out of his pocket and said, "Is the number the same as we used to leave the messages?"

"No," said Alice. "He's staying with Uncle Flambert. You need to phone his mobile."

She gave him the number and Moldie started dialling. He got through to Theo surprisingly quickly and handed the phone to Alice.

"Theo," she said, "It's Alice. There's someone here who wants to talk to you!" and handed the phone to me.

"Theo," I said, grinning at the others, "It's your mum. How are you, my darling?"

"Mother. Is that you? Is that really you? How are you? I'm good. Oh mum, it's so good to know you're safe."

I think he was crying by now.

"I'm perfectly fine," I answered, deciding not to worry him about my shoulder. "And the others are all here with me. We're hoping to be home fairly soon."

"When?" he asked, but I couldn't tell him.

"I'm not sure but we're hoping it will be soon," I said. "Give my regards to Flambert."

I asked him about my passport.

"I posted it off over two weeks ago," and he told me the address he had put on the envelope. I looked at Moldie, who nodded. It was correct.

"It hasn't arrived yet," I told him and he sounded a bit concerned.

"You should have received it by now."

We chatted for a few minutes before hanging up.

"He sounds okay," I said, "It was good to talk to him and hear his voice," and it had been good.

"We need to discuss what to do next in more detail," said Sam. "Clair, do you think that Bim Dram will come looking for you?"

Moldie answered for me.

"I think that Bim Dram would be very reluctant to do anything. He has too much to lose. If your kidnapping became known to the press and the general public, almost certainly he would have to step down as a minister, or, at the least, any chances of further promotion, say, to Prime Minister, would be down the chute. Do you agree?"

He was looking at me.

I wasn't totally convinced and said so.

"I think he is so desperately in love with me, or maybe just the idea of having me, that he might not be thinking clearly. I think it would help if I could talk to him and explain things. Not face to face," I said, as I saw the look of shock on their faces, "Just by telephone."

The others all agreed.

"We agree you should do that," they all said.

"He's away somewhere at the moment," I said, "And won't be back in Snuka till late afternoon, I think. I should phone him later."

Moldie and Sam and Stu went to the shops to buy some supplies, they said, but really to let us three girls have a good chinwag.

We talked about home and the charity work, but it soon became obvious to me that they knew about what I had been doing in the apartment in Redik. They were deliberately avoiding asking me any questions about my time there.

I decided to put the question straight to them.

"You know what I was doing in Redik, don't you?" I said.

They looked embarrassed.

"We're all grown up women," I told them. "Do you know?"

They both nodded.

"Yes."

"How did you find out?" I asked them.

"Theo discovered a short film on the internet. We think it was probably sent to potential clients to encourage them to visit you, mother," replied Alice, looking sideways at Pauline.

"Ah, yes, that film. I've also seen it. It's a good film. I think I look rather wonderful in it."

Alice looked shocked.

"Mother, how could you say such a thing? It's pure pornography."

"After what I've been through in the last few weeks, Alice dear," I said gently, "Nothing embarrasses me anymore. Moldie made it," I added, casually.

"Yet you are friends with him!" Alice sounded amazed.

I tried to explain.

"Moldie is a good man. In fact, he is a very good man. His main aim in life is to help his fellow people of Effghania, and they really do need help. There's a lot of poverty, and the money I've earned for Moldie and his friends really has made a tremendous difference to their lives. He figured that kidnapping me and then whoring me out to three very rich clients every week was the quickest and easiest way to make a lot of money to help them. I can't really blame him, to be honest. And it worked."

The two of them looked at me in total horror.

"Do you like him?" I challenged them.

"Well, yes, he seems a decent bloke, but that's not the point," said Alice.

"To you it might sound awful," I continued, "but it wasn't so bad, and after a while I actually started enjoying myself. I mean, what else could I do? And the amount of money I was earning was making such a difference to all the local people. Moldie took me out and showed me. Honestly, it wasn't that bad."

I don't think they really believed me. There was plenty of time for them to get used to the idea.

I changed the subject.

"You've both had your hair done differently," I accused them.

They both chuckled.

"It's a disguise. After the photos were taken of us at the lake, Bim Dram knew what we looked like. We weren't sure if he would come after us so Sam suggested we redo our hair. Nothing exceptional, just different and Moldie arranged for a lady to visit us. Do you like it?" asked Pauline.

"You both look very different, but still very pretty," and we all laughed.

The boys turned up later, with bags of shopping. Sam pulled out some workmen's overalls.

"Do you intend doing some painting?" asked Pauline, with a laugh.

"They're disguises for Moldie and your mum when they go off to visit Dave and Laura tomorrow," explained Sam. "I really don't think there will be any sort of problem, but any time spent on preparation is time well spent. That's what we were always told."

Stu nodded.

"There's some tins of paint and brushes and some cloths and covers in the boot. If you get stopped you are a decorator and his assistant off to paint a house somewhere. Moldie knows where there is a house being painted."

Moldie nodded.

"A friend is having his house decorated at the moment. I've

talked to him and he'll back up my story, but, like Sam says, I really don't think anything will happen."

Moldie had a pay as you go mobile phone which he thought couldn't be traced if we used it to phone a government official. Moldie reckoned, but wasn't totally sure, that the police monitored and recorded such phone calls so it was best, he said, to keep any phone calls short and sweet.

We all walked through to the garage. Sam and Stu were working on the car. Sam was dismantling the two large aerials which were fastened to the back wings and Stu was unpeeling some full length go faster stripes.

"We altered the look of her," said Sam. "Now we are returning her to Lady Sammy once again. We just need to put on her original number plates, and she'll be as good as new."

"Lady Sammy?" I asked.

Alice laughed.

"The car is a Lada Samara, and Pauline named her Lady Sammy. She's the most common car in Abacadia, and the most common colour, which is why we bought her in the first place."

There was another car parked on the drive. It looked identical to the other.

"Lady Sammy Two," said Alice, and I chuckled.

Moldie and I drove off in Lady Sammy to a different part of the city, twenty minutes away, so that if by chance the call was monitored, the police or whoever couldn't place it near the safe house.

Through his ODOE contacts, Moldie had the private phone numbers of all the Abacadian politicians, and this included Bim Dram. We stopped in a quiet suburb and Moldie switched off the engine. I phoned the number we had and a male voice answered in Abacadian.

"Ministry of Home Affairs," he said, "How may I help you?"

"My name is Lady Clair Hamilton," I replied, in my improving but still not brilliant Abacadian. Moldie had helped me with the words and pronunciations but it was still a bit of a struggle.

"I wish to speak with Minister Bim Dram, please."

There was a brief pause, then the voice said, "Please hang on," and then I heard a couple of clicks and Bim Dram spoke to me.

"Lady Clair," he said, sounding very formal. "What a surprise to hear from you. How are you?"

"I'm very well Bim," I said.

I didn't want the phone call to go on too long, so, rather than any informal chatting, I carried on immediately.

"I would like to make a suggestion. I suggest we both forget what has happened. Neither of us want it to become public knowledge. If the British press found out about what has happened to me here, it would be extremely embarrassing for me. I'm sure you can understand that. And if the Abacadian press were to find out what you have done, it could well ruin your political career. I understand you would deny it, but I have too much evidence against you and too many of my friends know about this, including some in England. I suggest you leave me well alone, and let me return to Britain."

There was a silence on the phone.

"Bim," I asked. "Did you hear me?"

"Yes," he said, and I could almost hear him sigh.

"I can hear you."

Another sigh.

"I agree. What happened between us will remain a secret. That I promise."

"Good, Bim. I'm glad you've seen sense."

It was the answer I expected from him.

"If you ever come to England, please don't bother to look me up. Goodbye Bim."

"Goodbye, Lady Clair," and he hung up on me.

Immediately Moldie drove off, turning onto one of the main streets through Snuka. Within seconds we saw a police car drive by in the opposite direction. Was it coincidence or was it sent by Bim Dram to try and catch us? We didn't know and we never would know.

However, that police car worried Sam when we told him later.

"It may be a coincidence, but we can't risk it. You two must definitely leave tomorrow morning after breakfast. I'll let Dave and Laura know."

The men had bought some groceries when they had gone shopping earlier and Sam and Stu offered to cook dinner but I took charge.

"I learnt some new skills in the kitchens in Heavenly Winds which I want to show you," I said. "Come on girls, let's prepare an Abacadian style Hamilton Hall dinner for our men."

Which we did. Washed down with some Cadian wine, of course.

Moldie and I made love that night. Despite all the sex I had had over the last few weeks, it was still nice to have Moldie making love to me. We seemed to bond naturally and it was once again very special for both of us.

And once again, as I drifted off to sleep afterwards, I wondered about me and him and the future.

Chapter 40 - Shadow and Kylie

Next morning Stu transferred the paint and everything from the boot of Lady Sammy to the boot of Lady Sammy Two. He had even opened a couple of the cans and spilt and splashed some paint over the rags and sheets and the paint brushes.

I said goodbye to Alice and Pauline and Sam and Stu. I had just been reunited with them, and now I was leaving them.

"It's just for a few days," said Alice, as I hugged her. "We'll soon be back at Hamilton Hall."

I climbed into the passenger seat with my meagre amount of luggage, one overnight bag. I had a cap on my head with my hair piled up underneath it and out of view. Pauline had used some dark blusher which she had applied on my upper lip. I was wearing the men's overalls, which now had paint splashed on them, and I looked like a teenage boy who was trying to grow his very first moustache. Moldie was also wearing paint splashed overalls and we looked like a man and boy off to do some building work.

That's what we hoped we looked like.

We stopped to fill Sammy Two full up to the brim with petrol and bought some bottles of Cadian wine to give to Dave and Laura.

As Moldie drove, I told him more about my time in Bim Dram's house, teasing him dreadfully with a detailed account of Mkubwa and his world record breaking member, and he kept apologising for letting me get kidnapped at Lake Lucinda. I told him not to worry about it.

I needed to tell Moldie about his brother, Flakey, and this seemed as good as a time as any.

"I have something to tell you," I said. "News about your family," and he stiffened, and looked at me.

"What about them? Is it good news or bad?" he asked.

"Well, good news. Nothing to be alarmed about."

"I'm sorry," he said. "Please tell me the news."

So I told him about Flakey being an army sergeant and working for Bim Dram but he amazed me by telling me he already knew.

"How do you know?" I asked, and he told me how Alice and Pauline had met him at Lake Lucinda and how he had actually seen him on Rum Hearty's yacht on Lake Bongadina.

"I also talked to the young girl who worked on the yacht, what was her name, Dragonfly?"

I nodded.

"She told me a bit about Flakey, and now I even have a phone number for him. I intended to try and contact him once you are safely back in England, Clair. What do you know?"

"All I managed to get out of him was that he saw one of your brothers a couple of weeks ago. He was also a sergeant but in another army unit, he said. He also seemed to be fairly sure that your mother worked as a cook in a restaurant in Snuka, though he didn't know where."

Moldie thanked me for the news, and there was silence for a while as we both thought our own thoughts.

After about an hour Moldie turned off the main road and onto a narrow dirt road. We travelled for a couple of minutes through beautiful countryside until we came upon a good sized house.

It looked slightly Dutch to me, with a very high and steep roof, and columns on a veranda. There was an immaculate lawn and I thought I saw a lake glistening in the near distance.

"Lovely place," I said to Moldie. "Is this where Dave and Laura live?"

"I believe so," he replied and then I remembered he had never actually been there before.

They came out to introduce themselves and directed us to sit on chairs on the lawn. Sam had told me that the house was bugged. They didn't seem that pleased to see us, but Sam also had warned me about their anxieties about losing everything, so I just kept calm and grateful.

We shared a pot of tea and some biscuits, but the

conversation was stilted until Dave asked us how I had been rescued and we told him the story we had decided on in the car. A very abridged story.

Dave chuckled and even Laura smiled.

"I bet you're so pleased to be free from that horrible man," she said, and reached over the table to squeeze my hand.

However, they seemed relieved when Moldie asked them if they could show us to the village and our hut.

"Follow me," said Dave. "It's a bit of a drive so I'll take my car as well, and drive back once you are settled in."

Off he went, we waved to Laura, and set off after him.

"I see what you mean," I said to Moldie. "They really don't want us here."

"It's only for a few days, hopefully," said Moldie, "Then we will be on our way."

We followed Dave for about ten minutes, maybe a mile or so, then came upon a village, which was in a clearing in a jungle thicket and shaded by Tamarind trees. There were about twelve huts, which were built on short stilts and constructed with wattle and daub walls and roofs thatched with coconut palms. They looked exactly like I expected them to look.

Picture postcard perfect.

Dave parked next to one of them, and signalled for us to pull up alongside.

"This is your hut," he told us as we got out of the car. "It's pretty basic but I think you will enjoy your stay. I'll introduce you to the elder. His name is Shadow. He'll look after you. We've had people staying here before so he knows what to do. Let me show you inside first."

He ducked in through the door, and we followed him in. It was gloomy inside. There was just one small window. The only furniture were two wooden chairs and a wooden table, and the bed, which was made of clay on a raised platform, with a sheet laid on straw. A blanket was folded up alongside two pillows. There was a lantern hanging from the roof, which could obviously be lit at night time.

"Basic," said Dave, "But quiet and safe. And it's only for a few days."

He looked at Moldie, who nodded.

"Just a few days," he answered.

Dave went outside and walked across a small open space to another hut, which was slightly larger than the others. We followed and noticed an old man sitting on a mat outside the door. He looked ancient, but was, I found out later, only sixty six years old. He had long white, white hair which hung in a pony tail and actually touched the ground. His beard, which was black, jet black, also hung down and also touched the ground. Very odd.

Dave squatted down next to him and they talked. Shadow looked up at us. He held out a hand in greeting, and grinned, showing a wonderful set of obviously false teeth.

Dave stood up.

"I'll leave you in Shadow's capable hands. Have an explore. His great granddaughter, who's called Kylie, after the singer, will come and find you when food is ready. Just let me know when you are ready to leave."

Moldie nodded.

"Thanks mate," and shook his hand. I also shook his hand, but then, on impulse, leaned forward and gave him a peck on the cheek.

"We really appreciate this, Dave. Thank you and Laura so much," and gave him my most dazzling smile.

He gave a sickly smile back.

"No problem. I'm sorry if I've been a bit grumpy, but we have so much to lose."

He drove off and I smiled at Shadow.

"Thank you for letting us stay here," I said to him in Abacadian, and he looked a bit shocked. Moldie laughed behind me.

"What do you think you have just told him?" he asked, chuckling.

"I thanked him for letting us stay here," I said. "Didn't I?"

Moldie laughed again.

"What you actually said was 'Thank you for cooking us till we are dead.'"

He chuckled again then spoke to Shadow, who also laughed. Shadow took my hand and smiled.

"It is good you try to speak our language," he said in very slow Abacadian. "During your stay here, we must talk together, you and me, and you can tell me about England and your bad weather and your Abacadian will get much better."

At least I think that was the gist of what he said.

Moldie had gone to the car and returned with a bottle of Cadian Wine, the last bottle that Stig de Silva had given me. Shadow took it with a nod, and placed it carefully beside him.

"We will share this later," he said.

Moldie and I changed out of our overalls in the hut and put on the traditional clothes he had bought for us. I put on a loose fitting white cotton shirt with a slight V neck and long dark baggy pants, held up with a wide blue band tied at the back. I put them on and felt very comfortable in them. Cool and free. I understood why the locals wore such clothes.

When I got home, I would suggest them to Danger Goodness. I think they could well become popular in England, especially during the summer.

Moldie had bought himself a plain cream coloured shirt and plain brown trousers. We both wore rubber sandals on our feet.

Moldie tied a think green silk scarf around my head to hide my blonde hair. The local women all had black hair.

He stood back to admire me.

"For a common peasant," he grinned, "You look quite stunning."

We went for a walk around the village. Apart from Shadow, the only people we saw were half a dozen children playing with a dog and an old woman who was obviously looking after them.

"Everyone else will be at work in the fields," explained Moldie. "They'll return at dusk."

We spent the day exploring the village and relaxing. It was good to relax. I was still finding it hard to believe I was actually free, and I kept holding Moldie's hand for reassurance. He understood how I felt and squeezed my hand and smiled.

Kylie, Shadow's great granddaughter, found us lying in hammocks hung between two palm trees beside a lake. We were watching hundreds of water birds squabbling and making quite a noise. She was a pretty little thing, possibly about twelve years old, and wearing nothing but a short grass skirt. She smiled shyly at me as I climbed out of the hammock, then curtsied.

"Hello Lady Clair," she said, and I was amazed that she spoke English.

I asked her about that and she told me that as a young child she had shown herself to be extremely bright so had been sent to boarding school in Snuka and had learnt English while she was there. She was doing well at school and wanted to go to university. She would be the first person from the village ever to go to university and everyone was proud of her.

"Food will be ready in one half of an hour," she said, and wondered if we would like to get ready?

The evening meal was a communal affair, with everyone sitting around tables in a large hut. It had open walls, and was right next to the lake. It was just about the most idyllic place I had ever had dinner.

There were big wooden bowls of rice in the middle of each table, to which we helped ourselves, using wooden spoons to pile the rice onto our wooden shallow bowls. There were two other bowls per table. One was full of hot spicy vegetable curry and the other was full of hot spicy goat stew.

"This is delicious," I told Moldie, who then told everyone else what I had said. They all laughed and clapped their hands in glee. I felt quite embarrassed.

We had some fresh melon for pudding and it was all washed down with fresh coconut water. It had a sweet, nutty taste, and Moldie told me it was the clear liquid that was tapped from the centre of young, green coconuts.

It was the best meal I had had, probably, considering the circumstances, ever.

When we had finished, Kylie shyly came over to us. She took

my hand and told me her granddad wanted us to share the bottle of wine with him. We walked to his hut and he was still sitting where we had left him. Kylie told us that food was brought to him. He invited us to sit next to him on two low wooden stools.

He had three small bark mugs with him and Kylie poured a miniscule of red wine into each. He toasted us, we toasted him, and he started asking me about England. He wanted to know about the queen and football and Manchester United, which seemed to be the only two words of English he knew.

Eventually we escaped, washed in the lake with everyone else, and retired to our hut. We cuddled down on our straw bed, which was surprisingly comfortable, and then Moldie asked me if it might be possible for us to make love again and I told him that I had never made love in a mud hut lying on a straw bed and maybe this is was the opportunity I had been waiting for and he said that I most certainly should grab this opportunity and I agreed with him so we made love and it was very nice despite the bit of straw which worked it's way up my bottom.

The next morning, Moldie and I had a long chat before we got up. He started it.

"Now that it looks like you'll certainly be back in England soon, do you mind if we talk about, well, things when you are there?"

"What sort of things, Moldie," I asked, though I had a good idea what was on his mind.

"Clair," he said, holding both of my hands in both of his, "Over the past few weeks you have earned a huge amount of money for my people and you have seen how that money has helped. It has made such a massive difference to so many of them, and I can't thank you enough. But, we could always do with more money. There is still so much to do."

"I will continue to raise money and awareness from home," I said.

I wasn't sure what he was hinting at.

"I have four job offers and I will happily give most of the

money I earn from them to help you."

"Four job offers?" he asked. "The ladies dresses and the wine. What else?"

"Golden Stud offered me a part in one of his films," I reminded him, "And I will get paid for that. And Sparkling Eyebrows wants me to star in more of her lesbian porn films."

Moldie chuckled.

"I had forgotten about them. Clair the film star. Clair the lesbian porn star!"

He became serious once again.

"I need to ask you this. I think I know the answer but I have to ask you anyway."

He looked embarrassed and I was wondering what was coming next.

"For the last few weeks, you have been a great success in our, eh, enterprise. We have another dozen or more clients who are willing to pay the $100,000 each to spend the night with you. That's another million dollars. Would you consider at some later time returning to the apartment for two or three weeks? I'm sorry, but I just had to ask!"

I sighed, laid my head back onto the pillow and thought about what he had said. I was a humanitarian. I hated to see people suffer, especially when it was through no fault of their own. Over the last few weeks it was true that I had earned a lot of money and the money really had made a massive difference to so many people. I had seen the differences with my own eyes.

But I had done it by whoring out my body to strangers. That couldn't be right, could it? But, and this was a big but, in all honesty, I hadn't minded. In fact, most of the time I had quite enjoyed myself. Some of the time I had really enjoyed what I had been doing. My mind flitted back over some of the lovers I had had and I smiled as I remembered the four virgins and the visits to Lake Lucinda and the Angel's Hair Falls and Puddle.

I sensed Moldie watching me. I think he expected a big no from me, but instead, much to his obvious amazement, I said,

"Let me think about it. I'm not saying yes but I'm not saying no. Let's see how my money-making efforts go back in England shall we? And I would need to talk to my family."

"Surely they wouldn't approve."

He was a bit taken aback, I think, by my answer.

"Probably not," I said, "But they might if I explained things to them properly. Let's talk about the other business offers. Would you act as my agent for me?"

I had been thinking about that and he was the perfect choice. By now I trusted him completely and knew he wouldn't swindle me. He was the only one who had all the contact details for Stig de Silva and his clothes and Danger Goodness and his wine and Sparky and Gold with their film offers. And the children could help and keep an eye on him.

He looked pleased with that suggestion.

"Yes, of course," and we left it at that.

Moldie and I spent eight idyllic days in our mud hut in the village. We spent time making love, as always, but also lots of time exploring. There were a couple of basic bicycles which we borrowed and cycled many miles around the local beautiful countryside. There were lanes and hills and woods and jungle and lots of lakes and streams and we enjoyed picnics, made by Kylie. There was a rock temple and intriguing rocky outcrops and caves to explore.

We borrowed a boat and rowed on the lake, fishing and swimming and bird watching. We laughed a lot together and my shoulder slowly recovered. The pain went, replaced by stiffness but Moldie massaged it for me and it soon felt almost as good as new.

The villagers went about their daily lives, mostly farming, and we offered to help but they gently refused.

"You are on holiday," said Kylie. "You should not be working."

It was an idyllic few days and I spent some time each day writing in my diary. Moldie helped.

Every day I phoned Alice and Pauline or they phoned me. They were pleased I was having such a good time but they were also enjoying themselves. Now that I had been rescued and the pressure was off, they could really relax and they were treating it as a real holiday.

There had been no sign of Bim Dram or any indication that he was searching for them or me.

And no passport.

Chapter 41 - Flower

Once mother and Moldie had left, we relaxed. Well, as much as four people can relax after what had happened. We acted like tourists and, to be honest, newly in love lovers. Most of our time was spent sleeping and bonking, but we did occasionally go out to visit shops and other things in Snuka.

Saying that, Sam and Stu still kept a wary lookout for anything unusual, and then, on about the sixth day since mother's rescue, they became a bit twitchy. They had noticed a car driving past the house. To Alice and me it looked like a normal car, but with darkened windows, which meant maybe that it belonged to somebody rich but there were many cars with darkened windows in Snuka. They kept the occupants out of the glare of the extremely bright sunlight.

Sam and Stu had noticed something else about the car.

"I am pretty sure," he explained, "That I saw a video camera of some sort through the window. I may have been mistaken but it's cause for concern."

"Yes," agreed Stu. "And why was it driving so slowly? It may be nothing, but it's definitely suspicious."

"What should we do?" I asked.

"Not panic. Not yet anyway, but I think we should warn your mum and Moldie and pack our stuff into Lady Sammy, ready for a quick getaway," which we did.

We packed three tents and spare clothes and basic cooking equipment and water and dried food and fruit and anything else we could think of. Stu examined the car carefully, checking the oil and water and brake fluid and the tyres, including the spare, and then took the car away and filled her to the top with petrol, and also filled two ten litre containers with petrol, and stowed those in the boot, which was now extremely full up.

Then, very early the next day, there was a knock on the front door. We were having breakfast and Sam and Stu looked at each other. They nodded and without a word got up and walked to the front door. Sam picked up a dart gun and stood to the side of the door as Stu opened it.

A young and rather scared looking young lady stood there. She was pretty with long black hair and looked very nervous.

Stu invited her in and led her through to the dining room. She looked around, obviously looking for someone, and her disappointment that they weren't there was evident.

"Who are you looking for," I asked her gently.

"Lady Clair or Moldie," she said, in a quiet voice. "I have news for them."

"My name is Alice," I said, smiling. "I am Lady Clair's daughter, and this is my sister, Pauline. These men are our friends. We are also good friends of Moldie Bedlam. They are not here at the moment, but anything you want to tell them, you can tell us. We will let them know that you visited and tell them your news. I promise."

She looked at each of us, obviously trying to make up her mind whether to tell us her news.

"Moldie and Lady Clair have told me about you," she said.

We waited.

"ODOE have heard news," she eventually said, "And they have asked me to tell Moldie or Lady Clair. I will tell you instead."

She took a piece of paper out of a pocket of her dress and read.

"There is a huge army presence at Winston Macmillan Airport and everyone is being searched thoroughly. The government say they are looking for some terrorists. They are also undertaking a house to house search over large parts of Snuka and will be coming to this part of the city in the next couple of days."

She put the piece of paper away and looked at us.

"That's the news," she said.

"Is your name Flower?" I asked her, and she nodded.

"Thank you, Flower, for coming to see us and trusting us with this news," I told her, "And we will tell Moldie and Lady Clair, I promise."

We let her out of the front door and she disappeared. We looked at each other.

"I believe her," said Sam.

"So do I," agreed Stu, and Pauline and I nodded.

Sam took control, as usual.

"We must leave," he said. "They may not be looking for us, but on the other hand, they may be. We can't take that chance. But where to go? Any suggestions?"

"Moldie will know of somewhere. We need to phone him and mother anyway," suggested Pauline.

"How are we going to get back to England?" I asked, and that made everyone stop still. How indeed were we going to get back now we couldn't fly from the country's only international airport. Yet another problem to be solved.

Chapter 42 - The café in Bugulla

The phone rang. It was Alice, and she sounded disturbed.

"Mother, we think Bim Dram may be looking for you."

"Why do you say that?"

I was concerned.

She told me that Flower had visited and the news that she had told them.

"We are leaving the house," Alice told me, "And need to meet up with you two and were wondering if Moldie could suggest somewhere."

"Let me think about it," said Moldie, "And tell Alice I will phone them back."

I hung up and Moldie and I looked at each other.

"Bugger," I said, "That bloody Bim Dram. He promised he'd let me go. Bugger."

I buggered a few more buggers then Moldie suggested that we also had to leave as soon as possible and I agreed.

"But where to?" I asked him.

"I'm thinking," he said, sounding a bit irritated. "We can't go back to Lake Lucinda or The Angel's Hair Falls. Too obvious. We need some forest I reckon. Somewhere away from Snuka, heading vaguely in the direction of Effghania. We have friends there. Maybe we could hide in the back streets of Redik. It shouldn't be difficult to keep hidden in one of the thousands of small houses there."

"If Bim gets wind of us being there, wouldn't it go badly for the local people?" I asked, and Moldie nodded.

"It might. Maybe we could do that when the hue and cry is over. First we need somewhere remote and I still think the forest is best."

He thought a bit more.

"There is a range of hills between here and Redik, but off to the west somewhat. They are well forested but not so far off the main road that Lady Sammy and Sammy Two couldn't manage

340

the tracks. I don't think anyone lives there, or not many people. It's called the Forest of the Slumbering Giants, because somebody, many, many years ago, reckon they came upon a giant creature, half man and half gorilla, who was sleeping. It was supposed to be over ten feet tall and dressed in shorts and braces and very hairy. It woke up and chased after the man, who only escaped by jumping into the river and swimming. The beast was unable to swim, it seemed. All utter nonsense, of course, but that is why the forest is called what it is."

He phoned Sam and told him about the Forest of the Slumbering Giants and we agreed we would meet later that afternoon at a café in a small village called Bugulla, which meant 'beside the field' in Abacadian.

"We need to pack up and go," I said, with some sadness. I had really enjoyed my stay in Dave and Laura's village. I wondered if I would ever return. I doubted it. Shame.

We packed our few belongings into the back of Lady Sammy Two and said goodbye to Shadow and Kylie and all the others. I gave Shadow my hairbrush, which I thought would be perfect for his long hair and beard, and I gave Kylie my make-up bag. She was absolutely thrilled.

"The other ladies will be so jealous," she said.

We drove up to the house where Dave and Laura lived and thanked them profusely. They seemed relieved that we were leaving, and made us a quick lunch and a glass of Cadian wine before we left. They already knew about the terrorist alert, but didn't think it had anything to do with me.

"We often get terrorist alerts," Laura explained.

Moldie offered them some money for their hospitality but Laura just laughed.

"It's been a pleasure to help," she said. "We're just glad you're free."

"Sam and Stu are old friends," added Dave, "And I know they would help me if the occasion ever arose. Good luck with getting back to England."

We found out later that as soon as we had left, Dave had

driven down to the village and spoken to Shadow. He explained that no one must know that a woman with long golden hair and her man friend had stayed in the village, and that if he told anyone about them, then they would all be thrown out of the village and would have to find somewhere else to live.

Some soldiers did arrive there the very next day, and Dave and Laura were questioned. They denied knowing anything about any terrorists, and so did Shadow and the villagers when the soldiers went there.

It seems they were just checking everywhere they could think of, and had no particular suspicion of Dave and Laura. They left after an hour or so, taking a crate of beer with them that Dave had donated before they found it, which he knew they would, and confiscated it anyway.

We drove away from their home and headed south. We switched on the radio and listened to the news and there was a brief mention of extra security at Winston Macmillan airport but no mention of me. Moldie and I looked at each other and I shook my head.

"Bim promised me he would let me go and not do this," I said, shaking my head. "The swine, the utter lying swine."

Moldie started telling me about the area we were driving through, mostly, I think, to take my mind of the beastly act that Bim Dram had done to me. I hardly noticed but the countryside was rather special, and we were slowly rising. The vegetation changed from an almost tropical jungle to a more English type woodland as we drove. We passed through a few villages of just a dozen or so huts and stopped twice to buy fruit. We saw very few cars.

Eventually we arrived at the village of Bugulla, which was very similar to many other villages in the area, though possibly slightly larger. Moldie stopped on the outskirts and phoned the others to see where they were. They would be there in about an hour or so, Sam reckoned, so Moldie said to me, "Come on, let's go and get ourselves a nice fruit drink and a sandwich."

We drove into the village centre and parked near the only

café. It was part café, part shop and, it seemed to me, also the home of the local doctor.

"The doctor also doubles up as the village priest," said Moldie with a grin.

We walked into the cafe, ducking under the low doorway, and sat down at a table. The café was empty, but then an elderly lady appeared from behind a curtain. She took one look at Moldie, and burst into a broad grin. Moldie stood up and they hugged and talked very quickly in Abacadian. I tried to understand but it was almost impossible.

Eventually Moldie turned and introduced me.

"This is my friend Clair," he said, in Abacadian, but slowly so I could understand. "This is an old and dear friend. Her name is Plengia, which translates into English approximately as Motherly and we have known each other for over twenty years."

She said something to me, but I didn't catch it, and Moldie spoke to her, telling her, I think to speak slowly as I was still learning Abacadian, and then she said, in exaggerated slowness and clarity,

"Hello Clair. It is good to meet you. Welcome to Bugulla. May I offer you a cup of tea?"

I smiled and said thank you and she disappeared through the curtains again.

I asked Moldie how he knew about this village and cafe.

"Do you remember how I told you how my family were captured when I was younger but I escaped and then a group of us founded ODOE?"

"Of course I do," I answered his question.

"Our aim at the start was just to offer help and aid to any Effghanians we could find and we are not far from Effghania here. Many Effghanians came here to escape the army and I spent a lot of time in the village. I used to stay with Plengia quite a lot, and got very friendly with her daughter, but she died of a fever. Occasionally I pop back here to say hello to old friends."

Plengia brought us a pot of local herbal tea, which tasted a bit of banana, and some home made biscuits, which were delicious. She sat down at the table, and speaking slowly so I could sort of understand, asked Moldie what he had been up to. My mind wandered and I wondered where the others were and how could Bim be so rotten. I was getting to really quite like him as well.

Chapter 43 - The Forest of the Slumbering Giant

I phoned mother, using Moldie's secure phone line, and told her the news. She sounded shocked, and grumbled about Bim Dram being a swine. Moldie phoned back later and talked to Sam and suggested we meet at a village called Bugulla. We could then drive on to somewhere with the odd name of The Forest of the Slumbering Giant.

"There is a little café in the village and I know the owners. They are friends of mine. It should take you about four hours if you leave straight away," he told Sam.

Sam wrote the names down and checked on the map, and agreed with Moldie's suggestion.

"We'll see you there in about four hours," he said.

Lady Sammy was already loaded with virtually everything we needed, and it took only minutes to finish packing. We left the house which had been our home for over three weeks, hiding the key under a stone in the back garden as Moldie had suggested, and set off for Bugulla. Sam drove at the same speed as the rest of the traffic, making sure he did nothing wrong.

"Blend in with everybody else," he told me, "And the chances are that you will be left alone," and we were.

We drove through two road blocks but they took us as ordinary tourists and let us just drive through.

Which was nice.

We were soon out of Snuka and driving through the countryside and it was only then that I realised that mother's passport still hadn't arrived. There was nothing we could do about that but maybe Moldie

could arrange for Flower to visit the house and pick it up.

We arrived at Bugulla village, saw Sammy Two parked outside a small café cum shop, and heaved a sigh of relief. We weren't sure if mother and Moldie would be there.

When the others did turn up, we said goodbye to Plengia, who gave me a big hug and slipped a bag of biscuits into my hand.

Sam took charge, as usual.

"I have been thinking about seating in the cars," he said. "I think that Stu and I should be in separate cars, and, if you don't mind, Moldie, we should also drive."

Moldie shrugged.

"That's fine by me. It'll be nice to be chauffeured."

"So, you and Clair can come with Alice and me in Lady Sammy, whilst Pauline and Stu will go in Sammy Two. We can change later. Does everyone agree?"

As if we wouldn't.

"Could I sit next to mother in the back?" asked Alice. "We have a lot of catching up to do," and Sam shrugged.

"Whatever. Stu, we need to arrange somewhere to meet up in case we get separated," and once again Moldie suggested somewhere and showed them on the map and that was settled.

We climbed into the cars and set off towards The Forest of the Slumbering Giants. Alice and I talked and talked in the back seat whilst Moldie and Sam chatted in the front. The road rose gradually into some hills and we saw almost no traffic. Eventually the tarmac finished and we drove along mud roads until Stu phoned and we pulled over to the side of the road.

Pauline got out and asked if she could swap places with Alice as she wanted to chat to me, so they swapped, and on we went.

Eventually Moldie drove off the main road and up a small, single lane track. We drove about two miles through thick deciduous woodland, still going uphill, until he pulled over once again into a small clearing, turned off the engine and got out of the car and stretched.

We all got out and joined him and he suggested that we set up our tents there. Sam and Stu looked about and shrugged.

"It seems like a good spot," they agreed. The clearing was vaguely circular, about 20 yards across, and vaguely flat and we set up the three tents close together near the middle. Moldie explained that there was nobody within twenty miles, probably, but Sam and Stu went for an explore anyway, before it started to get dark. They returned an hour or so later.

"We have explored the surrounding area,'" said Sam, "And haven't seen the slightest indication of any human activity for at least the last month or so. Then we climbed to the top of the nearby hill and looked out over the tree tops and still didn't see anything. We agree with Moldie. We should be safe here."

We lit a small fire and cooked an evening meal which we washed down some Cadian wine. Then we got down to some serious talking. I started it.

"What do we do now?" I asked. I really had no idea. I was hoping somebody else could come up with something.

"Let's sort out the facts," said Pauline. "We four have passports and can return to England, and you also, Moldie, if you want?"

Moldie nodded.

"My passport is up to date."

"Mother has an up to date passport also," continued Pauline, "But we don't know where it is. Theo posted it to us, but it hasn't arrived yet. It may arrive to the house in Snuka soon, but, taking the worse scenario, it may never arrive. If it does arrive, Moldie, can you arrange for someone to pick it up?"

"Of course. Flower will check everyday, and let me know if it is there."

"To add to our problems, we think Bim Dram has broken his word to mother, and is searching for us, saying we are terrorists. He has blocked off the international airport in Snuka and was conducting a house to house search when we left home.

"So," Pauline had taken charge and we let her get on with it.

"Either mother stays here in Abacadia or she has to be smuggled out illegally."

She looked around at us and we all nodded.

"That's just about it," I said.

"On the plus side," said Pauline, "Bim has no idea where we are, and we still have plenty of money left."

"If you have money problems," said Moldie, "ODOE have promised they will help out."

"Thank you Moldie," I said, giving him a smile.

Pauline continued remorselessly on with her conclusion.

"Basically, we have no plan what to do next."

She looked around.

"Does anybody have any thoughts?"

"We could contact the British Embassy in Snuka," suggested Alice. "Surely if we tell them what has happened they would give mother a temporary passport so she could get home. It's not as if she's done anything wrong."

I spoke then.

"If we go to the Embassy, they will want to know all about me, and inevitably I would have to tell them about Moldie and ODOE, and, to be honest, I don't want to do that. Let's keep the British Embassy as a last resort."

We hadn't really heard any comments from the men.

"Sam and Stu, what do you think?" I asked.

They looked at each other.

"I think," said Sam, speaking carefully, "That Moldie brought you out here, and it should be up to Moldie to get you back to England."

He looked at Moldie, and shrugged.

"Sorry mate."

We all looked at Moldie, and he shrugged.

"I may be able to do something," said Moldie. "I'll make a phone call in the morning."

He wouldn't elaborate.

That night we decided we needed to keep watch, and the men took it in turns to stay awake for three hour shifts, and us girls stayed up with them. I took the middle watch with Moldie, and we sat on a small log a short distance from the tents, holding hands, and looking up at the sky. I had never seen so many stars, and watched in fascination as the moon rose, crossed the sky, and then set behind the trees. I felt very close to him then, it was almost a magical experience.

The next morning, Stu and Pauline woke us with a cup of tea and a sausage sandwich and we carried on our discussions from the night before.

"I've been thinking and I think I can arrange for us to get home," said Moldie. "I'll just make a call."

He returned a few minutes later.

"I have spoken to ODOE," he said. "I have begged and pleaded with them, and they have agreed to help you, Clair."

"That's good, Moldie," I said, "Thank you."

"Yes," said Sam, "Thank you Moldie. Can you give us any more details?" but Moldie shook his head.

"It has to be done in complete secrecy. I'm sorry."

We all breathed a sigh of relief. At least we had some sort of plan to get home, even if it was known only to Moldie. We made some coffee, and relaxed, went for a short explore in the woods and made some lunch.

We were half way through lunch when both Sam and Stu jumped up, and grabbed their dart guns. They were both looking towards the woods, then everything changed. About one hundred soldiers had surrounded our little campsite without us being aware of their presence, and now suddenly they all appeared at the same time. Sam and Stu threw down their dart guns and put their hands on their heads. The rest of us stood up and did the same. Our capture was as easy and quick as that. Sam and Stu looked absolutely forlorn. Two experienced former SAS soldiers captured as easily as that. They must have been fuming with themselves.

The soldiers took out some handcuffs and, grinning, fastened our hands behind our backs and marched us away.

"Where are you taking us?" asked Moldie.

"To see the general," came the answer. "No more questions."

We walked through the trees in single file for about twenty minutes. Sam and Stu were muttering, I bet they couldn't believe how easily they were caught.

We rounded a small hill, and there, on the far side, hidden from the hill top Sam and Stu had climbed, was a small army campsite. We were led to a tent which was slightly larger than the others, and shown in to see the general.

Chapter 44 - Mud, again.

The general was sitting at a desk, strewn with papers, and looked up as we were led in. It was one of my clients in my previous life as a high class prostitute. General Mud Oneye. I recognised him immediately but not before he had recognised me. There was shock on his face, just for an instant, then he looked me in the eye and very, very slightly shook his head. Did he mean not to let on that I knew him. He put his finger to his lips in the universal sign to keep quiet in a discreet way so, he hoped, no one but me would notice.

"Who the cuffing hell are you?" he asked me, and I decided, as he knew anyway, I would tell him the truth.

"My name is Lady Clair Hamilton, and these are my daughters, and these men are friends."

"What the cuff are you doing here, Lady?"

"Just visiting, on holiday."

He turned to one of the guards.

"Take these five away, cuffing handcuff them together, and don't let them escape. Give them some water. I will give further cuffing orders later."

Sam spoke up.

"What are you going to do with Lady Clair? We would like to be all together."

"No cuffing harm will come to the lady, I promise you," said Mud, "Now, please, go with this cuffing guard," and they all reluctantly walked from the tent, looking back at me as they left.

I just shrugged.

"I'll be okay," I said, "Don't worry."

After they had gone, Mud came around the desk and undid my handcuffs and pulled up a chair for me to sit on.

"I'm not sure if I cuffing believe you about just being on cuffing holiday. You see, I have been ordered to search for some cuffing foreign terrorists, and there has been reports that they have been seen in this vicinity. You and your friends are not cuffing terrorists, are you, Clair?"

"You know we're not, Mud," I said.

"Hmm," he said, "I'll need more cuffing convincing than that," and immediately I cottoned on to what he meant, and I sighed. If I had sex with him, then he would let us go and not report us to his superior, probably Bim Dram. Why did it always come down to sex with men? But I supposed it was a small price to pay for the safety of my daughters and the others. Moldie would be upset. Poor Moldie, but what option did I have?

"How long will it take me to convince you, Mud," I asked him, and he chuckled and answered,

"I don't know, probably all cuffing night," and I laughed.

"You're a sexy old bugger, Mud," I told him and he laughed back.

"Almost as sexy as you, Clair, but less of the cuffing old."

Then he became serious.

"Clair, when I visited you a few weeks ago, you told me that you were there trying to earn some cuffing money to pay off death duties and keep your home, what was it called, Hamilton Hall, I think."

I nodded.

"That wasn't cuffing true, was it?"

I didn't say anything, just stared at him.

"Shall I tell you what I cuffing think? I think you had been kidnapped, and were being whored out and the money you earned was being used to help the poor cuffing people of Effghania. You are a well known humanitarian and so were happy to go along with the cuffing plan just to help. Am I right?"

I sighed and nodded.

"How do you know that?" I asked him.

"I'm a lot cuffing cleverer than I look," he said, with a laugh. "Actually, it wasn't that hard to reason out. So tell me what has happened to you since I last saw you and what the cuff are you really doing here?"

So I told him about Bim Dram and the kidnapping at Lake Lucinda and how I escaped from his house. I didn't mention anything about Rum Hearty, his Prime Minister.

"Bim Dram is not a cuffing bad man," he said, "Though many people think he is. He's actually a decent and caring politician. He must be absolutely cuffing besotted with you, Clair, to do what he did. If he gets found out, it could ruin his career as an MP and scupper any thoughts he had of becoming the next cuffing Prime Minister."

"Will you tell anyone what I have just told you?" I asked him, and he laughed.

"Minister Dram is my cuffing boss," he explained, "So no, I won't tell anyone. Do you want to go and tell your friends what the cuff is happening?"

I didn't want to go and tell them. I really, really didn't but I had to. So outside I went. They were sitting on the ground, all handcuffed together and looked up at me. I knew immediately that they knew what was going on, but I blundered embarrassingly on and left them to their handcuffs and their hard ground.

Mud looked at me as I re-entered his tent, and I think I detected some pity in his eye, but there was more amusement.

"Did that go well?" he asked with a chuckle. "I'm sorry, that was cuffing uncalled for. Would you like something to eat and drink? Don't worry, your friends will be fed, the same cuffing food as us, but they will have cuffing water whilst we have wine."

So I sat opposite him at his desk, and food was brought in, a stew, of course, and quite tasty, and we shared a bottle of Cadian wine. We talked, and talking to him was easy, but he wouldn't tell me the reason he was there.

"As I said earlier, searching for cuffing terrorists," is all he would say.

Eventually he laid two roll up mattresses on the floor and he undressed me and I undressed him and we did what he wanted us to do, and then he asked me a question.

"Will you marry me, Clair?" he said.

Of course I was a bit taken aback. Another Abacadian wanting to marry me.

He continued before I could answer.

"You are an extremely attractive lady, and I would be very honoured to have you as my cuffing wife," he said. "You will have to be on your own in my house near Snuka quite a lot when I am away cuffing working, but it is quite a nice house and I'm sure you would be cuffing happy there. I have a cuffing maid who comes in twice a week. What do you think?"

Out of the four proposals I had had in Abacadia, this one was the easiest to turn down, except it was the hardest. I mustn't upset him. My children and friends were lying on bare ground outside, all handcuffed together. I wanted us all to leave in the morning. What should I say?

He saved me from answering by bursting out laughing.

"Of course I would love to have you as my cuffing wife, Clair," he said, "But I'm already cuffing married," and he laughed some more.

Bastard.

So I slept in his arms,

Chapter 45 - A night in chains

After we were captured we were led into the tent and I saw a large man sitting behind a small desk wearing army clothing. He was introduced to us as General Mud Oneye.

It was immediately obvious that he knew mother. He tried to hide the fact but he wasn't much of an actor. He ever so slightly shook his head and put his finger to his lips, hoping one would notice. We all noticed.

He asked mother who she was, and she told him, making no effort to lie. She knew he knew her, and obviously decided to tell the truth. Then, after asking her what we were doing there, 'On holiday,' he told the guards to lead the five of us away, and told mother to remain. She seemed happy to do that.

We were led away, and all our hands were handcuffed together in a chain, boy, girl, boy, girl, boy with Moldie, who was at the end of the line, handcuffed to a small tree. Two soldiers, armed with dart guns, were left to keep an eye on us.

We talked, and Moldie admitted that General Oneye had in fact been one of mother's clients and he told us a bit about him.

"He's a good soldier and Clair got on well with him," he told us. "But then Clair got on well with everyone."

He sighed.

"He'll say he will let us go if she makes love to him," said Pauline, "And, of course, because she loves us all and wants no harm to come to us, she'll go along with him. Probably spend the night in his bed," and we all looked at Moldie, who looked somewhat sick.

"There was no need to be quite so blunt," he said,

"But I do agree with you. That's what will happen."

"He does swear quite a lot."

I shook my head.

"If you consider cuffing a swear word."

A few minutes later, mother was led out by a guard and came over to talk to us. Surprise, surprise.

"Er," she sort of muttered, obviously very embarrassed, "The general wants me to, er, have dinner with him. He says he will let us all go in the morning. I might not, er, join you until then."

She looked at Moldie.

"I'm sorry Moldie," she said and he just smiled weakly.

She turned and disappeared back into the general's tent, and we all sighed. Moldie looked sad.

Later, some guards brought us some food, stew, of course, and some water, but we were left outside all night. It was the middle of the summer, so the night wasn't cold, but the guards still brought us a blanket each. We tried to sleep the best we could, but it was difficult with us all being handcuffed together.

"Lie on your side," suggested Sam, "And dig a small hole in the soil for your shoulder and hip. I have found that that is the comfiest way to sleep in situations like this."

We thanked him, did as he suggested and it was a lot comfier, and in the end I slept quite well.

Two guards kept guard over us all night.

In the morning we were brought some more food, just bread and cheese this time, before Moldie was unfastened from the tree and we were all led back into the general's tent. He was sitting behind his desk in exactly the same position as he had been the last time we saw him. Mother was sitting opposite him, and stood up when we entered. She looked extremely embarrassed.

The general smiled.

"Your mother and I have had a cuffing talk," he said, "And she has convinced me that you are not the cuffing terrorists that I thought you were, so I am releasing you all. You may go on your cuffing way."

He was smiling. He had obviously enjoyed his night with mother, and was now enjoying her embarrassment.

He ordered one of the guards who had come in with us to undo our handcuffs, and we rubbed our wrists.

"So, we can go?" asked Pauline, and General Mud Oneye nodded.

We left his camp and walked quickly back to our tents. We packed up as rapidly as we could, climbed into the cars, and gratefully and thankfully drove away from General Mud Oneye and the Forest of the Slumbering Giant.

Chapter 46 - Flight home

As we drove away from the soldiers and Mud, I breathed a sigh of relief. That had been a really horrible experience and I had a nasty thought that I had handled it very, very badly. Had I really needed to sleep with Mud? If I had refused, would he have kept us locked up and taken us back to Bim Dram? I had a gut feeling now that probably he wouldn't and I had needlessly upset Moldie and the others.

But it was too late now. I had done it and there was no going back. The atmosphere in the car was the worst it had been since I had been rescued. Nobody was really talking. Oh dear, I would have to make it up to them somehow.

After an hour or so, Moldie, who had eventually condescended to hold my hand in the back seat, told us to pull over into a glade at the side of the road. It was a pretty spot, with a view through the trees to a small river.

Pauline pulled out a bag and made some sandwiches, whilst the boys made a small fire and boiled a kettle for some tea.

"Okay Moldie," said Sam. "How are we going to get back to England? Can you tell us?"

Moldie nodded.

"I can tell you sort of, but you must understand this is a complete secret. Don't get me wrong, I trust you all completely, but even so, I really can't tell you too much. I hope you don't mind."

"That's fine, mate," said Sam. "Just tell us what you can."

"As Clair knows, there is a secret route used by ODOE between England and Effghania."

He smiled at me. A weak smile, yes, but still a smile, and I smiled back.

"It is the route we used to bring her here in the first place," he continued. "We do have a few other secret routes, and I'm not going to tell you about those either, or the reasons why we have them, though I am sure you can guess."

358

We all nodded, though I couldn't think of any reason apart from smuggling attractive middle aged Ladies.

"The ODOE powers that be were very reluctant to allow me to do this but I reminded them how much money you had earned for us, Clair, and told them about your promise to help us raise money even when you get back to England and they have now agreed. We will be leaving this evening from a runway in this vague vicinity."

We finished the picnic, and all visited the trees, before we set off again. A few minutes later, Moldie stopped again, this time by a small van. A young man sat in the drivers seat with a young lady next to him.

"You don't need to know their names," said Moldie, smiling, and indicated that we climb into the back of the van.

We grabbed our personal belongings, one overnight bag each, said goodbye to Lady Sammy and Lady Sammy Two, and climbed in. There were bench seats either side, and we all sat. It was a bit of a squash, with our bags on our knees. There were no windows, and the only light snuck in through a crack where the back doors didn't shut together exactly. Moldie was sitting next to me and I reached for his hand.

"I'm sorry about the secrecy, I really am," he said, "But it will be like this all the way to England, I'm afraid. We'll be at the runway in about twenty minutes, and will be taking off almost immediately. The plane has been refuelled and there will be plenty of provisions on board to make the journey as comfortable as possible, but it's still going to be rather cold, noisy and boring."

I really needed to say something about sleeping with Mud and I reckoned now was as good a time as any, so I took a big breath and said, "Everybody, especially you Moldie, I'm so sorry for how I behaved with Mud Oneye. I thought at the time I was doing the right thing. All I was thinking was to do what was best so he would let us go. Now I'm not sure I was right."

Both the girls leant forward and hugged me and Moldie squeezed my hand. They all spoke at once but all said the same thing.

"Don't worry about it. We know you did what you thought was best. Forget about it," but I couldn't. I rested my head against Moldie's shoulder and he put his arm around me and kissed the top of my head.

"It's okay Clair," he said and I thought what a good man he was.

Twenty minutes later and the van stopped and the back doors were opened. We all climbed out to find ourselves at the edge of a large clearing surrounded by tall trees. A scruffy looking muddy brown aeroplane was parked nearby and Sam and Stu recognised it immediately.

"It's a Havvy Twin Otter," said Sam, the astonishment evident in his voice. "I haven't seen one of these for a long time."

"Sure brings back some memories," said Stu. "Do you remember ...."

"Later Stu, when we're in the air. But, now I've seen this, I really think we've got a chance of getting home."

Moldie had been talking to two blokes who I assumed were the pilot and co-pilot but turned and grinned when he heard what Sam had said.

"You know this plane? Good, hey?" and Sam and Stu nodded.

"One of the best. We have both flown them in the past," and Moldie looked astonished.

"You can fly them?"

"We learnt all sorts of things in the SAS."

Moldie introduced the two men. One was older, with a fine moustache that was twisted up at the edges, obviously copied from old World War Two films. He looked very competent. The other looked barely a man. He had no facial hair and I wondered if he needed to shave. Very young to be a pilot, I thought.

"This is Booka," Moldie said, gesturing toward the older man. "He's ODOE's number one pilot," and Booka grinned.

"And this is Mila. Mila is learning from Booka but is still a very competent flyer. Don't let his boyish good looks fool you," and he also grinned. They obviously both spoke English, which was good, and shook hands with Sam and Stu. They barely glanced at us girls.

"You knows the de Havilland Canada Twin Otter?" asked Booka but before Sam could answer Moldie interrupted.

"Plenty of time for talking when we are on our way," he said. "Booka tells me the plane is all ready to take off. Provisions have been loaded and all the pre-flight tests done. Now climb in."

A small stairway with only five steps led to a door and I climbed up and had a first look at the place that would be our home for almost the next two days. The pilot's cockpit was to my left, with it's multitude of switches and dials and two seats, and the cabin to my right. It was quite roomy, with six seats at the front and an empty space at the back. There were two piles of stuff tied down on either side. Provisions, probably, I thought.

"Put your bags just behind the seats," shouted up Moldie and then I sat down in a seat by the window and looked out. From here I could just make out a small building hidden in the trees, with a number of men standing and watching. Later Moldie explained to us that ODOE had two crews of mechanics to service this and another smaller plane, and the building was where they kept all the stock and supplies and fuel for the planes.

"We are in a remote part of Effghania," he said, "And the building can't be seen from the air. When the plane is parked up at the edge of the trees, we hide it from casual view with netting. It has worked so far."

When we asked who they were hiding it from, he shrugged and said vaguely, "Anyone who happens to be looking for it."

Everybody else climbed in, including Moldie, and sat down, as did the two pilots. Mila, the co pilot, pulled the steps up behind him and closed and fastened the door, then the engines roared into life, and the plane taxied to the very edge of the clearing. There was no obvious runway marked out.

"We keep it that way on purpose," explained Moldie. "As soon as we have taken off, the men will come out of hiding and clear away any signs that we have been here. If we need a night landing, then portable lamps are brought out of the building."

I wasn't quite sure why ODOE needed so much security, but didn't ask. Instead I watched the trees rush by and then we were in the air and the journey home had started.

Once we were safely on our way, Moldie told us some more details about our journey.

"I am not allowed to tell you much," he said, apologetically, "But I should imagine you will be able to work out most of the route yourselves. Sometimes I will ask you to draw down your blinds so you can't see out."

We nodded.

"No problem."

"The whole trip should take about two days, fingers crossed. We have done this journey a number of times and have had no problems so far, but, who knows. We will have to land three times to refuel. Please don't ask me where we are. On the second of these stoppages you will be able to get out and stretch your legs. There is plenty of food and drink at the back of the plane so we shouldn't go hungry, and   flasks of hot water for tea and coffee and soup."

He pointed to the back of the plane and we all turned our heads.

"This plane normally has eighteen seats but we have fastened twelve of them to the side of the fuselage," and I noticed what he meant. What I thought were curtains were actually the bottom of seats strapped, as he said, to the side of the fuselage, leaving the middle empty.

"There are six bed rolls and blankets and pillows over there, so hopefully we all should be able to grab some sleep during the trip."

He smiled at me.

"I've always wanted to join the mile-high club," he said, and winked, and we all laughed but I knew he was serious and wondered if we would get the chance.

"Behind that curtain is a portaloo. There is sanitising moisture provided."

He pointed to the two piles of stuff tied down by tarpaulins.

"These are goods to be exchanged for other goods needed by ODOE," he said. "Don't worry, if we get searched, it's all legal. Mostly fruit and other types of food."

He picked up two battered suitcases.

"These contain $10,000 dollars each and are bribes to help us keep our route open. When we land, maybe you two," he nodded at Sam and Stu, "Could keep guard over them, please."

Sam and Stu nodded.

"No problem."

"One last thing," said Moldie, with a sly smile.

He pulled a cloth off an object and underneath was, of all things, and exercise bike.

"On long journeys like this, legs can stiffen up and cramp set in. I find that by riding the bike for just a few minutes every now and then, it keeps the legs fresh and the blood flowing. Whenever you feel the urge."

Sam and Stu nodded.

"A good idea," they said.

"British Airways should have a couple on their long haul flights," I said. "It might cut back on deep vein thrombosis."

I looked out of the window. I thought we were flying north west-ish, and I always had a good sense of direction, I reckoned, so later we would be flying over northern Europe somewhere.

"Do you mind if we speculate where we are?" I asked Moldie and he told us we could speculate all we liked.

So we speculated.

"Stu, how far can this plane fly on one tank of fuel, can you remember?"

"I really can't remember. One thousand miles, maybe."

"I think you're about right, and it's, what, three thousand, three and half, from Abacadia to England?"

Stu nodded.

"About that."

"So," said Sam, "Four hops and three stops should do it."

Moldie looked amused.

"That's what I said."

"It cruises at about, what, 150 mph," pondered Sam, "So six or seven hours a hop. Add on refuelling three times and extra time for landing and take off, and Moldie's time of about two days seems just about right," and Moldie grinned.

"Just about right," he said.

Sam and Stu entertained us with SAS stories from previous flights they had undertaken on a Havvy Twin Otter and told us how they had learnt to fly a number of different planes. Then Moldie provided us with some sandwiches and some hot tea from the flasks.

Sam asked if we could visit the cockpit and Moldie looked at his watch and said they could but only for half an hour and please don't ask the pilots where we were because they had orders not to tell.

Eventually Moldie asked us all close our blinds, and we did, though I had one quick glance out. Below were some low hills and still yet more trees. Trees, trees, everywhere.

Then we started to descend and I felt the plane touch down, taxi, and eventually come to a stop.

"I'm very sorry, but you can't get out here," said Moldie. "You may open your blinds, though."

Outside it looked bleak and cold, though I couldn't really see much. More trees and a couple of small buildings. A small provincial airport or runway, I thought.

Moldie opened the cabin door and immediately I felt a cool breeze. It was refreshing after the stuffiness of the last six hours.

He pushed the steps through the door and almost immediately two men entered. They wore grey jackets and blue jeans and looked like they may have been Russian. I couldn't tell if they were carrying guns. They walked down the length of the fuselage with Moldie, peering suspiciously at the men and leering at us women.

Moldie had given one of the battered suitcases containing the $10,000 dollars to Sam and Stu with orders to keep it hidden under their seats, but he gave the other to one the men who opened it, saw the money, and grinned.

"Thank you," he grunted, and, after taking one more look at me and my daughters, they left and Moldie followed. He turned and told us he would be an hour or so and would we be so kind as to wait for his return and not try to get out of the plane. The pilots went out with him, and then the door was closed.

We pondered on our location but somewhere in North Eastern Europe was our best guess.

Sometime later, much more than an hour, and Moldie and the pilots returned.

"Sorry about the delay," said Moldie. "Nothing to worry about. I've brought on some hot food, which we will have as soon as we are airborne, and the flasks have been re-filled with boiling water. Oh, and they have donated some cold beers. Nice stuff. Seat belts on and blinds down, please."

Fifteen minutes later and we were all enjoying a spicy hot stew and a cold beer each, along with some thick slices of lumpy bread.

It was getting dark outside, and the internal lights were switched on where we were sitting. I was feeling tired and yawned and told the others I was going to try and get some sleep.

"The elderly have no stamina," joked Pauline, at least I hope it was a joke.

Moldie wasn't amused by the quip.

"Your mother is not old," he said. "She is in the prime of her life. Come on Clair, I'll help you get comfortable. It is almost seven hours until we land again."

He unrolled two of the bedrolls and laid them side by side, then produced two pillows and two thick blankets, and helped me get comfy. The mattress was not so thick and I could feel the cabin floor beneath me but it had been a long and stressful couple of days, and I was tired.

"I'll just talk to the pilots and be back in a couple of minutes."

I thought to myself that the others were probably thinking that they were not surprised I was tired as I had probably not got much sleep the night before whilst entertaining Mud Oneye and smiled to myself. Let them think.

I felt Moldie lie down next to me. He leant over and kissed me.

"I love you Lady Clair Hamilton," he whispered into my ear, and I whispered back that I loved him also, and at that moment in time, I really, truly did, and I drifted off to sleep wondering if we would ever live together in Hamilton Hall.

I slept the sleep of the innocent and was woken by Moldie with a cup of almost hot tea.

"We'll be landing in a few minutes," he said, "And you'll be able to get out and stretch your legs. There will be a toilet and a proper hot meal available."

"Thank you Moldie," I said, giving him a peck on the end of his nose.

I struggled up. The others were all sitting in their seats with the blinds up. They smiled at me.

"You slept well, mother," said Alice, "You must have been tired. We'll be landing soon."

I sat down, fastened my seatbelt, and looked out of the window. We were flying low over a massive field. I could see a huge flock of sheep. There seemed to be thousands of them. The only sign of human habitation was a very long fence in the distance.

We landed in the middle of nowhere. Basically just a landing strip, with a few out building and half a dozen houses. In the far distance I could now see some mountains, capped with snow, it seemed.

"You need to put on some extra clothes," said Moldie. "It's chilly out there."

He passed us a jumper and a woolly hat each, and we clambered down the ladder. Moldie was right, it was chilly. I breathed in the lovely fresh air, and saw Moldie talking to a couple of men, whose distinguishing features were huge bushy beards. They hugged and laughed and came over to shake our hands. Moldie didn't introduce them.

"Stretch your legs for a few minutes," he said, "Whilst we unload the goods I have brought for them."

"Would you like some help?" asked Sam, but Moldie shook his head.

"You just relax," and the three of them disappeared into the plane.

There was a duck pond and a small copse of trees nearby and we walked over to have a look.

"Where do you think we are?" asked Alice, but none of us had any idea.

"Poland, Ukraine, Russia?" suggested Sam. "Does it really matter. We're about half way home, that's all I know."

After about twenty minutes, Moldie called us over and we all trailed into one of the huts. There was a log fire burning and I was glad as I was starting to get cold. I hunkered down in front of it, holding out my hands, then followed the others by taking off my hat and jumper.

We all sat down at a table and food was brought to us. Roast lamb with potatoes and vegetables I didn't recognise. All topped with thick gravy and beer to wash it down. Possibly the best breakfast meal I had ever tasted.

The food was served by two women who didn't say a word and the two beardies ate with us. They spoke a sort of English, heavily accented, but I didn't recognise the accent and neither did Sam or Stu.

All too soon we were climbing back up the steps into the Havvy Twin Otter and taking off once again. We had spent over two hours on the ground and it had refreshed all of us.

Although one of the two piles of goodies had been unloaded by the two bearded gentlemen, there was now another pile of stuff in its place.

"Things for ODOE," said Moldie. "Just things for ODOE."

I couldn't even be bothered to wonder what the things might be.

"We are now over half way back to England," Moldie said, "And the journey is going well. However, we now have the trickiest landing ahead of us."

"What do you mean?" asked Sam.

"Well," Moldie seemed hesitant to tell us, but eventually said, "It is not easy to find places to land and refuel and keep it totally secret. The people at the next place we land know this and are starting to get greedy. Originally they would let us use their landing strip for Abacadian supplies, the same as the last stop, but then they wanted supplies and money, and now they insist on even more money. So there might be trouble."

He walked to the very back of the plane and pulled a sheet off a pile. Underneath were a number of dart guns, and some clubs.

"We may have to use these," he said. "I hope we don't but I just want us to be prepared."

"Where will we be landing," asked Sam and Moldie looked worried.

"I suppose I can tell you," he said. "We'll be in Northern Poland."

"Oh," said Sam, "I always found the Poles to be fairly placid chaps but you get good and bad in any nation."

Moldie gave a dart gun to all of us, even Alice and Pauline and me and Sam and Stu showed us exactly how to load and fire them vaguely accurately.

"I hope it won't come to anything," said Moldie, "But better to be prepared if you can. Isn't that what you always preach, Sam?"

"Time spent on preparation," agreed Sam, "Is time well spent."

Stu nodded.

"SAS motto," he confirmed.

"If we need to shoot with them," continued Sam, "Aim for flesh. Anywhere. Arms, neck, face, but try and keep away from the eyes. They could take one out. If in doubt, just shoot them in the chest. Unless they are wearing body armour, the dart should penetrate their clothing. If there are a few of them, try and notice who Moldie and Stu and I are firing at and chose someone else. If in doubt, just fire then reload and fire again."

We all looked very serious and I felt a bit sick. I had shot at rabbits and rats when I was younger, but never at a man.

"But I'm sure nothing will happen," he finished, but he didn't sound convinced.

Moldie also gave Sam and Stu a club each.

Just in case.

We slowly descended and I looked out of the window to see another flat and boring landscape, with trees stretching to the horizon. We landed gently and taxied to a large shed. Moldie opened the door and four men entered the plane. Booka and Mila, the pilot and co-pilot, left the plane, presumably to check on the refuelling.

The four men were all very jovial, overly jovial, over the top jovial, and they made me highly suspicious and nervous. They laughed and cracked jokes, some in English and some, I presumed, in Polish, which I didn't understand and shook everybody's hand and kissed all the girls on both cheeks. They leered provocatively at us and I just smiled back.

Eventually they got to the rear of the plane and Moldie gave them the suitcase full of the ten thousand dollars and showed them all the provisions we had brought from Abacadia, including many bottles of Abacadian wine. More smiles and back slapping and the money and the goods were unloaded.

The men came back in and the leader suddenly pointed at us women. All of them spoke a bit of English, it seemed, but the leader was fairly fluent.

"We want all the women for one hour," he said, "Then you can go."

"You can't have them," said Moldie, coldly. "They are not part of the deal."

The atmosphere changed, suddenly becoming cold and

unpleasant. We all had our dart guns hidden under blankets and I felt for the trigger on mine.

The four men stalked down the plane, and now Sam and Stu stood up. They were big men, and very tough looking, and the Poles stopped and grinned.

"We mean no harm," said the leader, holding his arms wide, but then he made a mistake. He made a grab for Alice who was in the seat next to him. Maybe he thought he could haul her out of her seat and use her as a hostage but he was far to slow. Sam instantly shot him in the neck with a dart and he collapsed onto the floor.

Stu shot another one who was attempting to pull a gun out from under his shirt, and Moldie and us girls shot the other two between us. Within ten seconds they were all lying unconscious in the aisle.

There was shouting outside and immediately Sam and Stu rushed to the door and carefully peered through. The rest of us looked through the windows to see Booka and Mila surrounded by men with guns. Then there was a shot and Booka screamed and collapsed to the ground, holding his left leg.

Sam ran back down the aisle, grabbed the unconscious leader of the group and dragged him to the door. He held a knife to his throat, and the shouting from outside stopped.

"Let go of the pilots," he shouted loudly but calmly.

"Now," and they let them go.

Mila hauled Booka to his feet. He lent on Mila's arm and the two of them staggered towards the plane. Stu jumped down and helped Mila to pull Booka into the plane. Sam saw he had been shot in the left thigh, and it was bleeding profusely.

"What happened?" asked Sam.

"They wouldn't let us finish refuelling. We are only half full, nowhere near enough to get to England," said Booka through clenched teeth. "They said they want more money."

"The took deliberate aim and shot Booka in the leg," said Mila. "The bastards. Why would they do that?"

""They want something and it's a warning," said Sam. "Stu,

drag up another one of those three."

Stu grabbed one of the other unconscious Poles and dragged him to the doorway to stand with Sam, a knife at his throat also.

"You," he shouted at the group of Poles who were looking at him with real hate in their eyes. "Finish the refuelling. Now," and the men reluctantly and slowly continued with the refuelling.

"Stu you go with Mila to check they are doing it properly."

Stu went to join Mila outside whilst Booka hobbled to a seat and I helped him sit down.

"I need to fly the plane," he groaned but Sam shook his head.

"You're in no fit state to fly, Booka. Stu will help Mila fly the plane. You sit there. Don't move, try and relax. As soon as we have taken off, I will look at your leg. Meanwhile, try and keep it still. Clair see if you can elevate it a bit. Put a bag or something under his foot. Alice, there are some strong pain killers in my pack. You know the ones I mean. Give Booka two with a bottle of water."

All the time he was giving orders, Sam was holding the knife to the leaders throat and looking out of the door. He grunted in satisfaction.

"Good," he said grimly, "They are doing as they are told. Good, good boys."

Within a few tense minutes, Stu shouted to Sam that the refuelling was finished.

"Right, come back on board," but the Poles outside lifted their guns and pointed them at Stu and Mila.

"We swap them for ours," said one of them.

"No," said Sam firmly. "Those two will come on board, we will taxi to the end of the runway, and dump these four men there. They are not hurt, yet, just sleeping."

"How do we know you will keep your word?"

"Why the hell would we want these four?" said Sam reasonably. "They are just scum. We will leave them over there. We don't want them."

The Poles glanced at each other, then nodded and lowered their guns.

"You have the money and the wine and everything else," shouted Sam, as Stu and Mila climbed up the steps and disappeared into the cabin.

"You can keep those."

Although Stu and Sam had flown Twin Otters before it had been a long time, it seemed, and Stu was a little bit rusty and so Mila, much to his delight, became the senior pilot.

"Just remind me what to do," Stu told him. "I'll pick it up quickly enough."

Mila started the engine and slowly taxied the plane to the far end of the runway. Sam kept the door open to show the Poles that we had no intention of taking off.

When we were furthest from them, Sam dropped the leader out of the door, holding him by the wrists at full length so as not to injure him.

"He's unconscious, and unconscious men don't injure so easily," he said.

He dropped the second one out whilst Moldie dragged a third to him. Pauline and I dragged the fourth and both of them were dropped out of the door. Immediately, Sam pulled up the steps and closed and locked the door and the plane moved forward. Alice had her arm around Booka, trying to comfort him. He was moaning and was obviously still in a lot of pain. The pain killers hadn't kicked in yet.

We all sat back down in our seats and put on our seatbelts and I looked out of the window. I half expected the Poles to shoot at us, but instead they were running to the pile of four unconscious bodies.

The plane built up speed and the wheels left the ground and we all breathed an audible sigh of relief. We had got away with it, but only just.

Sam immediately attended to Booka's leg wound. His trouser leg was saturated in blood, but Sam carefully and gently cut it away with the pair of scissors he always kept in his pack.

"Moldie," he snapped, "Pass me some water and a towel or a cloth."

He used a damp cloth to wipe away all the blood, then gently examined the wound. Booka moaned and tried to keep still, but his leg was jerking slightly.

"Move your toes," and Booka wiggled his toes.

"That's good," said Sam. "Nothing broken and no serious muscle damage."

"I hope," under his breath.

He gently moved the leg so he could look at the back of it.

"An exit wound. That's good news," he told us all, but mainly he was speaking to Booka, trying to reassure him.

"It's worse if the bullet is lodged inside the flesh and the muscle. That can cause swelling and infection. I'm sure you'll be okay."

He reached into his pack and brought out a bandage and a pad.

"I'm going to apply a pad to try and control the bleeding," he explained, and held the pad firmly against Booka's thigh.

I reached across and took hold of Booka's hand. He looked at me gratefully and tried to smile, but he was obviously in a lot of pain. I squeezed gently.

"You'll be okay, mate," I said. "You're in good hands," and I started to tell him about the dog bite I received when I was rescued from Bim Dram's house in Snuka. I reckoned it would take his mind off his own injury. I exchanged glances with Sam, who smiled and nodded.

After a few minutes, Sam said, "The bleeding is under control, Booka. I'm going to wrap your leg in a bandage to hold the pad in place. It may hurt a little bit. Then I'm going to lie you down on one of the mattresses," he indicated to Moldie, who unrolled two and laid them on the floor, one on top of the other, "And cover you with two blankets. This will help control the shock and the trauma."

He wrapped the bandages and, after checking they weren't too tight, picked Booka up in his arms and gently laid him on the mattresses, and covered him with two blankets.

"The pain killers should be taking effect," he said. "You need to sleep now. Sleep helps. As soon as we land in England, Moldie will take you to the local hospital. You'll be okay, I promise."

He looked at Moldie, who nodded.

Booka was trying to tell Sam something, but his voice was a whisper. Sam put his ear by his mouth and listened.

"Mila," he shouted, "Booka wants to speak to you," and Mila came trotting back.

"That Stu, him clever man. He know what to do."

He had a grin on his face but it disappeared when he saw Booka.

"Is he Ok?"

"He'll be fine," said Sam. "He's just in a lot of pain right now. Listen to what he has to say. I think it's important."

We all involuntarily craned forward but Booka spoke quietly in Abacadian. Mila nodded, then looked at Moldie, who nodded and returned to the cockpit to talk with Stu.

Moldie told us what Booka had said.

"From now on, Booka says it is vitally important that we follow exactly the height, direction and speed that is shown in the flight plan in the cockpit. Somehow ODOE have arranged with somebody to allow us to fly safely and without interference. We will be met by immigration officials when we land but otherwise we will be left alone."

Sam shrugged.

"I've never heard of anything like that but then I'm not an international pilot. As long as we get there safely and get Booka to hospital. Can you tell us where we will be landing in England?"

"As Stu is helping to fly the plane, you'll know anyway. It's in Norfolk, near a town called Fakenham. A van will be waiting for us there, I hope, to drive us to somewhere where a hire car will be waiting for you to drive yourselves back to Hamilton Hall. That's the plan, anyway."

"What will you do?" I asked Moldie. "Will you be coming with us?"

"Only in the van," he said, "Then I have to come back here. Normally we taxi the plane into a hangar, have it checked over and serviced and refuelled, then loaded with goods to take back to Effghania and then we'll leave again tomorrow night, but now Booka is injured, I suppose we'll have to try and find another pilot. Mila is good but he has very little experience. ODOE will sort that out for me."

He looked at me.

"I'd love to come back to Hamilton Hall with you, Clair. Maybe another time?"

He looked so sad and I squeezed his hand.

"No maybe about it, Moldie. You will definitely come and stay with me. And soon," and we both smiled at that.

Later, Sam went through to the cockpit to speak with Stu and Mila. He came back after a few minutes and told Moldie,

"That Mila seems like a good bloke. An old head on young shoulders. He could go a long way," and Moldie nodded.

"I agree and if he can get us down safely in England, it will look very good on his record. I'll give him a good report, don't worry."

"How old is he?" asked Pauline.

"He's twenty three, I think."

"The same age as me," said Pauline. Her eyes looked dreamy.

"And I've heard that Abacadian men have big cocks."

"Not all of them," I said, looking at Moldie and winking but thinking of Bim Dram and his tiny little penis.

Everybody laughed, even Moldie.

"You wouldn't be talking like that if Stu was here," said Alice, chuckling.

"Stu wouldn't mind. He knows I'm only joking."

Sam became serious.

"Moldie, I'm sorry about what happened back there in Poland. I don't think you can use that landing strip again."

Moldie shrugged.

"There's no doubt about it. We definitely can't go back there, but it was getting dubious anyway, as you saw. I think ODOE have other locations in mind. Somebody will sort something out. They always do. They are very good at that sort of thing."

He had a think, then looked at me.

"Mind you, with all the help that Clair has been giving us, things in Effghania are going much better than they were. Maybe ODOE will decide we don't need to do this flight anymore. This may be the last time."

I asked Moldie if this flight was simply to get goods and provisions from Britain to Effghania, and he said, "Mainly, yes. Most of the stuff is donated but now ODOE can afford to pay for essentials. But that's not my decision," and he wouldn't tell us anymore.

"For the time being, though," he added, "Please keep all of this a secret. Please," and we all swore that we would keep it a secret and not tell a soul.

Stu came back to see us. He looked like he was having a great time flying the Twin Otter but first he asked about Booka, who was now sleeping.

"He'll live," said Sam. "It's not serious. Where are we?"

"Over the North Sea. We should be landing in about seventy minutes. It will be pitch black but Mila doesn't seem to be bothered. He says there will be landing lights to show the runway and he has landed many times in the dark near Redik and that was with paraffin lanterns showing the way. With proper lights it will be, and I quote, 'Like a fully grown lion stealing a carcass from a bunch of hyena pups'. I tell you what, Sam, I am enjoying flying again. I may take it up as a career!"

"Nobody would employ you mate. You're too old and knackered."

I looked out of the window. It was pitch dark, and I couldn't see a single light, not even in the distance. I would be home soon, I thought, I hoped. How long had it been since Moldie had first kidnapped me? That had been June and now it was only early September. Two and a half months and so much had happened to me in that short time and now, I was almost home.

But in all honesty, I always thought I would get home one day. It never occurred to me that I wouldn't. I had always tried to be positive and I didn't think I ever got too depressed.

I thought of what had happened. I wondered if I could have done anything different. Not really, I reckoned. Fate and circumstances had dictated my actions and decisions. Self preservation a lot of the time.

I tried to work out how many different lovers I had had, and smiled at the memory of some of them. Then I tried to work out how many times I had had sex in Abacadia but that made my brain hurt. Too many times I thought but then decided that it wasn't too many times. You can't have sex too many times, I reckoned, not if you were willing and I had always been willing. Too willing?

I sighed and wondered about my return to Hamilton Hall. Would life be different now? Possibly, probably. Alice and Pauline and I had been drawn even closer together through our experiences. We had always been close but now there was a much stronger bond. That was a good thing.

I wondered about Theo. How we he feel about what I had been up to? It wouldn't be a problem, I decided. He was a good lad. Not a lad, a young man. I was looking forward to seeing him again. I would give him a big, big hug.

When we got back to Hamilton Hall.

I felt the plane start to descend and looked out of the window. In the distance I could see a few lights. It must be the coast of Norfolk. England, and my heart leapt. So close.

Moldie came from the cockpit and sat next to me, and took my hand. We smiled at each other, though his was tinged with sadness, I thought. Poor Moldie. He would miss me, but he would survive and find another woman. I knew.

Stu came back and told us we would be landing soon and would we mind if we did up our seatbelts, thank you.

We dropped lower and then there was the slightest of bumps as the wheels touched the ground and the plane slowed and stopped and I was back in England. I sighed in relief.

"That was a good landing," said Sam. "Perfect, I'd say, and in almost pitch darkness. You were right, Moldie, Mila does have a talent for flying."

Mila and Stu switched off the engines, and they came through to the back. Sam and Stu shook hands with Mila and Booka, congratulating them on their flying and wishing Booka all the best for the future. Us ladies gave both of them a big hug.

Moldie opened the door and we picked up our bags and climbed down the steps and I was standing on English soil once again. A nice feeling.

Two men were walking towards us and Moldie went to talk to them. He handed them a piece of paper which had all our details written on them. Then they came and talked to each of us, starting with Sam and Stu.

They came to me.

"You are Lady Clair Hamilton, of Hamilton Hall, Worcestershire?" one of them asked me, reading from the paper by the light of a small torch.

I nodded.

"I am."

"You don't have your passport on you?"

"No. It's been lost."

He stared at me for a moment and nodded, then went to my daughters and asked them a similar question.

And that was the extent of the immigration formalities. I was amazed but so many things had amazed me over the last few weeks and this was just another one.

Moldie led us over to a small van and we all climbed in the back. Once again there were bench seats. We sat down and the van started to move.

"Is it always that easy?" asked Sam.

"Usually," said Moldie.

We drove for about ninety minutes, then stopped and climbed out to find ourselves in a lay-by. A small car was waiting for us. A man climbed out, and shook hands with Moldie, who turned to us.

"This is your hire car to take you back to Hamilton Hall. We didn't have your details," he told Sam and Stu, "So only Clair and Alice and Pauline are insured to drive. We are near

Northampton. There is a Sat Nav in the glove box to guide you home. Somebody will visit Hamilton Hall in the next day or so to pick it up. Leave the keys under the front right hand tyre and I will arrange for your Jaguar to be returned as soon as possible, Clair."

It was time to say goodbye to Moldie. Alice and Pauline gave him a big hug. Sam and Stu shook his hand. He hugged me tightly and I hugged him back.

"We'll meet again, Moldie," I told him, looking him straight in the eye. "And soon. I promise."

He nodded. He looked very sad.

"I know we will."

I thought he wasn't going to say anything else, but he did.

"You are the most wonderful woman I have ever met," he told me quietly. "It has been an honour and a privilege to know you. I love you and I always will. Never forget that."

He hugged me again, then turned away and climbed into the van, which immediately drove off.

I watched it until it disappeared around a bend, then turned to look at the others, who were trying to keep straight faces.

I stuck my tongue out at them, and they grinned.

"Come on, let's be on our way home," Alice said with a chuckle. "Shall I drive?" and, without waiting for a reply, clambered into the driver's seat. Sam got in next to her. Pauline, Stu and I climbed into the back seat, whilst Sam checked the Sat Nav. He set a course for Hamilton Hall, and we were on our way.

An hour and a half later and we drove through the gates and up the drive and there was my beloved Hamilton Hall in front of me. I could scarcely believe I was home.

I climbed out of the car, and my legs felt shaky. Alice took my arm, whilst Pauline went to a flower bed and felt under a large rock. Triumphantly she held up a key. She gave it to me, and I opened the front door. There were tears in my eyes.

"There won't be anything in the fridge," said Alice.

"Straight to bed," suggested Sam, but I shook my head.

"No," I said. "I'm going to phone Theo first."

"Mother, it's four thirty in the morning."

"I don't care. I want to tell my son that we are home."

I phoned him, and eventually he answered.

"Who the hell is that?" he grumbled.

"Theo, it's your mother. I'm home. At Hamilton Hall. We're all home," and tears were flowing down my cheeks.

"Mum, you're home."

He sounded relieved more than anything.

"When did you get back?"

"Ten minutes ago. We'll tell you all about it when we see you. We haven't slept so we're all off to bed. Come for lunch tomorrow."

We all went to bed. As I lay in by own bed, I smiled to myself.

Home sweet home.

Part 2 - England

Chapter 47 - Frederick the Bastard

I woke at eleven twenty four. I know because my bedside digital clock told me so. There were noises from downstairs. I wondered what they were then realised it was probably the others doing something or other. I just lay there, in my big, soft, four poster double bed. I was home.

I must have dozed again but then heard a knock on the bedroom door which opened and Pauline walked in with a cup of tea and some of my favourite biscuits.

"Sam and Stu have been to the local shop," she explained. "Did you sleep well?"

"Like an innocent little baby," I said and she chuckled.

"We thought you might like a soak in a nice bubble bath. Theo and Uncle Flambert will be here in an hour."

I had forgotten about Flambert. He had been a big help to us, I remembered.

"Thank you sweetheart. Yes I'd love a bath."

"I'll go and run it for you."

It was wonderful to hug my little baby son, who was now a fully grown man, an hour later. We held each other close and I looked into his eyes. They were wet with tears, as were mine.

"Oh mum," he said. "It's so, so good to have you back home," and he hugged me again, then hugged his sisters and Sam and Stu.

Then I hugged Flambert, who hadn't changed one bit since I had last seen him. He held me at arms length and looked into my eyes.

"You are still the most beautiful girl in the whole world," he said.

He embraced Sam and Stu, and kissed Alice and Pauline. We

sat down to a picnic lunch, and we told Flambert and Theo some of what had happened. The whole story would have taken all day and part of the next.

After lunch, Alice and Pauline popped into Kidderminster to do a supermarket shop, then cooked an evening 'Abacadian style' meal, with couple of bottles of Cadian wine they had discovered. The meal was full of laughter as I told them more of my adventures.

It was truly wonderful to be home. I could scarcely believe it as I looked at the six of them sat around my large oak table, smiles on all their faces. I wanted to cry with happiness, but I didn't.

Flambert had offered to drive Sam and Stu home, and eventually the time arrived for them to leave. Once again there were more hugs and kisses. I thanked Sam and Stu but they laughed off my thanks.

"It was a pleasure and a lot of fun. Wouldn't have missed it for the world."

I was expecting tears or something from Alice and Pauline when they said goodbye to their men but they were too excited and thrilled to have me home, it seems, and all the men got from them were a quick hug and kiss each and a "See you soon."

We waved goodbye as they drove away, then opened another bottle of wine and talked and laughed and answered Theo's questions into the early hours. It was possibly the happiest evening of my whole life.

Inspector Hector came to see me the next morning. How he knew I was home I don't know, but there he was. I had to make a statement and explain what had happened. He wasn't a happy Inspector at all.

"You shouldn't have gone off like that," he scolded Alice and Pauline. "It is a criminal offence to keep information from the police. It is within my rights to arrest you and charge you."

"But you're not going to, are you?" asked Pauline.

"Probably not," he answered. His frown slipped a fraction.

"However, I would like to say something before I leave," he

continued, looking at Alice and Pauline.

"You really should have kept me up to date with everything you were doing. You really do need to trust the police. You might not believe it, but we really are on your side and we really do want to help."

He turned back to me.

"Lecture over, Lady Clair. I would like to say how pleased we all are to have you back safe and sound in Hamilton Hall. Good day, ladies."

And he left.

Pauline and Alice let out a big sigh.

"Thank goodness he didn't hear what we called him before we left for Abacadia," said Pauline, and the two of them burst into laughter.

That afternoon the girls and I walked to the local church, St Mary's, to visit my late husband's grave. I had always tried to visit once a week, to talk to him and to weed and trim the grass. Normally I went on my own, but this time I took Alice and Pauline with me.

I knelt down, and fussed about the grave, tidying away a couple of blown leaves and pulling up some small weeds.

I read the inscription, as I always did.

Lord Alfred Hamilton
'Alfie'
Beloved husband and father
Everybody's friend
Taken too young.

We stood by the grave, and bowed our heads and remembered him. Then I spoke.

"I loved you, Alfie. I still do. I miss you so much and wish you were still here with me. But, and I'm sure you will agree with me, life must go on. I have met another man. He is a very, very good man. He's almost as good as you were. I think I may have fallen in love with him. I wanted to tell you."

I turned and walked away and the girls followed me.

"There," I told them. "I've said it. Now you know. I think I love Moldie."

We spent the next two days catching up on work. Theo went back to Print-U-Like in Kidderminster and us three girls attempted to catch up on the orders they had received for their homemade soaps.

On the second morning I woke up and drew the bedroom curtains to look outside. I had always done this, but now I was back home it gave me even greater pleasure. And this morning even more pleasure than normal.

Sitting in the middle of the drive was my beloved silver blue 45 year old E Type Jaguar. I squealed, dragged on my dressing gown and slippers and ran down the stairs and out of the front door. The keys were in the ignition and I couldn't stop smiling.

Alice and Pauline had followed me out and were also grinning.

"Do you know anything about this?" I asked them.

They shook their heads.

"Moldie must have arranged it all," said Pauline. "Good old Moldie."

I climbed in and drove it down the drive and back up again. I snuffled back a couple of tears. Grown women don't cry when they drive a car, even their favourite car, but my E-Type was like an old friend. No, not just an old friend, more like one of the family.

The hire car was gone.

There was also many letters concerning my charity work and the usual household bills. I paid all the bills, but only quickly read through the charity stuff. I wouldn't do anything about that until I had talked to the rest of the Lady Clair Hamilton Trust.

So, two days later I phoned Marjory Hacket, my best friend in the whole world, and a member of the committee, to tell her that I was safely returned.

"Oh, good," she said, sounding not at all enthusiastic about hearing from me.

384

"Are you well?"

"Not too bad, Marjory. Is everything okay?"

"Eh, well, er, Clair, the charity committee want to talk to you as soon as possible. As soon as you have recovered from your ordeal," she added hastily.

"I'm fine now," I told her. "I can meet you all anytime you like, just arrange it. What's this all about?" but she wouldn't tell me, just said she would get back to me and hung up as quickly as she could.

I wondered what was wrong. I discussed it with the children over dinner but none of us could think of any reason why they would want to see me so soon and why Marjory was so cagey and so obviously upset.

"Would you like us to come with you when you go?" suggested Alice.

I said I thought that would be a good idea.

Marjorie phoned me back again the next morning.

"Clair. Could you meet at the Frederick's house tomorrow evening at 7.30?" she asked.

She didn't sound a very happy lady.

Frederick Pondermoor OBE was the chairman of the Lady Clair Hamilton Charity Trust. I had given him the position. I had also okayed the other four members of the committee, including, of course, Marjory.

I told her I would be there.

"Can you tell me what this is all about Marjory?" I asked her, but once again she wouldn't. She just said goodbye and hung up.

The next evening, Alice and Pauline and I drove to Frederick's house in Alice's little Morris Minor. It was only a couple of miles away. He lived in a detached house in the middle of a two acre beautifully manicured garden. Alice parked up by the front door and we all climbed out.

I knocked on the door and was surprised when it was opened by Marjory. She didn't seem very happy to see Alice and Pauline there.

"We weren't expecting you two," she said.

"Well, they're here and they're coming in with me," I told her.

She shrugged and stood back to let us pass. Then she suddenly grabbed my arm and pulled me to one side. She hugged me and started weeping.

"I'm so sorry Clair," she sobbed. "This is not my idea," and she let go and disappeared into the toilet.

I watched her go and wondered what was about to happen. I looked at the girls, who just shrugged.

I followed them into Frederick's sitting room. The rest of the committee were already sitting there, and they also didn't seem very happy to see my daughters with me.

Frederick stood up.

"Welcome Lady Hamilton," he said.

Lady Hamilton? He had never ever called me Lady Hamilton before. It had always been Clair, not even Lady Clair.

"We weren't expecting Alice and Pauline. Maybe they would like to wait in another room?"

"No," I said, "They stay. They have always worked with me and whatever you have to say is for their ears also. I keep no secrets from them."

Frederick sighed and asked Marjorie, who had just come into the room, if she could bring two extra chairs in from the dining room. I sat on the only empty chair and, when Marjory returned, Alice and Pauline sat either side of me.

"Well, Freddie, why have you invited us here?"

He hated being called Freddie. I smiled sweetly at him.

Suddenly he looked embarrassed and tongue-tied but then he took a big breath and said, "Lady Hamilton, it has come to our notice that you have been in Abacadia for the past few weeks."

"That's true," I said, "But how do you know that?"

I looked at Alice and Pauline but they just both shrugged again.

Frederick ignored my question and just bulldozed on.

"And we understand that during your whole time there, you acted as a prostitute, and that you had your wanton behaviour professionally filmed. We think that is not the behaviour of someone who we want to be in charge of our charity organisation. We are unanimous about this. We have contacted the Charity Commission and they agree with us. Therefore, your licence to run a charity such as the Lady Clair Hamilton Charity Trust has been taken away from you. We have voted for a the name of the charity to be changed to Central Worcestershire Charity Trust. You have been removed from the committee and you will not be invited back."

All this came out in one mad rush. I don't think he drew breath from the first word spoken to the last.

At that moment I felt a huge mixture of emotions running through my mind. Anger, obviously. Hatred, yes. Frustration, indeed. But one of the main emotions was relief. Relief that I no longer had to deal with these petty minded, small people.

I stood up. Alice and Pauline also stood up. I looked at Frederick and smiled. A sick smile I agree but a smile nevertheless.

"If that's your decision, Frederick, then that's fine by me. Goodbye."

I turned and left the room. Alice and Pauline followed me. I walked to the car, overcoming, just, the urge to slam the front door behind me. We all got in and Alice drove off.

Alice said, "Mother, are you okay?"

I shrugged.

"Oh Christ," I sighed.

I shook my head.

"Oh God!"

It came out as a moan.

Alice squeezed my arm. Pauline leant over from the back seat and gave me a big hug.

"They are just silly petty minded little people who have a jumped up opinion of themselves. Please don't let them upset you mum. It's not worth it."

I turned and smiled at her, though tears were running down my cheeks.

"I'll try," I said, but I thought it would take me a while to recover.

"I wonder how they found out?" Alice asked.

"I was wondering about that as well."

And I was.

"It wasn't any of us three," said Pauline. "Who else knew?"

"Sam and Stu knew," I suggested, but both Alice and Pauline shook their heads.

"No," said Alice. "It couldn't have been them. We didn't tell them until last week, and anyway, they just wouldn't. They're in love with us. They wouldn't."

"What about Moldie?" asked Pauline.

"I don't think so," I said. "Why would he want to do that? Sam and Stu are in love with you two, but Moldie is in love with me. His main concern is for the people of Effghania. How would telling Frederick help his cause? I just can't see it."

"Is there anyone else who knows?" Alice wondered.

"Theo and Flambert. Surely not. They're family."

I couldn't even consider that possibility.

We all wondered but there wasn't anyone else. Apart from, of course, Inspector Hector.

"Could it be Inspector Hector," Alice suggested. "He knew you'd gone to Abacadia."

"But did he know what I did there?" I mused.

"He may have found The Tape of you on the internet. Moldie's tape," suggested Alice.

"But he was so reasonable the other day," I said. "Either he doesn't know or he is the world's greatest actor. I don't think it was him."

Alice agreed with me.

"He can be a bit of a twat," she told us, "But I do think he is an honourable man. I can't see it being him."

"There is one other," suggested Pauline. "Bim Dram. He's probably very upset with you. He might well want revenge. It wouldn't have been difficult for him to find out all about your charity work, and to find the email addresses of the committee. Everything is on your website and also on your Facebook pages.

He also has a copy of The Film. It would have taken just one email to Frederick to get his revenge."

We thought about that and couldn't come up with any other possible culprits.

I slept badly that night. My mind was in a turmoil. Full of bad thoughts about Frederick and the rest of the committee.

"Bastards," I kept thinking. "The utter bastards."

The next day, I phoned Moldie. He was already back in Redik and pleased to hear from me.

"I'm glad you got home safely," he told me. "I miss you already. Is everything alright."

Firstly I thanked him for returning my E Type Jag.

"Oh good," he said. "Was it okay?"

"Fine. Not a scratch, thanks."

There was me thanking him for returning something he stole off me in the first place. Oh well.

Then I told him what had happened at Frederick's house. He was horrified.

"You don't think it is me, do you?" he asked, sounding even more horrified.

"No, of course not, you wally," I told him. "We think it's probably Bim Dram, trying to get revenge. We can't think of anyone else."

"A few people here in Abacadia have seen The Film," he said, "But I think I agree with you. It must be him. What a rotten thing to do."

He told me about the further progress that was being made with my money. Things were going well, but they really needed some more money, and fairly soon.

"Money has started trickling in from other sources," he told me, but not sounding too excited about it.

"They showed the news film that I showed you a couple of weeks ago on American television, but it didn't have as much effect as we hoped. I think it's because the film shows things are improving and I assume that the public and other charities would rather send their money to other countries, where things aren't going so well."

"I'll see what I can do about getting hold of some money," I told him. "Moldie, I miss you. I wish you were here to support me."

Immediately he said, "Do you want me to fly out. I could be with you in a couple of days," but I told him no.

"I've got Alice and Pauline and Theo with me, and anyway, you're needed in Redik. I'll be okay soon. I'm just feeling a bit down at the moment."

Later that day and we were sitting around the dining room table having lunch when Alice spoke.

"Mother," said she, in a very serious tone of voice. "What happens if The Film gets into the general public domain? It could easily become viral. What then?"

This was something that had crossed my mind. And it was something that could easily happen. And it almost certainly would become viral.

"I don't think you could really deny it. It's very obvious that it is you," went on Alice remorselessly.

"I'm not ashamed of what I did," I said, and I wasn't ashamed. "I really didn't have any option."

"We know that. But how will the public react. You've seen what Frederick and the committee think about it. I'm sorry to hark on about it, mother, but it's something that we all have to take seriously. It could easily happen."

I had given this scenario a bit of thought. Not a lot of thought because the thought depressed me and as I couldn't think of a solution I decided not to think about it.

But now Pauline had brought up the subject and I had to think about it. I chickened out by saying, "What are your thoughts?"

"I think you should write the story about your adventures and I think you should do it soon. You need to put your point of view and you need to do it before somebody else does. That's my opinion."

I sighed and swore at Moldie. If only he hadn't made The Film I might have been able to keep everything under wraps.

Damn him.

"I think you may be right," I replied to Pauline. "Let me think about it," which meant I was putting it off until another time. The cowards way out.

But I did start thinking about my previous charity raising efforts here in Worcestershire. The last event I organised before I was kidnapped was a big success and raised £4,000. I was so proud of myself but I would have to organise 20 or more of them to earn the same amount of money that one night's loving in Redik had earned.

It made me think.

Very, very briefly I thought about carrying on my whoring ways here at Hamilton Hall. I daydreamed about having the occasional rich gentleman staying for dinner and sleeping in my big soft warm double bed with me and paying lots and lots of money for the privilege. Just as I had in the Redik apartment, but this time I would be in charge.

I remembered some of the lovers I had had and fantasised about having new lovers here at home. Then I wondered if Moldie would mind. Maybe he would, maybe he wouldn't.

Then I thought of what my children would think. They had just about accepted that I had no choice in Redik but here in Hamilton Hall? I thought that they would probably disown me.

Mother, the High Class Prostitute.

Nope. No way.

So it remained just an idle fantasy.

What really concerned me though was the family finances. In the last two months, none of the children had earned any money. Theo had taken unpaid leave from his printers shop job, and we still had his university fees to pay.

Alice and Pauline had been in Abacadia and spending money, quite a lot of money, not earning it. There were the few orders for soap that we had sent off since we got back, and a few more trickling in, but the finances were not good. We had got into debt and needed to get hold of some money.

And soon.

Chapter 48 - Danny Dumbles

I needed to start taking advantage of the contacts I had made in Abacadia. I phoned Moldie again to tell him.

"I am going to start with the Cadian Wine adverts," I said. "Danger Goodness suggested we made some here in Hamilton Hall. I'll remind him about that. If I hint at a bit of bedroom action as part of the bargain, I'm sure he will come over fairly soon."

"I wish I was getting a bit of bedroom action," said Moldie, and I could sense a bit of jealousy in his voice.

"I'm sure we'll get together soon," I soothed. "I have decided to give half the money we earn to you. It was going to be more, but the family here are a bit short of cash at the moment. I need to put some into our bank account."

Moldie perked up at the talk of money.

"Do you want me to contact Danger?" he said, "And suggest it to him?"

"Yes please, Moldie. Ask him to phone me here at Hamilton Hall."

Two days later, Danger Goodness phoned me.

"Hello Lady Clair," he said. "I've been thinking about you," and he chuckled. I wondered if he had been thinking about the adverts or my bottom. Probably both.

"I see you have returned to England. Is there anything you have in mind?"

"I have been thinking about adverts for Cadian Wine," I told him. "I think we could make some really good adverts here at Hamilton Hall. I would play myself, all dressed up in my posh dresses, and my household could play the bit parts. All you would need is a camera crew. I'll send you some ideas, if you like."

He agreed that he would be happy to receive some ideas from me. He seemed even happier when I added, "I am sorry to say, though, that if you do visit, I don't have a spare bedroom and you would have to sleep with me in my large four poster soft double bed. I do hope that that wouldn't be a problem."

He generously decided that he could put up with that minor inconvenience.

So, that evening after dinner, I gathered the children around and told them what I wanted. They thought it was a great idea and sounded like a lot of fun as well as an opportunity to earn some money.

The quality of the adverts we were going to send to Danger Goodness didn't have to be brilliant. They were just sample ideas. I had thought of filming them on my mobile phone, but Theo had a better idea.

"I'm sure I could borrow a decent digital cine camera from Worcester uni," he said. "I could take the part of the director and the university could help me edit them and then we could send the finished adverts off to Abacadia. I'm sure the university would be even happier if they knew that they would get a mention in the finished film."

We agreed that sounded a good idea and the following day Theo turned up with a smart looking camera and a baseball hat with the word "Director" written across the front.

We filmed a number of scenes. Theo pretended to be in charge, but I was really. I had to be the star. I was the celebrity in Abacadia. It was me that Danger wanted in the adverts. It would be me he would be paying.

In the first advert, I was standing outside Hamilton Hall's front door, looking very posh in my poshest dress.

"Hello," I said, smiling sweetly. "I'm Lady Clair Hamilton, and this is my family home, Hamilton Hall, in England. Tonight I am having a dinner party. The main course will be pomegranate and chicken stew, here being prepared by my daughter, Pauline."

There was a short visit to the kitchen, where Pauline pretended to be a cook, wearing an apron and smiling shyly at the camera whilst stirring a big pot of stew on the Aga.

Back to me.

"I need a nice wine to compliment the chicken, and I have chosen this white chardonnay, produced in Abacadia by Cadian

Wines."

I held up a bottle of Cadian wine that we had bought from the local supermarket, and smiled.

"It's golden in colour with a gold medal taste. Easy to drink with an overture of melon ."

The advert finished with the four of us sitting around the dining room table, sipping the wine that was being poured by Pauline and making appropriate noises of appreciation. I took a sip of mine and said to camera,

"Cadian wines. Make your dinner party just that extra bit special."

We also filmed other versions for the different wines. Sam and Stu visited and were roped in. I suggested they were just coarse ignorant men, with no subtlety or education or taste and only drank beer, but I forced them to try a Cadian red wine, and they actually quite liked it.

Then we filmed me in the kitchen talking to Pauline, our chef, and after I left, Pauline having a secret drink of rose wine, to appeal to the 'more common' viewers, and one of me enjoying a glass whilst deeply emerged in a bubble bath, to appeal to the more sex-starved viewers.

We attempted to film a copy with me speaking Abacadian. I know it wasn't top quality Abacadian but I told Danger that I could get it right with a bit of help from him and some practise.

Theo edited them at university, and when we were satisfied, he sent them off to Danger Goodness in Abacadia, and we waited for a reply.

The following week, Marjory Hacket came to visit me. I hadn't heard from her and was becoming worried.

Annie and Pauline thought it was best that I waited until she contacted me. Give her time to make up her mind about what to do.

She rang the front door bell, something she didn't normally do. In the past she had wandered around to the kitchen and let herself in. Ringing the front door bell told me that things still weren't back to normal.

I could see she was still very upset, so I gave her a big hug. I sat her down in the living room and made us both a cup of tea.

"Marjory, whatever happened, I still think of you as my best friend. Nothing has changed. You are still my best friend."

"Oh Clair," she bleated. "I'm so glad to hear that. I really don't deserve you. It's been horrible, really horrible. I've cried myself to sleep every night. I didn't know what to do and there was nobody here at Hamilton Hall."

There were tears in her eyes so I got up and hugged her again and she hugged me back.

Then she told me what had happened.

"We all knew you had been kidnapped, of course. The children and the police had questioned us to see if we knew anything, but we didn't. We were all concerned for your safety. We had no idea where you were.

Then one day Frederick showed us The Film," she continued. "I was horrified. I couldn't believe my eyes. There was you, Lady Clair Hamilton, my best friend, acting like a total wanton whore. I couldn't believe it."

She didn't have to be quite so blunt, I thought.

"The others wanted to dump you immediately. I tried to stick up for you, saying we should wait until you return and we could hear your side of the story, but they wouldn't listen to me and it was four against one. We had a vote, I was outvoted and that was it. I couldn't do anything. I tried, I argued, I pleaded, I begged, but they were adamant. You had to go. I'm so sorry."

She was in tears. I told her not to worry.

"You did your best. Don't worry. Do you know where he got hold of The Film?" but she shook her head.

"I'm sorry. We did ask him but he refused to tell us."

I suspected as much and said, "Now, do you want to hear the true story," and I told her everything that had happened to me, leaving out nothing. She was my best friend, we had known each other for years, but I think even she was a bit shocked at what had occurred and what I had got up to.

"Please don't tell anyone," I asked her, and she promised she wouldn't.

She stopped for lunch and a glass or two of wine and we caught up on the rest of the news. She told me what charity work had been going on, and all the local gossip. It was good to catch up.

When she eventually left, I let out a big sigh. Not because she had gone but because The Film hadn't spoilt our special relationship. If anything, it had made it even stronger, and I was glad about that. I needed all the friends I could.

Things took a turn for the worse the very next day.

I had a phone call.

"Hello," said a local Worcestershire voice, "May I speak to Lady Clair Hamilton please?"

At least he was polite.

"Speaking," I answered. "How may I help?"

"My name is Danny Dumbles. I'm a reporter from the Daily Window and I was wondering if I may come and talk to you, please?"

"Eh, what about?" I asked, immediately suspicious.

He didn't answer my question, which made me even more suspicious.

"I won't keep you for long."

I sighed.

"Yes. Of course. When would you like to visit?"

He came that same afternoon. He was only young, well, in his late twenties probably, with curly hair and a goatee. He wore a smart shirt, no tie, and smartly creased trousers.

I offered him a cup of tea, as I did to all my guests, and he thanked me with a smile.

"What can I do for you?" I asked him as I poured and he came straight to the point.

"Lady Clair," he answered. "I have received a short film, about three minutes long, which appears to show you acting as a prostitute in Abacadia. I ...." but I held my hand up as I felt my heart give a flip.

"I would like my daughters to hear what you have to say," I

396

said. "They're in one of the outbuildings. I'll go and get them. Please will you hang on for just one minute?"

Oh God, don't say Bim Dram had sent a copy to a journalist. And the Daily Window. Why them? They loved stories about celebrities, and didn't care whose reputation they ruined. The juicier the better.

I needed Alice and Pauline with me.

I went through to a small building toward the back of the hall, and found them packing up parcels of soap, ready to be posted off.

The looked up at me and the look on my face showed them something must be wrong.

"Mother, what's wrong?" asked Alice.

"I have a major problem. I think Bim Dram has sent a copy of The Film to a journalist from the Daily Window, and he's here now. He wants to interview me. Will you come and give me support, please?"

Immediately they stopped what they were doing, washed their hands and followed me through to the sitting room.

"I'm sorry to keep you waiting," I said to Danny. "These are my daughters, Alice and Pauline. This is Danny Dumbles, a journalist with the Daily Window," and he politely stood up and they shook hands.

"Please start from the beginning again," I said. "Anything you would say to me you can say to them. We keep no secrets from each other."

He nodded, looking serious.

"I have received a short film by email and it appears to show you acting like a prostitute in Abacadia. I ...."

"Who sent it to you?" interrupted Alice, looking extremely angry, but Danny Dumbles shook his head.

"To be totally honest, I don't know, but even if I did know, I wouldn't be at liberty to tell you. Do you deny that it is you in the film?"

"Before I admit or deny anything," I said, "What sort of journalist are you? Are you reputable? Do you have any

397

examples of your work? Do you have any references?"

He sat up straight and pulled back his shoulders.

"I assure you, lady, that I am proud that I adhere to the highest possible journalistic standards. I do not make up stories and I do not write tittle tattle. If you wish to check with my editor, then please do so. If you wish to Google me, you will find out the same thing. I am a proper serious journalist."

I held up my hands.

"Whoa," I said. "I meant no harm but in my position I need to be sure. I wish to talk to my daughters alone. If you remain here just for a couple of minutes more, please," and we all walked out of the living room and into the dining room.

"Well, what do you think?" I asked them.

They both nodded and Alice said, "It was bound to happen sooner or later. It might as well be him. He's young and he's local and he seems genuine," and we walked back into the room.

"Danny." I deliberately used his first name. "Would you like an exclusive interview?"

"Of course," he obviously replied. "What have you got to tell me?"

"Before I say anything, you would have to agree to allow us to read everything before it is printed and make any alterations as we think suitable."

"I'm not sure if I can do that," he said. "If that was the case, it wouldn't strictly be my work, would it?"

"You must agree, otherwise we will get someone else to write my story who will agree," I said.

"I don't have much option then, do I?" he said. "Okay, I promise, nothing will get printed until you have agreed to it."

Alice brought out a sheet of paper and wrote on it,

'I Danny Dumbles, hereby agree that I will not publish anything I write about Lady Clair Hamilton or her family without them first agreeing to the article.'

He read it over, sighed and signed and we all signed as

witnesses.

"Now, what have you got to tell me."

"What do you know about me?" I asked him.

"I have Googled you," he said, "And I know about your family and your husband, Alfie, and your charity work. That's about it really."

"Do you know that I have been recently kidnapped and held hostage in Abacadia?"

His eyebrows really raised high.

"I hadn't heard that. Is that to do with the film?"

"It is. Look, this is very sensitive, which is why we are being so cagey and why we got you to sign that promise. We understand that there is a very good chance that what has happened to me will become public knowledge sooner or later, and we want it to come out from our point of view rather than through rumours or told by somebody else. Do you understand what I mean?"

He was looking really interested now. I think he was beginning to understand that there might be quite a good story brewing.

"I understand," he said. "Perhaps you should start from the beginning. Do you mind if I record this conversation?"

"Not at the moment," I suggested. "Let's just have an off the record chat first and take things from there."

"Okay. No recording and no notes."

He seemed happy enough with that.

So I gave him a brief outline of what had happened. As he had a copy of The Film, there was no point in keeping the sexual part of the story from him, though I didn't go into too much detail.

He listened without interrupting, as did the girls. The story didn't take long and ended with us landing in Norfolk.

"I see," he said. "It is quite a story. Just wondering, do you have any proof to back up everything that you have just told me?"

"I could get all the proof you need," I told him.

Moldie would send me some bits of the films he took of me in the apartment and at the lake if I asked him.

"Much of what I did was filmed, and I have access to them if I want."

He nodded.

"Sounds good enough."

"One other matter," I said. "We are a little bit short of money."

"I understand," he said and went off to discuss the matter with his boss at the Daily Window. He returned the next day with an offer of money. It was not a bad offer but it wasn't that good either. I told him that for the story I was about to tell and the extra sales and publicity it would bring the Daily Window, I wanted more money than they were offering.

A lot more.

Especially, I thought to myself, as I was going to give half to Moldie. Actually, Alice and Pauline weren't that keen on me giving half the money to Moldie.

"He's the bloke who kidnapped you and took The Film and it's because of him that you are in this pickle," they said, but I wouldn't agree with them.

"I promised him," I said, "And anyway, the money is not for him, it's for the people of Effghania," and that was the end of that argument.

Eventually we came up with a deal that both the Daily Window and we were happy with.

"As long as the story is as good as you promised," said Danny Dumbles.

He brought along a contract and we both signed it.

So, for the next few weeks, Danny Dumble came to visit Hamilton Hall, five days a week, (I need the weekends off to replenish my batteries, he said), and for two hours every morning. We sat in the dining room, around the table, and I talked and he recorded and the more he heard the broader became his grin.

"This is quite a story," he said.

"This is going to be one of he biggest stories of the year" he said.

Then every evening Alice and Pauline and I would sit down and decide what to tell him the following day.

I used the notes from my diary and Alice and Pauline did their bits from memory. Sam and Stu would come over occasionally to read what was written and to put in their suggestions and memories.

We changed the names of most of the people I had been involved with, including Moldie and all my clients. And I changed the businesses of dress and wine making to hat and tea making, to keep Danger and Stig happy, I hoped. I wondered whether I should change Bim Dram's name and in the end decided I would, to Bomb Drain. He had, after all, lied to me quite badly. I also made him a successful businessman, rather than and MP. I thought it would make the story more acceptable.

I did, however, describe the sex in quite graphic detail. I figured that the kind of people who read the Daily Window were the kind of people who would quite enjoy reading about the sex life of Lady Clair Hamilton.

Every few days Danny would bring us something to read. To be fair, he did a pretty good job and we didn't have to change or edit much.

Moldie sent me various photographs that I asked for. Some of me in the apartment, one or two of both of us at Lake Lucinda, and a couple of before and after views of Redik and the improvements. We got many other pictures from Google and the Abacadian Embassy in London.

It didn't take Danny and the rest of the Daily Window management to realise that they had a gem of a story on their hands. They paid me quite a lot of the money upfront, and suddenly the family were financially sound again, which was a big relief to us all. I sent half the money to Moldie in Effghania. It was the first load of money I had sent him since my return, and he was delighted.

The paper decided to publish my story in a weekly serialisation, starting in a couple of weeks time. Every Saturday there would be a two page, or more, spread in the middle of the paper, with plenty of colour photographs, mostly of me. They did it weekly because it was taking us quite a while to write down our memories, and to make sure everything was correct.

I thought about changing my name. I thought of Lady Eleanor Kensington-Smythe. I liked the ring of that, but eventually decided that it would be a waste of time. With modern technology, it wouldn't take long before it got generally known that Lady Eleanor was, in fact, little old me.

Changing my name would have made it seem that I was embarrassed by what I had done, and I wasn't embarrassed at all. So I decided to use my own name.

Chapter 49 - Daily Window

Meanwhile, back in Abacadia, Moldie had contacted Stig de Silva, the dress designer, for me, and one day Stig phoned me.

"It was good to hear from Moldie," he said. "I'm so glad you are still interested in promoting my dresses for me in England. Have you any ideas about how we could proceed?"

"I have two grown up daughters," I told him, "And they are both as pretty as me."

I was going to say they were a lot prettier than me, but I didn't think he would believe me.

"'We have discussed your dresses, and think it wouldn't be too much of a problem to set up a fashion show either here or in Worcester, the local city. Then we thought, why bother hiring models when we could model them ourselves?

If we send you our measurements and tell you which dresses we want, could you make them to fit us? I'm sure one of the fashion magazines would send a photographer and a journalist to Hamilton Hall for a photo shoot and an article."

Stig thought this was a great idea. We had already had our measurements taken professionally by a local dress maker, and had picked out a dozen of his dresses each we liked. I had deliberately gone for a slightly older look, the kids had gone for young and trendy. All the dresses we had chosen had a touch of Abacadian about them.

We sent the measurements and choices off to him, and then waited for the dresses to arrive.

I decided not to tell him about the upcoming Daily Window articles. He was such a gentleman that the story might put him off using me to promote his dresses. I was hoping that once he had discovered how good I was at promoting them, with the girls help, that he would overlook the articles.

I figured, in all modesty, that the extra publicity from Danny Dumbles's articles would almost certainly bring would actually help the sales tremendously, and I was hoping he would come around to the same opinion.

I had the same hopes for Danger Goodness and his wines.

Alice and Pauline were seeing quite a lot of Sam and Stu and they all seemed to be getting on very well together. They often came round for dinner or went off for a meal or the cinema or an adventure weekend. Whenever they had any free time they seemed to be with them.

That was fine by me. I liked them both a lot and we got on well together. I was thinking that we needed some real men around the place, especially if any of my business propositions started becoming successful. I was trying to think of some way I could use them, apart from a bit of muscle. Neither of them were super bright, but they weren't stupid either.

Then, one evening, the girls were looking excited over dinner.,

"Come on, tell me, what's up?" I asked. "You two look like you've won the Abacadian lottery."

"Better than that," said Alice, grinning at Pauline, who grinned back. "Sam and Stu have asked us to marry them."

Was I surprised?

No.

"And what did you both say?" I asked, teasing.

"We both said yes, of course," grinned Pauline.

Then she went serious.

"You do approve, don't you?"

It did briefly cross my mind to tease a bit more but realised that maybe this wasn't the right time, so instead I said,

"I'm delighted for you both. They're both lovely men and I'm sure you'll all be happy together," and gave them both a big hug.

"When's the happy day? Will you have a joint wedding?"

They said they hadn't decided on a date but, yes, they probably would have a joint wedding.

"Maybe here at Hamilton Hall?" suggested Alice.

I smiled.

"That would be fine," but deep down I felt a bit jealous and a bit lonely. I didn't really have a man in my life. I was sure that all I had to do was invite Moldie to visit and he'd be over in a flash, but I was now having second thoughts about him. All the problems I was having due to The Film that he made was making me wonder if I could actually live with such a man. The memories would always be there.

Alice was still talking.

"It won't be for a while, mum, not until everything is sorted out with The Film and the Daily Window and the Cadian Wine adverts and the dresses. We're not going to abandon you."

It didn't take long before Danger Goodness got back in touch with me about the potential advertising campaign we had suggested to him for his Cadian Wines.

"I was very impressed," he said. "If the quality of the film had been a bit better, we could almost have used them as they were. I would definitely like to visit you and bring a camera crew and film them please."

I was pleased about that. The sooner they were filmed the sooner we would feel the benefits of the money we desperately needed. I had sent half the Daily Window money to Moldie and with half the money gone to Abacadia, we weren't as well off as we hoped we would be.

"We haven't talked about money yet, Danger," I said to him. "How much do you have in mind?"

"The first advert, the one we filmed in Abacadia, was very successful," he said, "And I think these follow up adverts could be even better. Plus, we will be using Hamilton Hall and your family will be the actors. I thinking of a good basic fee plus an additional bonus every time one of the adverts is shown on TV or cinema."

I had expected him to make suggestions to keep the fees down, but here he was, building me up as if he wanted to pay me more. I think the offer to share my bed had sweetened him up.

I was very happy with the amount he quoted me and told him so.

"I want half the money paid to me here in England, and the other half paid to Moldie Bedlam in Abacadia, please. And that includes any repeat fees from television."

He agreed that that wouldn't be a problem.

"When do you want to visit?" I asked him.

He arrived with a camera crew of three men the following week. That evening we entertained them all at Hamilton Hall. We had prepared some pomegranate and chicken stew and we washed it down with some Cadian wine, of course.

I had asked Marjory Hackett if she would like to be involved in the filming, and she looked very pleased.

"You would have to pretend to be my cook," I told her. "Your parts would be filmed in the kitchen," and so she was there for the meal and got a bit tipsy.

Alice drove the crew to a local inn where they were going to sleep for the duration of their stay. They were given strict orders not to get too drunk. Then she took Marjory home and told her not to be late the next day.

Danger Goodness climbed into my big soft four poster double bed with me.

I was very sexy that night. I know I was. It had been ages and ages since I had slept with Moldie in Abacadia and I had become very frustrated.

And Danger was the poor man who had to extinguish my frustrations.

I shagged him this way and that way and then this way again until he begged me to let him sleep.

"Darling Clair," he said, "Tomorrow we have some adverts to make and I need to have my wits about me and you need to look very pretty. We need some sleep, please," so, reluctantly, I left him alone and we slept.

Next morning we shared a shower together, then went down for breakfast, where the children acted as if it was perfectly normal for me to spend the night with a rich Abacadian businessman. I'm sure they must have heard one or two noises coming from my bedroom.

The camera crew turned up in time for coffee looking slightly pale, as did Marjory, and we showed them where Theo had filmed the previous demos. Danger looked all over the hall but eventually decided that he had been so happy with our demo's that he would film them again almost exactly the same.

So we all got dressed into our finest and started filming.

Danger had brought some different Cadian wines with him, and we used them for the adverts. We filmed each advert five or six times, with various variations and I spoke my dialogue both in English and appalling Abacadian. Danger coached me with pronunciations and seemed happy enough with the finished products, but I know my Abacadian was not good.

"Your posh English accent gives your Abacadian an air of mystery," he said.

Marjory's acting part involved no dialogue, which was just as well, because every time she heard me speak Abacadian, she giggled. But she played the part of a simple peasant very well, and when I told her so, she giggled some more.

We actually made eight different adverts, which took five days to do. Danger re-did all our original ideas plus a couple more ideas of his own.

So Danger shared my bed for six nights of passion, and it was great. It was better than great, it was wonderful. He was such a gentleman, so kind and so caring. My mind started wondering about being with him for the rest of my life. He was unmarried but he wouldn't tell me why.

Then I realised he would never leave Abacadia to come and live here in Hamilton Hall with me and I would never leave Hamilton Hall to live anywhere else, so living with Danger was just a short lived fantasy.

On the last morning he was with us, whilst we were lying in bed, I told him about the Daily Window articles. I thought it was only fair. He acted very calmly towards it.

"It's not a problem," he said. "If anything, the extra publicity could really help the sales."

"I think exactly the same," I agreed, and made love to him one last time, to show him how much I agreed with him.

I had enjoyed having Danger Goodness at Hamilton Hall, and when he left I had a feeling of sadness.

"Without a man again," I thought.

It was just after that The Daily Window published the first of the stories about my kidnapping and capture in Abacadia. They had made quite a big deal about it, and had been advertising the story for a couple of months beforehand on the front page of every Saturday edition. Then the story was advertised every day for the week leading up.

The whole of the front page of the Daily Window on the first Saturday was made up of one big headline.

Kidnapped
A true story
Lady Clair Hamilton reveals all

There was a photograph of me underneath, looking posh and sexy in one of my posh and sexy frocks.

The article-cum-story was a tremendous success. It made the local news stories in the local press and also on local radio and it was even mentioned on the local news. There was no mention of any sex in this first article, though it was hinted at for the next week's addition, so everybody was very sympathetic towards me.

Some of my neighbours who had never even talked to me suddenly became best buddies and called around to see me and offer me sympathy. Old friends who hadn't contacted me since Alfie's funeral became mates once again. It was all very strange, but it was not something I couldn't handle.

I plucked up courage and phoned Stig de Silva in Snuka. I was hoping by then that the dresses he had promised would have arrived and I could have started promoting them for him before I had to tell him about the articles.

But the timing didn't work out like that.

But I needn't have worried.

"To be honest, Clair," he said, "I had already guessed something like that. It's not a problem. In fact, the extra publicity might actually help the promotions you are organising. Don't worry about it."

And it made the news in Abacadia. Moldie phoned me to tell me. I had changed his name from Moldie to Doughy in the story, after the song Mouldy Old Dough, and that tickled him.

The money flowing into Effghania had reduced to a trickle, but now Moldie didn't seem that concerned.

"We are now growing most of our own fruit and vegetables," he said, "And drugs and medicine are being donated and foreign doctors and nurses are working for a pittance. Basically board and lodgings. So the people are a lot healthier.

Our next aim is to start some industries and we are looking towards wood based businesses. In the drought, many trees died and there is an abundance of wood. Any money you could get for us would go towards producing cut timber and eventually building new housing and schools. Keep up the good work."

Chapter 50 - Fashion Show

Theo went back to university to continue his full time studying for his degree in Computer Science, and he seemed to be doing okay. He also now had a steady girlfriend. She was on the same course as he was, and was called Olwen. I had met her a couple of times and she seemed nice enough. A bit shy, but nice enough. He had got her a part time job at the printers in Kidderminster where he still worked part time, Print-U-Like. Seeing the two of them together just made me feel more jealous and lonely.

I talked to my best friend Marjory about the problem. She was happily married but was most understanding.

"You are an extremely attractive and desirable Lady," she told me with a smile. "There must be millions of men who would go out with you."

"If that's the case," I said, "Where the bloody hell are they all?"

"What we need to do is to organise some dates for you. I can do that, if you like."

Of course I was horrified at the idea, but she was my best friend and somehow talked me into going out with a 'gentleman' she knew. His name was Andrew and he was a bit strange. Sort of good looking, I suppose, with a funny beard. Not a fully, bushy, manly beard but with hair only above and below his mouth. Nothing to the side. A bit like Billy Connolly in his prime, but not so witty. And he had a fat beer belly.

He worked as a manager of a local bottle making factory and had some funny ideas. He didn't like the Beatles, weird, or any proper music with a tune, weirder, but only liked to listen to synthetic music, which he did with one ear piece in and one ear piece dangling. Weirder.

He was nice but not nice enough, if you know what I mean, and not a touch on Moldie. We only had the one date.

I told Marjory that he was lacking in personality so she lined me up with a man who was completely the opposite. He was small and round with a full bushy beard. His name was Moony. A strange name but after all the strange names I had encountered in Abacadia, I wasn't that surprised.

He had personality coming out of his ear holes. Talked a lot, never shut up in fact, but he was very amusing and we did laugh a lot together. He almost laughed me into bed, but not quite. I was Lady Clair Hamilton, and I knew I could do so much better than him. I just had to keep looking.

Then, for a couple of days, I was the host to a real and proper Prime Minister, who stopped at Hamilton Hall for a weekend. It was Rum Hearty, the Prime Minister of Abacadia.

The phone rang one day and a voice with an Abacadian accent said, "Is that Lady Clair Hamilton?"

"It is," I replied, "Who is that?" but the voice with the Abacadian accent said, "Would you hold the phone for the Prime Minister please?" and then a voice I immediately recognised.

"Hello Clair," said the voice I recognised. A calm and gentle voice.

"Hello Rum."

I was a bit surprised but delighted to hear from the Prime Minister of Abacadia.

"What a pleasant surprise to hear your voice. Are you well?"

He told me he was extremely well, thank you, and asked me how I was, and I said fine. I was waiting for him to explain why he had phoned me.

"I bet you are wondering why I have phoned you," he said, on cue. "I am visiting London for a meeting and I have a couple of days free of duties. I wondered how I could spend those two days and the thing I would like to do most of all is visit you, Clair."

The randy old bugger meant he wanted to share my warm, wide, soft double bed with me, but I didn't say that, instead I said,

"Wow, Rum, it would be great to see you. Would you like me to book a room in the local inn or would you rather sleep in the spare bedroom here in Hamilton Hall?"

"Eh, well, I was wondering if I, eh,........"

I laughed.

"I'm joking Rum. Of course you can share my warm and soft double bed with me. I would be upset and insulted if you didn't," and I heard him sigh.

We made the arrangement, and I told the children, who were delighted, especially when I told them that I wanted them to join us for dinner on the Saturday evening.

"Would you mind stopping with Sam and Stu until then," I asked my daughters and they kindly said they would.

The following Friday the Prime Minister of Abacadia turned up at my house in a chauffeur driven Rolls Royce. I walked out of the front door to meet him and felt a real pleasure when I saw him. He was beaming and we kissed, and walked together into my living room. I served up a traditional tea and biscuits and we caught up on each other's news.

I had, obviously, taken a keen interest in anything on the news about Abacadia, and that regularly involved Rum, so I knew what he had been doing, and he, it seems, had taken a keen interest in me, so the conversation was easy and wide ranging. I showed him around the hall, and he seemed genuinely interested, especially in my four poster double bed. I showed him around the gardens, and could see he was impressed by the place.

He had brought a parcel with him, quite a large parcel, and now he gave it to me. I opened it up and inside were ladies clothes. The clothes he had given to me when I left his yacht, Heloise. I had left them in Bim Dram's bedroom when I was rescued, and Bim, to his credit, had given them to Rum, who now gave them to me.

I held a dress up in front of me and posed in front of him.

"I enjoyed my time on Heloise," I told him. "Thank you for bringing these to me."

"Bim was somewhat shocked and upset when you escaped," Rum told me, chuckling. "Serves him right."

That evening I took him to the local pub, The Old Volunteer, for dinner, driven in the back seat of his Rolls Royce by his chauffeur. I had booked a quiet table for two in a corner of the snug bar, and he tried some of the local ales. The pub did a platter of ales, three different beers in third pint glasses and he seemed to enjoy them all. He ate steak, I ate scampi and the evening continued with a singer and we got up and danced along with most of the pub and had a wonderful time.

The chauffeur dropped us off back at the hall and went to his room in the Volunteer. Rum and I had a nightcap then went up to my bedroom. We shared a shower then climbed into bed, and did what we both liked doing best. In the morning we did it again.

I took Rum for a drive in my E Type Jag around the lovely Worcestershire countryside, ending up in the Clee Hills and a traditional English cream tea before heading home. Alice and Pauline and Sam and Stu joined us for dinner, which the girls had prepared earlier, and all six of us had a great time. One big happy family.

The next morning, Rum asked me if the two of us could go for a walk around the gardens together. We sat on the bench by the fountain, and he took my hand and asked me a surprising question.

"Clair. You are a wonderful woman, as lovely as my late wife, Heloise. I don't want to upset you or her by saying either of you are better so I will say that you are equally smashing."

He was rambling on, obviously nervous. The Prime Minister of Abacadia, nervous. It seemed strange and I was wondering what he was going to say.

Eventually he got around to it. He knelt down on one knee in front of me, the Prime Minister of Abacadia, on his knees in front of little old me, and he proposed.

"I love you, Lady Clair Hamilton," he told me in a clear, sincere voice, whilst looking me straight in the eyes. "Will you do me the honour of becoming my wife?"

I was shocked. I hadn't expected this at all. I knew he liked me, and I liked him, I really liked him, but marry him?

"I am sure the people of Abacadia will accept you," he

continued, "Even though you aren't Abacadian. You will make the perfect First Lady for me, and I really, truly do love you."

He had a lot going for him, I realised. A very good job. Prime Minister is a very good job, with a huge amount of respect going with it. And I would share that respect. A big house and a big yacht. But all in Abacadia.

I was tempted. I really was. But then I looked around the garden, and knew I would miss Hamilton Hall and the children. It was a hard thing to do, but I said, "Thank you Rum. I like you, a lot, I really do, but I'm sorry, I can't marry you. Thank you for asking me," and he sighed.

"Is there anything I can do to make you change your mind?" he asked, but I shook my head.

"This is my home, Rum," I tried to explain. "After everything that has happened to me, I want to live here in Hamilton Hall in Worcestershire. I really am so sorry, but, no."

He chuckled. Bless him.

"I understand," he said. "Oh well, I tried and I could never have forgiven myself if I hadn't. But we will remain friends?"

I leant forward and kissed him on the end of his nose.

"Always."

He left that Sunday afternoon, and later on I phoned Alice and Pauline and told them the news.

They chuckled.

"What did you say?"

"I was tempted, but I turned him down. I didn't want to live in Abacadia, not even as the wife of the Prime Minister. I want to live in Hamilton Hall. Did I do the right thing?"

"Yes mother, you did the right thing," but I lay awake that night wondering if I had. I had turned down a marriage proposal from a Prime Minister. Was I mad?

Two more articles about my kidnapping had by now appeared in the Daily Window. The second article included quite a lot of the sex, and my visits to the two beauty spots of Lake Lucinda and Angels Hair Falls. There were photos of both places, dug up from some archives, it seemed, but they didn't do either of them real justice.

I think almost everybody in the country read the stories and I was becoming a bit of a minor celebrity.

I gave interviews to all the local newspapers, and appeared live on the local radio station. The interviewer, a bloke, tried to embarrass me by asking me so-called questions of morality.

"Are you ashamed by how you acted?" he asked me.

"No," I answered. "I had no choice."

"You could have refused," he said.

"No I couldn't."

"It seems from the articles that you actually enjoyed the sex."

"I did."

"Do you feel hatred towards the kidnappers?"

"No I don't."

"Why not?"

"I just don't."

If he was going to ask stupid questions to make me look an idiot, then I wasn't going to co-operate.

Eventually I said to him, "Look, mate," (I had forgotten his name) "If you ever want me or anybody else back on this poxy little show of yours then you need to improve your interview technique, because at the moment you are a complete and utter dead loss."

I smiled sweetly at him over the microphones. I know I shouldn't really have done it, not on live radio, but he really was getting on my nerves. I think he expected me to get up and walk out then, but, out of spite, I stayed.

"Now then, do you want to start again?"

He was looking daggers at me, but then laughed.

"You are right, Lady Clair, and I apologise. Let's start again," and this time he asked proper questions and the interview went a lot better.

Rival radio and TV stations thought the interview was a hoot and replayed it on their news and I was becoming rather popular.

The family just chuckled.

Then one Wednesday morning the dresses arrived from Stig de Silva. He had sent us thirty, ten for each of us, and we had great fun trying them on. They all fitted perfectly, but I wasn't surprised about that, and they looked really good, we thought.

"Right," I said, "We need to organise that fashion show."

We decided to hold it at the Guildhall in Worcester. I contacted Worcester City Council who readily agreed to the suggestion and we arranged a date for midday, two weeks later.

We started on the advertising campaign, contacting every local and national newspaper, including the Daily Window, and inviting them along the fashion show. Every major fashion magazine, and all the local magazines were contacted and the Guildhall put up plenty of notices outside and inside the building.

We invited the Daily Window to come along to Hamilton Hall for an exclusive preview of the fashion show we were planning there. Danny Dumble and a lady fashion reporter, called, oddly, Polly Parrot, turned up, along with a very professional looking photographer.

It was a lovely day, and we sat them all outside in the garden with tea and cake and told them all about the dresses and Stig de Silva and what we had planned.

Then we took it in turns to put on some of the dresses and allow ourselves to be photographed outside and inside the hall, wherever the photographer wanted us. I asked Polly what she thought of the designs.

"They are very different," she said. "A mixture of Western and Eastern styles, but I like them. I'll give you a good write up, don't worry."

Theo also filmed us as we strutted our things. He had studied the camera crew that came to Hamilton Hall to make the adverts for Cadian Wine, and talked to them, getting hints and tips on film making. He had become very keen, brought his own cine-camera and, though I say it myself of my only son, rather good. Olwen had become his sound girl and assistant, and they made a good team.

The dresses had a full two page spread in the Daily Window the following week, and it was good. Very good and they mentioned the fashion show at the Guildhall the week after.

We hadn't bothered selling tickets for the show. We were going to be just grateful if anybody turned up, but the hall was absolutely packed over an hour before the show was supposed to start at noon. All the seats were taken, and every spare inch of space was full of people standing and trying to get a glimpse.

I now think that maybe a lot of the people who turned up were there just to get a glimpse of me. I had become a bit of a curiosity, I think.

Anyway, we quickly realised that there was a problem, and after a brief discussion with the council, decided that we would have to put on a second show in the afternoon, starting at 3.00 pm. Many people left, but then did turn up later so we had two full up shows.

Theo and Olwen had designed and printed hundreds of glossy catalogues for us at Print-U-Like. They had photos of all the 30 dresses, and order forms. Ladies just had to chose the dress and enter their measurements, and payment, and the dresses would arrive a couple of weeks later.

Both shows were huge successes. Alice and Pauline and I took it in turns to walk up and down on a red carpet laid on top of stout, sturdy tables, with hasty dress changes in between. Marjory, my best friend, did the commentary for us. She had a posh, aristocratic voice, and was used to public speaking, and did it well.

We took dozens and dozens of orders, and Olwen and Marjory helped to sort them all for us. Even Sam and Stu helped and they seemed to really enjoy themselves.

A few people, mainly men, said they would only order a dress if they could be photographed with me and if I would sign the brochure for them. So, as soon as the forms were filled in and payment details included, I posed and signed, and, occasionally, gave a cheek a peck.

Anything to help the sales.

Meanwhile, Theo filmed it. We were not sure why it needed to be filmed, but Theo was keen and had his new cine-camera and filmed it anyway.

We had a great time, and Stig de Silva was there. He had flown over a couple of days before, and was stopping at Hamilton Hall, sleeping in my bed, with me, obviously.

He was absolutely delighted with everything, and kept clapping and smiling with pleasure. His dresses were a big hit, with lots of orders, lots of publicity, and he was sleeping with me.

He was a very lucky man.

"Whilst I'm here," he said, "I was wondering if it might be possible to film some adverts for my dresses. I've looked at the work Theo has done. It's very good. I was thinking that we only need to film a bit of you talking to camera, and we could lace that together with parts of your Daily Window photo shoot and the fashion show, and we could make many top quality adverts for the dresses.

The trouble is, I've only just thought of it and a bit of help with the dialogue would be appreciated."

Between us, we came up with some words for me to speak and Theo filmed me speaking them in English and Abacadian.

"When I get back to Abacadia I'll get some producers to patch some adverts together, but I'll send you some copies before we show them, to get your opinions."

He held me at arms length and said, "Lady Clair, Meeting you in Abacadia was the best thing I have ever done. You are a remarkable woman. I am sure that my business will grow and grow because of you. Thank you."

He returned to Abacadia and once again I was without a man to share my bed.

Which was a shame.

Chapter 51 - Back to Abacadia

The press were getting on my back about the Daily Window articles. Lots of stories were being written about me and my whoring times in Abacadia. Some of the stories were sympathetic but most of them were not good and I wasn't sure how to handle everything. The children tried to help me.

"Mother," they said, "You really don't have anything to be ashamed of. You had no option at all except to do what you did."

"I know that," I said, "But I still performed like a whore. And enjoyed it," I sighed. "I'm thinking I should just stick my fingers up at everybody, contact Gold in Abacadia and suggest he helps me make a film about my adventures. I could star in it, and he could play the part of Moldie, maybe. What do you think?"

"You mean you would be willing to make a porn film?" asked Alice, sounding nowhere near as shocked as she should have.

"It's just a thought," I said. "I'm sure, with all the publicity surrounding me at the moment, that it would be quite popular and would make plenty of money. It's just an idea."

I mentioned it to Moldie. He thought it was a great idea.

"Think about it Clair," he said. "We have most of the sex scenes filmed already. I think the quality would be good enough. We would just have to film the other bits. Your kidnapping in Worcestershire, the trips to Redik and the beauty spots, and your capture by Bim Dram and escape.

Actually, thinking about it, there is quite a lot to film. No need to use Gold, though, I could play myself."

It was a silly idea I know but I was under pressure.

Alice and Pauline and I were in my kitchen one day, preparing a dinner for Sam and Stu, who would be visiting later. We had regularly produced Abacadian style meals, which were spicy and hot but a different taste from English type curries.

"I enjoyed my time in the kitchen at Heavenly Winds," I told the others. "I learnt quite a lot about Abacadian cooking techniques from Waving Grass and I even thought about writing an Abacadian recipe book. Now, with all my publicity, I think it could sell quite well. Would you two be interested in helping me?"

They said they would be delighted to help, but had had other ideas on the subject.

"When we were in Snuka, we visited a couple of Abacadian style coffee shops," they told me. "We really liked them. They were different and so was the coffee. We have discussed, half heartedly, opening an Abacadian coffee shop-cum-café-cum-restaurant here in Worcestershire somewhere. It might do well."

We discussed the idea and decided it wouldn't be so hard to do.

"Who would run it and who would do the cooking?" I asked.

"Well, we would, between us," answered Alice.

I wasn't so sure. We weren't proper chefs and had had no formal training. It would also mean we were tied down to one place.

"Let me have a think about it," I told them. "I may have an idea."

I decided I needed to get away for a while. A visit to Effghania. On my own. To see Moldie and see for myself the good work that was being carried out there. I had no doubt that good work was being carried out and that the money I was sending to Moldie was being put to good causes and not lining the pockets of top ODOE officials but it would be nice to see for myself.

Whilst I was there I could organise to see Stig and Danger and even The Golden Stud.

But not Bim Dram.

Alice and Pauline asked me if I would like them to go with me, but I shook my head.

"Thank you but no. I need to go on my own and hopefully get the place out of my system. Moldie is meeting me and he assures me that everything will be fine."

Alice made a suggestion.

"Whilst you are gone, why don't we employ Sam and Stu to help us run things. All the businesses are growing rapidly and we think that we need someone to help, even if you weren't going to Abacadia. We need someone hard working and honest, and who knows something about what we are doing, and Sam and Stu are all of these things. We could sort out payment for their labours later. What do you think?"

I didn't even hesitate. I had had the same thought.

"Go for it," I told them. "I agree with you entirely," and they beamed with delight. They would have their men with them a lot more of the time.

Lucky devils.

There was no problem booking the flight from Birmingham. Moldie met me at Snuka airport. He hadn't changed. He was still as handsome as ever, though he had shaved off his moustache. It made him look younger.

He still had the Lada Samara, Lady Sammy, that he had driven before I left Abacadia with Alice and Pauline and Sam and Stu.

"I would have thought you could have bought something a bit better," I teased him.

"I love this old car," he said, patting the bonnet. "I've had it serviced and it goes really well. And it brings back happy memories."

The house that we had stayed in before wasn't empty, so Moldie had booked us into a posh hotel.

"You really needn't have booked somewhere so posh," I told him. "This must have cost you a fortune!"

"It's owned by an Effghanian company," explained Moldie. "It hasn't cost me a penny. Even the meals and any drinks will be paid for."

The double bed was king sized and comfy and got a lot of use and not all of the use was sleeping. The first day, we didn't even leave the room. We had our meals brought up to us.

We enjoyed ourselves!

In Snuka we visited Danger Goodness and Stig de Silva. They

were delighted to see us. Both of their businesses were flourishing, and I say this with due modesty, thanks to me. Sales of dresses and wine had increased three or four fold in Abacadia, directly due to my adverts, and sales in Britain were also starting to take off. Both companies were looking to expand to USA and Australia.

The fact that I had become a celebrity in Britain also helped. My story was big news in Abacadia and this had definitely helped local sales.

Danger and Stig were two very happy men.

I also took the opportunity to visit The Golden Stud, the famous actor and film maker, well, famous in Abacadia. He was also pleased to see me, though I think he would have been happier if I had been on my own and not had Moldie in tow.

He took us out to lunch to his favourite restaurant, and, after the usual chitty chitty chat chat, I told him about my problems in England with the circulation of The Film. He sympathised, but knew all about it, and said he could understand about how it could ruin my reputation as an English charity-working lady.

"It could also, though," he added, "Add to your reputation. I am sure you will make a huge number of new fans and those who disapprove, well, forget about them. They sound like what we call in the business, Good News Friends. They only want to be acquainted with you if things are going well. As soon as you take a drop in your fortunes, they leave you well alone.

True friends, like Moldie, and myself, see you for what you are and will stick by you at all times. You have friends like that?"

I thought of my family and of Marjory and nodded.

"I do," and could see where he was coming from, and it made me feel quite a lot better.

"Talking about The Film," I continued, "And that's one of the reasons I've come to see you. The story of my kidnap and imprisonment," I smiled at Moldie, "Is being serialised and published in one of England's top daily papers."

"I know that as well," he said. "I've read them. I think most people in Abacadia have read your story."

"Oh. I should have guessed. Anyway, I was thinking that there would be an opportunity to make a film of my adventures and I was wondering if you might be interested?"

He pondered the thought.

"Hmmmm," he pondered.

"Maybe. Yes, I would be interested. It couldn't be until next year though. I'm busy at the moment. Would you want me to produce it or just act in it?"

"I don't know," I said. "It was just a thought."

"Okay, I'll think on it. It definitely has promise. Changing the subject slightly, and I think I may have promised you a walk on part in one of my films."

I nodded.

"I think you may have."

"Could we film at Hamilton Hall?"

"You could."

"My latest film is another action thriller. It wouldn't be too hard to write in a short story line involving an English Lady, and you would certainly add star quality to the film. I'll get back to you on that as well."

We left Gold with promises of further correspondence. Moldie seemed a bit off. I couldn't help but tease him.

"The Golden Stud is very good looking, isn't he? And he wants me to act in a film with him . Lady Clair the film star. I like the sound of that."

He pulled a face and I laughed.

"I'm only joking. Come on, what are you going to do with me for the next couple of weeks, or is that a silly question?"

That night whilst we sat in the hotel bar with a drink each, Moldie told me that he had some news to tell me. He sounded happy and serious at the same time.

"Do you remember my brother, Flakey?"

"Of course," I said. "A decent man."

"Yes, he is."

He signed and chuckled.

"You also remember how I hadn't seen him since we were young boys. How he and the rest of my family were kidnapped from our family farm in Effghania?"

I nodded.

"I remember."

"Then he suddenly appeared, working for Bim Dram as an army sergeant and was involved with your kidnapping from Lake Lucinda."

"Of course I remember all this, Moldie. What are you getting at?"

"After you had returned to England, I decided to try and meet him. I had a phone number, and spoke to him. The meet took a bit of arranging, but we managed it, and we met up in a bar in Snuka a few weeks ago."

"How did it go?"

"It was really good to see him, and we got on very well together. We swapped addresses and details and have met up regularly since then. We are making a joint effort to contact our other brother, who is also in the army, and our sisters."

"I'm pleased for you Moldie."

And I was. It is always nice to catch up with old friends and even better to catch up with family you haven't seen for a while.

"There's more," he said.

He was now actually grinning like a Cheshire Cat.

"Between us we managed to find our mother. As Flakey guessed, she is working in a restaurant in Snuka. We visited seventeen restaurants between us and eventually found her. She is in fine health and has remarried, to the owner of the restaurant where she works. We are going to meet them tomorrow for lunch in their restaurant," and I was thrilled for him, I really was.

So next day we had lunch in a restaurant called Grumpy's, and I met his mother, who was called Cora, and her new husband, who was called Grumpy, but wasn't. They knew all about me and seemed delighted that I was Moldie's girlfriend. Cora, who was one of the happiest people I have ever met in my life, asked me if I was going to marry her son, and laughed when I told her that we were just very good friends.

The following day we headed off in Lady Sammy to visit Dave and Laura Gulldred. We swapped news. They told us that there had been no follow up problems after our stay in the village. We told them to give our best wishes to Shadow and Kylie.

I told them that Sam and Stu were to marry Annie and Pauline.

"Those two scoundrels settling down! I wouldn't have believed it. Not those two."

He laughed, then looked at Laura, his lovely wife.

"Mind you, if you get the right woman, it is heaven. Get the wrong one, and it can be hell!"

Laura punched him on the arm, and he pretended it hurt.

"So I've been told," he added hastily.

We carried on in Lady Sammy and, somehow, ended up at Lake Lucinda. That was a strange experience. Mixed emotions? I should say. I had been there twice. The first visit was wonderful, the second time I had been captured by Bim Dram's army thugs.

We checked but there was no one about, so we headed for the bay and stripped off and swam in the nude and frightened the water birds and made love on a blanket and had a picnic. Exactly as before.

Then we drove to Angel's Hair Falls. We arrived in the evening and Moldie pitched a small tent right next to The Angel Tears Puddle. He made a small fire and we cooked some chops and drank some wine.

We swam after dark. The water was still nicely warm. The only light was a small flickering from the fire, and a tiny twinkling from the stars, of which there appeared to be millions.

We swam slowly towards the sound of the falls and ducked underneath and crawled up onto the ledge. We held hands and I said, "This is still the most perfect place in the whole world. I will remember it until my dying day. Thank you for bringing me here again."

My visit there with Bim Dram wasn't mentioned.

We were so happy there that we stayed for two nights.

After leaving the falls we drove to Redik, and Moldie showed me around. We used the clapped out old Landrover so I could get a better view from the higher seat position, and the two gorillas sat behind us. It was as if nothing had changed.

"They're here for your protection this time," explained Moldie. "Everybody in Redik knows that you are to thank for most of the good work that is being undertaken. They know what sacrifices you made and they worship you like a goddess. The gorillas are here just in case anybody gets too friendly."

Redik was becoming a proper town again. Nearly all the electricity had been restored. Many, many shops were open and most of the roads had been repaired. A proper wooden hospital building had been built though most of the wards were still tents. A new motel had been built and the bus station repaired.

"Next year we are hoping to promote some tourism in Effghania, though this may be difficult to get started. There will still be opposition from the Jakalamnian government, despite all the international press and TV coverage that had taken place recently. All started off by you," Moldie said, smiling.

The tented village which I had seen on my last visit and looked like a refugee camp, had greatly reduced in size, to maybe half.

"Where have all the people gone?" I asked, hoping he wouldn't say they had all died.

"We have found accommodation for them in the town," he said. "Many of the dilapidated houses have been refurbished, often very basically, but made liveable. Much better than a tent. But a few people have died or left."

He showed me an area where some large wooden sheds were under construction.

"Do you remember I mentioned that we are hoping to start timber and wood working businesses. To start with they will be sited here."

I asked Moldie if we could visit the same restaurant we had previously, called Loaves and Fishes. I wanted to speak to the young Welsh lady who ran it, Eileen Edwards.

She remembered me, of course, and seemed honoured that I wanted to talk to her.

"When does your contract here run out?" I asked her.

"In four months time," she said.

"Will you stay here then or go somewhere else?" I asked her.

"I want to go home," she said, looking at Moldie, and giving a tiny shrug. "I've been away for almost two years and I miss my family and I miss Wales."

"What will you do when you get back?"

"I thought about opening my own Abacadian restaurant in Cardiff, but I don't have any capital," she told me, "And it might be difficult to get started."

I told her about the similar plans that Alice and Pauline and I had about opening a café-cum-coffee house in Worcester and how we were looking for someone to run it.

She sounded very interested. Worcester was only an hour or so from her home.

I made another suggestion.

"Maybe we could run it as an equal partnership. I would supply the finance and you would manage it and do the cooking. Worcester is quite touristy and I'm sure we could make a success of it."

She seemed extremely interested now, and promised to contact me on her return to Wales. I would wait to hear from her.

Moldie and I spent a few days living in the apartment together. It hadn't changed a bit, and some of my clothes were still hanging in the cupboards and smellies in the bathroom. Moldie slept with me every night.

He told me he would like to spend the rest of his life lying next to me, but I thought I noticed a slight lessening of his passion for me.

I was certain he was going to ask me to marry him and I had decided to say no. I'd rather just stay friends. But he didn't ask me. In the end it was me who brought up the subject.

"Moldie," I said, one morning, over breakfast in the apartment. "Have you found a lady friend?"

He looked a bit shocked.

"Eh, well, yes," he said. "I have. How did you know?"

"Female intuition," I chuckled. "What's her name? Who is she? How did you meet? What's she like? Can I meet her?"

"You're not upset?" he asked, staring straight at me, eye to eye.

"Moldie," I said, "You really are the most wonderful man I have ever met, and I think I include my late husband in that, but you are Abacadian, I am an English Lady who is almost old enough to be your mother. I want to live at Hamilton Hall, not here in Effghania, and if you came to live with me, you would be constantly pining for Effghania. I am very, very fond of you, but I don't think a long term relationship between the two of us could ever work. I'm sorry."

He sighed, but smiled.

"You're right, of course. I'd come to the same conclusion. But we can remain friends, and visit each other regularly?"

It was my turn to sigh. We both felt the same and would remain friends, possibly lovers, but with no hard feelings.

"Of course," I said. "Of course we will remain friends," and kissed him on the tip of his nose.

"Now then, who is the lucky lady?"

He smiled a smile of happiness.

"You know her," he said.

"I do? Do you mean Pebble?"

Pebble was the maid who had looked after me in the apartment in Redik.

"No," he said. "But she is well and still works for us. Somebody else."

He was enjoying teasing me, but I couldn't think of anyone else.

"I give up," I said.

"Do you remember the cleaner at Bim Dram's house."

"Flower? Of course I remember her."

I looked at him and smiled.

"You and Flower are a couple?"

"Yes. I would like to marry her but first I needed to talk to you."

"Oh Moldie, dear Moldie," I said, "I'm delighted for you. Of course you must get married. I mean, you are getting on a bit," I teased.

Then I had a thought.

"Have the two of you been living here in this apartment? She's moved out for me, hasn't she? Oh Moldie, you shouldn't have done that. Now you've made me feel really bad."

It was his turn to comfort me.

"Clair," he said, "After what you have done for the people of Effghania, it was the least we could do. Don't worry about it. Would you like to meet her?"

"Yes please," I said. "I didn't get to know her very well, but she did seem very nice. Very clever, I remember. And very pretty. Too clever and too pretty for you, Moldie, I would have thought."

He laughed.

"How about inviting her over for dinner this evening. You're leaving tomorrow."

I was feeling a bit uncomfortable when she arrived. I mean, I had spent the last eight nights sleeping with her fiancé and had been bonking him senseless. How would she feel about that? I know it wasn't my fault. I didn't know he was engaged but even so, I wasn't looking forward to meeting her.

But everything went okay. She either wasn't bothered or pretended she wasn't bothered. I think the fact that I was leaving the next day, and would probably never return, made things a little easier.

As it was, we got on fine. We chatted about our time in Bim Dram's house, laughed about the escape and what we had both done since.

She never returned to Bim's house. Everybody agreed that that would have been far too dangerous. Moldie got her another job with another politician. The Minister for Health. She re-styled and dyed her hair, becoming hazel, and changed her name to Nellie, on the odd chance Bim Dram visited.

"I had to sleep with the minister," she said. "He was elderly, almost 50, and horribly overweight. I had to close my eyes and imagine he was someone else. I found myself wishing it was Moldie. That's when I realised I had fallen in love with him."

She shrugged her shoulders, and chuckled.

"And now I am to become his wife."

She smiled.

"I am very lucky," she said simply.

"Not as lucky as me," said Moldie, smiling at her, then looking at me and blushing. He started to stutter, thinking he may have inadvertently upset me, but I held up my hand and smiled.

"I'm very happy for both of you," I said. "I'm sure you will be very happy together. When are you getting married?"

"As soon as we can."

"Any time you want a holiday or even just a break away from all this," I said to the two of them, "Come and visit me in Hamilton Hall. We always have a spare bedroom and you both will be very welcome."

The next morning Moldie made love to me for the very last time. We both knew it would be the last time. It was gentle and loving and sad. Neither of us mentioned Flower.

Over breakfast, we talked about our future. From now on it would be a working relationship. He would still be my agent in Abacadia, spending the money I sent him and spending it wisely.

"Use a small amount of it to buy a place for you and Flower to live," I told him. "You have earned it."

Moldie drove me to Snuka airport. It was a long drive, over four hours and we stopped for a picnic on the way. At the airport we held each other and kissed.

I looked into his eyes, and smiled.

"See you about," I said.

He smiled back.

"See you about."

As the plane took off, I looked out of the window at Snuka and Abacadia spread out beneath me. I wondered if I really would ever return. Maybe that part of my life was over, and I needed a new start. Maybe I would now always be linked to Abacadia and it's people.

Chapter 52 - Him, Again

I got back home to find that Theo had moved out. Olwen, his girlfriend, and he had rented a small flat near Kidderminster and seemed very happy in their little lovers paradise. I visited them weekly and was very pleased for them both. They were obviously very much in love, and I felt pangs of jealousy. Everybody was in love, apart from me.

One day a couple of months later I had a phone call at Hamilton Hall. It was a phone call I never expected to get, but after my visit from Rum Hearty a few weeks previously, I wasn't that surprised. It was from Bim Dram. I almost dropped the phone in shock.

"Lady Clair Hamilton," said a familiar voice. "This is Bim Dram. I am presently in England on Abacadian governmental business and I was wondering if it might be an opportunity for the two of us to meet up again, for old times sake."

I was tempted. A mischievous streak in me made me think about it. He would have to come here, on his own, and I would make sure Pauline and Alice but most important Sam and Stu were here when he arrived.

And I wanted to know if he was the one who had sent the emails and The Film to Frederick and the Daily Window.

"Phone me tomorrow," I told him.

Alice and Pauline were horrified, but the men laughed.

"The cheek of the man," said Sam.

"He would have to come here on his own and all of you would be here with me. I'm sure he wouldn't do anything. And I want to find out if he sent The Film."

So, Bim Dram arrived at Hamilton Hall two days later, on his own, in a hired posh BMW sports car. He looked well, wearing a posh suit and even posher shoes. I had forgotten how good looking he was.

I had made a special effort to look my best and I looked a

432

million dollars. Not one hundred thousand dollars but a million dollars. I was hoping to make him jealous and when I saw the look in his eyes, I knew I had succeeded. I introduced him to the family.

"These are my daughters and these are the men who rescued me from your house on Queen Victoria Avenue," I told him. "They are former SAS."

"It was one of the easiest and most enjoyable jobs we have ever done," grinned Sam. "If you ever want proper security, please contact us."

He wanted to sleep with me. I could see it in his eyes. Pure lust when he looked at me. Did I really have that effect on men?

We sat outside in the English autumn sunshine drinking English tea and nibbling on cucumber sandwiches and chatted about unimportant things. I could see he wanted to ask me if he could stay the night, but not in front of the others.

Eventually I said, "Bim, where are you staying tonight?"

"I, er, ………."

"Or where you hoping to stop here?"

"Well, I, um ………."

"Bim," I said and gave him my sweetest smile. "I am going to ask you some questions. And we all want you to answer them honestly. Do you think you can do that for me, Bim?"

He looked suspicious, but nodded.

"Of course."

We were all staring at him, intently.

"After I escaped from your house, I phoned you. Do you remember?"

"Of course," he said.

"You said you wouldn't stop us from leaving Abacadia and flying back to England."

"I did say that," he said, looking slightly puzzled.

"So why did you accuse us of being terrorists and surround Winston Macmillan Airport with security and send the army to chase after us?"

Now he looked genuinely puzzled.

"I didn't," he said.

Now I was confused. I expected an admission and a grovelling apology.

"We were told that everyone was on high alert for some foreign terrorists."

"That's right. We were on a high alert. Members of the Rahul Amin Terrorist group had been seen in both Snuka and Redik and it was them we were looking for. What made you think that it might have been you?"

The family all exchanged glances. I believed him and so did the others. I could see it by the expressions on their faces.

Then I realised that Mud Oneye, the general of the army who I had slept with, had tricked me. He had implied that he was looking for us, and he would only let us go if I spent the night with him, which I had done. Or had he? Or had I just imagined that is what he had said. I chuckled. The cunning old devil. And then he had proposed to me. I chuckled again, and noticed the others were all staring at me.

"Okay Bim. I apologise. I believe you. But, something else I want you to be honest about. Did you send copies of the promotional film about me to my charity chairman and the Daily Window newspaper?"

The look in his eyes told it all. He smiled but only after his eyes had said everything.

"Bim, you promised to tell the truth."

"I feel ashamed, but yes. I wanted revenge on you for escaping and thought this was a good way to hurt you."

So it had been him. We had been right all along. I wasn't surprised.

Anyway, to cut a long story short, and much to the disgust of Alice and Pauline and the further amusement of Sam and Stu, Bim Dram spent the night at Hamilton Hall, in my big soft double four poster bed, with me.

Which was nice.

We talked gently during the night whilst I lay in his arms.

"Did you really think I would let you into my bed?" I asked

him, "Seeing as how you did actually kidnap me and hold me as a prisoner for a few weeks."

He chuckled.

"I think you have a soft spot for me," he answered, and it was my turn to laugh.

"Well, do you?" he asked, and I realised I probably was vaguely fond of him.

"Maybe," I said. "But how do you feel about what you did? Do you regret the way you treated me?"

He sighed.

"Yes, of course, but I was so in love with you. I just lusted after you. I wanted you so badly. Thinking of you was affecting my work, everything. I couldn't help myself. I'm sorry, I really am but, well, it wasn't that bad, was it?"

It was my turn to sigh.

"No," I said, "I suppose not. Being locked in your bedroom was very boring but I enjoyed your country house, Heavenly Winds, and the time on Rum Hearty's yacht, Heloise."

I thought I'd mention that just to wind him up a bit.

He grunted.

"Rum told me once how much he enjoyed having you stop with him. I think you helped him get over the loss of his wife."

A short silence whilst I remembered my time on Rum's yacht. A good few days being he guest and the lover of the countries Prime Minister.

"What did you think when you returned to your home to find me gone?" I asked. "I hope the soldiers who were guarding me didn't get into trouble."

He chuckled.

"I was shocked, I must admit. I shouted at them a bit, but that's all. I actually think they did all they could. Now I've met Sam and Stu, I'm not surprised the soldiers didn't recapture you. They both seem very competent."

"They are," I said and fell asleep against his chest.

But I didn't sleep well. I think it was because I was worried about something Bim had said that evening. A vague memory was troubling me and I couldn't work out what it was. I delved and searched my memory all night, but it was over breakfast, a breakfast that Alice and Pauline refused to attend but Sam and Stu enjoyed, that I eventually remembered.

It was the name Rahul Amin. That was what had been bothering me. Bim and Sam and Stu were having a general conversation about terrorists and terrorism when I remembered, and I gasped involuntarily. All the men stared at me and it was Bim who said,

"What's wrong, Clair?"

"You said last night that you were looking for members of the Rahul Amin terrorist group."

He nodded.

"That's right. What of it?"

"Did you catch them?"

"Most of them," he answered. "They were all hung or hanged in the main square of Snuka. A huge crowd turned out to watch. You may have read about it in the news. Why?"

"Most of them? You caught most of them?"

"Yes, but unfortunately the leader, Rahul Amin himself, escaped. We think he may have left the country. Why?"

I could feel my pulse racing and I think I may have turned pale.

"Clair, are you all right?"

All three of them were looking concerned.

"I met Rahul Amin," I said.

"When?" asked Sam, and then all three of them cottoned on at the same moment.

"Oh. Do you want to tell us what happened.

So I told them what had happened, how he had tried to throttle me and how Moldie Bedlam had shot him with a dart gun and dumped him out of the boot of the car near Snuka.

Bim Dram looked horrified, as did Sam and Stu, who had stopped grinning about the fact that Bim had spent the night with me and now looked deadly serious.

Sam asked Bim Dram the question I dare not ask.

"Do you think he may have come here, to England?"

"I wouldn't have thought so. But, well, who knows."

I asked a question I did not want to ask.

"Do you think he may come here, to Hamilton Hall, to ………."

My voice trailed off.

"I think the girls need to be here," said Sam, and Stu jumped up.

"I'll go and get them," he said, and disappeared.

"Do you have any idea, any idea at all where he might be?" Sam asked but Bim shook his head.

"He could be anywhere. We have, however, given all his details to Interpol, the international criminal police organisation, and also Scotland Yard and every major police and security organisation around the world. He is one of the top ten wanted men on Interpol's list now. He hasn't been seen since he escaped from us in Snuka last year."

Just then Alice and Pauline turned up, looking very serious.

"I've told them about Rahul Amin," Stu said.

Both of my daughters came over and hugged me.

"Oh mother," they said, "How horrible."

They walked around the table to Bim Dram and shook his hand, and he nodded and said, "Thank you. I will do everything I can to protect your mother, but I'm not sure how much that is. We, the Abacadian security forces, have already informed everyone we can but I will inform Scotland Yard that we think he may be either heading for England or already here," and the girls gasped.

"Do you think that?" asked Alice.

Bim shook his head.

"No I don't think that, not for one moment, but there is no harm in telling them, is there? Do you want me to tell them about you, Clair?"

I had no idea. This was becoming way out of my league. I looked at Sam and Stu.

Sam spoke. Instead of answering Bim's question, he said, "What is he actually wanted for, Bim?"

"Drug smuggling, mostly, and armed robbery, but he is also known for murdering at least four people who crossed his path, probably a lot more we don't know about. Look, when I get back to Snuka, I'll send you a copy of his police profile. Meanwhile, may I make some suggestions?"

I nodded.

"Please Bim, suggest all you like."

"You two," he nodded towards Sam and Stu, "Are former SAS?"

They nodded.

"That's good, very good."

He thought for a moment.

"Look, we really have no idea if he'll come looking for you Clair. Probably not, but I suppose there is a chance. Let's assume worst case scenario and he does come looking. There are two options."

Sam and Stu nodded. They had a good idea what Bim was going to say.

"You can move away from here and go into hiding. He would probably never find you. The trouble with that is, how long for? And you would still always be wondering. Always looking over your shoulder."

"I agree," said Sam. "Stu and I have experience of putting informants into secret hiding, and it is not a nice experience for them. Very stressful."

"Exactly," said Bim. "I think, and this is just my initial thought, that you should stay here in Hamilton Hall. Sam and Stu and Alice and Pauline should move back into their old rooms, to be near at hand. Increase the security. Extra locks on the doors and windows, maybe bars on some of the more vulnerable windows. Security lights and alarms, that sort of thing. There will be a local security firm who will do this for you. I have experience of this in Abacadia."

Sam and Stu grunted.

"I know you rescued Clair very easily, but I have increased security since then and I think you would find it much harder now."

"That all makes sense," said Sam. "We'll move in today, if that's all right with you, Clair?"

I felt a sense of relief. I felt much safer whenever Sam and Stu were nearby.

"Do you have access to guns?" Bim asked, and Sam nodded.

"There is no problem with guns. I must admit though, Bim, I did become very fond of your dart guns in Abacadia. I really like them ...."

"No problem. I'll send you a couple with plenty of darts when I get back to Snuka."

He smiled.

"Diplomatic immunity."

We all laughed.

"I'm glad you like them," continued Bim. "That was mainly my doing, you know. I was so fed up with all the murders and serious injuries caused by ordinary guns with bullets that I really pushed for dart guns in parliament and won the day. One of my proudest achievements, I think."

I leant over and took his hand.

"Well done, Bim," I said, and felt a real warmth for him at that moment.

The others all nodded. I could see Alice and Pauline chilling out a bit towards him.

"The argument that finally clinched it for me," continued Bim, looking pleased, "Was the fact that if you just wounded someone with a bullet, then they could still escape. Wounding with a dart, and it still works and they still fall asleep and they still get captured."

Sam nodded then took charge, as always.

"We'll all move in this afternoon, and start on the security arrangements immediately. Bim, you'll contact Scotland Yard, and when you get back to Snuka, send us all the details you have about Rahul Amin and a pair of dart guns and darts. Okay with everyone?"

We all nodded, and Bim stood up.

"I have to go," he said. "I have a lunch meeting in London and I am already running a bit late."

He held out his hand to Sam and Stu, who shook it firmly.

"Thanks mate," said Sam, "It really has been a pleasure to get to know you. I mean that," and Bim smiled.

"Yes, thank you," agreed Stu.

Alice and Pauline actually gave him a big hug.

"Thank you Bim. Have a good trip back to Snuka."

I walked him to his car, holding his hand.

"It's been really good to see you again, Clair."

"And you Bim," and I kissed him and we hugged for a few seconds.

"Anytime you are in England, please come and stay with me," and he climbed into his hired BMW sports car.

Then he climbed out again holding a brown envelope. He handed it to me.

"A present for you Clair," he said, with a grin.

The writing on the envelope was the address of the house we stayed in Snuka and it was in Theo's hand writing. I would recognise it anywhere, and I knew immediately what was in the envelope. I opened it and I was right. It was my passport.

I stared at Bim.

"I thought I would keep it safe for you," he said, gave me another peck on the cheek, climbed back into the car and was gone. I felt tears in my eyes as he drove away.

Bugger.

I wiped the tears away, and headed back to the house. The others looked up when I walked back into the dining room.

I showed them the passport.

"Bim has just given it to me. He didn't tell me how he got hold of it."

The others all chuckled then Alice said, "Mother, we want to take back everything we said about Bim Dram. He is actually a really nice man."

"He is, isn't he," and I sighed to myself. He was a nice man, a very nice man, but he lived in Abacadia and I lived in Hamilton

Hall and I couldn't live in Abacadia, I didn't think, and he couldn't live in Hamilton Hall, I reckoned so, that was that.

And anyway, he still had a very small penis.

Chapter 53 - Security measures

The four of them moved back in that afternoon and I phoned Theo to tell him what was happening. I told him everything and he was horrified.

"We'll move back in with you now," he said, but I disagreed with him.

"There is nothing you can do, Theo," I told him. "The others have got everything under control. How's Olwen?"

I left all the security arrangements to Sam and Stu and they got to work immediately. First, they explored every single inch of the house, probing here and looking there, and making notes. They decided on what should be done, made suggestions to me, to which I just nodded and said 'Get on with it,' They phoned a security firm of whom they knew the owner very well, 'Former SAS,' they told me, and two days later, Hamilton Hall was more like Fort Knox.

They showed the rest of us, including Theo and Olwen, what had been done.

"Inside, we have changed some of the locks, and added some more. Each door now has two separate locks, a Yale and a deadlock. They also have bolts top and bottom. Nobody is going to get in through the doors. And look, spy holes in each one, so we can see anyone who is standing by the door. The windows also have locks on them, and also we have installed these window shutters."

On either side of the windows were shutters, which could be swung across the windows at night, and fastened with a bar which went fully across. They showed us how they worked.

"It will be almost impossible to get through these windows from the outside," they proclaimed.

"We have also had interior alarms installed. There are a number of infrared beams which will set them off."

They showed us where they were and gave us an example. I

expected the alarms to be loud and noisy, but they weren't. There was an alarm in every room and they were quiet, more like an electronic alarm clock.

"These should wake us up," explained Sam, "Without Rahul Amin or anyone else realising what is happening. If he comes, we want to catch him. If he escapes, then he may return. We have also put bolts on the inside of each door upstairs."

We climbed the stairs to have a look.

"There is a new secure lock on the bathroom and one on the inside of each bedroom. These are also alarmed and will go off if forced. There is also an intercom system."

Stu and Alice disappeared into their bedroom whilst we went into mine. Sam pushed a button and Stu answered from their bedroom.

Alice and Pauline and I looked at each other. We were impressed. Surely no one could get in through all these alarms and locks and bolts.

"Let us show you what we have done outside," and we all trundled into the garden.

"There are night-time cameras installed to cover all areas of the garden. They are movement sensitive and the pictures can be seen on small TV screens in every room."

"We thought about having guard dogs," said Sam. "We have an ex-SAS friend who would loan us two trained dogs for a small fee, but we decided against it. We want to catch this bloke, not frighten him off and dogs would do that."

"That's the security," continued Stu, "And it's mostly aimed at night time. The problem might be if he comes during the day, and he might. We have to be vigilant at all times and Sam and I have come up with some rules which we all must follow religiously."

He started to number them off on his fingers.

"1 - You girls must never, ever go outside on your own. There must always be one of us with you, even in broad daylight.

2 - We must all make doubly sure that all the doors and windows are locked at night.

3 - We must keep our eyes and ears open at all time and report anything, and I mean anything, that seems odd or unusual or out of place.

4 - You three girls must learn some basic self-defence. Lessons to start immediately."

I nodded, and so did Alice and Pauline and that very afternoon we started our self-defence lessons. Sam and Stu were very good teachers. It had been one of their jobs when they were in the SAS and they made it fun, and as we girls were all fairly athletic, we learnt quickly.

Chapter 54 - Rahul Amin

The following is a greatly edited account of Rahul Amin's story after he was shot with a dart gun in the apartment in Redik by Moldie and taken away. The source of this story will be explained soon.

After he was dumped by Moldie Beldam from the boot of the car near Snuka, Rahul Amin wanted revenge on somebody. He had a high opinion of himself and felt humiliated by what had happened. He wanted revenge.

He didn't know who Moldie was but he did know all about Lady Clair Hamilton and the fact that she lived in Hamilton Hall in England. A grudge inside him burnt and burnt and he wanted to get back at her.

But he didn't know where about in Abacadia she was. The whole meeting with her had been kept totally secret from him.

He was a terrorist, and knew the police were after him, but he was confident of not being captured. He was the leader of a gang and they had committed crimes of robbery and rape and murder in various parts of central Asia. They had perfected a trick of exploding a bomb an instant before they committed their crime, making the crime easier to commit.

They were planning to cross the Abacadian border to commit another robbery, letting off bombs and in the confusion, rob a bank or a rich house. They had heard about a large consignment of gold transported in secret and decided to bomb and rob that but one of them talked to a prostitute, the age old story, and the police raided their safe house.

Four of the gang were captured but Rahul Amin and two of the gang got away. They separated and using a false passport with the name Naida Rudella and dressed as a woman, he escaped. Eventually he found his way to England and studied a map to find out where Hamilton Hall was. Using public transport he arrived in Kidderminster still dressed as a woman wearing a niqab, which covered his face leaving only eyes visible. He had travelled as a woman before and so was quite good at acting as a woman. He had a slim build with large eyes which made the make up easier. He actually enjoyed being a woman and he sometimes wondered if he was a woman in men's clothing, but he most certainly was not a homosexual.

He made a complete inspection of the gardens and the outside of Hamilton Hall using binoculars he always carried with him. Spying and examination like that was something he had done many times and he was very good at it, whilst remaining hidden. He noticed the high security in the house and how Sam and Stu were always there. He saw they were very competent and thought they may have been retired soldiers or security guards.

He decided it would be too difficult capturing Lady Clair at the hall so started concocting an alternative plan. He realised it might take a while but he was in no hurry and had plenty of money hidden in a money belt around his waist hidden by his loose female clothing. He rented a cheap room in a house for one month and kept himself to himself.

He didn't really know what he would do if he ever caught her, but he would probably rape her and torture her and then murder her, sending her severed head to the family. He chuckled when he fantasised those thoughts.

He noticed that twice a week the whole family left in one of the cars, returning about three hours later. They took bags with them which he thought might be a change of clothes or a towel, and concluded that they might be going to keep fit. He noted the type and colour and number plate of the car, and waited in Kidderminster, the nearest town with a gym, and kept a look out.

The very next time they visited, he spotted them, and joined the same gym-cum-leisure centre as a woman using the passport with the name of Naida Rudella.

He explored the centre, noting where the ladies changing rooms were. He discovered a store room with a door to it from the ladies changing rooms. The door was locked but it and the lock were old and it was easy enough for him to unscrew the lock and sneak into the storeroom. He replaced the screws with very short screws so the door could open easily. The door opened inwards and he discovered it could be jammed shut by wedging it with a chair. There was a *ventilation duct in the store room and when he examined it, discovered that the grill pulled off very easily and then he could, if need be, climb through it and find himself outside on the far side of the centre. Perfect.*

Then he waited for Clair and her daughters to appear. He had checked on Wikipedia who they were. He sat quietly in a corner of the changing room, pretending to pray or meditate. Then, when he saw Clair was on her own, he dragged her into the store room, with one hand over her mouth and a knife at her throat.

Clair continues with this part of the story.

We had noticed the Muslim lady sitting in the corner of the changing rooms before. She seemed to be meditating, or possibly praying, we couldn't be sure. She just sat there, motionless and silent. A bit odd, we thought, but harmless.

We had been in the gym for an hour, and now we were hot and sweaty, and decided to go for a swim. I preferred to have a quick shower before I dived into the pool but Alice and Pauline didn't bother.

There was no one else in the changing rooms when I stepped out of the shower, and reached for the towel, water in my eyes. I felt somebody grab me from behind, one hand over my mouth and felt a knife at my throat. I was half dragged, half carried to a door saying store room which was pushed open and I was dragged through and door shut behind us and barricaded with a chair wedged behind the handle.

"My name is Rahul Amin," said the woman in a man's voice, "You stole a lot of money from me and humiliated me in Abacadia. Now I want repaying. I'm going to rape you, then I'm going to torture you and then I'm going to kill you and cut off your head and send it to your daughters in a paper bag."

I was the most terrified I had ever been in my life, and for a few seconds I was certain I was going to die.

He removed the knife from my throat, and used it to start to cut away my bathing costume, and moved his hand from my mouth and held me in a choke hold with his arm across my throat. I still couldn't shout, I could barely breath, and I reacted as Sam and Stu had taught me.

I moved my hips to the left, stuck out my bum, ducked and swivelled my head down and around and my head easily slipped out of his grip. I grabbed the arm that had been holding me and jerked it up behind his back viciously and he let out a soft grunt. It must have really hurt. It had happened in an instant, taking him completely by surprise and I blessed Sam and Stu for training me.

I kicked the chair away from the door which swung open and there, blessings, were Alice and Pauline, and, more importantly, Sam and Stu were with them, in their swimming trunks and dripping water. The girls had returned just as the storeroom door was closing. They couldn't see me and had called the boys from the swimming pool who had come running.

They saw instantly what had happened, and Sam stepped into the room and kicked Rahul Amin in the balls and, as he bent over, chopped him on the back of his neck, knocking him unconscious. He pulled off the niqab and whistled when he saw that it was Rahul Amin.

"Close the door," said Sam, breathing heavily. "Are you okay, Clair?"

"He grabbed me as I came out of the shower, and held a knife to my throat."

I was starting to tremble with shock.

"Then he moved the knife and put me in a choke hold and I instinctively used the throw you taught us last week and it worked."

Alice and Pauline hugged me, and Sam said, "Well done Clair."

I thought I deserved a bit more praise than that.

"How was he going to escape?" asked Stu. "There is always an escape route," and Sam walked over to the ventilation grill and grabbed it and it came away in his hands. He peered through and said, "Through here. It looks like it leads to the back of the centre."

He thought then made a decision.

"We need to get him back to Hamilton Hall," he said. "I want to question the bastard before we hand him over to the police. Alice, Pauline, take your mother, and get yourselves dried and dressed and drive the car to the corner of the car park, as close as possible to this duct. Park with the boot to the hedge, but not too close. Do it quickly but try and act normal. Keep an eye on your mum, she may start suffering from shock. Stu, go to our changing room and come back with our clothes. I'll stay here. Now go."

Sam's clear and concise orders calmed my nerves, and the three of us got changed and went outside and drove the car to the corner of the car park, as ordered. As soon as we got there, we saw Stu peering around the corner of the centre. He nodded, and said, "Open the boot," and disappeared and seconds later he reappeared with Sam and they were carrying Rahul Amin between them. Another quick glance then they dumped him into the boot and closed it and climbed into the back seat of the car.

"I've given him an injection of anaesthesia," said Sam. "He should be asleep for a while. Now Alice drive back normally to Hamilton Hall."

Alice drove us away, and Sam asked me what had happened in more detail and when I told them, was full of praise, as were the others, and although I agreed with everything they said, I had reacted magnificently, I still felt myself blushing.

Back home and Sam and Stu carried Rahul Amin into the dining room and undressed him down to his shorts. They sat him down on the chair at the head of the table. This was the heaviest and strongest, and had arm rests. Then they tied his wrists to the arm rests and his ankles to the chair legs, both of them checking that he couldn't get free. They blindfolded and gagged him, checked he could still breathe, then examined his money belt.

They whistled. It contained a lot of money. Over ten thousand pounds. His passport was in the name of Naida Rudella and he looked quite feminine and rather pretty in the passport photograph. There was a key, probably to the room he was staying in somewhere and nothing else.

Sam took most of the money, leaving just a couple of hundred pounds, and gave it to me.

"I don't want it," I said.

"Give it to a local charity," said Sam, and I nodded and took the money. Better for a charity to have it than the police, I thought.

"Time for lunch," suggested Sam, when all of this had been done. We ate lunch with Rahul Amin slumped over the chair at the head of the table, a weird experience, whilst we discussed what to do with him.

"I think we should hand him over to Inspector Hector," said Pauline. "We were pretty horrid to him by not trusting him and heading off to Abacadia without telling him. It would make his day to announce the capture of one of the world's ten most wanted terrorists and he would be our friend for life. Always good to be lifelong friend with the local police inspector."

We all agreed that that would be the best course of action.

"I would like to interrogate him first though," said Sam. "I think Stu and I would be able to get information out of him by using techniques which a, um, policeman might find a bit, er, illegal and unethical."

"What do you mean by that?" I asked, not sure about what he was suggesting.

"We can use a truth drug. It's a barbiturate called scopolamine. It was used regularly until about thirty years ago but now it's illegal because it has side effects but we have been taught how to use it in the SAS. Combined with a bit of gentle torture, and we should be able to get almost everything out of him."

"Oh," I said, looking at Alice and Pauline but they just shrugged.

"He has just tried to rape you, mother, and then threatened to torture you and cut off your head and send it to us in a paper bag. A bit of gentle torture doesn't seem so bad," said Pauline.

I shook my head but said, "Okay, as long as I don't have to be here."

"And you don't tell anyone about this," said Sam, and we nodded.

As if.

Rahul Amin stirred on the chair and lifted his head and groaned.

"He'll have a bit of a headache," said Sam. "Now, if you three girls would like to leave us alone for about half an hour?"

We went to the kitchen and made a cup of coffee each and then to the living room, where we sat and talked. We heard just one scream, sharp and piercing before it was cut off abruptly, and I shivered.

Forty minutes later and Stu appeared at the living room door.

"All finished," he said, sounding horribly cheerful. "He's freely confessed everything, and it's all been taped, in duplicate. Sam is wondering if you mind if he phones Inspector Hector now."

Inspector Hector arrived about forty minutes later with sirens blaring and lights flashing, accompanied by six armed police officers. By this time, Rahul Amin was dressed again in his Muslim ladies clothes, and was lying on the floor, with his hands tied behind his back and his ankles secure. He had been given some water to drink and the paleness in his cheeks, which he had when I looked at him thirty minutes earlier, had darkened back to their normal colour.

"Rahul Amin," said the good inspector, very formally, "You are under arrest for international acts of terrorism. You need not say anything but anything you do say will be written down and may be used in evidence against you."

He didn't bother waiting for an answer, but turned to us, and his grin was the grin of a very, very happy police inspector.

"Would you like to tell me how you captured him?" he asked and Sam said, "No, not really", and handed the inspector a CD.

"There is a full confession on here," he told the inspector, "Willingly given before five witnesses. I will come and visit you at the police station tomorrow, if that's okay with you?"

The inspector, who was so happy he would have agreed with anything, nodded.

"That's fine," and he marched Rahul Amin away to spend the night in a Kidderminster prison cell.

The following day Sam went to the police station to make a statement on how we caught him, of which only maybe twenty percent was true. There was no mention of dart guns and truth drugs or the fact that it was me who actually caught him. We thought it was probably better to have two former soldiers capturing him than a helpless middle aged woman.

Later, Rahul Amin was found guilty of numerous terrorist activities, partly thanks to Sam and Stu's freely given confession, and locked away for many, many years.

Which was nice.

The Final Chapter

With Rahul Amin's capture and confinement, it was safe for the others to move out of Hamilton Hall, which they did, and once again I was on my own.

Financially, things were going well for us at that time. With all the Abacadia kidnapping publicity, our soap business had become popular and various shops were now selling them for us.

Sales of Cadian Wines had also taken off. Danger Goodness's adverts, starring me, were regularly shown on television and we got money every time they were shown plus a small nominal fee for every bottle sold and lots of small nominal fees together become an income.

The same with the Stig de Silva's dresses. A regular income from them. And a small income from Abacadia from the same things.

I was still paying half to Moldie, but we were doing okay.

We were still waiting to hear from Eileen Edwards about opening an Abacadian restaurant and coffee shop, but had high hopes it would work out eventually.

Lots of money was coming in and I didn't have to do much to earn it. It just came in.

I was feeling down. I was bored and my past was beginning to haunt me.

The Daily Window had finished publishing all the articles about my Abacadian adventure. Opinions on the story were divided. Lots of people were horrified and disgusted with me and my behaviour. An equal number were delighted with me. Whatever, I was big news.

The BBC asked me to appear on NightNews, their late night news programme, where I was interviewed by Jonathan Jacksman. He was a proper interviewer and asked proper questions properly and I actually quite enjoyed it.

Then Channel 4 did a full one hour programme about me, with the families co-operation. They did it from the point of view of

Moldie Bedlam, though Moldie refused to appear on it, and interlaced interviews with me with bits of film that Moldie sent me plus some bits with actors and actresses. It was shown at peak time and was quite sympathetic towards me.

During both these appearances I made sure I mentioned Effghania, and all the good work that ODOE were doing.

"There is still so much to do, however, and any financial help would be gratefully received."

Theo had constructed a website for me, called 'Help Clair to help'. Anybody could donate any money straight to it.

"Every single penny donated, and I mean, every single penny, will go to help the people of Effghania," I said, and it did. Theo had arranged it all for me, and that sent another steady trickle of money to Moldie.

Despite, or maybe because of these appearances, I was lonely. I had my family and I had Marjory but that was it. I didn't have a man, I didn't have a lover, and I was lonely. I didn't know what to do with myself.

I was seriously thinking about returning to Redik and whoring myself in the apartment again, but it wouldn't have been the same. Moldie was with Flower, soon to marry her. That idea remained a day dream.

I thought about doing charity work again, but my experiences with Frederick and the rest of the committee had put me off that. I needed a new challenge. And I needed a man to share my life with me.

I had had five (ish) proposals of marriage in Abacadia, all from men who had something (ish) to offer. In England, nothing.

'Oh well', I thought to myself whilst sitting in the garden on my own, drinking a cup of tea and watching a bumble bee collecting nectar from a flower in the mid-morning sunshine. '

'I'm Lady Clair Hamilton of Hamilton Hall. Something will turn up.'

The End

Also by Simon Bonsai

Surviving Polly

Simon Bonsai produces and sells what are almost certainly the most beautiful Bonsai trees in Britain. He is hard working, intelligent and very talented. He chooses with care and much forethought the shows and markets he will attend. He should be successful and rich, but he is not.

Surely this can't be the fault of his eccentric yet strange girlfriend, Polly, who hinders him as they travel the length and breadth of Britain together? Have caravan, will travel …….. Off they go again.

This is a wickedly humorous and detailed account of a year in their life together. Read it to discover the secrets of their relationship; meet many of their equally odd friends and visit with them various vaguely interesting places on their travels.

This book is definitely a one off. Find out how the other half lives. Love it or hate it, I promise you, you won't be able to put it down.

Lightning Source UK Ltd.
Milton Keynes UK
UKOW03f0837120317
296377UK00001B/8/P